THE STRIP

J. J. Salem is the *USA Today* bestselling author of *Tan Lines* which has been published in several languages. He lives in Mississippi and is currently at work on his next novel.

Visit his author website at www.jjsalem.com.
Connect with him on Facebook at J.J. Salem.
Follow him on Twitter @jjsalemwrites.

Praise for The Strip

'J. J. Salem delivers yet again. *The Strip* is a fun, fast, furious and sexy read. I loved it!'   Jackie Collins

'Deliciously sinful – I loved it'   Tilly Bagshawe

Praise for Tan Lines

'Escapism with a feminist edge'   *Sunday Telegraph*

'Deliciously juicy – a peach of a holiday read'
                                        Tasmina Perry

'Sexy beach trash of the highest order'   *Elle*

'Wickedly sharp and clearly well-researched, it's a salty beach read with legs'   *Daily M*

'A really great be

By the same author

Tan Lines

THE STRIP

J. J. Salem

PAN BOOKS

First published 2011 by Pan Books
an imprint of Pan Macmillan, a division of Macmillan Publishers Limited
Pan Macmillan, 20 New Wharf Road, London N1 9RR
Basingstoke and Oxford
Associated companies throughout the world
www.panmacmillan.com

ISBN 978-0-330-45329-5

A CIP catalogue record for this book is available from
the British Library.

Typeset by Ellipsis Digital Limited, Glasgow
Printed in the UK by CPI Mackays, Chatham ME5 8TD

For Tim, Betsy, and Jennifer
There is nothing like the connection
of brothers and sisters . . .

ACKNOWLEDGEMENTS

Some special thanks are in order for people who helped make this novel possible ...

Jennifer Weis – The Diva Editor. Her insightful – and at times brutal – assessment of my first draft was just the kick in the ass I needed to become a better writer and craft a stronger story!

Madeleine Buston – The Super Agent. She was patient and supportive during a difficult period, and we emerged with an exciting future intact!

Jenny Geras – The New Lady Boss. Her keen take on the second version of the manuscript and incredible support for its potential and future projects transformed my career!

Elaine Newton – The Vegas Doyenne. Her holiday party provided an essential up close look into Las Vegas society and the schemes and dreams that make that city so wonderfully iconic!

Jackie Collins – The Queen. Her gracious support for my work and encouragement all around has been the stuff of dreams. If there is a woman in the world with more class, style, humor, and killer work ethic, I have not met her yet!

PROLOGUE

Fucking a married man who traveled to Las Vegas on business was supposed to be fun, hot, and uncomplicated.

'Looking for these?'

Gucci Marlowe glanced up.

Nick Burke was twirling her Cosabella thong around his index finger, flashing a dimpled smile that made her want to forget the dead body she was leaving him for. *Not fun.*

'Keep them. As a souvenir.' She scooted on her skin-tight jeans, stepped into a pair of snake-embossed ankle boots, and slipped a vintage Poison rock tee over her head.

He made quite a show out of bringing her panties to his nostrils and inhaling them like an addictive drug. *Not hot.*

Gucci vaulted into the bathroom to swipe on some lip gloss and to style her dark, shoulder-length mane away from the up-all-night-having-sex look.

Suddenly, her gaze fell upon a loose photograph propped up against the mirror. Nick's kids – two boys, both under ten. *Very complicated.*

She wondered if they would grow up to do the same thing one day – cheat on their wives. The same way that their father was cheating on their mother, the same way that Gucci's father had cheated on hers. Gripping the marble countertop, she zeroed in on her own reflection. *Come on, Marlowe. Get your act together*.

One night during her regular game of craps at Caesars Palace, Nick had casually made an approach. He flirted. She flirted back. The action moved to the bar at Pure and an hour after that, upstairs to his room. Months later, they were still meeting at his hotel whenever work brought him to her city, which seemed to be every four to six weeks.

'You don't play fair,' Nick called out.

Gucci finished a quick Listerine rinse before answering. 'How's that?'

'You insist that I turn my phone off, but yours stays on.'

She reappeared to grab her Kooba bag and give him a withering look. 'That's because I work homicide. Besides, the day I have to sit around like a little mouse while you lie to your wife is the last day you'll ever see me naked.'

He let out a sigh and gave her an irresistible smile. With sleepy eyes and his own sexy case of bed head, Nick possessed the no-worries bearing of a naughty frat boy the morning after a keg party. 'Can't we at least have breakfast? I feel so used.'

'There's a murder victim at the Wynn. I don't have time for coffee and scrambled eggs.' She started for the door.

'What am I supposed to do about this?' He pointed to the impressive hard-on that was tenting the top sheet draped over his lean body, which was deliciously dark with the perennial tan of an outdoor sportsman.

Feeling a potent mixture of temptation and self-loathing,

Gucci let her eyes skate from Nick's face to his crotch and back again. 'Not my pig, not my farm.'

She walked out with the solemn determination to stop answering his dirty texts and late-night calls. He was a husband. He was a father. And Gucci Sofia Marlowe was better than this.

Leaving Nick's den of sin at the Bellagio, she drove north to the Wynn, a five-star casino hotel bursting with pricey luxuries unattainable to mid-level-salary mortals such as herself.

A thick-uniformed patrol officer stood guard at the entrance to suite 3641 and wordlessly handed Gucci a clipboard that held the crime scene log.

She scribbled her initials and badge number onto the third line. The first name on the sheet belonged to Doug Lanvin, the coroner; the second name was Jagger Smith, her partner.

Gucci ducked under the barricade tape.

Jagger was right there to whisper conspiratorially, 'Play nice, detective. Lanvin's going through a nasty divorce.'

'Yeah, well, until the asshole stops getting married, he'll always be going through one,' Gucci replied in an equally hushed tone.

Jagger had been her partner for just over a year, and their bond was already sealed in the crucible of annoying department bullshit. She was an attractive woman with a swimsuit model's body. He was a gay black man so good-looking that Blair Underwood could be his ugly brother. Together they covered almost every boneheaded ism and intolerance. But they were a stronger team for it.

A torrent of familiar sensations hit Gucci all at once –

a loud, eerie silence, an acrid odor of corroded copper and cheap quick-sale hamburger, and a faint whiff of gunpowder.

She surveyed the carnage on the bed. The victim was a white twenty-something male – six-foot-four, incredibly handsome, chiseled-bodied, and naked.

'Live fast, die young, and leave a beautiful corpse,' Gucci murmured.

'Hey, that's from a Lil Wayne song,' Jagger remarked.

Gucci looked at him sharply. 'What are you, *twelve*? James Dean said that.'

Doug Lanvin spoke up. 'Actually, Dean lifted it from an old Bogart movie called *Knock on Any Door*.'

Gucci cut him an annoyed glance.

He shrugged. 'I read it on Wikipedia.' Doug stepped toward the body and pointed to the victim's forehead. 'See this stellate pattern? Muzzle was held against the skin. Single shot. No exit wound. Our vic's got a thick skull. And the firearm was small. I'm guessing nine millimeter.'

Jagger moved in for a closer inspection. 'This is Cameron Lawford.'

'Never heard of him,' Doug said dismissively.

'*Cam* Lawford?' Jagger tried.

Now Doug's face was blank *and* annoyed. 'Still haven't heard of him.'

'He was a football star at Penn State,' Jagger explained. 'Lasted half a season with the Dolphins before a career-ending injury.'

Doug gestured to the semen stains on the sheets. 'He went out with a bang. In more ways than one. With a cock that size, who wouldn't?'

'Interesting observation,' Jagger teased.

'I'm just saying.' An instant splotch of red stained the coroner's cheeks.

Gucci ignored the boys as she carefully surveyed the scene. The duvet was slung onto the floor. The sheets were twisted into a passionate mess. A half-burned lime basil and mandarin Jo Malone candle sat on the nightstand, along with an iPod stereo paused on Diana Krall's 'Peel Me a Grape,' an empty bottle of Ferrari-Carano Chardonnay, and next to that, a single wineglass.

'Time of death?' she asked.

'Sometime between seven and eight last night,' Doug replied. 'Housekeeper found him this morning.'

Gucci checked the bathroom and closet, discovering an elaborate male toiletries kit and an expensive set of street clothes – black Armani slacks, a finely laundered Thomas Pink shirt, spotless Prada shoes.

'He was a gigolo,' she announced matter-of-factly.

Jagger raised an eyebrow.

Doug pointed to the dead body. 'Well, if he ended up like this, I guess she didn't come.'

Gucci was staring at the Andy Warhol *Flowers* print that adorned the salmon-colored wall. 'No cell phone?'

Doug shook his head.

She reached into her bag and fished out a pair of latex gloves. 'This is a seduction scene. He'd keep the cell out of sight and on silent.' She stepped back into the bathroom and carefully retrieved an iPhone from the side pocket of the toiletries case.

Jagger suited up with latex gloves as well. He splayed out his hand.

Gucci turned over the device. 'You're faster with these things.'

He worked the touch screen with expert, nimble fingers. 'Most recent call was outgoing to a Jennifer Payne. Last night at seven twenty-two. Checking out the calendar now ... four appointments in the last few days – Jennifer, Billie, Mrs. S, and Kristin for the weekend ... I'm in the contact links now ... mobile numbers, e-mail addresses, lists of their favorite things ... Jennifer likes to be dominated ... Billie is into erotic massage ... Mrs. S has a car fetish ... Kristin enjoys role-playing.'

Gucci took in a deep breath. 'He was a smart manwhore. At the end of the day, it's all about customer service.' She stepped back into the main part of the suite, quietly ruminating over the details.

'Jesus,' Jagger remarked, following her.

'He was a client, too?' Doug cracked. 'This guy really was good in bed.'

Jagger continued working the iPhone obsessively. 'When I say Billie and Kristin, I mean *Billie Shelton* and *Kristin Fox*.'

'Speak of the devil,' Gucci said, gazing out the floor-to-ceiling window to see a mega-sized billboard advertising Billie Shelton's wildly successful *Rebirth* show at the London Hotel.

'Who's Kristin Fox?' Doug wondered.

'She's a bestselling novelist,' Jagger offered. 'That HBO show *Come to Bed* is based on her book.'

'The one about all the suburbanites fucking each other?' Doug asked.

Jagger nodded.

Gucci stepped closer to the bed and stared at Cam Lawford. His eyes were open, seemingly looking through her and on into infinity. She didn't turn away. A powerful feeling seized her gut. It was the kind of instinct that never let her down.

'I know that look,' Jagger said.

Gucci continued staring into the victim's shocked and dead eyes. 'This was an intimate murder,' she said quietly. 'There was no struggle. He was at his most vulnerable. And he never saw it coming. I think a woman killed him.'

'Maybe an obsessed client?' Jagger ventured.

Gucci glanced at her partner. 'Or maybe one with something to lose. Two of his most recent dates were high profile – an entertainer, a successful writer. What's the story on the others?'

Jagger was already there. 'Nothing on the Mrs. S. For Jennifer, the name and number match a marriage and family therapist's office on Paseo del Prado.'

Gucci raised an eyebrow. 'Obviously, she was his client. Maybe he was hers, too.'

Doug snorted derisively. 'Guys like him don't see shrinks. They don't need to.'

Jagger traded a meaningful look with Gucci. 'Not necessarily. He crashes and burns one season into the NFL and ends up screwing for money on the Strip. I'd need therapy.' He went back to the business of iPhone forensics. 'Hey, check this – turns out Cam Lawford had a book deal in the works. It's called *Stud Diaries*. No lie.'

Doug cackled. 'Now I've heard it all.'

Gucci sighed and glanced at the victim once more.

'I miss the old days when hookers just had a lamppost.' One beat. 'Anything on the security tapes?'

'The manager's working on that,' Jagger said. 'He's not happy.'

She rolled her eyes. 'Well, I'll raise his unhappiness with a dead guy in the prime of his life. Guess who wins?'

'So where do you want to start?' Jagger asked.

'Where else? With the women who paid him,' Gucci said.

Part One

FANTASY

Six Weeks Earlier

> **Las Vegas is the only place I know where money really talks – it says, 'Good-bye.'**
> **FRANK SINATRA**

CHAPTER ONE

Even Cam Lawford's nipples were exquisite. This was the first thought that came to Kristin Fox when her eyes fluttered open. She let out a soft, satisfied moan. 'How long have I been asleep?'

'About twenty minutes,' he whispered. 'But you earned it. That was quite a workout.' His fingertips skated down her naked torso.

Kristin stretched languidly, feeling a delicious soreness that would linger for days. It was still amazing that her tiny body could accommodate him. She was only four-foot-eleven. She weighed ninety-eight pounds. And Cam was the most well-endowed man she had ever been with. To say his prized asset was practically the size of a wine bottle would only be a mild exaggeration.

'Our time's up.' Gently, he extricated himself from her embrace and swung around, planting both feet on the floor. The man was a stickler for keeping a schedule. Two hours was two hours. Not a minute more, not a minute less.

She watched him dress back into the cop uniform, complete with handcuffs, Taser X3, and fake badge. His body was a marvel – the perfect V shape, the sculpted muscles, the taut, tanned, naturally smooth skin. If there was a single physical flaw, Kristin could not find it.

Cam discreetly pocketed the red envelope on the desk. 'As always, it was a pleasure, Mrs. Fox.' He started for the door. 'Think about a new scenario for next time. I could get my hands on a soldier's uniform or a firefighter's suit.'

She stared after him, half shocked, half appalled, all the way titillated.

Cam gave her a hot and final look. 'Call me.' And then he walked out.

In the silence that followed, the thousand dollars it had just cost her to feel this good seemed like a bargain. She was positively glowing – inside and out. That she was paying for the pleasure did not make her feel the slightest bit desperate. With her highly toned petite frame, long blond hair, and delicate features, many remarked that she resembled pop songstress Kylie Minogue. Finding a man who would sleep with her for free was not her problem. But like everything else, you get what you pay for.

Suddenly, she was struck by a sharp pang of loneliness, private shame, and a wave of guilt. And once again Kristin wondered, *What in God's name am I doing?*

She was slumming at the Flamingo, one of the oldest hotels on the Strip. The rooms were inexpensive. Ugly tourists lined up elbow-to-elbow at the casino's slot machines. Hookers staked out the elevators. Even the property's newly remodeled Go suites were quintessential Vegas tacky. The white vinyl upholstered ceiling-high headboards, posh carpeting, and sleekly modern décor touches gave off sci-fi vibrations in the vein of the Jane Fonda camp classic *Barbarella*.

Still, the paradox gave Kristin a frisson of smug satisfaction. Her husband, Hart Fox, was a top executive at the London Hotel, the Strip's sprawling new mega-property competing for a share of a tightening hotel, gambling, and entertainment market.

And here she was at the Flamingo, dropping cash for a room booked under her maiden name, making time with a stud-for-hire. It was the kind of tacky, scandalous, and selfish behavior that powerful, accomplished, and high-profile men typically indulged in. She allowed herself a moment of secret celebration. This one was for the fed-up wives of America.

Every husband had secrets. Every wife had them, too. In fact, writing about such matters had made Kristin rich and almost famous. Like a character from one of her popular novels, Hart believed that her appointment for private Pilates instruction was actually private Pilates instruction. The subterfuge always provided a quiet, if temporary, thrill, especially in light of the fact that her husband could be such a mean son of a bitch.

This is purple prose romance crap for sexually frustrated housewives.

Years later, she could still hear Hart's dismissive voice inside her head. He had never supported her writing ambitions. His complaint was that she wasted valuable hours that could be better spent on their two children and other household concerns.

But Kristin had refused to give up. She began to work surreptitiously, stealing fragments of time during Lily's gymnastics classes or Ollie's soccer games, slipping out to early-morning yoga classes that were a front for sixty-minute writing and coffee binges at Starbucks. And she took advantage of every possible moment in between.

On some level, Hart's lack of support was an important factor in her success. The combination of resentment and determination to prove him wrong became unstoppable fuel. It changed her writing dramatically. Kristin stopped echoing the styles of other authors and found her own unique voice. She crafted wicked observational tales about what she saw around her – asshole husbands, unfulfilled wives, slutty neighbors, incompetent parents, and messed-up children.

The result was *Come to Bed*, a raunchy exposé on the rise in spouse swapping among upscale suburban dwellers. After years of self-doubts, unpublishable drafts, and industry rejections, everything happened at a dizzying pace.

The first agent she queried signed her immediately. Within days, the novel garnered such intense interest that it went to auction and sold for $500,000. HBO snapped up television rights and put the project on a fast-track development schedule. Just months after the hardcover edition reached the upper echelon of every bestseller list, the premium pay cable channel was airing a series based on her novel. Critics dismissed it as 'Sex in the Suburbs.' But the ratings were huge.

Kristin Fox had officially become a minor cultural phenomenon. Just like Jackie Collins once blew the lid off Hollywood social mores for a voyeuristic public, Kristin did very much the same, only her excavation was the moral rot that existed inside well-heeled suburbia.

But the controversy surrounding *Come to Bed* was mild compared to the incendiary reaction that greeted her second novel, *The Guy Next Door*, which chronicled the secret gay society of conservative Southern married men attending a megachurch called Pine River. Though right-wing crusaders attacked her with a vengeance, the outrage only spurred sales and attracted more readers.

No matter her success, Hart still dismissed Kristin's career as an indulgent hobby. He only saw the way that it stood in the path of her responsibilities to him, their children, and home.

Leave the selfish bastard.

This was a thought that rolled around in Kristin's mind almost every day. She had the reasons to say good-bye. She had the money to finance her exit. But she just could not bring herself to put a plan into motion.

More than anything, it was Ollie and Lily that gave her pause. The children adored their father. And while failing her in so many ways, Hart had been reasonably good to them. Plus, a gut thing told her that Ollie would insist upon living with Hart in the event of a divorce, a move that she felt sure would risk derailing her already struggling twelve-year-old son.

Beyond her concern for the children, though, Kristin had to admit that the idea of starting over alone was paralyzing. So much of her life had been spent loving Hart, then enduring him, ultimately resenting him. But was this destined to be the rest of her life, too? If Hart knew how she had spent her morning, the things she had done to Cam Lawford, the things she had begged him to do to her . . .

Her BlackBerry chimed with a text alert.

OLLIE FOX Bring me some lunch. Subway sounds good.

She stared at the message. Ollie was growing up to issue rude demands just like his father.

KRISTIN FOX Sorry, have an appt. Eat at school.

OLLIE FOX This sucks!

KRISTIN FOX Children have survived worse.

The communication halted. Ollie would probably sulk over her refusal to cater to this instant whim. And he would likely complain to Hart, who in turn would attack Kristin with something like, 'The boy has to eat. What were you doing that was more important?'

She would be so tempted to answer, 'I had just finished fucking a twenty-four-year-old. It was an inconvenient time.'

Kristin dressed quickly, covered her long blond hair with a Pucci scarf, donned face-swallowing Oliver Peoples sunglasses, and slipped out of the Flamingo, into the parking garage, and away from the Strip.

Traffic crawled along Las Vegas Boulevard. She suffered through it, alternately touching up her lipstick and checking e-mails as Kings of Leon's 'Sex on Fire' blared at deafening volume in her moonbeam-colored Bentley Continental GT.

Kristin had chosen this particular make and model because she had announced to Hart that she was buying a car and paying cash for it with her first royalty earnings for *Come to Bed*. When she drove the vehicle home, the look on his face – total shock mixed with constipation – had been worth the outrageous sticker price.

Finally, the gridlock gave way. Kristin reached Nevada 589 and picked up speed. Ten minutes later, she was pulling into a Pueblo Revival-styled office court and rushing inside a second-floor suite.

A bell on the door announced her arrival into an unstaffed waiting room. She sat down long enough to anxiously thumb through several pages of *Architectural Digest* before Jennifer Payne opened an adjoining office door and invited her inside with a warm smile.

Nancy – a fluffy, Alpine white, immaculately groomed Bichon frise – greeted her affectionately.

Kristin assumed her place on the chocolate-brown leather sofa. The initial moments of every therapy session were always fraught with awkwardness. Out of sheer politeness, she sometimes felt compelled to engage in banal small talk, even though her preference was to get right down to it. Fifty minutes could go by in a flash.

'How are you?' Jennifer said, and unlike most people who asked the question, she really wanted to know.

And that's when Kristin started to cry.

CHAPTER TWO

The irony never escaped Jennifer Payne. At thirty-five, she was a marriage and family therapist who specialized in relationship issues. Clients – most of them women – came to her seeking coping tools for emotional rescue. And yet her own union – going seven years weak to a man she could barely tolerate these days – was pushing her to the brink of frustration.

But like failed novelists could teach novice writers and like unsuccessful thespians could mentor student actors, Jennifer knew that she still had something worthwhile to offer her clients.

Kristin Fox fascinated her. The woman was an ever-changing kaleidoscope of love and hate, liberation and imprisonment, confidence and insecurity.

'Over the years, I've seen a number of clients in conventional marriages who seek out affairs,' Jennifer said quietly. 'One of the similarities is that they more often than not choose men who are not good lovers. At least not better than their husbands. They sacrifice sexual satisfaction to be appreciated again, to not be taken for granted. I'm curious. How does Cam make you feel?'

Kristin reflected for a moment. 'He makes me feel enti-tled . . . monstrously entitled.'

Jennifer was intrigued. 'Go on.'

'I get to the hotel first and wait. The anticipation of hearing that knock on the door is so exciting. And I love it when he takes his money. I feel like I'm in control.' She opened her mouth to say more, then seemed to think better of it.

Jennifer always allowed for silence. Therapy was not talk radio. Filling every second with sound did not necessarily move a session forward.

'He's in awe of the fact that I'm a bestselling author. He doesn't want me to be some bored little housewife. I read to him, mostly new pages that I've written. It's the most intimate I've ever been with a man . . . it's more intimate than the sex.'

'Explain to me the sense of entitlement,' Jennifer said.

'For those two hours, he's mine. I own him. He works hard to please me. He feeds my feminine ego, my writer's ego, too. And he's this young, hot, hard-bodied . . . *toy*.' Kristin gestured for Nancy to join her on the couch.

Jennifer watched as Kristin indulged the dog with gentle caresses. Nancy was a partner of sorts in the private practice. Her presence comforted clients and seemed to encourage them to share more of themselves.

'Why should men like Tiger Woods have all the fun? I think more married women should cheat. I believe we should act on our horniness just like men do. Does that make me a terrible person?'

'Of course not. It's . . . complex,' Jennifer said, employing one of her favorite terms. The word was nonjudgmental, and it bought the necessary time and space to explore more deeply. 'Perhaps this is an assertion of power. You have the economic independence to choose a man for precisely the purpose you desire. But this is also being driven by the lack of satisfaction in your marriage.'

'It always comes back to him, doesn't it?'

'On a certain level, yes,' Jennifer confirmed. 'You're having an erotic adventure. All the rebellion, secrecy, and naughtiness make it fun. In a sense, you're getting everything that you want. You're using the money from the career that Hart has always disparaged to go out there and be unfaithful. You're making a fool of him. Meanwhile, Cam is a flesh-and-blood fantasy. He offers sexual pleasure. He appreciates your talent and accomplishments. I understand how satisfying that must be. But it's not exactly real. How long can it last? And what will you do when it ends?'

Kristin just sat there for several extended, preoccupied seconds.

Jennifer noticed the time. She generally liked to conclude each session by reflecting on the work done, but sometimes the clock simply ran out. 'We're going to have to stop here for today.'

Six clients a day was Jennifer's limit. She preferred fewer than that, particularly when dealing with a DC – therapist vernacular for *difficult customer*.

There was one on her current caseload – Billie Shelton, the rock star turned tabloid tragedy turned Vegas act. One session could leave Jennifer spent and feeling useless. Her sense was that Billie was keeping secrets – perhaps dangerous secrets – and that made the process of emotional discovery almost impossible.

Thinking about Billie's case, Jennifer noticed an envelope between the sofa cushions. It belonged to Kristin. Jennifer typically requested that clients bring in photographs of the family members, lovers, and friends whom they discussed in therapy.

People were often different than the way Jennifer envisioned them or the way clients described them. She flicked through Kristin's snapshots. Hart Fox was sexier and more handsome than she imagined. In her mind, he was bald, stocky, and rigid with intensity, the kind of man whose emotional expressions were limited to anger and lust. The subject in the photo was far more captivating. His tall, athletic frame, dark hair, and brooding intensity brought to mind actor Jon Hamm's Don Draper persona from *Mad Men*.

Ollie had been painted as a mirror image of his father in look and attitude. There was a certain resemblance to Hart, but Jennifer saw a sullen, overweight boy struggling with a low self-concept. Only Lily, the nine-year-old, lived up to the sweet, angelic girl that Kristin promoted.

The next snapshot gripped her attention and raised her temperature. There had been no exaggeration or off-base descriptors in Kristin's assessment of Cam Lawford. He was a gorgeous man with an underwear model's body and a brazenly sexy attitude. Kristin had captured an image of him in bed, with the top sheet barely up to his waist. The hooded look in his piercing blue eyes seemed to convey a carnal campaign promise: *I'm the best time you will ever have in bed.*

Jennifer could not stop staring at the photograph. Generally, the sight of nude or semi-nude men did not turn her on. But something about Cam Lawford's pinup looks and guy's guy brawn had her body pinpricking with arousal.

Shamefully, she shoved the pictures back inside the envelope and sat down at the desk to establish her equilibrium, opening her MacBook Pro to scan e-mails and surf *The Daily Beast*. But she found herself Googling 'Cam Lawford.'

Dozens of hits materialized – sports items from his Penn State career, stories chronicling his brief appearance with the Miami Dolphins ... and a single entry for his own Web address.

Jennifer's thumb hovered over the click-bar that would activate the link. Just as her finger made contact and brought the site onscreen, she experienced a stab of regret ... yet she did not turn back.

It was basic. Some photographs, a list of services that included massage, fitness training, and personal entertainment, a contact number and e-mail address, and a very large, very bold WOMEN ONLY disclaimer.

She was astonished that her curiosity had allowed her to go this far. But Kristin had been so explicit about her encounters with Cam. She talked endlessly about his stamina, his vigorous way with intercourse, his insatiable passion, and his impressive endowment.

Jennifer closed her eyes. The months had stretched on to almost a year. That's how much time had passed since Patrick had made love to her. She craved the warmth of a man's touch. In fact, her body ached for it. But even acknowledging this natural desire brought on a crushing guilt as she considered her husband.

Patrick was in a career slump and suffering from a depression that seemed impossible to overcome. He managed it with Lexapro. The drug stabilized his moods, but the side effects – decreased libido and delayed ejaculation – frustrated him to the point where he had lost all interest in sex. And he refused to talk about the problem or even consider trying a different medication.

As a couple, they were in a dangerous place – utterly disconnected, sharing nothing but space. Only their amazing and beautiful daughter, five-year-old Mia Sara, brought them joy. The rest of their world was an endless cycle of lifeless nights watching Patrick fall asleep on the sofa in front of Fox News. Jennifer's soul was slowly dying. She could almost feel it wasting away.

When she lifted the receiver and heard the dial tone, her stomach lurched. The obvious next step was to punch in the number. She hesitated, then reluctantly jabbed in the digits.

To even fantasize about contacting Cam Lawford was wrong. Not to mention unethical, imprudent, professionally reckless, and an affront to the sacred vows of her marriage. But the anxiety gave her a rush. The sensation of risk and danger and abandon was so intoxicating. She was that desperate for something exotic and erotic.

He picked up on the third ring. 'This is Cam.'

Her first instinct was to simply hang up. Instead, she just remained on the line.

'Hello?'

Jennifer took in a deep breath and promised herself that

she was only calling him for a massage. That was a legit-imate therapeutic concern. And the private lie gave her the courage to speak out loud. 'I heard about you from a friend . . .'

CHAPTER THREE

Billie Shelton belted out the Tina Turner classic 'What's Love Got to Do with It' torch style, accompanied only by piano. She rolled around on the custom-designed leopard-print baby grand in a red gown, daring a slit that went all the way to the moon. Her goal: To give it to them so hot that Michelle Pfeiffer's 'Makin' Whoopee' number from *The Fabulous Baker Boys* would seem about as sexy as a colonoscopy.

She finished off with a note that stretched on and on. Any Broadway bitch would've conked out thirty seconds ago. Her voice was more evocative than ever – raspy, haunting, vulnerable. And it should be. Every lyric was directed at March Donaldson, the right wing's motor-mouthed media stud and the man whose presence in her life had left a little shard of glass that pierced her heart whenever he came to mind.

But no dreamboat asshole was enough to ruin her incredible instrument. The same went for the lost years of drugs and alcohol and the nightmare that had come close to killing her. Billie Shelton was a goddamn survivor.

Her favorite dancer was right there to whisk her off the piano and onto the stage floor for the next number – a moody, slow-building, intricately choreographed cover of Adele's 'Chasing Pavements.' She hit her mark to perfection, moving like a seasoned showgirl.

'Girl, you are *fierce*!'

Billie beamed proudly at David Dean, answering him with a high-flying kick.

He howled with laughter. David was the youngest in the troupe – a baby at twenty-one and a Vegas newbie by way of Utah, fresh from being cut off by his Mormon parents for coming out. He did everything he could to make it on his own – dancing in her show, teaching kick-boxing classes, and doing product modeling gigs at conventions. A real hardscrabble Sin City dreamer.

The sound check was over. Curtain would go up at 7:30. With an hour to kill, Billie made a quick retreat to her small backstage dressing room, tossing off the dress and towering heels in favor of a luxurious cashmere robe and her favorite pair of Uggs.

Lindsay Lee, the perpetually crabby wardrobe assistant, stormed in to reclaim custody of the expensive Marc Bouwer dress. 'Oh, look, it's piled on the floor like old gym clothes. Ann-Margret never pulled this kind of shit. Now there was a lady who cared!'

Lindsay was on the other side of sixty, rough looking but clearly a beauty in her youth. Years of hard drinking and smoking had aged her considerably. An unlit cigarette dangled from her fleshy lips.

'You know, if you light that thing, I might take a drag or two,' Billie hinted.

'No way. I'm trying to quit. But it helps to have something in my mouth.'

Billie smirked. 'I'm not going to say a word. It's just

too easy.' This was their routine – complaints and insults delivered with an undercurrent of affection.

Lindsay groaned her irritation, snatched the gown, and walked out.

Billie was alone for maybe forty-five seconds.

And then Carly McPhee came in to deliver a stainless steel travel mug of green tea with honey and lemon. 'Randall expects you back at the penthouse for dinner no later than nine thirty.'

Billie accepted the tea and nodded wordlessly, seized by a miserable feeling as all sense of control evaporated. She sipped slowly, allowing the caffeine-free concoction to coat her throat. 'How does the house look tonight?'

'Six hundred eighty-seven at last count. It should tick up to seven hundred by showtime.'

Billie's *Rebirth* spectacular played six nights a week at the Palladium Showroom in the London Hotel, which had finished construction just before other developments began to freeze.

It was precarious timing to open an extended-run show. Las Vegas tourism had dropped by double digits. With decades of phenomenal growth stopped cold, the city was gripped by ominous financial fears.

But *Rebirth* was garnering rave reviews and passionate word of mouth. The London's aggressive promotional efforts continued to stand out in a hypercompetitive entertainment market. Hart Fox had promised Billie a kick-ass campaign, and for once, a corporate asshole had actually delivered on his big talk. Apparently, hell had frozen over, and pigs were flying.

Tragic. Utter waste of talent. Lost cause.

Those had been the public declarations about Billie Shelton from industry executives, music critics, and famous peers. Yet here she was, proving all the doubters wrong. The validation should be sending tingles throughout her body. But Billie felt absolutely nothing.

'*Vegas* magazine is interested in doing a feature,' Carly announced crisply. 'But they won't commit to the cover, so Randall wants to wait.'

Billie shrugged, brooking no argument as Carly continued on in clipped tones about a recording session for a charity Christmas CD by Vegas stars and an upcoming interview alongside Randall for his segment on *Metamorphosis*, the popular cable series about plastic surgery.

Shut up, bitch.

Billie wanted to scream out the words but instead seethed silently, betraying nothing. She hated Carly. Randall's uniquely devoted personal assistant had become her unofficial handler, scheduler, and privacy invader. It was at once suffocating and demoralizing.

The few hours Billie could claim to herself were her sessions with Jennifer Payne, her massage therapy appointments, and occasional outings with Kristin Fox. But just maintaining those freedoms remained a constant struggle as Randall's penchant for control grew worse.

Carly stood there in her regulation St. John suit, pouty lips pumped full of a branded hyaluronic acid called Captique, pert California Natural breast implants jutting out like two scud missiles ready for launch. The walking iceberg smoothed a well-manicured hand through her over-processed blond hair as she inspected her BlackBerry. 'The recording session conflicts with your next massage.'

As disappointment crashed hard and fast, Billie made an effort to appear unfazed. 'I'll reschedule.'

'No need. I've already booked an in-room massage for later that afternoon,' Carly said. 'Natasha comes highly recommended by the London Spa.' There was a brief pause. 'And Randall prefers this arrangement.'

Billie's internal panic was total. She couldn't lose her access to Cam Lawford. The idea was unthinkable. 'Carly, please, I'm more than capable of scheduling my own massages.'

'It's already done.'

'I need ... I ... would like to retain the same therapist.'

Carly gave her a suspicious look.

'I *finally* found someone who can work on my back without causing me unbearable pain. I need these treatments to keep up with the show night after night. I'm sure whoever you found is great, but I can't start over with someone who doesn't know my body and risk going through all of that agony again.'

Carly appeared unmoved.

'You should see the X-rays of my back,' Billie went on, managing to keep the desperation out of her voice. 'It's a miracle I can even stand up straight. I was thrown down a flight of stairs and kicked to hell and back. I found a massage therapist who can gently navigate around the damage. Don't take that away from me.' She gave a final, imploring look.

With a slight huff, Carly fussed with her BlackBerry. 'Fine. I'll try to explain to Randall.'

'Thank you.'

Once Carly left, Billie breathed a quiet sigh of relief. Drinking deep on the tea, she approached the dressing table and lowered herself onto the cushioned seat that faced the mirror.

Her nerves were fraying at the edges. The teeth grinding started up again. Her legs began to shake. She glanced at the reflection and suddenly found herself engaged in an intense staring contest.

Billie Fucking Shelton.

That woman no longer existed. Once upon a time, she'd been a hell-raising ballbuster, the indie music scene's It Girl of the moment. Her provocative debut, *Dick Magnet*, was still considered a minor classic, though the praise always came with a disclaimer about potential career promise ruined by clichéd rock star excesses.

The cynical pricks were right. Billie had run the gauntlet faster than most. Hit record. Sold-out tour. Alcoholism. Sophomore slump. Drug addictions. Scorched-earth love affairs. Trashed friendships. Public meltdowns. Bankruptcy. Arrest. Emergency room death watch. All the essential elements for *Memoir of a Train Wreck* were there. She just needed a book deal and a ghostwriter who gave good cautionary tale.

Gazing at the stranger in the mirror, Billie tried to reconcile the fact that she was indeed that person from those days. But nothing quite connected, especially when it came down to the reflected image. Her physical identity had been completely altered, the old world and indulgent freedoms she once knew abruptly cut off.

Wincing at the memories, she touched her resculpted face with tentative fingertips, wracked by a terrible foreboding. Someday soon, Randall Glass would kill her. Of this Billie was certain.

When your husband woke you up in the middle of the night, shoved a gun into your mouth, and swore that any reason might be good enough to pull the trigger, a wife could do only one thing.

Take the sick bastard at his word.

Confessions from the Man
Who's Satisfying Your Wife

By Cam Lawford

Things I Can Tell Just by Looking at Her

Women will pay for sex. I'm not talking about old, ugly, or fat chicks. The ones keeping me in business are beautiful, successful, and at their sexual peak.

Sometimes they want to be kissed and held and told how attractive they are. Sometimes they want to play out a fantasy that's been living inside their head for years. And sometimes they just want the freedom to unleash their inner bad girl.

People are always curious about how I got into this kind of work. I used to play tight end for a pro team. One Sunday night I caught a pass up the middle, got taken down, fell the wrong way, and ripped my ACL. My future in the game was over before it really started. I've had blow jobs that lasted longer than my NFL career. But I got my Divisional ring. Sometimes I still wear it. Big piece of jewelry. You can't miss it. And women love the idea of being with a guy who played pro ball.

After I got discharged from the team, one of my old fraternity brothers invited me to hang out in Vegas. We called him Tabasco back in college, and the redneck, Mississippi-born party animal hadn't changed a bit. He still woke up every morning, worked out like crazy, played poker most of the day, and blew coke up his nose all night.

Tabasco was five-foot-ten with easily forgettable good looks, the start of a receding hairline, a less-than-average-sized cock, and a booming male escort business. I figured if this dickhead could generate a regular customer base of generous females, then I'd have women beating down my door.

One night he was too loaded to keep an appointment, so I filled in. The client was blond, early forties, fighting a wide ass and a midsection thick with stubborn post-baby weight, but still gorgeous. She spent the first half hour complaining about her husband. He rarely showed her any affection. The guy would come home after a three-day business trip and give her nothing more than a dry kiss on the cheek and a platonic sideways hug. She was starving for it. That night I made her come so hard she nearly scratched the skin off my back.

Then she told her friends about me. It's a given that a lot of girl talk is bullshit. They lie to each other all the time. But when a woman praises a man for being a champ in bed, other women pay close attention. And in this industry, word of mouth is everything.

CHAPTER FOUR

A nude woman was screaming for her life as a menacing man in full coal mining gear chased her with a pickax. Once close enough, he sliced the weapon through her head with a murderous rage.

Kristin stood frozen with disbelief, shocked by the bloody, gory scene in front of her.

Ollie was kicked back in a plush, quilted black leather recliner, transfixed by the carnage as his orange-stained fingers dug into a three-quarters-down bag of cheese puffs.

'*What* are you watching?' Kristin demanded.

'*My Bloody Valentine*.' He mumbled the answer, never taking his eyes off the hundred-inch HD flat screen.

Kristin seized the remote and fumbled to find the right buttons. The volume shot up to a near deafening level, then went silent as the screen turned solid blue.

Ollie lurched forward. 'Mom!'

'You know better than—'

'Dad said I could!'

'I don't care what your father said. You're not watching that kind of garbage in this house.'

Ollie rose up in hostile protest. 'Oh, but it's fine for you to *write* garbage in this house!'

Kristin glared at him, experiencing a flash of dislike for

her own son. The moment shamed her. 'Go shower and get ready for bed.'

'I'll just finish watching it when Dad gets—'

'Ollie,' Kristin cut in, her voice a low hiss. 'I've had enough of your nasty attitude. What I say is not open to debate or reconsideration by your father.' Spotting his iPhone on the arm of the recliner, she snatched it. 'And until I feel like you fully understand that . . . no cell phone privileges.'

Ollie attempted an indifferent shrug, even as his nostrils flared. 'I don't care.' His eyes narrowed into slits, and he stared Kristin down for several long, hateful seconds before miserably trudging out of the state-of-the-art media room, muttering curses under his breath.

Kristin sank down onto one of the recliners and stared blankly at the blue screen. Ollie was only twelve. What would he be saying to her at sixteen?

Woof! Woof! Woof!

Sinatra, their Harlequin Great Dane, was barking excitedly, a special rhythm and timbre that he reserved for Hart's arrival.

It was just after ten o'clock.

Kristin's stomach knotted, anxiety settling in her chest as she ventured down to greet her husband.

Hart was standing in front of the open refrigerator door. 'Did you cook dinner?' He gave her an irritated, blood-shot-eyed glance.

She shook her head. 'Lily's spending the night with a friend, and Ollie wanted Taco Bell.'

'That explains why he's getting so fat.'

There was an open bottle of Mollydooker's Carnival of

Love Shiraz on the kitchen island. Kristin poured herself another glass. Obviously, she would need it.

Hart continued scowling into the refrigerator. 'I come home, and there's not a goddamn thing to eat.'

'It's after ten, Hart. And you didn't even call.'

He slammed the stainless steel door hard enough to rattle its contents.

Calmly, Kristin sipped her wine. 'Sinatra needs to go for a walk.'

'So take him. I've been dealing with shit all day. I shouldn't have to come home and pick up his shit, too.' He leaned against the counter, ran a hand through his thick hair, and let out a deep, stressed, world-weary sigh.

Knowing that the London had opened in the weakest tourism climate to hit the market in decades, Kristin felt herself thaw toward him. 'There's some rotisserie chicken salad. I could make you a sandwich.'

'Don't bother.' Hart rubbed his eyes. 'I'll just have a drink.'

'What happened today?' She asked this, honestly wanting to know, but secretly resentful that he never considered how her day might have gone.

'More of the same. Everything's down – occupancy, the casino, the restaurants. Billie's show is the only good news. She sells out every night. But we have to cut rates again. The Paris and Caesars are booking rooms for seventy bucks. Trump is advertising at less than a hundred *and* giving out spa credits. It's a bloodbath.'

'Why don't you take a shower,' Kristin suggested. 'I'll walk Sinatra, and when I get back, I'll fix something for both of us.'

His lips curled into a cruel smirk. 'Is this your half-assed attempt at playing the supportive wife?'

Kristin looked at him sharply. 'I'm just being pleasant, Hart. You should try it sometime. You might find that it requires less energy.'

'Pleasant for me would be a decent meal and a blow job, preferably at the same time.'

'You're disgusting.' Desperate to get out of the house, she put down her wineglass, grabbed the leash and a few plastic supermarket bags, and searched the first floor for Sinatra, finding him sprawled out on a sofa in the formal living room.

The laziest dog in the world did not budge.

'*Sinatra*. I know you have to poop.'

Reluctantly, he lumbered toward her, his feelings hurt, his enormous head hanging low in embarrassment. He was also the most hypersensitive dog in the world.

Hart appeared and attempted to intercede. 'I'll take him.'

Kristin gripped tightly on the leash. 'No, I need some air.'

Hart started to walk away.

'We have a problem with Ollie,' Kristin announced.

He turned around. 'Besides the crap diet you enable, what is it?'

Kristin sighed with frustration, half inclined to abandon the conversation altogether. But she decided to force the issue. It was too important. No matter how much their own relationship had deteriorated, there had to be some solidarity where the children were concerned.

'He's disrespectful. He fights me on everything. His angle is always to go to you in order to get his way. Tonight I walked in the media room, and he was watching a naked girl get hacked to death in some sick R-rated movie. He tried to tell me that you said it was okay.'

Hart's expression was pure annoyance. 'It's just a movie, Kristin. What's the big deal? Guys Ollie's age want to see tits and gore. It's normal.'

She stared at him incredulously. 'You can't actually believe that.'

'I promise you he won't grow up to be a serial killer.'

Kristin looked away for a moment. He could be such a patronizing son of a bitch. Sometimes she truly hated him. 'A movie like that isn't appropriate for a twelve-year-old. But you would say otherwise just to disagree with me. Next to golf, that seems to be your favorite sport.'

'You're making too much out of a stupid movie,' Hart snapped. 'Maybe Ollie wouldn't be so goddamn fat if you worried half as much about what he ate.'

Kristin felt the flush of anger start at her neck and rise up to her cheeks. 'Oh, so his weight is *my* fault? It has nothing to do with the fact that he doesn't exercise or play any sports?'

'He plays soccer.'

'Ollie hasn't played soccer in over a year. But how would you know? You never attended a single game, which is probably why he lost interest and quit.'

Hart's face registered real, unexpected hurt. He was speechless.

Kristin felt a certain satisfaction for having earned a moment at her husband's expense. Those occasions were rare. She tugged at Sinatra, dragging him through the front door and into the Nevada night.

The Great Dane trotted obediently beside her, walking proudly, sniffing at the air, enjoying the cool desert mountain breeze.

They lived in a six-bedroom/eight-bath seven-thousand-square-foot home in Red Rock Country Club, a guard-gated community nestled at the base of Red Rock Canyon and lavishly situated around two Arnold Palmer-designed golf courses.

'I don't envy you!'

One of their neighbors, Elaine Dayan, was across the street with Sonny and Cher, two adorable Coton de Tuléars. She stopped to point at the enormous pile of shit Sinatra was producing.

Kristin carefully arranged her plastic bags to prepare for the gross but necessary cleanup chore. 'Believe it or not, this isn't the worst part of my day!'

Elaine laughed airily. 'I don't know how you manage! It's like horse dung! Where's Hart? He should be out here doing this!'

'I don't mind,' Kristin remarked. 'It's a gorgeous night.'

'Are you working on a new book?'

'Yes, I'm close to finishing. It should be out next year.'

'Well, I was just wondering,' Elaine said. 'I see you come and go during the week, and you're always so dressed up. You don't seem to be spending a lot of time at home in your office.'

It was the kind of seemingly innocent observation that, if overheard by Hart, might trigger a storm of invasive questions.

'Oh, I'm active at Ollie and Lily's schools and with a

few charities as well,' Kristin said, hoping to satisfy Elaine's curiosity and neutralize the subject at the same time. 'Sometimes it helps my creative flow to write away from the house, too.'

Elaine returned a supportive nod. 'Well, I can't wait to read the next one! Good night!' Cooing baby talk to Sonny and Cher, she ventured back toward her big, empty house. Elaine was a recent widow, lonely, and enjoyed meandering conversation over tea.

Kristin made a mental note to invite her over soon. It had been too long between visits, and she should – and could – make the time for the dear woman.

Hart was just exiting the shower when Kristin entered the master bedroom. He toweled off quickly, parading around naked as he flossed and brushed his teeth. Just one year away from fifty, he stayed in impressive physical shape through regular weight-lifting sessions, running, and golf.

She ignored him as she removed her makeup and slathered Crème de la Mer onto her face and neck.

The turgid rap beat of Eminem's 'Not Afraid' cut into the tense silence.

Kristin scooped Ollie's iPhone from her front pocket and powered down the device.

'That sounds like Ollie's ringtone,' Hart said.

'It is. I took away his phone.'

He snickered. 'That should improve his attitude.'

She glared at him through the mirror.

Hart responded by pressing his body against her and bringing his mouth down to the nape of her neck. 'I'll talk to Ollie tomorrow,' he whispered thickly.

She felt his arousal and stepped away. 'I have some work to finish.'

'What's your fucking problem?'

Kristin turned on him hotly. 'You come home after ten. You don't bother to call to say you're going to be late. Every word out of your mouth is either an insult or an argument. And then you actually think I would want to have sex with you. The better question is what's *your* fucking problem?'

She left him standing there with a strong erection and no place to put it. In most instances, Kristin passively accepted Hart's lustful embraces, so refusing him tonight was empowering.

Retreating to her writing office, she flicked on the Bose stereo to muffle the sound of her phone call to Cam Lawford. As Rihanna's 'Russian Roulette' played in the background, she whispered into the receiver, 'It's Kristin. I want to see you again. Try to get your hands on that soldier's uniform . . .'

CHAPTER FIVE

'You next.' The stern woman wearing a white nurse's robe spoke in a thick Hungarian accent.

Jennifer hesitated.

'*You next!*'

Flustered, Jennifer stood up quickly and followed her into a small treatment room.

'Strip. Get on table. Legs up.' She barked the orders like a drill sergeant.

Jennifer nervously slipped off her shoes, slacks, and underwear, her mind buzzing with a verbatim memory from Kristin's vagina monologue.

When it comes to grooming in Las Vegas, I don't trust anyone but the Gestapo Sisters. Cam says I have the most beautiful pussy he's ever seen.

The woman was staring at Jennifer's crotch and making no attempt to edit her disapproval. 'Your bush too long. Need trim before wax.' She reached for an electric hair-clipping device and flicked it on.

Hot with embarrassment, Jennifer closed her eyes as the necessary preliminary work commenced.

Kiss's Salon on East Tropicana was nothing exceptional on the aesthetic front, but the establishment – operated by twin sisters Julianna and Magdolna – appeared clean enough.

We learn from the strippers.

Another bit of wisdom Jennifer had picked up from Kristin – and other clients who were wives of high-ranking casino executives. There were no class barriers in Las Vegas when it came to personal upkeep. If a socialite on the planning committee for the Black and White Ball found herself sitting next to a pole dancer from Treasures at Salon Rojo, then she knew she was getting her hair colored at the right place.

'You want Brazilian, yes?'

Jennifer nodded. There were other options – the bikini wax, the G-string wax, the Hollywood wax. She had no idea what each entailed. All she knew was that Kristin had talked at length about Cam's preference for the Brazilian, which removed all hair except for a landing strip at the front.

Suddenly, Jennifer could feel the sensation of the warm wax being applied. It was strangely soothing. Her anxiety began to subside, even as the pressure of the cloth strip signaled the inevitable next step.

RIP.

'Oh, God!' Jennifer cried. The pain arrived with a ferocious intensity. She knew that the hair was gone. But it felt like the skin might have gone with it. Beads of sweat dotted her forehead.

'Be quiet. I'm working.'

RIP.

The agony shot up a notch. Tears formed in Jennifer's eyes. She held her breath for the next one.

Kristin had spent the better part of a session discussing the perfect Brazilian wax and its positive impact on her sexual confidence. But she never mentioned the pain.

'Why you crying? I don't understand.'

'It's excruciating,' Jennifer whispered, her voice quivering. 'You have to stop.'

'You no leave like this. Just one side finished. I have reputation.'

RIP.

Jennifer clenched both fists as the pain shot through, sharp and fast.

'Turn over.'

She just lay there, frozen.

'Worst pain top of vulva. That done. Turn over.'

She did precisely as she was told, suffering silently through the rest of the procedure, hoping the results would be worth it.

Cam Lawford was *the* most desirable man Jennifer had ever seen, and it seemed unlikely that she could ever be desirable enough for someone like him, even if she were paying.

Finally, the torture ended. The woman tossed some baby powder onto the inflamed area. 'Get dressed. Come back four weeks. Next time not so bad.'

Later that night, while relaxing in a warm tub perfumed with Chanel No. 5 Velvet Milk Bath, Jennifer could not stop touching herself. It was so soft, so smooth, so gorgeous. The little rush of more blood flowing down there was undeniable. For the first time in a long time, she felt sexy. And not just sexy . . . but very, very sexy.

She heard Patrick making his way toward the master bathroom.

'Are you still in there?' His tone registered annoyance.

Boldly, Jennifer stood up. She was naked, dripping wet . . . waiting.

Look at me, Patrick. Show me some sign that we're more than ambivalent roommates. Give me a reason not to go through with my plan.

He gave Jennifer a cursory glance as he stepped into the water closet and released a seemingly endless stream of urine, no doubt brought on by the consumption of beer that accompanied his ritualistic evening viewing of *The O'Reilly Factor* and *Hannity*.

When he stepped out, he gave her a strange look. 'Do you need a towel or something?'

Hastily, Jennifer covered her body with a bath sheet. 'I got a Brazilian wax today. Not that it matters to you.'

Patrick stared back at her with dull, black eyes.

'I can't even remember the last time we made love. Does that bother you at all?' Jennifer knew this was the wrong approach. It was an attack, an interrogation. Questioning a man about his lack of interest in sex would only push him away. But hurt and frustration overrode her more sensible instincts.

Patrick shrugged wearily. 'It's late, Jen. I'm tired and a little drunk.'

'Really?' She gave him a contemptuous look. The truth was, she wanted to fight – about his flat-lined libido, about his endless zombie act in front of the television, about anything at all. But Patrick refused to engage that way.

Jennifer knew that sexual desire was intricately linked

to how well a couple could argue. Without it, there was just a dangerous buildup of unexpressed anger. She routinely explained this to her clients. And now she was living it in her own marriage.

At thirty-six, Patrick appeared to be going through some kind of early midlife crisis. He had dramatically abandoned his once preppy persona in favor of jeans and T-shirts, long hair, and a biblical beard. The turnaround brought to mind the late '70s look of actor-singer-songwriter Kris Kristofferson. She had to admit that the transformation actually flattered him. There was a sexy, edgy, rebellious quality to his reinvented style.

Patrick was openly bored with his career covering local politics for the *Las Vegas Review-Journal*. The major daily, like most traditional newspapers all over the country, was responding to a declining readership with savage cost-saving measures – staff cuts, furloughs, reduced benefits. His future employment there was tenuous. But he lacked the energy and ambition to do anything about it. He was a recession-battered, stuck-in-a-rut white man in America. Basically, an angry cliché.

Sometimes Jennifer believed Patrick was completely unreachable. But then she would see him interact with Mia Sara. The tender manner in which he tucked her in at night, the lovely way he whispered entreaties – he responded to his daughter's vulnerability with heart-melting devotion.

This soothing quality reminded Jennifer of the reasons she married him. They had been part of their own wonderful romance once, before his depression, career stagnation, and impotence set in. When he looked at her now, all signs of connection seemed to shut down. It was as if he only saw in her someone who might judge him, someone who stood ready to unleash therapy talk that he did not want to hear.

In a sense, he was right. She desperately wanted to examine their issues. Sometimes she felt like a pathologist searching for the source of a deadly disease. Whenever she tried thoughtfully to approach him, everything Jennifer said seemed to take on a shrink-like spin. But improving their marriage would make them both happier. It would make them better parents, too. So how could he not care enough to do anything about their problems?

Jennifer knew that with his shaky career and lower salary, Patrick considered himself the weaker partner in their marriage. She also knew that he was vetoing intimacy as a way to assert some kind of power and status in the relationship. Her feelings of anger, resentment, and loneliness had become unbearable. It seemed as if she were slowly eroding from the inside.

This frustration at home triggered a certain envy for the clients who came to her with their great love affair catastrophes, the kind that were – all at once – passionate and hurtful, dramatic and ecstatic. Jennifer classified these events as wipeouts, and she encouraged the survivors to be thankful for the intensity of feeling, both good and bad. Wipeouts made life interesting, and they usually provided important self-revelations.

'Patrick, *please* . . .'

He pretended not to hear her as he crawled into their king-size bed and immediately fell into a deep sleep.

Suddenly, Jennifer felt more emboldened than ever.

Tomorrow she would keep her appointment at Salon Rojo for a cut, color, and style, as well as her booking at Tanning Vegas for an airbrush tan. And the day after that, she would keep her appointment with Cam Lawford.

She needed a wipeout of her own. Even if it only lasted for two hours.

CHAPTER SIX

Randall Glass was a meticulous creature of habit.

His dinner hour was precisely 9:30, and he always insisted upon the same meal – a New York strip steak cooked very rare, garlic mashed potatoes, sautéed asparagus, and crème brûlée for dessert.

Billie and Randall were eating on the balcony of their penthouse at the London. The 1500-square-foot, two-bedroom, two-bath towering palace had been negotiated as part of her compensation package for headlining at the hotel's Palladium Showroom.

The view at the top was incredible. Las Vegas was brilliantly electric – a jeweled city of flash and neon. Billie was amazed by how it could be two things at the same time – a decadent oasis for the privileged top two percent and a bargain-rate paradise for the put-upon everyman.

The glittering lights proved hypnotizing as she sat there, suffering through another somber dinner with her control freak husband. She'd just endured the grueling seventy-minute set that was the nightly irony called *Rebirth*. With one show blurring into the next, Billie had no idea what day it actually was. Did it even matter? Las Vegas was a black hole when it came to time.

She watched Randall stab a bloodred piece of beef and

shove it into his mouth. He was a short, exceptionally thin man with fiercely intelligent brown eyes and small, almost childlike hands. Except for a thatch of coarse, wiry black follicles on his scalp, he was completely hairless and prone to sweaty dander. By all conventional standards, Randall Glass was an ugly creature.

He glanced briefly at her chest, then concentrated on cutting his meat as he said, 'Your breasts need some attention. We should do a lift and implants. Soon.'

Billie just sat there, moving the food around on her plate as much as eating it. Randall had a laser eye for body imperfections, both present and future. He would no doubt be slicing her open again at the first available break. Of course, she had every confidence in his skill as a plastic surgeon. His work was flawless. But with each passing day that she spent as the wife of Dr. Randall Glass, Billie began to wonder: Would she have been better off being left as a free beast than being transformed into a trapped beauty?

It seemed a lifetime ago that she performed the disastrous New York showcase at Lotus with rapper/producer/ex-con Domestic Violence. Fresh from being dropped by her recording label, it was part of Billie's drugged-out plan to forge a new career direction in the arena of hip-hop.

She could still hear the cacophony of jeers from the standing-room-only crowd. Something about the constant refrain of 'You suck!' was painfully indelible. The Lotus debacle was followed by her arrest for attempting to assault her former manager with a liquor bottle. But the real Armageddon was still to come.

Billie defied bail restrictions and followed Domestic

Violence and his entourage to Las Vegas for more of the drinking, drugging, fighting, and making up that had come to define their brief union. By linking up with him at all, Billie was stubbornly ignoring the wise axiom, *When people show you who they are, believe them.*

Domestic Violence had crafted his stage name from his own dark history. He was a Rikers Island regular, having served three separate sentences for beating former girlfriends, even going so far as to boast about it – and make a fortune doing so – in his misogynistic hit, 'Yeah, I Did That.'

Billie was operating under the delusion that Domestic Violence would never make her the target of his abuse. The first punch during an argument over cocaine proved her wrong. It sent her tumbling down a flight of emergency exit stairs on the twenty-seventh floor of the Mandalay Bay Hotel. And then he proceeded to beat and kick without mercy until she blacked out completely. When a housekeeper discovered her eight hours later, she was barely alive.

His intention had been to kill her. Proof of that was in the sheer brutality of the attack. Billie's face was destroyed – a broken nose, fractured jaw, shattered cheekbones, ripped eyelid, and extensive dental damage. She also suffered cracked ribs, a collapsed lung, a concussion, and multiple contusions.

The incident had been closely chronicled by Norm Clarke, the eye-patched, man-about-town gossip columnist for the *Las Vegas Review-Journal*. His coverage piqued the interest of one of the city's most prominent plastic surgeons – Dr. Randall Glass.

Billie had been captivated by Randall's intensity. When he announced, 'I'm going to make you more beautiful than you were before,' she believed him. The interest he bestowed was devotional, and she found herself depending on him for everything.

Randall cared. He showed up. And week after week, surgery after surgery, his determination to make good on his romantic promise seemed to grow exponentially. Quite simply, Randall paid attention. It was the purest form of love Billie had ever known.

Her relationship with March Donaldson hardly qualified as that. The conservative politics pinup boy had just used Billie for sex, the kind of sex his proper fiancée wouldn't give him, the kind of sex an upstanding, God-fearing patriot wasn't supposed to have. And when feelings bubbled up to threaten the no-strings fun – *her* feelings, because the ambitious bastard was too selfish to have any for someone else – March cut her out of his life like a cancer.

So Billie's decision to say yes to Randall's marriage proposal came easy. She moved into his immaculate four-bedroom, four-bath home in the Scotch 80s, one of the oldest master-planned residential communities in central Las Vegas. It was there that she recovered from the endless cosmetic procedures under the controlling care of Randall and the watchful eye of his personal assistant, Carly.

Billie went through rhinoplasty, cheek restoration, jawline surgery, extensive Restylane and Juvederm soft-tissue fillers, an eyelid replacement, skin resurfacing with a Fraxel laser, and dental work that included not only a mouth full of perfect porcelain veneers, but a smile lift that pushed her gums upward to expose more teeth.

The final results were fascinating and unnerving. Looking into the mirror, Billie saw a completely different person. Her face was more trapezoidal in shape, wider at the cheeks than at the jawline, the very definition of classic beauty. Randall hadn't oversold his abilities. She was gorgeous. But the dramatic transformation triggered a strange kind of mourning. On a purely physical level, Domestic Violence had killed her, and Randall had brought her back to life. But she still found herself grieving the death of the old Billie.

When the perpetual distraction of surgery and recovery subsided, Billie began to see how truly isolated her life had become. She rarely left the Scotch 80s house. Randall closely monitored her comings and goings. Except for cosmetic procedures performed at his office, he strictly forbade most outings.

Without the focal point of the reconstruction of her face, Randall revealed himself to be cold and distant. He didn't like to touch or be touched. His idea of lovemaking was insisting that she watch while he masturbated. The sight of his small hand choking his even smaller penis left her disgusted and humiliated. But Billie's discomfort only seemed to heighten his arousal.

Randall obsessed over what he believed were flaws on her face and body. His criticism was eroding what little confidence she was building back, and she pleaded with him to leave her alone. But he insisted on more surgery, first to address the contours of her cheeks.

That procedure was done with hydroxyapatite, a form of coral with the same chemical components and porosity as human bone. Mixed in granular form with blood and collagen, he injected it directly onto her bone surface and molded her cheeks to his vision of perfection. Randall's artistry, as always, was exquisite. The results further enhanced Billie's already stunning features.

As a surgeon, Randall was a savior. But as a husband, he was a monster who grew more twisted and paranoid by the day. In fact, the marriage was so miserable that going another round with Domestic Violence seemed like the better path. Billie recognized this with stone-cold sobriety, for she had given up drugs and alcohol and weaned herself off painkillers.

Randall was shameless about exploiting Billie as his masterpiece, seizing every publicity opportunity to show-case before-and-after photographs. It was a bizarre form of celebrity that had little to do with her as a person, as a survivor, as a talent. The focus was the disfiguring attack and Randall's efforts to make her beautiful.

But as Billie discovered, Randall's zeal to pimp her tragedy had more to do with business than ego. His practice had plunged 50 percent in the aftermath of the economic down-turn, which was hitting Sin City with sledgehammer force. As extravagance morphed into frugality, new tits and Botox were no longer top household priorities.

Randall's push to get her back on the stage was just another way to wield control. He floated the idea of creating a splashy Vegas spectacular called *Rebirth* at one of the better hotel properties on the Strip, setting up a series of meetings and assuming the role of agent and manager. Hart Fox convinced him that the synergy of debuting the show in synchronization with the London's grand opening would guarantee them the most exposure.

Billie passively went along as Randall negotiated the deal, conceptualized the show, restricted her access to money, and limited her freedom to see other people. The idea of resisting seemed futile. He was making all the rules now.

Randall dictated everything about *Rebirth* – the set list, the stage banter, the costumes. Any songs from Billie's landmark *Dick Magnet* album were forbidden. His master plan was to bury her indie rock girl past and remodel her into a sexy, sequined chanteuse. And it scored a direct hit, as one reviewer gushed: 'Billie Shelton is an edgy throwback to the kind of Las Vegas razzle-dazzle that has gone missing in recent years. A new star on the Strip is born.'

Nobody from her past would recognize her today. This new version of Billie Shelton was surreal. Her whole life had been thrown out the window. She watched – in the role of detached observer – as everything about her was changed ... because Randall said so. She was beginning to feel bolder, though. Some defiance from the original bitch remained. And it was like a slowly simmering pot, just waiting to come to a rolling boil.

'It's almost time to renew your contract for *Rebirth*,' Randall announced. He started on his crème brûlée, considering her carefully. 'When did you last see Kristin Fox?'

Billie shrugged vaguely. 'I don't know. A few weeks ago maybe.'

'It's time to exploit that relationship.' He consulted his Droid smartphone. 'Carly sent me your schedule for tomorrow – a massage, a session with your shrink. Call Kristin to get together after the show. I'll allow you to skip our regular dinner.'

Billie nodded, revealing nothing, even as the words *I'll allow you* burned like acid. She let it go. The fact that he glossed over the massage appointment with Cam Lawford was the important thing.

'Get Kristin loose with a few drinks,' Randall went on. 'She might reveal something that could inform the negotiation.'

Billie managed a dutiful nod. Randall thought he knew everything. But sometimes he didn't know shit. As a work assignment, a night out with Kristin Fox was hardly a shift in the mines. Kristin was a strong, talented, intelligent, and successful woman. They shared more in common than he realized – the same gigolo, the same therapist, the same desire to helicopter out of a miserable marriage.

If Randall wanted them to enjoy a girls' night out, then the crazy bastard would get his wish. Oh, yes. Billie was desperate to shake off the blues. And with Kristin by her side, they could do it for bedeviled women everywhere.

Confessions from the Man Who's Satisfying Your Wife

By Cam Lawford

The Midnight Cowboy Test

Women want sex just like men do. I know this because they don't pay me for companionship, and they don't pay me to talk. That's what poodles and therapists are for. When a woman calls a guy like me, she wants one thing.

I stopped advertising a long time ago. Few real customers came my way. Most turned out to be bullshit. I'd get skittish women who just wanted to send endless e-mails back and forth. Men would hound me, too. Some straight escorts do gay-for-pay. Not me. I'm not that desperate for cash.

Dealing with crazies is part of the business. Sex and money can be a dangerous combination. One time a husband hired me to screw his wife while he watched. Hot-looking couple. They lived in a swank five-bedroom house in the Vistas subdivision of Summerlin.

I figured he was one of those cuckold types who got off on seeing another man please his wife. But when he realized that she loved it too much, he pulled a gun out of the nightstand drawer and threatened to shoot me in the balls.

The wife started to laugh. Yeah. I'm about to get my dick blown off, and this bitch thought it was funny! I managed to talk the guy down. Then I scrambled out of there and vowed never to take another residential appointment. Too much can go wrong at a private home. Hotel dates are safer.

One of my regular customers is a successful writer. Her books are bestsellers. Sometimes she reads to me in bed, usually the racier parts of whatever she's working on. It's cool. You'd think that she'd get enough of fantasy land creating her novels, but this woman is heavy into role play. I've been everything from a cop giving a speeding ticket to a college student being seduced by an English professor.

Another one of my regulars is a headliner at a big hotel on the Strip. Drugs and alcohol used to be her thing. Now she's addicted to me. Last week she paid me with a Cartier watch that she stole from her husband. I call that nice work if you can get it.

A select few buddies know what I do for a living. They're always pressing me, 'Dude, what's it like? Should I get into it?' I tell them to put *Midnight Cowboy* in their Netflix queue, and if they think they can handle being a gigolo after watching that, then go for it. Cash in. Make some money. You're only young once.

CHAPTER SEVEN

'I'll say this, baby – when you do it for your country, you really do it for your country.' Cam Lawford was nearly out of breath, slick with sweat, and smiling the kind of sensual smile that short-circuited Kristin's should-I-be-doing-this interior dialogue.

She laughed. 'What can I say? I'm very patriotic.'

He pointed to the bread-crumb trail of soldier uniform pieces and military accoutrements that started at the door of the small MGM Grand suite and led all the way to the edge of the bed. 'Remind me to deploy more often.'

Suddenly, Kristin experienced a strange feeling. Somewhere out there were real men, women, and families dealing with the stress, atrocities, and tragedies of war. And she was using the theme as a backdrop for a silly sexual fantasy. In the aftermath of the heat of the moment, it just seemed wrong.

'There really is a war going on,' she murmured. 'It's easy to forget sometimes, the way we so casually go on about our lives. Isn't that terrible?'

He adjusted the bed pillows and propped up on one elbow to face her, smoothing a hand down her slender arm with intimate affection. 'Two guys I went to high school with died in Afghanistan this year. I found out on Facebook.'

Kristin was struck by how young Cam sounded. He was still years away from his ten-year reunion. His source for news was a social networking site. Oh, God, he really was a twenty-four-year-old . . . *boy.*

Aside from the fact that he was a star college player at Penn State and a first-season casualty for the Miami Dolphins, she knew very little about him. 'Where did you grow up?'

'California.'

'Rich kid?'

The question made him smile. 'Why? Do I act like one?'

He was so sexy when he asked this that Kristin practically melted into the sheets. 'Not necessarily . . . but you do have a certain unencumbered air about you.'

'My dad's an insurance adjuster, and my mother's a teacher. We were comfortable, nothing more than that.' He paused a beat. 'What about you?'

She searched his movie-star handsome face. 'Are you really interested in knowing?'

Again with that adorable smile. 'If you want me to be.'

Kristin grinned. 'Let's just say I consider my childhood a survival period.'

He looked quizzical for a moment, then took in the naked sight of her with bold admiration. 'You know, customer or not, what we just did ranks up there with some of the best sex I've ever had.'

She felt the warmth of a blush hit her cheeks. The compliment gave her a palpable sense of well-being, as if she were suddenly a better person because Cam Lawford had just declared her good in bed. 'When did you start?'

'Having sex?'

She nodded.

'I was fourteen. How old were you?'

'Nineteen. I was a nice girl.'

'Gone bad now.' He gently tweaked one of her nipples. Playfully, she slapped his hand away.

'It's crazy ... why a woman like you needs someone like me. If I were your husband ...'

'But you're not. Isn't that the point?'

'You know what I mean.' He rolled onto his back and sighed as he stared up at the ceiling. 'What's the old saying? For every beautiful woman, there's a guy who's tired of fucking her.'

'Henry Kissinger said that.'

'Who's he?'

She winked at him. 'Seriously?'

Cam grinned. He stretched out to reach his watch on the nightstand. It was a Cartier worth thousands. 'We've got a little time left. Will you read to me? I love that.'

Kristin beamed. This meant so much more than the sexual praise or the reference to her being beautiful. Hart never showed any interest in her work. In fact, he had never even read one of her novels from beginning to end. If he could ignore a national bestseller and a popular television series, he could ignore anything.

She slipped out of bed to snatch a sheaf of papers from her vintage Hermès Birkin bag, twirling around with delight. 'I just happen to have some new pages with me.'

Cam kicked back, propping his hands behind his head, a move that emphasized his incredible biceps. He stared at her with amused and animated interest. 'I'm ready. I hope it's dirty.'

'Not really,' Kristin trilled. 'But there's sort of the promise of something dirty later.'

His eyebrows danced lasciviously. 'Almost as good.'

Her new novel was called *Kiva Dunes Road*. It concerned a group of longtime neighborhood friends whose family-like bond bitterly implodes under the pressure of business entanglements, sexual secrets, toxic resentments, emotional gamesmanship, and religious hypocrisy.

Kristin cleared her throat and began to read. 'Emily couldn't stop staring at his body . . .'

'This must be about me,' Cam cut in. 'I want a percentage of the royalties.'

Giggling, she started over, never looking up until she finished the chapter.

Cam was staring at her with rapt attention. 'That's all? You're killing me. What happens next?'

Her look was coy. 'Isn't it obvious?'

'Read the part where they nail each other.'

'I haven't written that scene yet.' She grinned. 'Maybe next time.'

He regarded her for a long, indulgent moment. 'This is sexy – you standing there bare-ass naked, reading to me. It's something new that you wrote, right? Nobody else has seen it?'

Her silence was her answer.

Cam nodded his head as if grooving to a beat that only he could hear. 'That's fucking hot.'

Kristin presented an envelope containing ten crisp hundred-dollar bills. 'Flattery will get you . . . *this*.'

He tossed the cash onto the nightstand, not bothering to count it. 'Tell me what happens. Does the husband find out about the affair? Do the guys lose their shit in the real-estate deal?' He reached for her hand and pulled her closer. 'I'm hooked.'

Kristin smirked. 'Says the man who watches *Gossip Girl*.'

He looked exposed for a moment. 'Did I tell you that?'

'Yes. But don't be embarrassed about it. Be embarrassed about *The Jersey Shore*.'

'Why? That's good television.' He said this with a straight face, yanking her closer to spank her bottom.

They laughed and wrestled playfully for several seconds.

Cam spied his watch again and sighed with what sounded like real regret. 'I need to go. I should hit the gym. And I have another appointment later.'

Kristin was suddenly afflicted with a brooding silence. Only a nanosecond ago she had been struck by how nice Cam made her feel. Now she was preoccupied with the reality of his profession. In just a few hours, another woman would be forking over the bucks for the same nice feelings.

The realization brought on immediate jealousy. It was irrational. Kristin knew that. But the feeling could not be denied. Her own hyped-up image of herself as a private sex star began to dim just as doubts began to swirl over whether the passage from her novel was really that good. Would Cam tell his 4:00 booking that she was a Jenna Jameson in bed, too? Would he listen to her bad poetry and pretend to enjoy it? Was any of this authentic? Or was it all just a pay-by-the-hour scam?

Cam dressed quickly, kissed her good-bye, and left. The moment he shut the door, isolation closed in around her.

There was no lonelier feeling than being in a hotel room alone after he left. Kristin hated this part.

When her BlackBerry rang, she felt flooded with relief and rushed to answer it, surprised to see BILLIE SHELTON CALLING on the ID screen. 'Hi, Billie.'

'I've come up with a fantastic idea. What are you doing tonight?'

Kristin thought about it. Every night was always the same for her. 'Nothing special. I'll be at home with the kids, probably working.'

'Come out with me after the show. Two hot married women like us should be able to find some trouble.'

'I agree,' Kristin said, instantly grateful for the company and the break in routine. 'Sounds like fun. Count me in.'

'We can be Thelma and Louise,' Billie said.

Kristin let out a throaty laugh. 'Well, this sounds dangerous. They drove themselves off a cliff at the end.'

CHAPTER EIGHT

'He proposed to me on a golf course,' Kristin said. 'God, that feels like a million years ago.'

Jennifer noticed her client wince at the memory. She thought it important in today's session to press Kristin for information about her relationship's past, hoping it would provide some insight on its dysfunctional present. 'How did you meet Hart?'

'We met at work.' Kristin sighed. 'I'd just graduated from UNLV with a hotel management degree and been accepted into the training program at the Mirage.'

'Those are highly competitive slots, as I understand it,' Jennifer said.

Kristin nodded. 'Las Vegas was coming out of decades of decline. It was a hot and sexy and fashionable destination again, a really exciting time, especially for the hotel business.'

Jennifer could recall the pageantry and ceremony of the Mirage's grand opening on the Strip in 1989. She remembered this because her prom had been held in one of the ballrooms the following spring. At that time, the $630 million construction budget made the Mirage the most expensive hotel and casino ever built.

The credit went to developer Steve Wynn, who had a

vision to create a resort that would rival any tourism property in the world. His personal zeal for eye-popping extravagance and over-the-top glamour made him an instant legend and the unofficial mastermind of what had become modern Las Vegas. Back then – and even now – Jennifer enjoyed observing the glitz factory from a distance.

'I was twenty-two,' Kristin continued. 'The starting salary was shit, and they worked us to death, but I still felt like I'd . . . *arrived.*' She smiled. 'I lived with another guy in the program – Jeffie. He was hilarious and smart and skinny as a rail . . . and gay, of course.'

'Why of course?' Jennifer inquired.

'Can you imagine a straight man going by *Jeffie*?'

Jennifer returned a wry grin. 'Point taken.'

'We were like Will and Grace before Will and Grace,' Kristin went on. 'Our apartment was a dump. But it didn't matter, because the hours were insane. We were hardly ever there. When we were home, we ate Ben and Jerry's on the couch and watched tapes of *Seinfeld*. Usually, we were out on the Strip drinking.' She let out a wistful laugh. 'That's one of the happiest times that I can remember. My life was completely my own, you know? The future was this exciting and promising thing. And then I met Hart.'

'You make it sound as if all those positive things stopped,' Jennifer observed. 'Is that how you measure your life – before Hart and after Hart?'

Kristin considered the question thoughtfully. 'Sometimes.'

Jennifer nodded earnestly. 'Tell me about him. What were your immediate impressions?'

Kristin pursed her lips as she searched for the memory.

'He was handsome, brash, intimidating, full of swagger and confidence . . . and sexy, I must admit. He was the Mirage's newest executive, fresh off a divorce, and twelve years older than me – thirty-four.' She laughed a little. 'At the time, that seemed ancient.'

Jennifer smiled and nodded for her to go on.

'My attraction to him was instant and electric . . . almost chaotic. Within twenty-four hours, we'd already kissed in front of the hotel's artificial volcano and shacked up in a corporate suite. The next morning I showed up for work and Hart had put in for me to be immediately transferred to the training program at Treasure Island. That's a sister property. He said having me remain on site at Mirage would be distracting and lead to staff conflict. So just like that I was gone, away from Jeffie, all the other coworkers I'd grown close to, and the environment that I loved.'

'How did that make you feel?' Jennifer asked.

Kristin stared blankly for a moment, as if reliving it. 'I was stunned. I was humiliated. I should have said no. I should have threatened him with a sexual harassment suit. But I accepted the transfer and kept on seeing him.' She let out a bitter laugh. 'And then I married him.'

'We need to stop here for today,' Jennifer said. 'But this is good work. I want to continue on this path.' Going about the business of filling out an insurance claim form, she could feel Kristin's eyes on her.

'You look so different,' Kristin commented. 'Amazing, in fact.'

Standing up, Jennifer smiled and handed over the paperwork. 'I was long overdue for a personal makeover of sorts. I constantly preach self-care to my clients and realized that I was ignoring my own advice.' She paused a beat. 'We'll pick up where we left off next week.'

The moment she found herself alone, Jennifer felt seized by a sudden anxiety and took in a deep breath to calm her nerves. She was a jangled mix of fear, shame, uncertainty, and erotic anticipation.

A luxury suite had been booked at the Venetian. There was a lunch reservation at Wolfgang Puck's Postrio restaurant. And Cam Lawford was scheduled to meet her at 1:00 for a two-hour appointment.

Jennifer had prepared for this as if it were the most glamorous event of the year, first suffering through the Brazilian wax, next enduring the indignity of a nude airbrush tan, then visiting a third salon for a cut and color. All the wisps of gray were gone. Now her hair was darker – chestnut brown with golden caramel highlights – and styled in a modern curly shag cut with side-swept bangs.

Yesterday she had dropped four hundred dollars on a red confetti-print Diane von Furstenberg silk wrap dress that teased cleavage with a V neckline. And the spending splurge did not stop there. She turned over seven hundred dollars for a gorgeous pair of Oscar de la Renta open-toe pumps. Add to that a three-hundred-dollar Neiman Marcus cosmetics spree and an application lesson from a national makeup artist. Counting the cash withdrawal for Cam's escort fee, Jennifer estimated the overall damage for this secret rendezvous to be about three thousand dollars.

The shock of the bill triggered immediate alarm. Her behavior was manic, irresponsible, grossly indulgent, financially destructive, not to mention completely at odds with her value system. And yet she could not even begin to entertain the idea of stopping herself. That is how much she wanted to go through with it.

You look pretty, Mommy. I know Daddy thinks so, too.

This morning Mia Sara had uttered those words during the drive to Montessori Visions Academy.

Jennifer had scarcely been able to look at her own daughter. Mia Sara was only five years old, but the child knew. She could sense the emotional distance between her parents, and she was attempting to narrow it with that sweet little lie.

A stab of sadness and self-loathing pierced Jennifer's heart. For Mia Sara's sake, she tried hard to mask the troubles with Patrick. But the emptiness was right there in her eyes, and that did not escape the keen perception of a bright girl like Mia Sara.

Here she was at five years old, taking on the relationship baggage of her parents, trying to carry what she could to make things better, to bring happiness to all of them. It was incredibly unfair.

Nancy jumped off the sofa, trotted to the door, and gazed back at Jennifer expectantly.

'Is it time to do your business?'

At the sound of Jennifer's baby talk voice, the Bichon frise whirled into a fluffy white ball of excitement.

Jennifer led Nancy into the office park courtyard, purging family dysfunction from her mind as she factored out the rest of the day. She had arranged for early check-in at the Venetian. The opportunity to get comfortable in the room before meeting Cam seemed essential. Afterward, there would be time to shower and make it back to the office for her late-afternoon session.

'Jennifer, is that you?'

She turned and smiled as Kurt Taylor approached. On the finishing end of his regular lunch-hour run, he was sweaty, short of breath, and boldly checking her out.

'Holy smokes! You look great!'

Jennifer tucked her hair behind her ear, glancing down at Nancy. 'Thank you.'

Kurt laughed. 'You must be having an affair.'

Jennifer gave him a cross look, instantly resenting him for tossing off a dumb joke with such sharpshooter accuracy.

Kurt picked up on her irritation. 'I'm kidding. God, what an ass I am. It's just ... the hair, the tan ... that dress.' His smile was more than a little flirtatious. 'You really do look great ... like a young Diane Keaton. That's a compliment.'

Jennifer merely grinned, experiencing a sensual confidence that was refreshing, new, and quite wonderful.

Kurt favore Christopher Meloni from *Law & Order: SVU* with his receding hairline, handsome face, intense blue eyes, and lean, muscular body. He was a dentist with an office in the same building, married to a successful divorce lawyer, and the father of five rambunctious boys.

'I don t mean to imply that you didn't look great before,' Kurt assured her. 'It's just ...'

Jennifer raised a halting hand. 'No, I understand. And I was actually making a real effort to look my best, so the fact that you noticed is ... nice.'

Kurt bent down to rub the top of Nancy's head.

'So ... how are the boys?'

Kurt stood up. 'Great. Crazy. All over the place. We

spend most of our time driving them back and forth to baseball games and music lessons and birthday parties. It's insane.'

Jennifer smiled, feeling a twinge of envy. She and Patrick would probably never know the crazy energy that multiple children living under one roof could bring. 'It sounds like fun.'

Kurt beamed. 'It is. How's your little girl?'

Jennifer widened her eyes in mock fear. 'Far too wise for her years. Sometimes it's frightening.'

Kurt grinned. 'Hey, look at it this way. I've got five Tasmanian devils running around that could easily end up in the juvenile system. And you're probably raising a future president.' He laughed. 'Man, I always wanted a girl. We kept trying for one. But after Colt was born, Diana sent me in for a vasectomy.'

'And after giving birth to five children, she gets to do that!' Jennifer pointed out lightly, feeling a surge of female solidarity for this superwoman whom she had never met.

Kurt shrugged and opened up his hands in that classic comic pantomime of helpless male guilt. 'She wanted to stop at three. But I was sure Dalton was going to be a girl. And then I was *damn* sure Colt was going to be a girl.' He smiled. 'My credibility was pretty much shot at that point. I think I was in recovery with an ice pack on my nuts before Colt even came home from the hospital. That's how fast it happened.'

Jennifer laughed, really laughed. It struck her how much she had been missing this kind of interaction. As a man, Kurt was devastatingly attractive, intelligent, funny, sexy, observant, virile, kind, capable, a dedicated father, an accomplished athlete, the list went on.

She found herself responding to him in an almost primal way. In fact, her desire to prolong this encounter worried her. 'I need to run, Kurt. I'm sorry. It's so nice to visit, but I have an appointment.'

He nodded easily. 'No problem. This economy is killing my business, and I'm afraid I have too much time on my hands. I hope I didn't keep you.'

'Not at all.' Jennifer managed an empathetic smile.

'Your practice must thrive in times like these,' Kurt said.

'My line of work is always steady. In good times or bad, relationship issues seem to persist.'

'We should have lunch sometime,' Kurt said.

Jennifer hesitated. 'Okay.'

He narrowed his eyes with faux suspicion. 'I've never shared a meal with a therapist before. You won't try to analyze me, will you?'

Jennifer tugged gently on Nancy's leash and started walking away. 'Oh, I've already done that.' Her voice was teasing.

'No fair!' Kurt called out. 'So what's the diagnosis?'

Laughing, Jennifer turned back to look at him. 'It's beyond my training!' she joked. 'I'll have to refer you to a specialist!'

Kurt laughed heartily, waved good-bye, and broke out into a slow jog toward the stairs that led to his suite on the second floor.

Jennifer could not stop smiling. Her body thrummed with kinetic energy. It amazed her how rewarding a harmless episode of flirtation could be.

She thought of Patrick. They no longer shared light-hearted moments. The exchanges between them were perfunctory and lifeless. In fact, Jennifer could feel herself already living for the simple possibility that a lunch with Kurt might happen, even as she got into her Toyota Camry Hybrid and drove toward the Strip with the full intention of paying a male escort for sex.

Months and months of Patrick's indifference had brought her to this point. All of her choices for dealing with it were wrong. Intellectually, Jennifer knew that. And at several points along the way to the Venetian, she even considered turning the car around. But she never did. The compulsion to feel something – to feel anything – propelled her forward with a force all its own.

CHAPTER NINE

The pretty hostess led the way through the inner sanctum of Postrio. Wall-mounted fireplaces gave off a soft glow, enhancing the rich, minimalist color palette of chocolate brown, white, rosewood, and olive-green leather.

Jennifer was seated in the restaurant's café, which offered a front-row view of the entertainment at St. Mark's Square, the courtyard of the Venetian's massive Grand Canal Shoppes complex. A gaggle of tourists gawked gleefully at the painted mimes and jugglers.

She ordered a glass of the house white wine and waited, nervously watching the crowd for Cam Lawford. Her eyes fixated on a tall handsome man in a dark suit striding past the Gandini boutique.

'Jennifer?'

She glanced up, startled.

The man standing over her was taller, more handsome, and doing things for a white polo and a pair of lived-in jeans than should be illegal. He extended a large hand. 'I'm Cam.'

Yes, you are.

His shake was firm, his skin warm, his gaze direct. He sat down just as the waiter returned with Jennifer's wine.

She could not bring the glass to her lips fast enough.

Cam never averted his eyes, even as he politely declined to put in a drink order and dismissed the waiter.

Jennifer let out a short, nervous laugh. 'I can't believe I'm actually doing this.'

'Just try to think of me as a personal service provider. It's no different than having a relaxing massage.' His smile was mischievous. 'It's just more fun.'

She drank deep on the wine.

'I'm safe,' Cam assured. 'Unlike a lot of escorts, I'm straight, I get tested regularly, I've never had any kind of STD, and I'm careful about the women I take on as clients. Most of my business is of the repeat variety. I know how to satisfy.' He grinned. 'But someone referred you to me, so you already know that.'

His oblique reference to Kristin made Jennifer consider bailing out. This was wrong ... on so many levels.

Cam waved a hand, flashing his football ring. 'I was in the NFL. Some women get into that. Maybe they had a crush on the high school or college quarterback but never got a chance with him.' He smirked. 'Look no further. And I even went pro.'

She could easily have thrown up at that moment. It was the guilt, the shame, the nervousness, the narcissistic come-ons.

Suddenly, Cam leaned across the table. His cologne was spicy and warm but not overpowering. Like the physical part of him, it was perfect. 'So did you book a room, or is this just a getting-to-know-you?'

Jennifer simply looked at him.

'Don't get me wrong. I'm cool either way. Time is time,

though. I bill by tenths. You know, like a lawyer. One tenth is six minutes. And I charge five hundred an hour.'

'So that explanation alone probably cost me fifty dollars,' Jennifer remarked.

Cam's sensual lips curled into a cocky grin. 'Something like that.' He eased back to observe her for a moment, taking notice of her wedding ring. 'So what's your story? Is your husband a dud in the sack, is he just not paying attention, or is this revenge sex?'

'Does it matter?'

'Not really. I'm just trying to figure out where your head is.'

'Don't concern yourself with that,' Jennifer said coolly. 'I have that part covered. I'm a therapist.'

'A shrink?' Cam looked genuinely surprised.

Jennifer snapped open her new python clutch, retrieved a pair of Venetian key cards advertising the Blue Man Group, and placed them on the table. Her hands were shaking. 'It's a luxury suite. Room three-five-two-eight.'

Cam gave her a confident nod, as if suddenly making up his mind about something, then reached out to claim one of the room keys. 'The last thing you need is to sit here and talk to somebody. I bet you do enough of that.'

She considered bolting at that moment. Maybe it was not a paid escort that she needed. Maybe it was an appointment for couples counseling.

'I want you to go up to the room and take off all your clothes. Except for those shoes. Wait for me in front of the window. I'm going to give you exactly what you want and need.'

His bold orders were an instant turn-on. Jennifer wanted to be told what to do. Somehow Cam instinctively knew that. Still, she hesitated.

'Move along, baby,' he said, downing the last of her wine. 'I'll join you in a few minutes.'

She dug into her clutch for a twenty-dollar bill to cover the drink and tip, then hustled out of Postrio in a trance-like state. Reaching the room, she followed his instructions to the letter, peeling off her wrap dress and underwear and stepping in front of the floor-to-ceiling window.

Jennifer was naked, gloriously naked, wearing nothing but the obscenely expensive Oscar de la Renta peep-toe heels. She gazed out at the incredible view of the Strip and the towering Mirage and Treasure Island hotels across the boulevard, feeling more sensual anticipation than she had ever experienced.

Sex was one-dimensional and meaningless when cut off from emotional connection. That was the point Jennifer so often made to her clients. But already the sense of danger and excitement had her heart racing, her blood pumping, and her body tingling.

Perhaps it was the decadent freedom – no baggage, no strings. With Patrick, there was a toxic history and an awkward familiarity. With Kurt, there would be the heavy consideration of two people selfishly and recklessly putting their families at risk. But Cam Lawford was just a big gorgeous escape that Jennifer could indulge in for a few hours and walk away from. Transactional infidelity. At the moment, it seemed like a smart and sensible solution to her unsatisfied life.

When Cam stormed into the room, he proceeded to tear off his shoes, shirt, jeans, and boxer briefs as if they were burning his skin.

Jennifer stopped breathing.

The photographs of his body did not do him proper justice. They failed to capture the tremendous vascularity of his arms and legs. Veins popped out like ropes. His eight-pack abdominals looked as firm as concrete. And his cock – the same cock that Kristin had waxed rhapsodically about in more than one session – was already rock hard and pulsing with intensity.

Cam zeroed in on the Hungarian woman's handiwork, unleashing a lusty sigh as he stepped down into the sunken living room. 'Look at that beautiful pussy.' He dropped to his knees in near worship and instantly buried his face between her legs.

Jennifer was paralyzed by the shock and pleasure of his thick tongue plunging into her very core. The potential danger of falling backward disappeared, even as her bare ass planted against the windowpane with a loud bang.

Cam reached up to caress both of her breasts. He drew back slightly, then stood up, towering over her. 'I'm going to fuck you right here. And I'm going to fuck you so hard that every second it's going to feel like we're about to crash through this glass.'

They were on the thirty-fifth floor. No balcony separated them from the sky. Just the idea of peering down gave Jennifer a vague sense of vertigo.

'Does that scare you?' Cam asked.

She managed a brief nod. The erotic madness of the moment consumed her. She was dreading the act. But she was craving it, too. And his dominant way of calling the shots was driving her crazy ... in a good way.

'Trust me. When you come, it's going to be like nothing you've ever felt before.' Kissing her neck, he cupped her ass with both hands. 'Are you ready for this?'

'Yes,' Jennifer answered.

Cam smiled at her. 'Yes is all I needed ...'

CHAPTER TEN

'This town was built on hopes and dreams. You're always one roll of the dice away from a jackpot. Even the losers believe that. That's why I love it here.'

Billie sank deeper into the plush facerest of the portable massage table as Cam Lawford philosophized in a low, soft voice. She inhaled the lush candle scent of honey-infused citrus and bitter orange wood. Dido was lulling her with the quietly percolating 'White Flag.'

Cam's hands were – as always – exquisitely soothing and arousing. He rubbed in the fragrant warming oils with such amazing skill that an involuntary sigh escaped her. The scene was close to perfect.

Sometimes it stunned Billie how hungry she was for human touch. Randall displayed no affection. Occasion-ally choking her while shoving a gun into her mouth was the extent of their physical relationship. Although they did sleep in the same bed, he stayed distantly to one side, coiled into a fetal position. It was all so sick.

Cam's hands slid down her body with a deliciously familiar slyness, moving from the small of her back, to the exposed cheeks of her bottom, and then in and around her inner thighs, all in one teasing, serpentine movement.

Suddenly, Randall and the prisonlike existence that was her life seemed inconsequential.

Billie let out a faint moan, finally giving in, totally immersing herself in the pleasures of Cam's talented touch.

'You have an amazing body . . . a showgirl's body . . . it's so sexy,' he whispered.

Billie murmured her thanks as she anticipated his next move. It would happen any moment now . . . the middle and ring fingers of Cam's right hand would slide inside her and proceed to bring her to a convulsive climax so intense that she'd begun to think of a man's cock as just a useless appendage that dangled between his legs.

She could feel the warmth of his hand hovering at her opening . . . teasing her . . . then ultimately denying her as it slid back onto her thigh and up and along her torso. When he began to concentrate on the knots centered in the back of her neck, the almost-erotic turning all-the-way therapeutic, she was confused.

'You're so tight here,' he observed clinically, increasing the pressure in the most boring of places.

Billie could hardly believe it. She turned over in a fit of frustration, exposing her breasts in the process. 'Are you fucking kidding me?'

Cam gave her a mischievous smile, then leaned in to kiss her on the mouth.

The gesture left her feeling surprised and vulnerable.

'So demanding,' he clucked. 'You just won't relax until you get your orgasm, will you?'

Billie pulled up the sheet to cover her chest as the indignities tumbled over themselves. Was the fact that she wanted it so much a joke to him? She needed to know. 'Am I as pathetic as your other clients? Customers, whatever you call them.'

'None of the women I see are pathetic,' Cam said. His tone was earnest, not defensive. 'They all have their reasons for needing my services.'

'And what do you think mine are?' Billie asked.

He gave her a penetrating gaze that radiated a level of warmth and insight that made her uncomfortable. 'I think you're lonely. I think you're starving to be touched. And I think you're scared of something.'

She scoffed at him. 'You're much better with your hands than you are with armchair psychology.'

'Well, my massage training is limited, so that must make me a really terrible psychologist.' His smile was self-deprecating charm at its most devastating. There was something behind it, though. Cam Lawford knew that he'd touched a nerve. 'You're not taking advantage of what I do best, Billie. You should let me make love to you.'

'The last man I made love to beat me within an inch of my life, and the one before that broke my heart. I don't need a lover. I need a release.' And with that, she ripped off the sheet, returned her face to the table's cushioned headrest, closed her eyes, and waited.

'What about your husband?' Cam asked. 'He doesn't make love to you?'

'He never touches me in bed. Only in the operating room.'

Cam hesitated, as if to let the bizarre admission sink in. And then his hands found their way back onto her body and began to move in the sensuous rhythm that Billie had come to expect, ultimately bringing her to a pulse-quickening, voluptuous, and rapturous climax.

As she lay there, completely spent, Billie held Cam's cock in her hand. She didn't want it inside her. She didn't want to taste it. She just wanted to feel its heat, hardness, and power. Finally, she let go.

Cam unleashed a low, frustrated groan. 'You're killing me, Billie. At least finish me off.'

'I was under the impression that our time together was about my pleasure,' she murmured.

'My pleasure could be your pleasure. Ask around.'

Smiling, she rose up from the table and draped herself with the sheet, feeling relaxed, tingly, and quite wonderful.

Cam lived in a small, sparsely decorated one-bedroom in the Dancers Ghetto, a tenement of apartments and rental houses located near the Strip. By comparison, her old walk-up in New York had been a little palace.

'Nice place,' Billie remarked. 'Maybe you should ask Kristin Fox to give you a raise. I'm sure she can afford it.'

Cam just shrugged as he stood there, gloriously, outrageously nude. Being naked was comfortable for him. He could do anything in the buff – rub her down, make her come, sing the national anthem, whatever. 'You're the only client I see here. I usually schedule dates at hotels.'

'I guess I'm special.'

He reached out to touch her face. 'You are special.'

Billie drew back a little, sidestepping the moment of intimacy by taking in the surroundings. She noticed sweaty workout clothes in a pile on the floor and dirty dishes stacked up in the sink.

Cam strode over to the refrigerator and pulled out a large bottle of Smartwater. After gulping down a third of it, he offered the rest to Billie. 'You should hydrate after a massage.'

She took a few generous sips. 'Why do you live in such a dump? Do you send all your escort money back home to poor relatives or something?'

He grinned at her. 'You're funny.'

'Well?'

'There are certain perks.'

'Like what? It's obviously not the free maid service.'

'A lot of showgirls and burlesque dancers live here. It makes hook-ups easy and uncomplicated.'

'Don't you ever get tired of sex?'

'No,' Cam said matter-of-factly. 'I don't get tired of sex, and sex doesn't get tired of me.'

'I take it you don't read much.' Billie started to get dressed. With Carly sidelined by a sinus infection and Randall occupied with surgeries, this had been a rare afternoon of true freedom. But she still had to exercise caution.

Carly maintained a meticulous record of mileage on the leased BMW 7 Series sedan that Randall allowed Billie to drive. Billie had suspicions that the vehicle was being tracked with a hidden GPS device, too. Luckily, David Dean also lived in the Dancers Ghetto. It was that coincidence that gave her the courage to venture there. If ever confronted, she had a plausible reason for being in the area.

She finished buttoning her Tory Burch blouse.

Cam was staring at her. 'Do you remember playing a Penn State concert at a club called Lulu's Nightspot?'

'I played a lot of college gigs,' Billie said. 'They're all

one big blur. Back then I was drunk or high most of the time. Why?'

'I was there.'

'Really?' She gave him a wan smile. 'So how was I?'

'You were wild.'

'Those were wild days,' Billie said, feeling an odd sense of detachment from her rock bitch persona of yesteryear. God, it felt like several lifetimes ago. She put her brain computer to work searching for the memory. 'Wait a minute. I think I actually remember that gig. Lulu's didn't have any seats. It was one of those standing-room venues, right?'

Cam nodded. 'The capacity was six hundred or so, but a lot more were packed in that night. We could barely move.'

Billie recalled it vividly now. 'There were no barricades. The body surfing got out of control. That was a fun show.'

'One of my fraternity brothers loved your music. He used to play *Dick Magnet* all the time. We doubled with two girls from the skank sorority, and they ended up blowing us right there on the floor during one of your songs.' He smiled, the enthusiasm of party boy youth all over his handsome face.

'I must've only been semiwasted that night,' Billy said ruefully. 'That could've easily been me doing that. If I had a dollar for every college guy that I . . .'

She trailed off and reached into her handbag, dug around until she found Randall's Tiffany Mark T-57 automatic chronograph, and tossed it in Cam's direction.

He caught it in midair and gave the gleaming stainless steel face an appreciative once-over as he slipped it on. 'Oh, baby, you shouldn't have.'

'I started to bring you his Rolex, but it's one of those link bracelet numbers, and my husband has a wrist like a little girl.'

Cam stood there admiring the expensive timepiece on his arm. 'You're spoiling me.'

'You can say that again. That watch retails for over seven grand.'

'He won't miss it?'

'If he does, I'll just blame it on one of the sticky-fingered maids.'

Cam stepped closer and rested his hands on her bare hips. His Paul Newman-blue eyes sparkled with amusement. 'You've got everything figured out, don't you?'

'Not really.'

His kiss surprised her. It was soft, yearning, and passionate – a lover's kiss. Their mouths fit perfectly together, and when he parted her lips with his tongue, Billie found herself giving in completely. He came up for air and traced the outline of her cheeks with his fingertips.

'Do you kiss Kristin like that?'

Cam revealed nothing. 'That's private.'

'What – are you bound by some kind of stud–client confidentiality?'

'Maybe. If you want to know, ask her yourself. But why does it matter?'

'I'm just wondering if all these moves of yours are original.'

'Every woman is different. I've told you that.' He pressed his lips to the tip of her nose. 'You're annoying.' His tone was light.

Billie scooted on her jeans and began searching for her shoes. 'I've been gone too long.'

'He really keeps you on a short leash.'

'More like a cage,' Billie corrected.

'I was twenty years old when I saw you at that concert,' Cam said, watching her intently. 'You were rocking out and flying into the mosh pit. I'd never seen a woman so wild and free. What happened?'

Billie found her shoes and slipped them on. 'Near death and marriage happened.' She located her keys and started for the door.

'Don't bring me any more watches,' Cam said to her back. 'I feel like I'm stealing from you.'

'It's hard for me to get my hands on cash.'

'Then put my conscience at ease and get your money's worth next time.'

Billie turned to face him. God, he was the most beautiful man she'd ever seen. 'Maybe I will.' And then she walked out.

For a long time she sat frozen in the front seat of Randall's BMW, focusing on her breathing, trying to make sense of her life, her choices, her feelings. Suddenly, Billie lost all composure and proceeded to beat the steering wheel in a fit of tearful fury. 'Fuck ... fuck ... fuck!'

A tall redhead with incredible legs was walking past the car at precisely that moment. 'Honey, are you okay?'

Billie waved her off. The nosy bitch was probably one of Cam's convenient showgirl lovers.

Oh, God! Sometimes the despair just hit her from out of nowhere, as if by lightning bolt. She cheated death for this? To be monitored, controlled, and abused as Randall's porcelain doll property? To sing cover songs in a cabaret act night after night to a ballroom full of dreary slot-machine gamblers?

Everything in her life was a lie ... everything except Cam Lawford. He was real with her. Billie was real with him. They were real together. It wasn't enough to sneak away for a lousy hour once a week. She wanted more. She needed more.

In the past, far lesser things had sent Billie straight to her favorite bar, to her coke stash, to her medicine cabinet, to her friendly neighborhood meth dealer. Those cravings were long gone, though. Now she just wanted her freedom. But how to get it – and how to stay alive in pursuit of it – was what she had to figure out.

Part Two

SEDUCTION

What do you do in Las Vegas? You
gamble – and you go to strip clubs.

SCOTT CAAN

CHAPTER ELEVEN

Seven hot guys in dinner jackets, open-neck shirts, loose bow ties, and tight pants were bumping and grinding to the Four Tops classic 'Reach Out I'll Be There.'

'Take it off, baby!' the fat bridesmaid from Michigan screamed.

Her partners in bachelorette crime – equally drunk, just as overweight, and swirling neon green martinis – squealed with raucous laughter.

Kristin leaned in toward Billie. 'They must think that clichéd outburst was original.'

Billie grinned. 'Stop being such a bitch and let them have their fun. Can you imagine the boring lives they're going back to?'

'Now who's the bitch?' Kristin countered, surveying the near-capacity female crowd in the Thunder from Down Under Showroom, which hosted the Australian all-male dance revue for nine shows a week. The small theater also doubled as a venue for Louie Anderson's let-me-tell-you-about-my-crazy-childhood comedy shtick.

It was all happening at the Excalibur Hotel and Casino, a rundown family tourist trap from the same developers who brought Circus Circus to Las Vegas. The trick was to overstuff the properties with enough arcades, juvenile live shows, and themed restaurants to occupy the kids while parents blew past their credit-card limits at the casino. Just being here reminded Kristin of the time that Hart had banished her to work at Treasure Island, a far more upscale version of the same thing.

Billie giggled as one Motown smash gave way to another – Marvin Gaye's 'I Heard It Through the Grapevine.' She moved her body to the psychedelic soul beat. 'So, do you think all of those hunks are true Aussies?'

'The show probably started out that way,' Kristin said dryly. 'But by now having seen *Crocodile Dundee* on cable probably counts.'

Billie cackled. 'It's official. *You're* the bitch.'

Kristin laughed, covering her face in mock horror as the beastly bridal company broke out the Dicky Lickies and began fellating the candy-colored penis-shaped lollipops that lit up like little phallic Christmas trees.

'Wow,' Billie remarked. 'Check out the older one who looks like a teamster. She really knows how to deep throat.'

Kristin made an effort to ignore the tacky floor antics and watch the muscled, waxed, and supremely confident men on stage. She sipped on her overpriced, watered-down drink. 'Remind me why we came to this again?'

'*Him,*' Billie answered, pointing to the last man standing.

The six others had cleared out, leaving a tall, dark-eyed, milk chocolate Adonis with a clean-shaven crown to bask in the solo spotlight.

'One of my dancers has been to this show at least ten times,' Billie explained. 'He's obsessed. I thought we'd see what all the fuss was about.'

'It's all starting to make sense,' Kristin murmured, unable to stop staring at the model-perfect face and *Men's Health*-cover-ready body. The phrase 'Black Is Beautiful' came to mind. But it certainly failed to do this man justice.

He was a merely good-enough dancer, going through the obligatory do-you-really-want-me-to teasing moves, which easily drew out near-deafening encouragement from the horny ladies in the house. Ultimately, he stripped down to a butt-baring thong, all to the subtle sounds of Justin Timberlake's 'Sexy Back.'

The authentically Australian emcee – charming in that cute, cocky, funny guy who's fun to date for only a few months kind of way – bounded back onto the stage. 'Give it up one more time for … *Black Diamond*!'

Shrieks of approval came roaring back.

'Some women have tried to smuggle him out of Vegas,' the emcee went on. 'But as you can see, ladies … the package is too big.'

His joke was answered by peals of naughty laughter.

'What do you think?' Billie inquired.

'Well, I can understand the commotion,' Kristin said. 'He's quite gorgeous.'

'Definitely,' Billie agreed, pursing her lips in deep thought. 'I'm not sure he's a strong enough dancer for my show, though.'

Kristin did a double take. 'Wait a minute. We're here scouting for *Rebirth* chorus boys?'

'One of the guys has a prescription drug problem,' Billie explained. 'He's off to rehab for thirty days, so I need a fill-in. David begged me to give this guy a chance, but I don't think he could keep up with the choreography.' She drained the last of her club soda. 'Besides, people come to *Rebirth* to see *me*. I don't want them distracted by some Mr. Wonderful who makes Denzel Washington look like an average Joe.'

Now the long-haired member of the group was front and center, barely covered by a medieval costume and showing off some impressive swordplay to the dramatic theme from *Gladiator*. For the women who got off on the Renaissance Fair scene – and apparently there were many in the room – this was the equivalent of live porn.

'Vegas is a tough town for dancers,' Billie said, vaguely watching the naked warrior on stage. 'You wouldn't think so, but the entertainment has become so specialized. Almost every show is a fucking Cirque du Soleil production. If you're not double-jointed or blessed with the ability to dance underwater, forget it.'

They stayed for what remained of the short set, the worst part being the emcee leading the loud Midwestern fatties through a fake orgasm contest. The future bride – hardly able to stand upright on her Payless shoes – took top honors and for her drunken effort won a Thunder from Down Under tiara and a kiss from the dancer called Adam Blue Eyes.

There was a steamy *An Officer and a Gentleman* routine from the military type before a crowd-pleasing Village People group number closed out the show. The final curtain call still left Kristin smiling. In spite of the many cheeseball moments, she had to admit that it was a dirty fun time and worth the ticket price.

The emcee gave the hard sell to a photo opportunity with one or all of the guys. 'Just twenty bucks, ladies.

And we can even make it a fuck-you Kodak moment if there's a particular jerk in your life who needs to learn a lesson.'

Billie dashed to the front, pulling Kristin along and waving a crisp bill in the air. 'This slut wants a picture with Black Diamond!'

Before Kristin could react, Billie pushed her onto the stage, snorting with laughter but still managing to say, 'Her husband's an asshole. Give her the fuck-you special.'

Everything happened at dizzying speed. Black Diamond – even more stunning up close – was suddenly upon her, a towering god at six-foot-three and smelling of clean sweat and Kiehl's Musk.

The photographer stood perfectly positioned, his eye in the viewfinder, his finger hovering over the shutter release.

And as fast as the button could be pressed, Black Diamond positioned Kristin's hand onto his crotch and his luscious lips onto her mouth.

Snap. Flash. Print.

The Girls Gone Wild moment was over in a nanosecond and fully documented.

Black Diamond smiled, revealing Colgate dream-white teeth. 'What's your name?' His voice was smooth, and even in those few syllables it rang the timbre of a highly intelligent man.

'Kristin.'

For a moment, she just stared, practically transfixed. There was something instantly fascinating about him, a sense that he had lived an important, productive existence before this period in his life. As a novelist, as a creator of characters, she wanted to know his story.

'I hope you enjoyed the show, Kristin.' He paused a beat and then added gently, 'You can remove your hand from my crotch now.'

'Oh!' Mortified, she snatched it away as if she had touched a hot burner, moving quickly out of the queue to make room for the stumbling Fake Orgasm Queen and her ghastly court.

'I want one with *all* of the beef slabs,' the bride-to-be slurred.

Kristin pantomimed choking Billie as they waited around for the instant picture. 'I am no longer the bitch,' she scolded. '*You* are! And a low-down bitch at that!'

Billie was nearly doubled over by a hysterical giggle fit, a condition that only got worse once actual evidence of the embarrassment presented itself.

The photograph was just as appalling as Kristin imagined it might be.

Billie pleaded for a closer inspection.

But Kristin refused and shoved the picture into her handbag. By now they had ventured outside the showroom and into the shabby, noisy Excalibur. The hotel was overrun with out-of-control kids. 'I need a change of scenery. For starters, a place that only serves drinks to good-looking adults.'

'Let's go to Tramp,' Billie suggested.

Kristin wavered. There were other options – LAX at Luxor, Haze at Aria, Lavo at Palazzo, Blush at the Wynn, Ghostbar at the Palms – whereas Tramp was part of the London Hotel. Did she really want to settle for the one choice that was official Hart Fox territory?

'It's more exclusive,' Billie reasoned. 'Less club trash. Not free of it, of course. But certainly less to deal with.'

Reluctantly, Kristin agreed. After all, it should hardly matter. Hart was at home with Ollie and Lily. They reached an exit and escaped into the Vegas night – and into fresh air. The weather was glorious. It was close to midnight. Kristin had not been out this late in ages. These were typically writing hours for her.

Her gaze zeroed in on the MGM Grand. An alternative popped into mind. 'We could also just cross the boulevard and go to Tabu.'

Billie pulled a face. 'The music is better at Tramp. Tabu plays too much house. After thirty minutes, that shit gives me a headache.'

Kristin went along easily. There was no avoiding the London tonight. The next decision was whether to jump in a taxi or walk the Strip. No matter their nosebleed designer heels – Giuseppe Zanotti on Kristin, Christian Louboutin on Billie – they chose to travel the hard way.

'Are you still seeing Cam?' Billie asked casually.

Kristin glanced at her, a sly grin curling her lips. 'Are you?'

'This afternoon,' Billie confirmed.

'This morning,' Kristin admitted.

'Does he kiss you?'

'Actually, he does something even better than that,' Kristin replied. 'He listens to me.'

Billie twirled her chain-strap Dior bag and sang, 'Every girl has her kicks.'

Kristin smiled. 'Do you realize that we share the same therapist and the same . . .'

'*Julian*,' Billie filled in. 'That was Richard Gere's name in *American Gigolo*.'

Kristin laughed.

'Well, it sounds better than gigolo, escort, stud-for-hire, male prosti—'

'I agree,' Kristin cut in. 'Let's stick with Julian.'

The Jennifer Payne connection was mere coincidence. But Kristin had shamelessly endorsed Cam Lawford as a fantastic lover the first night that she met Billie. And she had done so as easily as recommending a favorite hairstylist.

They had been having dinner at the London Hotel's Waterside Inn to celebrate Billie's opening night of *Rebirth*. It was a foursome – Kristin, Hart, Billie, and Randall. Talk turned to Kristin's writing career, and Hart went on the attack, dismissing her novels as 'beach and subway trash for the semiliterate,' and her HBO series *Come to Bed* as 'unwatchable soft-core porn.'

To avoid an ugly scene, Kristin left the table to compose herself in the ladies' room. Billie joined her there a few minutes later. As they went about the business of reapplying lipstick in the luxurious dressing room mirror, Billie inquired about the radiant glow to Kristin's complexion. She wanted to know her skin-care secret.

'Phenomenal sex,' Kristin told her.

'Don't take this the wrong way, but your husband seems like a colossal prick,' Billie replied. 'He must give great apology.'

'I didn't say the phenomenal sex was with Hart,' Kristin shot back. 'There's a guy. He's young, hot, a former professional athlete. Now he does other things . . . *professionally*.'

Billie's mouth dropped open in amazement. 'You're fucking with me.'

'No, I'm fucking *him*,' Kristin corrected. 'And judging from what I've seen of your creepy little husband tonight, you're probably going to want his number.'

It had been a reckless, indiscreet, out-of-character moment. But Kristin was so goddamn angry, and she immediately sensed in Billie a kindred spirit. They were both creative and talented women married to controlling assholes. Why not confide in and trust each other?

Now they were walking along the crowded boulevard in easy silence. Kristin stared up at the electric spires rising in the night. She thought about the writer Tom Wolfe's observation that Las Vegas was the only city in the world with a skyline made up of signs – huge, glittering, neon signs.

Up ahead, she could make out a JumboTron advertising *Rebirth*. The video footage showed Billie singing and dancing and entertaining her guts out. Also in the distance was a billboard for the new season of *Come to Bed* on HBO. The lead actress, Jenny Barlow, was standing nude on a well-manicured suburban lawn, draped loosely in a white sheet. Hovering above her seductive expression were the words, WHAT WILL THE NEIGHBORS THINK?

Kristin pointed to the proof of their success. 'It never stops being surreal, does it?'

Billie seemed less impressed. 'I see that, and it doesn't feel like me – the sequins and the dance routines and the cover songs. Even when I was playing dive bars, the other musicians and I used to make fun of crap like that. Now I'm actually doing it. And it's a huge success, so I'm trapped.

Part of me wishes the show had tanked. But Randall is hot to sign a new contract. Maybe I should just demand outrageous money, some insane amount that Hart could never agree to. Then he'd be forced to find a replacement, and I'd be free.'

'That strategy might backfire,' Kristin said, keeping a watchful eye on a black limousine slowing to a crawl. 'Your show is the only part of the London that's meeting sales projections. In fact, it's surpassing them. I can see Hart paying anything to keep you there.'

'Christ,' Billie groaned. 'Me and Elizabeth Taylor.'

Kristin gave her a quizzical look.

'Back in the early sixties Liz wanted no part of the movie *Cleopatra*, so she blurted out, "I'll do it for a million dollars!" And the studio was so desperate for her that they said yes. At the time it was unheard of.'

Suddenly, three rowdy conventioneers rose up through the moon roof of the lurking limousine. They were white, middle-aged, drunk, and determined to live out the ubiquitous tourist creed, 'What happens in Vegas, stays in Vegas.' If ever there was a slogan to encourage leaving home, acting like an idiot, and never feeling guilty about it, that was it.

'Hey, girls, want to party?' the ringleader shouted, still wearing an adhesive-backed name tag that proclaimed him KIMBER. 'There's plenty of room, and the beer's cold.'

A fast look and Kristin had him all figured out. This one had peaked in high school. His easy good looks and cool-guy demeanor had secured him a circle of bland friends who never challenged him, a meaningless but well-paying job, at least two marriages, and enough sexual attention from other women to maintain his cocky brio and keep him in the gym. His type was cradle-to-grave in the same zip code. She could write about him, but her books were longer than a single boring page. Good-bye, Mr. Cardboard.

Kristin waved dismissively and continued walking.

'At least show us your tits!'

This triggered guffaws from his name tag buddies ANDY and SCOTT. Eventually, the limousine picked up speed and blended in with the bumper-to-bumper main-drag traffic. It was Friday night on the Strip. And the thrill-seekers were out in full force.

'Those morons are three other good reasons to go to Tramp,' Billie said.

Tramp Las Vegas was a near clone to the legendary original located on London's Jermyn Street. Founded in 1969 by nightclub masterminds Johnny Gold and Oscar Lerman, Tramp established instant and sustained rule as party scene central for the glitz crowd, and *the* exclusive celebrity haunt.

Membership to Tramp could not be bought. No way, no how. Such a privilege could only be *recommended* by management. This discerning guest practice led to a strict door policy that left A-listers feeling oh-so-special and no-listers flapping in the wind.

Inside, it was anything but an ordinary bar/club/disco. Tramp gave off sophisticated gentleman's basement vibrations with its dark wood paneling, sconces, chandeliers, fresh flowers, and unique concept of hiring tuxedo-clad, impeccably mannered, older white-haired men as hosts. Male club-goers constantly joked that they left Tramp feeling a bit like Bruce Wayne. After all, an Alfred type had been serving them fine Scotch throughout the evening.

Finally, Kristin and Billie reached the London Hotel, only to encounter a body crush lined up to get inside Tramp Las Vegas. By Hart's money-crunching standards, this would be a good crowd. But he needed a great one to offset the so-so numbers hitting virtually every other revenue source on the property.

Billie surveyed the situation. 'I'm the talent, and you're the executive's wife. Fuck these people.' She started to push through. Once a rock star, always a rock star.

'There's an easier way,' Kristin said, holding her back and tapping out a quick text.

KRISTIN FOX It's Kristin, Hart's wife. Standing outside Tramp right now with Billie Shelton. Need a rescue!

The reply was instant.

JAB HUNTER On my way.

And in a blink he was right there, greeting them with a dazzling smile as he smoothly ushered them inside and away from the mini mob. 'What a pleasure to see two very beautiful and talented women. Will Mr. Fox be joining you?' If there was a more handsome man in the nightclub, then he was hiding in the loo. And he would have to be Brad Pitt.

'Not tonight,' Kristin answered. 'Girls only.'

Jab nodded. 'Of course. Follow me.' He strode toward a premium spot overlooking the dance floor, moving as sleekly as a tautly muscled jungle cat in his slim-fitting black Armani suit. Already on the table were two sterling silver buckets – one icing down a bottle of Louis Roederer Cristal, the other icing down three bottles of Fillico. The designer water was blinged out with frosted glass, Swarovski crystal accents, and ornate gold caps in the shape of the Queen's crown.

'We have the Fillico flown in from Japan,' Jab informed the women proudly, gesturing gallantly for them to sit down. 'It's sourced there from a Kobe spring. I hope you find it refreshing.' He opened a bottle and poured a generous amount into two clear glasses. 'Samuel will be around shortly to uncork your champagne. May I arrange for anything else?'

'Promise you will never leave us,' Billie said dreamily, her very first words since encountering him.

Kristin laughed.

Jab's smile was bright with gracious amusement. 'I'm never far away.' And then he was gone.

Billie gave Kristin a dramatic look. 'Where did you find him? I want to have his baby. As long as he takes care of it.'

Kristin laughed again. 'Hart discovered him. His last job was tending bar at a restaurant called Silk Electric in Miami. Hart put him through some kind of overseas finishing school. Now every nightclub on the Strip is trying to hire him away from Tramp. Oh, and the most important thing – he's dating Jenny Barlow.'

Billie made a face. 'I've never liked her.'

Kristin tensed. 'She plays Didi on my cable series. Jenny's a lovely person. And she's a very good actress.'

Billie sampled the Fillico. 'Why all the fuss? This could be Evian or Voss.' She shrugged. 'Maybe it's just the association. Jenny starred in *Watch Her Bleed*, and if it wasn't for that piece-of-shit movie, my friend Liza would still be alive.'

Kristin nodded sympathetically. The reference required no explanation. A disturbed young film student had become obsessed with the slasher flick and set out to continue the on-screen killings of powerful, feminist-minded women. His first and only victim was Liza Pike. He stabbed her to death in a Hamptons summer share on Labor Day only a few years ago.

'I never met Liza,' Kristin said quietly. 'But I feel a kinship with her. She wrote for New Woman Press, too. Toni Valentine – the publisher – discovered both of us and made our careers happen.'

A remix of Cheryl Cole's 'Fight for this Love' began pumping through the state-of-the-art sound system just as Samuel swooped in to open the Cristal and pour a single glass of the delicious bubbly – for Kristin only.

'Oh, he's good,' Billie said, referring to Jab, who not only possessed the knowledge that she no longer drank alcohol but had the agility to pass it on to their host in time to avoid the awkward decline.

'I know,' Kristin sighed. 'I wish Hart would send *himself* to that finishing school.'

Billie snickered.

Kristin glanced around the club, taking in all of the drinkers, dancers, high-class call girls, celebrities, seducers on the make, and reality show fame whores burning out their fifteenth minute.

'The last time I was at Tramp in London I got so wasted that I passed out in one of the bathrooms,' Billie said. 'When I woke up, the place was closed. I was locked in. My cell phone was missing and getting a call out was impossible because of the password-protected phone system. It was crazy. Anyway, the cleaning crew finally showed up. They told me that the same thing happened to Mama Cass once. Can you imagine? Me and the big whale from the Mamas and the Papas!'

Kristin laughed and drank deep on the champagne. It was so cold and so smooth. Cristal would always be her favorite.

Samuel was right there to refill her delicate flute, and, as if by magic, gone again.

'So where do you think our Julian is tonight?' Billie wondered. 'I'm sure he's not sitting at home doing laundry. Some lucky bitch has him booked.'

Kristin made more bubbly disappear. If it was Samuel's goal to keep her glass full, then he might be well advised to stand right beside her with the bottle in his hand. She thought about the husband she was growing to hate and the Julian she was growing to ... *love*? Oh, God, no. Anything but that. Suddenly, Billie's question began roaming around in her mind. In fact, Kristin became totally pre-occupied by it.

Where *was* Cam Lawford tonight?

Confessions from the Man Who's Satisfying Your Wife

By Cam Lawford

Beautiful Can Be Ugly

I arrived at the Encore suite just before midnight. A first-time client named Tricia Leigh (not her real name) answered the door and went right back to cutting coke lines without so much as a hello.

She snorted once, twice, three times – all in quick succession. Her stash was almost gone.

'Get it while you can.' Her warning came out in a sexy Southern drawl. She was a former Miss Tennessee and still beautiful – meticulously colored blond hair, gorgeous deep green eyes, and a tip-top body with big, perky fake breasts. Her style was Chico's window mannequin all the way. But I could get over that.

I joined her for the last hit to be polite.

Tricia Leigh boasted that back in college at Vanderbilt the frat boys used to call her the Blond Dirt Devil. I could definitely see why. But she also admitted that there was open debate as to whether the nickname was in reference to her greedy cocaine manners or her reputation as the Kappa Alpha Theta who gave the best blow job on campus.

On this particular weekend she was living it up in Vegas to celebrate a sorority sister's fortieth birthday. And Tricia

Leigh was determined to take advantage of every minute of freedom before going home to her demanding kids, boring husband, and mind-numbing suburban routine.

Her friends were at a prearranged tourist trap that included dinner, *Phantom of the Opera*, and a midnight helicopter ride. So she decided to play hooky and spend some time with me.

Money was no object. Tricia Leigh had recently discovered that her husband's four-night Florida golf vacation with the boys also included two nights with a Hooters waitress. I was her revenge.

With that in mind, I insisted that we go downstairs to the Encore's swanky nightclub XS. For starters, I knew the bar tab would murder the family credit card.

XS was standing room only. The Encore's answer to over-the-top Vegas nightlife is arguably the hottest after-hours spot on the Strip. And definitely the most spectacular. The place is massive. It features an in-club lagoon, a casino, cabanas surrounding the perimeter of the pool, multilevel bars, stripper poles at every turn, and the sick sounds of DJ Create.

We bypassed the endless line and slipped inside because I knew one of the bouncers. Tricia Leigh was really turned on by the VIP treatment. This was Las Vegas. XS was a mob scene. Model-perfect twenty-year-olds were in a clusterfuck to get inside, and this forty-year-old nobody went strutting past them like Paris Hilton. It gave her quite a thrill. Shit, where Tricia Leigh came from, her jackass husband commandeering a choice table at Applebee's was called a good connection.

Mariah Carey's 'Obsessed' was blasting to such deafening effect that the bass line vibrated in my chest like a second heartbeat. The dance floor was packed solid. Typical XS scene. Filipino boys showboating their hip-hop moves as if they were auditioning for *So You Think You Can Dance*. Check. Rich Asian girls in regulation Fendi shaking their flat asses and flirting for free drinks. Check.

We did Grey Goose and Red Bull, plus a pair of Crystal Head Vodka shots to get things moving in the right direction. In no time Tricia Leigh was feeling the alcohol, giving me an impromptu lap dance, and generally making a spectacle of herself.

I ordered more Grey Goose, plus a bottle of Dom Perignon. When the charge showed up on their account statement, this woman's dipshit husband was going to lose his mind. Fucking a guy's wife was one thing. Fucking his American Express Gold was quite another.

Tricia Leigh tipsy became Tricia Leigh drunk. She rambled about being a member of something called the Glamour Klan and scowled at the rainbow of nationalities partying around us. And then she went on a rant. I couldn't believe the backwoods bullshit that spewed out of her mouth.

She considered herself to be a sophisticated racist and wished that segregation had never been abolished. Most of her friends shared the same attitude. They loved the Deep South but hated living among so many poor and uneducated blacks. To claim membership, the wives in the Glamour Klan had to own a pair of Chanel sunglasses. Tricia Leigh thought this was funny.

I forced a smile, drank down some Dom, and wondered if five hundred dollars an hour was worth this. We went back upstairs to her room, and she asked me to ditch the condom. My firm policy with new clients was to go raw for fellatio but to always slip on a Magnum when it came time for the big event. Tricia Leigh started to whine that she wanted the real feeling.

For a moment, whatever I had to do to satisfy this MILF, get my money, and get on with my life seemed worth it. Besides, she seemed safe enough – a prestigious state beauty title, a thirteen-year marriage, a couple of kids, a leader in her Southern Baptist church. What could be wrong? The short answer was any fucking thing. The good-on-paper show-boats were usually the worst offenders.

I got a strange feeling in my gut and excused myself to step into the bathroom. That's when I saw it – a prescription for Valtrex made out to Tricia Leigh. My stomach dropped. She had genital herpes. And to think I was *this close* to . . .

I flung open the door to read her the riot act, but she had already dozed off. Maybe it was better this way. I was putting on my clothes when she woke up and complained about feeling sick. Then she wanted to know why I was leaving.

'I have to go. I'm sorry.' My voice was tight. I didn't want a scene. I just wanted out of there.

Tricia Leigh was instantly offended. 'This is the nicest hotel in Vegas. You've got a better place to lay your head?'

I decided to just come out with it. 'I saw your prescription.'

Her eyes were cold. 'So?'

'How could you push me to go without a condom?'

'You have sex for money,' Tricia Leigh said viciously. 'If you don't have herpes now, you'll get it from somebody soon.'

I just looked at her in disbelief.

She snatched an envelope full of cash from the night-stand. 'And I ain't paying unless we fuck.'

I checked my Cartier watch. 'It's been ninety minutes. We can call it quits with a one-hour fee.'

'That's five hundred dollars!' she shrieked. 'All you did was horn in on my cocaine and drink on my dime.'

'I got you into the club. The door there is brutal. Without me, you'd still be standing outside.'

The fake tan on Tricia Leigh's unnaturally smooth face was turning fire-engine red. 'Nobody *gets me in* anywhere,' she said haughtily. 'I'm a Miss Tennessee!'

Yes, she was – two decades and at least three plastic surgeries ago. And I bet the only other person who remembers that crown is her mother. But I stayed quiet.

All of a sudden, Tricia Leigh's overly made-up eyes filled with tears, and she started bawling.

God, she was a mess. A pathetic, bigoted mess. But in a strange way, I felt a surge of sympathy. Her best days were behind her. It was probably her husband who brought home the herpes and not the other way around. I approached the edge of the bed and sat down. 'You know what? Forget the fee. This date's on the house.'

She looked at me with little black rivers running down her face.

I gave her my warmest smile. 'But only if you promise to use the money for one of those racial sensitivity classes.'

This made her laugh a little, and for a fleeting moment, the humor reached Tricia Leigh's sad, heartbroken eyes. 'How is it that the whore in the room has all the class?' Her voice broke on the last bit. She slowly slid the money in my direction. 'Take it. I was an awful person tonight. You earned this.'

'Not entirely,' I said. And then I slipped off her shoes and proceeded to give her one of my special foot massages.

Seconds into the rub her head was back on the pillow and faint mewls of pleasure were escaping from her lips. 'Oh, Lord ... don't take this the wrong way, darlin' ... because I'm sure that you're *very* good at what you do ... but this is better than any sex I could ever have.' And just a few minutes later, Tricia Leigh was sound asleep.

I gently draped a blanket over her, kissed her mascara-stained cheek, and walked out.

If I'm lucky, one out of ten appointments is a no-drama sex date. Why? Because most married women's lives are a fucking disaster. Lusty is one thing. I can always handle that. But adding lonely, needy, and generally unstable to the mix is sometimes too much.

Nights like this make me stop and wonder. What will happen to me if I don't get out of this game?

CHAPTER TWELVE

Dale Munso looked like a man who might lose his cool at any moment, over any little thing.

Jennifer quietly observed him as he strode into her office. He was blandly handsome and oozed a jock's bulletproof confidence as he settled onto the sofa and checked his BlackBerry without apology. She took in the polyester-knit corporate polo, the belted khakis, the Submariner Rolex, the lightly scuffed brown shoes. If arrogance were an odor, he would stink up the room. The only thing missing was a stamp on his forehead that read EMOTION-ALLY INCAPABLE.

Dale was here because his employer, MDK Furnishings, strongly suggested a psychological consultation. His response to uncovering his wife's cyber adultery had been to check into a Marriott Courtyard, punch the wall with his bare fist, and lock himself in the room with a gun.

'Thank you for coming in, Dale,' Jennifer began earnestly. 'I want you to feel as comfortable as possible about this process. It's important—'

'How much?' Dale interjected.

Jennifer just looked at him, determining that his eyes revealed a particular coldness.

'How much do you charge?'

'One fifty per fifty-minute session.'

'I think the best move for me is to just go out there and have some fun of my own. Do I get a discount for knowing the answer?'

'Is it important for you to know the answer before we start?'

He gave her a smug smile. 'Nice shrink trick.' His gaze swept over the room, taking in the modest décor, finally acknowledging Nancy, who regarded him warily from her cushioned bed in the corner.

An instinct told Jennifer that he wanted to say something. More often than not, a period of silence brought those things to the surface. She waited him out.

When Dale began to talk, he unconsciously massaged the broken skin and light scabbing on his knuckles, obviously battle wounds from taking on hotel Sheetrock. 'None of this is surprising. Julie made out with an old boyfriend at her high school reunion right in front of me. Another time I watched her come on to one of my best friends at a restaurant. And there was a married guy at her office – Barrett. He ended up moving to North Carolina, and for a few weeks that's all she talked about. She wanted us to move there, too. I actually considered it. I just wanted her to be happy. It was only later that I figured out what was going on.'

'What are you feeling as you talk about this?' Jennifer asked.

The expression on Dale's face was pure cockiness. 'I'm feeling she's not nearly as discreet as I am.'

'What does that mean exactly?'

He shrugged. 'My job keeps me on the road two or

three nights a week. Julie's not interested in sex. At least not with me. You figure it out.'

'You say that *she's* not interested.'

'If I wanted a blow job at home, I'd have to suck my own dick. And when we do have sex, she just lies there like a coma patient.'

'In situations like this between a husband and a wife, the problem is usually a matter of connection,' Jennifer pointed out gently. 'Men are more inclined to be caring and attentive when their sexual needs are being considered. And women need to feel appreciated and cared for in order to respond sexually. This is a classic chasm.'

Dale shook his head in disgust. 'She lost twenty pounds for this asshole – Sean. I'd been encouraging her to exercise and lay off the pizza for months, and she just ignored me. This guy comes along and she drops the weight in no time.'

Jennifer knew the background. Dale's wife, Julie, had been exchanging sexually explicit e-mails with Sean, an out-of-town work colleague.

He scrolled through his BlackBerry. 'Listen to what she wrote to him: "I look at Dale, and I just want to go to sleep. He makes me tired and bored. And then I think about you, and I have the energy to stay up all night."'

Jennifer was ambivalent about the new social technology. It could facilitate connection, but it could also amplify hurt. E-mail, texting, Facebook, and Twitter seemed to cause more relationship problems than they solved. 'It's not healthy to read something hurtful like that over and over again. You should delete it.'

Dale's expression turned to granite. 'I don't care. I've

got women in my sales territory. All I have to do is send a text – *I'm in town*. They can't get enough of me.'

Jennifer glanced down at his damaged knuckles. 'Tell me about the injury to your hand.'

'I punched a wall. If I get mad enough, that's what I do.' He said this with a note of masculine pride. 'Better a wall than someone's face, right?'

'And how mad do you have to be to take the gun out of your sedan's console?'

Dale was silent.

'Did you have suicidal thoughts that day?' Jennifer pressed.

'I thought about shooting myself. I thought about finding Sean and shooting him. I thought about going back home and putting a bullet in my wife's idiot brain. I thought a lot of things. But that's all they were ... just thoughts.'

'How often are you troubled by these kind of thoughts?'

Dale shook his head, laughing a little. 'Let me clear this up – for you and the HR people. I was just pissed. I took off, I got hammered, I acted out, and then I came to my senses. Why should I let my wife and her online boyfriend have that much control over me? He's fantasizing and jerking off like some thirteen-year-old. Last week I nailed a sales girl from one of my L.A. accounts and another girl who works at the Marriott I stay at in Phoenix. Does it sound like I'm a danger to myself or anyone else?'

Jennifer said nothing. But she believed that he was not – physically, at least. Emotionally, he seemed to be a one-man wrecking ball.

Dale stared blankly across the room. 'Maybe I should

just chuck it and move away. Start over somewhere else. I've always liked Florida. Sarasota's nice.'

'Aren't there children to consider?'

He nodded. 'We have one – a boy. But Julie and her crazy mother would keep up so much bullshit about custody and visitation that I'd rather start over.'

'You could just walk away from your son?' Jennifer struggled to edit her incredulity.

'I can walk away from anyone. That's just the way I am.' He snapped his fingers. 'I can cut it off that fast.'

Jennifer surmised Dale to be a surface dweller who thrived in superficial relationships and struggled with deep connections. She wondered what he had witnessed in his household growing up, the framework of his previous relationships. 'Tell me about your first marriage.'

He opened up about a woman named Nadine and boasted about thrilling her with his sexual prowess while under the secret influence of cocaine. One day he introduced her to the source of his extra boost, and they began using together. But while Dale had the physical and mental discipline to use casually and remain functional, Nadine became an addict. So he walked out and divorced her without looking back.

Jennifer had treated men like Dale before. Internally, they were ice on ice. The deeper she would dig, the colder they would get. It was tough work with minimal progress – unless they truly wanted to change. Her sense was that Dale did not.

She recalled his birthday from the preliminary file. He was a Virgo. And true to form, he came off tightly wound, intense, withholding by nature, and possessed of a capacity to make brutal decisions about people. It was sad. She felt for Julie, their son, and anyone else in his life longing to break through the hard surface.

Jennifer glanced at the clock. 'We're going to have to stop.'

Dale stood up and peeled off two large bills from a money clip. 'If I want another appointment, I've got your number.'

When he left, Jennifer's thoughts drifted to Patrick. She could envision him reacting the same way if ever faced with knowledge of her infidelity with Cam Lawford – taking off, acting out, considering something horrific.

But the difference was that Patrick possessed none of the arrogance, emotional frigidity, and misogyny that characterized Dale. Those qualities served as a protective force field against the inadequacies that haunted him. By contrast, Patrick was more vulnerable. He pretended not to care about their marriage. But losing it could be the tipping point of failure in his life.

If confronted with a moment of personal despair similar to Dale's, she wondered what Patrick would do. Just think about pulling the trigger? Or actually do it?

Jennifer sat there, disturbed by the session and haunted by the scenario. Her mind started to play tricks, flashing images of Dale Munso in a Marriott Courtyard with a gun in his hand. And then the vision changed. Now it was Patrick in his place. Her husband. Mia Sara's father. A chill went straight to her bones.

Desperate to hear his voice and take his emotional

temperature, she called Patrick at the newsroom. It rang into voice mail. She hung up and tried his cell number. Same thing. She left a message and hoped to hear from him before her next appointment.

CHAPTER THIRTEEN

Patrick Payne saw JENNIFER CALLING on the screen and shoved the phone back into his pocket. He was at the Coffee Bean on Flamingo Road, nursing a double espresso and waiting for his screenplay critique meeting to start.

Technically, he should have been sitting in his cubicle at the *Las Vegas Review-Journal*. But his story for the day – a piece on a food bank called Three Square – had been written, polished, and proofed. All he had to do was file it by deadline. Patrick covered local politics, and hunger had become a hot-button issue in Las Vegas. With the unemployment rate edging past 14 percent, children, seniors, and even middle-class families needed social services like never before.

The group's usual suspects – Van Bryan and Robbie Breslow – showed up and joined Patrick at their regular table, a four-top nestled in the back.

'I had to buy this loser's coffee – *again*,' Van announced as they sat down.

Patrick looked at Robbie.

The struggling comedian from New York was ready with his excuse. 'I'm strapped, man. The Nugget canceled my gig last weekend. Can you believe they offered me free chicken-fried steak to do a shorter set? I may be hard up, but I'm not working for food. Not yet anyway.' He gestured to the empty seat. 'Where's the new chick?'

Patrick shrugged. 'It's just a few minutes after two. She said she'd be here.'

'I'm still not sure about this,' Van said. 'Have you read this girl's e-mails? She can barely spell. And I don't think she's ever learned the concepts of capital letters and punctuation.'

'Sounds like me,' Robbie said. 'I e-mail and text like that. Don't judge until you see her script pages.'

Van looked unconvinced.

Patrick nodded his agreement with Robbie, then addressed Van directly. 'We could use a female perspective. Right now it's just two guys and a retard.'

Van laughed.

'Hey, you can both eat my load,' Robbie said as he pantomimed jerking off. 'But if this is our new member walking up, that offer's revoked. I'll save it for her.'

A porn-star-chic stunner approached. She had expensively bleached hair, gorgeous fake breasts, and inflated lips that resembled two satin pillows, not to mention a banging body poured into a pink velour Juicy Couture tracksuit that accentuated every sinful curve. 'Is this the screenwriting group?'

Robbie gave the newcomer a horny grin. 'If it wasn't, sweetheart, it is now.'

She managed a hesitant smile.

Patrick offered her the empty chair. 'Don't pay any attention to him.'

She sat down and stacked four scripts fastened with brass butterfly clips on the corner of the table, her gardenia-heavy fragrance wafting all around them. 'Sorry I'm late. I have a club shift later, so I had to get my tanning in.'

'Where do you work?' Van asked.

She sighed. 'Everywhere. I co-manage the Seven boutique in the Forum at Caesars. I do an early evening shift at Crazy Horse. And then I'm in the late-night show *Bite* at the Stratosphere.' She pretended to bare fangs. 'I play a dancing vampire.'

'That's a topless show, right?' Robbie asked, giving her an amphibious leer.

'Yes,' she answered dryly. 'And I dance naked at Crazy Horse, too. But if you come to see me at Seven, I'll have my clothes on.'

'I'm not much of a shopper.'

She rolled her eyes.

Patrick was impressed. It looked as if their new member had already written a complete screenplay. None of them could say that. As a threesome, they had been writing and revising the first acts of their scripts for months.

They went around the circle to make introductions and offer brief summaries of their respective projects. Patrick jumped in first. He was writing a script called *Neon Underground*, a dark and twisted drama about a group of young addicts who reject the establishment and create an alternative society in the tunnel system underneath Las Vegas.

Van laid out his idea to turn *Twenty Years*, a short documentary he produced and directed about his high school reunion, into a full-length dramatic feature. Then he blathered on about the prestigious festivals that had accepted the original short and the special screenings taking place across the country.

Robbie talked about *Mancation*, his gross-out comedy effort about a travel booking error that sends four straight guys on the make to a remote island paradise that happens to be a gay-only resort.

Eva Lick chimed in last. She was saving money for a permanent move to Los Angeles, where she intended to break into the adult film industry. Her master plan was to market herself exclusively as a girl-girl performer, gain popularity, and then cash in as a porn superstar with boy-girl scenes. Eva also wanted to write the movies she acted in and give fans a compelling story in addition to great sex scenes. Her first attempt was *Angels Vs. Sluts*. She passed out a draft and asked for notes at the next meeting.

There was a long, awkward silence.

Patrick noted that the screenplay formatting was spot-on. If nothing else, the girl knew the basics.

Robbie held up the script and said, 'Any of this on video yet?'

Van cleared his throat and began thumbing through the initial pages. 'I don't think this group is the best fit for someone like you.'

Eva looked at him sharply. 'Why not?'

'We're interested in legitimate films.'

'Adult films are legitimate,' Eva countered. 'Last year they grossed over thirteen billion. How much did documentary shorts pull in?'

Van turned to Patrick for help.

But Patrick left him hanging. He liked Eva. She was sharp, bold, and demonstrated a killer work ethic. As far as he was concerned, this was her group now.

Eva stared at him strangely. 'You look like an actor. I

saw one of his old movies on cable a few weeks ago. I think it's called *A Star Is Born*. That lady with the big nose who sings is in it. What's his name?'

'Kris Kristofferson,' Robbie offered.

'That's him!' Eva yelped. She pointed at Patrick. 'He looks just like him, don't you think?'

Van glanced upward as if in need of God's strength. 'By the way, the woman with the big nose who sings is *Barbra Streisand*. You should probably know that.'

They talked shop for another fifteen minutes. Van dominated the conversation with talk of a friend of a friend who was going to get *Twenty Years* into the hands of filmmaker Steven Soderbergh *and* get Van a cameo on the last season of HBO's *Entourage*.

Robbie broke in with a story about having a one-night stand with Billie Shelton when he lived in New York. 'This was before getting beaten up by that rapper and all the plastic surgery,' he pointed out. 'If I get another shot, it'll be like sleeping with a different girl!'

The meeting ended, and Patrick – in no hurry to get back to his miserable cubicle – lingered with Eva after Van and Robbie shuffled out.

'I don't think Van likes me.'

'He'll come around,' Patrick assured her. 'He's a little full of himself, but he's a nice guy. I wish he would give up on that documentary, though. I think he's been flogging that thing for five years.'

'I don't get it,' Eva said. 'I mean, who cares about a high school reunion that's not their own? Unless it's a bunch of famous people. Anyway, staying with one creative project too long is amateur hour. You have to move on to the next one. It's the only way to grow and build momentum.'

Patrick grinned. 'All good points.' He paused a beat. 'What did you think about Robbie?'

'Well, he's a tool, obviously, but his *Mancation* idea is actually pretty impressive. It's just the sort of high-concept dumb-guy humor that studios are looking for. Kind of like *The Hangover.*'

Now Patrick was smiling. 'It sounds like you know more about the industry than they do.'

'I read *Variety*. There's a producer who comes into the Crazy Horse every week, and he brings me his old issues.'

Patrick placed a hand on her script and promised to read it right away. 'You put me to shame. I'm still on the first act of *Neon Underground.*'

'The trick is to keep writing,' Eva said. 'If you obsess over one section, you'll never go the distance.'

'You're right.'

'I really like your idea, too,' she went on. 'It sounds like it has the kind of edgy vibe that would attract an awesome cast of young and talented actors. When those movies work, they become cult classics. You know, like *A Clockwork Orange.*'

Patrick could feel his own eyes brighten. 'I love that movie. I've seen it at least a dozen times.'

Eva's smile was warm and supportive. 'Maybe someone will be saying that about *Neon Underground* in a few years.'

Patrick never talked to Jennifer like this. She knew nothing about his screenplay dream. She knew nothing about his critique group. His default mechanism was to shut her out completely. Maybe it was his way of punishing her. But for what exactly he did not know.

Eva was looking at him conspiratorially. 'Do you want to go somewhere and get stoned?'

Patrick's pocket started to vibrate.

Slipping out his phone, he saw JENNIFER CALLING again. Twice in the same hour? This time he answered, fearing Mia Sara might be sick or hurt. 'Hey, is something wrong?'

'No, I'm just checking in,' Jennifer said. 'How's your day going?'

'Fine . . . busy.' He glanced at Eva. 'Listen, I'm chasing down some quotes for a story. Can you pick up Mia from school?'

'Sure,' Jennifer said. 'My four o'clock just canceled, so it's not a problem.'

'Thanks. I'll see you at home later.' He returned the phone to his pocket. 'Sorry about that.'

Eva giggled and stood up. 'By the way, those *quotes* you're chasing down? They're at my house.' She started for the exit.

He followed her gleaming red Lexus SUV in his rundown Saturn that needed a wash and an oil change.

Eva lived in a planned community called Silverado Ranch in southeast Vegas, roughly six miles from the Strip. She led him through a majestic clock-tower entrance and into a deserted cul-de-sac.

Patrick knew the area well. He had written about it. The neighborhood was a foreclosure nightmare. Only a few residents remained, and most of those were tourists occupying party rentals on the weekends.

Eva pulled into the driveway of the only home on the street that did not have brown grass. Her yard was landscaped a beautiful green. She disappeared inside the garage, appearing again moments later when she opened the front door with a flourish.

Her house was a show palace – a sunken living room with a tricked-out wet bar, a bay of floor-to-ceiling windows overlooking a sparkling pool, a fully equipped Viking kitchen. It was much nicer than the home Patrick and Jennifer shared.

'Wow.' And then the rude question spilled out of his mouth before he could stop it. 'How do you afford this?'

'I don't. At least not anymore. I haven't made a mortgage payment in fifteen months. The bank hasn't said a word. But that doesn't mean I won't get kicked out any day now. Everything was fine until the economy crashed. I make about half of what I used to.'

He looked at her in marvel. 'How old are you?'

'Twenty-two.'

She zipped out of her track jacket, revealing a white tank that barely contained her luscious breasts.

Patrick could see right through the thin material to her large rosebud nipples.

'So I take it you're married.' She moved to the wet bar and busied herself with a sleek, brushed-aluminum gadget that looked like something out of the Hammacher Schlemmer catalog.

Patrick held up his hand to display his wedding band. 'Guilty.'

'How many kids?'

'Just one, a girl.' He pulled out his phone to proudly display his screensaver.

Eva stopped what she was doing to look, touching his hand as she studied the small image. 'She's precious.'

Patrick beamed. 'Her name's Mia Sara.'

'She's got Daddy's eyes.' Eva went back to her mysterious task.

'What about you?' Patrick asked. 'Any kids?'

'Oh, God, no. Maybe in ten years or so. I have other plans for this body between now and then. I was engaged once. But his parents thought I was a slut. He broke up with me on a Christmas Eve and married a *proper* girl. So now I hate the holidays, and he's working for a division of her family's construction business somewhere in Louisiana. *C'est la vie.*'

His eyes fell on a small gun sitting on an open shelf behind the bar. 'What's up with the firepower?'

Eva looked at him, then back at the pistol. 'Oh, that. It gets scary at night sometimes. I'm the only person living on this street.'

'I might need to borrow it sometime,' Patrick joked. 'You know, to keep Robbie in line.'

'Well, you know where it is if you need it,' Eva said absently, checking her strange contraption's digital temperature gauge.

'What is that thing?' Patrick asked.

'*This*,' Eva said proudly, gesturing like a television spokesmodel, 'is a Volcano Vaporizer. It lets you inhale the marijuana without smoke. My personal trainer swears by it.' She deposited about half a gram of pot into the small chamber. Attached to that was a large bag with a mouth-piece.

Patrick was fascinated. He had heard about this from a college buddy who lived in Boulder. The machine pushed hot air through the cannabis, which not only released a smokeless, almost odorless vapor, but also delivered an amazing high without carcinogens. It was every health nut's dream method of getting stoned.

'This little baby is made by Storz and Bickel,' Eva said, admiring the device. 'It's the Mercedes of vaporizers. I think it costs around a thousand. One of my regulars at Crazy Horse gave it to me for Valentine's.' She smiled. 'This is going to blow your mind. Are you ready?'

Patrick nodded. He had known Eva Lick for less than two hours, and already she had provided him more excite-ment than he had felt in years. Her sex goddess looks, her film industry savvy, her on-the-edge lifestyle – the combi-nation of it all thrilled and stimulated him. For the first time in a long time, he felt vibrantly alive.

'All you have to do is press this button,' she instructed in a soft, breathy tone. 'That releases the vapor into the bag. And then you just suck it in through the mouthpiece like this.' She performed a demonstration for his benefit.

Patrick watched her intently, seeing the impact of the drug play out in Eva's pale blue eyes. It was as if she had teleported from this dreary, economically ravaged street to some blissful private heaven that people only dream about.

'Oh, God, that's *good*,' Eva sighed. 'You can actually taste the herbal essence. I'll never smoke again. I'll only vaporize.'

Patrick mimicked her actions. After a minute or so, he did it again. And then he greedily stole a third attempt as Eva giggled at him.

It was the purest high Patrick had ever known. The wonderful floating sensation went beyond his head and spread throughout his entire body. What an amazing feeling! 'How long does it last?' he managed to ask.

'A long time,' Eva promised dreamily. 'But you might want to take it easy. Some first-timers get—'

For a millisecond the room spun, and Patrick stumbled. '*Really* stoned,' Eva finished.

Patrick laughed. In fact, he could not stop laughing. He experienced another moment of dizziness and almost fell. But this only made him laugh harder.

'I think you need to lie down,' Eva said, taking his arm as she led him into her bedroom.

Patrick was preoccupied by the indulgently girly décor – a sanctuary of pink and lace and collectible Barbie accent pieces. With Eva's assistance, he eased down onto the bed and practically waded in a sea of soft, frilly pillows.

'I have to leave for the club,' Eva was saying. 'But you're welcome to stay for as long as you need to. There's plenty of food if you get hungry. And the front door will lock behind you.'

Patrick could hear Eva's melodic voice. He could take in the full import of her words. But she sounded so far away, so distant. Rising up slightly, he searched the room for her with lazy eyes. All of a sudden, he froze.

She was dressing inside the explosion of clothing, shoes, and underwear that constituted her closet.

He studied the string of her thong and the way that it

bisected her perfect ass. Oh, God! Why did he have to be some idiot news writer? How amazing life would be if he could just be that string. After all, there looked to be no better place on earth than where that string was right now.

Suddenly, Patrick felt movement – a stirring where it counted. Months had gone by since he had felt anything down there except for the regular need to piss. His cock had just been a flaccid and useless symbol of his general dissatisfaction with life. But right now he sensed the beginning of an erection. Wait. Not anymore. This was a full hard-on. A raging boner!

Eva was dressed and rolling a small suitcase toward the bedroom door. She stopped, looked, and laughed. 'There's some lube in the nightstand drawer if you need to take care of that. But please clean up after yourself. And don't read my script until you come down from this high. I want a clear-headed reading!'

Patrick just grinned and fell back onto the pillows again, staring at the ceiling and the billowy curtains wrapping around the canopy, preoccupied by sexual desire, lost in the comfort and the quiet.

He needed to get up. The Three Square story had to be filed by deadline. The paper was looking for any excuse to cut people loose these days. Any little fuckup could get a staffer shit-canned.

But Patrick found it impossible to move. All he wanted to do was lie here in this beautiful woman's bed and touch himself. The beast had been sleeping for a very long time. It was awake now, though. And it was roaring! As he reveled in this, he slowly felt himself drifting away . . .

CHAPTER FOURTEEN

'He took three wedding rings from random women in the audience,' David Dean explained with awestruck enthusiasm. 'Then he dropped them into a wineglass, waved his hand over it, and suddenly they were all interlinked!'

'Amazing,' Billie grumbled. 'Maybe he could do a trick and make the waiter appear. I need more tea.' Finishing off the last bite of broccoli-cheese quiche, she bemoaned her current fag hag existence.

Here she was, lunching at Payard in Caesars Palace with David, her favorite dancer from *Rebirth*, and his much older boyfriend Jagger Smith, who happened to be both a police detective and, apparently, the long-lost twin brother of Blair Underwood.

'He's a real magician!' David insisted in a way that reminded her that he really was a sheltered refugee from one of the red states.

Jagger laughed a little. 'No, the guy is a bullshit artist. His best trick is that he's not in jail. Now that's magic.'

David pushed away his beef panini and fumed silently, like a teenage girl who'd just been told that the Taylor Swift concert was sold out.

'I've heard stories about him, too,' Billie put in. The

subject was Andrew Wiggs, the headlining illusionist at the London's Magic Cavern theater. 'He likes to choke women during sex. He freaked out the niece of one of the executives. There was talk of canceling his contract. In the end, though, I think the buyout was too expensive.'

Jagger nodded confirmation.

'That's just gossip,' David hissed. 'I was blown away by the magic.'

Billie rolled her eyes. 'Does he still turn the white French poodle and the black Labrador into one dalmatian?'

Jagger laughed again. 'I forgot about that trick.'

Billie admonished David with a dumb look. 'That theater is specially designed to make the hocus-pocus look real. Magic is when your fat Uncle Daniel convinced three women to share him as a husband.'

'Whatever,' David snapped, always pissed whenever someone made a remark about his family. He slid off the creamy white leather banquette. 'I need a cigarette.'

Jagger watched him leave the bistro in a huff. 'Always a flair for the dramatic.'

'He's a sweet kid. But he's still a baby. What do you see in a runaway gay Mormon from Utah?' Billie didn't wait for him to answer. 'Hey, you're a cop. Maybe you should arrest yourself for pedophilia.'

Unfazed, Jagger drank what remained of his iced tea and coolly motioned the passing waiter for refills all around. 'He's twenty-one. We met at the nightclub Krave. It's not like I cruised him in a high school parking lot.'

'How old are you?' Billie asked.

'Thirty-three. And we wouldn't be having this conversation if David were a twenty-one-year-old *girl* who'd left home. I like younger guys.' He shrugged. 'So what? That doesn't make me a perv.'

Billie softened. It was a reasonable answer. She eyed Jagger Smith carefully, finding him increasingly perplexing. Her gaydar could usually pick out even the most fiercely closeted homosexual cases. But it read nothing on the gorgeous man sitting across from her. She leaned in to ask, 'How do you manage to live so openly and work in a police department, of all places?'

'It's not easy,' Jagger admitted. 'But my partner's a beautiful woman, and it's not easy for her, either. I take a good bit of ribbing here and there. Nothing I can't handle. Being great at the job helps.'

Billie smirked. 'So modest.'

'Don't worry about your dancer boy. I'll take care of him. I don't know how long this will last, but at least it's a healthy relationship. David knows now that he's worthy of being loved. And he didn't come into this feeling that way.'

Billie sighed wistfully. 'Where were you when *I* was twenty-one? All the guys I met just wanted to get me drunk and naked as fast as possible.'

Jagger grinned. 'Look at you now, though. Sober. Big Vegas show. Married to a doctor. You did okay.'

'It all looks better on paper.' Billie noticed him studying her face. 'He's good, isn't he? My husband, the plastic surgeon.'

Jagger was visibly chagrined. 'I didn't mean to stare. It's just ... I saw the evidence photographs that were taken after your attack. I've never seen that kind of brutality before.'

Billie fell silent as she wondered what Jagger would say if she told him that Randall Glass was potentially more abusive than Domestic Violence, just in a different way. But the brilliant doctor was free to torment and to bask in the praise of his surgery skills while the dangerous rapper served out a twenty-year prison sentence at a maximum-security facility somewhere in Nevada.

'Has anyone told you about Ely State?' Jagger asked.

Billie shook her head.

'That's where he's serving his time. The joint is famous for a gang of Aryan warriors incarcerated there. They rule from the inside and dish out cruel and unusual punishment to inmates like Domestic Violence. I'll be surprised if he survives as long as two years. Sending him to that lockup was like throwing meat to wolves. Prison is a true hell on earth for him. I don't know if that's a comfort to you or not.'

Sometimes Billie hated him for not killing her when he had the chance. A few more savage kicks and sadistic blows would've finished the job, only Domestic Violence stopped just short of that and left her there to be discovered, to endure the agonizing recovery, and to ultimately fall under the sick tyrannical rule of Randall.

'Maybe I shouldn't have brought that up,' Jagger was saying. 'I hope I didn't upset you.'

'No, I'm fine,' Billie murmured. She focused her attention on him. 'Are you familiar at all with the Liza Pike case?'

Jagger nodded. 'I followed it. Did you know her?'

'She was a good friend.'

'I'm sorry. Everyone here was pissed when that son of

a bitch got away with an insanity defense. He deserved the death penalty. Or life in solitary.'

'At least he's locked up.'

'For now.'

'They won't let him out.' Her tone was absolute.

Jagger gave her a cynical look.

'They won't.'

'If you really believe that, then you should have more faith in the magic of Andrew Wiggs.'

Billie experienced a tension in her chest as the sinister image of Leonard Tidwell's mug shot flashed in her mind. 'That sick fuck stabbed Liza fifteen times.'

'He's at the Mid-Hudson Forensic Psychiatric Center in New York,' Jagger said. 'It's a maximum-security hospital, but the average stay there is just eight or nine years, even for murderers. If he follows the rules, he might move on to another facility with less security and eventually become an outpatient. It happens all the time.'

Billie just sat there, shocked. 'Let me get this straight. Liza is six feet under. I'm living it up in Las Vegas. But Leonard Tidwell could still end up doing less time than Domestic Violence?'

'Sometimes the system is fucked. I hate it, too.' Jagger checked his watch and impatiently scanned the area for David. 'Is he smoking the whole pack?' His cell phone buzzed. He glanced at the screen. 'I have to run. My partner's crawling up my ass. Tell David I'll see him at home later tonight.' He made a move for his wallet.

Billie halted him. 'No, it's my treat.'

Jagger grinned. 'Okay. Thanks for lunch. Have a great show tonight.'

Billie watched him go, her mind still reeling from the news about Liza's killer. The survivor guilt cranked up again. She needed to talk with Jennifer Payne. That woman had a gift for helping sort out the past.

David stalked back into Payard full of bitchy attitude.

'You just missed him. He had to leave.'

'What the fuck?' David roared, checking his cell phone. 'He didn't even text me!'

Billie resisted the urge to vomit. 'Stop acting like a girl. You happen to be dating a real man. Bullshit drama like this will chase him away. Is that what you want?'

'No,' David mumbled before slumping down on the banquette. 'It's just—'

Billie cut him off. 'Don't. I'm already bored. By the way, I saw the Thunder from Down Under boys the other night.'

David's eyes widened with interest. 'What did you think of Black Diamond?'

'I think he needs dance lessons. And he's too damn good-looking. If there's going to be a distracting beauty onstage, it better be *me*, not some Chippendales knockoff.' She put out an impatient hand. 'Give me your phone and a cigarette.'

Obediently, David turned over his T-Mobile Sidekick, a Hello Kitty lighter, and a pack of Virginia Slims. 'Be quick about it. I have to teach an exercise class.'

Billie hustled toward the outer edges of the casino floor and lit up the skinny cigarette. She preferred Marlboro Lights but refused to buy them. Quitting entirely was her ultimate goal. But until that stuck, she bummed a smoke if the craving hit strongly enough.

She dragged deep. Her life was shit – hanging out with

a May-December gay couple, living under Randall's constant watch, performing the same fucking show six nights a week. Jesus Christ! The only relief – the only true sense of joy – came from her time with Cam Lawford.

Getting sober had recalibrated Billie sexually. The hard-core carnality of her drug and alcohol period had given way to different needs. Aggression didn't turn her on anymore. Now she responded to skillful touch. And Cam's hands could do things to her body that provided some of the most intense pleasure she'd ever experienced. It was amazing how quickly and reliably he could bring her to orgasm. And that kiss. Oh, God, that kiss! He could do that until her lips were cracked and bleeding, and it still wouldn't be long enough.

She tried his number again. From her own phone, Billie disciplined herself to make only one call around appointment time so as not to generate any suspicion from Randall and Carly, both of whom monitored her call activity. But with David's phone, she practically burned down the cellular tower.

Billie scanned the area, looking past the out-of-shape daytime gamblers as she searched for Carly. Sometimes the freak would just show up and observe from a distance. And if she ever saw Billie with David's mobile, another crumb of privacy would be snatched away.

Constant paranoia. What a way to live. Maybe this was God's punishment. Liza got the easy street of being dead and buried. Billie got this miserable existence.

She tried him again. It rang and rang until the outgoing voice mail message played.

'Hi, this is Cam. You know what to do.'

Billie took in a deep breath, preparing to say something light and funny when she noticed a woman trudge by wearing an ill-fitting promotional T-shirt advertising HBO's *Come to Bed* and its name-above-the-title star, Jenny Barlow. That goddamn bitch was everywhere.

She killed the connection and fired up another cigarette. It was prime time for the Las Vegas wives. Their executive husbands were hunkered down in the casino bunkers, sweating the numbers and strategizing ways to put a tourniquet on the hemorrhaging gaming market. That left the women time to shop, pamper their bodies, complain to their therapists, and maybe – for a select number, the ones who were in the know and courageous enough – spend a few thrilling hours with Cam Lawford.

Billie puffed away. He was with one of them right now. She felt sure of it. And the question began to consume her as she stood there courting cancer.

Which lucky bitch was having him for lunch today?

CHAPTER FIFTEEN

Kristin could not get enough of him. Cam's body was like candy from the devil – sweet, sinful, impossibly addictive. She had never found fellatio so infinitely pleasurable with any other man. His length, his thickness, his incredible hardness, the delicious taste of his flesh – it all motivated her to put everything she had into the act.

'*Damn*. Maybe I should be paying you.'

Kristin flashed him a naughty smile as she lay back, basking in the praise, allowing her head to fall over the edge of the bed. She took in an upside-down view of the faux Eiffel Tower. She had booked a cut-rate-priced suite at the Paris, a rival to her darling husband's similarly themed London property.

Propped up on one elbow, Cam was watching her with amused interest, a sensual grin planted on his handsome face. 'Where did you learn to give head like that?'

Kristin giggled, still tingling from the sexual aftershocks. 'I'm not always that inspired. Trust me.'

He reached out for her hand and ran his thumb across the holy-shit-sized emerald-cut diamond on her wedding ring. 'How long have you been hitched?'

She sighed. 'Fourteen years.'

'Happy ones for him if he gets what I just got on a regular basis.'

'He could only wish.' There was an instant bitterness to Kristin's tone. She rose up to meet Cam's gaze. 'I'm here to forget that I have a husband.'

His eyes blazed into hers. 'What husband?'

She smiled and rolled over onto her stomach.

As if by instinct, Cam placed a proprietary hand on her ass. Playfully, he slapped one cheek. 'Bad girl.' And then the other. 'Very bad.'

The slight stinging sensation provided a delicious little thrill. Kristin was afraid to glance at the clock, even as she wondered how much time remained. They had made love twice, and then Cam had settled back like a king to enjoy her finest oral ministrations. She was constantly amazed by his sexual stamina, the way that he recharged so quickly. He really was a nonstop love machine.

Shaking her head in awe, Kristin got up and raided the minibar for a Perrier. The intense carbonation was refreshing. And with her body nearly dehydrated from the X-rated workout, the fluid was essential. She climbed back into bed and offered him the bottle.

Cam took a greedy gulp and passed it back.

She could not stop smiling at him.

'I've got a question for you, brilliant lady.' He reached out to cradle her face in his hands. 'A very important question.'

Kristin moistened her lips as she waited for it, suddenly meta-aware of how much he satisfied her.

'What's happening at *Kiva Dunes Road*? I'm dying to know.'

She practically squealed in response, molding herself to his rock-solid frame. 'Oh, Cam, do you know how that makes me feel?'

He laughed at her passionate display. 'Pretty good, I take it.'

'I love sharing my work with you.'

He studied her for a moment. 'You don't ever share it at home?'

'It's not appreciated. I'm not appreciated.'

Tenderly, he kissed the tip of her nose. 'You're too successful, baby.'

'It's not that.'

'Then what is it?'

Kristin struggled to come up with an answer.

Cam offered one. 'Money equals sex equals manhood. You're all over a billboard on the Strip – *based on the novel by Kristin Fox*. A guy can't live that down on the golf course.'

'So what am I supposed to do – stop writing? Or divorce him and marry some day laborer who'd never have the presence of mind to be jealous of my career?'

'It's too late to do anything. What's done is done.'

Kristin thought about the Oscar curse and all the Hollywood marriages that had ended mere months after the wives won Best Actress at the Academy Awards – Helen Hunt, Hilary Swank, Reese Witherspoon, Halle Berry, Kate Winslet, Sandra Bullock. And she was certain there were others. 'I don't understand. Why does it have to be a contest? Why can't he just be proud of me?'

'It's a matter of degree,' Cam said philosophically. 'Some

success makes him feel pride. Too much success makes him feel castrated. Is he cheating on you?'

Kristin was surprised by the question. She had never harbored any suspicions. In fact, she had never even considered the fact that Hart might be sleeping with someone else.

'He probably is,' Cam went on. 'Cheating is every angry guy's first chess move.'

She stared at him, both disturbed and intrigued by his insight. 'Is that what you would do?'

He nodded. 'It would be my way of taking control. The issue would no longer be the woman's success but my whoring around. That way it's not her decision to leave *me*.'

Kristin cast her eyes downward, tracing the hard ripples of his abdominal muscles with her fingertips. 'I don't want to talk about him. This isn't why I came here. I'm paying you to escape my husband, not to understand him better.'

Cam pulled her down onto his chest and began stroking her hair.

For several seconds she just listened to his strong heartbeat.

'You're the smartest woman I've ever met,' Cam whispered. 'You write these big complex novels, and you know the ins and outs of all your characters' problems . . .'

'But I can't figure out my own,' Kristin finished for him. 'That's why I write, I guess.' A single tear began rolling down her cheek.

Cam stopped it with his tongue and licked it away. 'Read to me.'

An intense feeling washed over her. All of a sudden, the

two-hour appointments here and there seemed like a Cam Lawford Starvation Diet. For a nanosecond, Kristin wanted to leave everything behind and run away with him to some remote tropical island. The fantasy passed, and she tumbled out of bed to fetch the new pages folded up in her handbag.

Cam adjusted the pillows to maximize his comfort and just sat there with a charming smile on his face, as if anticipating the greatest show on earth.

Kristin stood naked in front of him and read the newest chapter from beginning to end.

Cam was staring at her with riveted interest. 'So the married guy is making it with his wife's gay friend, and she's doing it with her husband's best buddy.' He grinned. 'I think I might need a scorecard for all the shit going down at Kiva Dunes Road.'

Kristin laughed. 'Welcome to suburbia.' She crawled back into bed and snuggled against him.

He wrapped his arm around her, pulling her in closer. 'So is the husband really gay?'

Kristin shook her head. 'No, he's more shamefully curious.' She paused a beat. 'Have you ever been with a man?'

'Never.' His tone was absolute. 'Why?'

'I only ask because of your age. People of your generation are more fluid with their desires. Experimentation or even declared bisexuality doesn't carry the same stigma.'

'I only love women. I guess you could say that I'm old school.'

She peered up at him and brushed a tendril of hair away from his eyes. 'If you've always looked like this, then certainly guys have fallen for you. Don't tell me you have one of those supermodel sob stories about being an ugly duckling and not having a date to your prom.'

'No, I never had any trouble getting dates.' The easy smile on his face said that being the best-looking person in the room was normal to him – the most beautiful baby, the most beautiful boy, the most beautiful man.

'There was one guy in Miami when I played for the Dolphins,' Cam began. 'He was a sportscaster for the NBC affiliate. He interviewed me a few times, and we became friends. One night we picked up a girl at a club in South Beach. The original plan was a threesome, but he just sat off to the side and watched us. It was weird. After that I would sometimes catch him looking at me with a lovesick expression.' He paused. 'Kind of like the way you are right now.'

'Oh, you pompous ass!' Kristin roared with good humor, pinching his nipple.

Cam playfully wrestled her down and pinned her arms overhead, kissing her forehead, her eyes, her nose, and, finally, her lips. 'Do you have any idea how beautiful and talented you are?'

'No,' she teased. 'So you're going to have to explain it in very detailed terms.'

He nuzzled his face into her neck, then looked at her as if in awe. 'When I listen to you read, it feels like your characters are real people. Do you think of them that way?'

'Very much,' Kristin answered, her mind tripping off into another place as she remembered her dear friend Jeffie. He was the inspiration for one of her new characters. In some small way, she was making up for the terrible past.

Jeffie had been her best friend, a surrogate sibling, her platonic soul mate. And if Kristin had learned anything in life, it was that having one special connection like that was worth more than a thousand acquaintances or casual friends. They used to laugh at the dumbest things, annoying the people around them, and they could spend hours deconstructing everything and everyone in their lives.

Why had she been so stubborn in her refusal to save the relationship? That was, and probably always would be, one of her deepest regrets in life. All those lost years. All that wasted time. Fate was such a tricky monster. If only she had reconciled with Jeffie. Perhaps he would not have been searching for the transfer that took him as far away as Acapulco, a move that secured his career with the hotel conglomerate that eventually sent him to New York and to his heartbreaking end . . .

'You look sad,' Cam said, interrupting her reverie. 'What are you thinking about?'

'An old friend. His name was Jeffie. He's the inspiration for the gay friend in the story, actually. Things ended badly between us.'

'So make things right. Give yourselves a happy ending on Kiva Dunes Road.' Cam grinned at his own suggestion. 'And while you're at it, baby, make me a Super Bowl winner.'

Gently, he pushed her legs apart with his knee and settled his body between them, craning his neck to check the clock. 'I feel a round four coming up. But it's going to have to be a quickie.'

'Someday I want to spend the night with you.'

He grinned. 'That can be arranged. I'd offer you a good deal on an overnight.'

'Not here in Vegas, though. I want to go somewhere. A real getaway.'

Cam's grin got bigger. 'Now you're talking my weekend rate. I know a place in Malibu. It's on the beach. You'll love it.'

Kristin was already thinking ahead. She could make up a speaking engagement in the Los Angeles area. It would be so easy. The thought of two nights and three days with Cam sent her spirits soaring. His price did not matter. She would pay anything.

'Just tell me when.'

'*Soon*,' Kristin murmured, tilting her pelvis to seductively brush up against his once half – now full – erection. 'What about next weekend?'

'How could I turn down my favorite writer?' Simultaneously, he entered her body and crushed his mouth onto hers. It was over in five minutes. But thirty seconds of that was an orgasm she thought would never end.

While they were getting dressed, Kristin's BlackBerry chimed, alerting her to a text message. She retrieved the device from the nightstand.

HART FOX Meet me for a late lunch at the pub? 2:00?

It was rare to hear from him during the business day. Her mind jumped into conspiracy overdrive. This could be some kind of test. What if he knew where she was and what she was doing? Or maybe he was just attempting to throw out some crumb of kindness.

KRISTIN FOX Ok.

She pressed the Send key with an immediate sense of deflation and regret. Why had she agreed to meet him? Even if he were on his best behavior, the encounter would leave her wanting. When it came down to their relationship, nothing Hart did was ever enough. And nothing ever would be. She knew this. But too often she found herself responding somewhat desperately to his rare attempts at outreach, hoping things might be different.

'Everything okay?' Cam asked, zipping up his Zegna trousers and fastening his Prada belt.

'Everything's the same,' Kristin answered, tossing the BlackBerry into her purse and secretly relishing the thought of showing up to meet Hart fresh from a marathon session with Cam Lawford.

CHAPTER SIXTEEN

The Audley was the London's crown jewel for British atmosphere and standard English eats. A faithful re-creation of the Victorian pub in Mayfair, it featured polished, dark wood-paneled walls, imported Persian carpets, and mahogany ceilings with meticulously carved floral motifs along the moldings. At this hour, a good day would mean a line spilling out into the faux Tube station. But the establishment was half full at best.

Kristin found Hart in one of the dark red leather-and-pin booths, furiously jabbing away on his BlackBerry.

'You'd think I could avoid getting involved in housekeeping bullshit.' He gestured to the drink in front of her. 'I ordered you a glass of wine.'

It was Montana Marl, a light New Zealand vintage with hints of spice and citrus. Kristin preferred something more full bodied, but this would do. She drank it down easily.

'I can't remember the last time we had lunch together – just the two of us.'

Kristin stared at Hart impassively. He was making an attempt. And deep down she resented him for it. The effort came off as phony and patronizing. In fact, she almost preferred him acting like an asshole. At least that was authentic.

His BlackBerry buzzed. He glanced at the screen. 'Maybe it's time to give Ollie his iPhone back. He's texted me a hundred times in the last few days from other kids' phones.'

Though the suggestion irritated her, Kristin had been thinking the same thing. She shrugged her agreement.

'There's a new crop of management trainees that just started,' Hart said, his voice suddenly animated. 'One of the girls is young and smart, very pretty, too. Reminds me of you the first time we met. She hangs out with a gay guy in the group. They're like Frick and Frack.' He smiled. 'Just like you used to be with Jeffie.'

Kristin winced at the mention of his name. The loss was still acutely painful, and she carried so many regrets. Eleven years of estrangement. She had sacrificed a wonderful friend for an unhappy marriage. And now Jeffie was dead.

'Do you remember our first time in that corporate suite at the Mirage?' Hart gave her an intimate grin. 'That was pretty hot.'

She drank more wine and wondered how she would get through the next hour. At times like this, she could not will herself to meet him halfway. Instead, a kind of paralysis set in.

The denial, lack of honesty, and general disregard was so similar to her relationship with her parents. Those were the dynamics that Kristin had grown up hating as a child and yet had married into as a wife.

Kristin Fox was born Kristin Elizabeth Miller, the daughter of a college professor and visual artist whose complete absorption in each other left very little for their only child. William and Abigail Miller were like Ronald and Nancy Reagan in that they shared an all-consuming love affair and a penchant for mutual codependency that rendered everyone else an outsider. This included their daughter.

Growing up in Richmond, Virginia, Kristin never felt truly loved by her parents. She merely felt ... *tolerated*. The Millers were fiercely dedicated to their work, her father as a business professor, nonfiction author, and corporate consultant, and her mother as a painter of landscapes and still lifes.

On the subject of company, a tension permeated the Miller household. Their home was not a neighborhood gathering spot or even a place for friends to occasionally visit. From an early age, Kristin had coveted the rich, happy, and boisterous lives that other families seemed to enjoy.

The mothers of friends captivated her most of all. They were warm, welcoming, inquisitive about her interests, and delighted to offer snacks, serve as chauffeurs to movie outings and parties, and facilitate any reasonable request for fun. This stood in such stark contrast to the quiet, emotionally unpredictable, non-child-focused environment created by her mother.

One memory would burn forever in Kristin's psyche. The incident happened at dinner on her seventeenth birthday. William and Abigail dominated the conversation with talk of his new book and her decision to donate a painting to a charity's silent auction. Unable to sit there and pretend any longer, Kristin chose that moment to express her disappointment.

'It's my birthday dinner, and it's like I'm not even sitting here. Would it be such a big deal to invite some of my friends? I've never even had a real birthday party!'

'You ungrateful little bitch,' Abigail snapped. 'Sometimes I look at you and wish that I'd had an abortion.'

The words left Kristin feeling poleaxed. She could still remember looking to her father for protection and seeing him stare back as if the horrible abuse had never been spoken.

In that moment, she let go of her parents almost completely. Kristin selected a college – the University of Nevada, Las Vegas – far away from home and a field of study – hospitality – that she knew would disgust them.

Her biggest regret was not exploring her interest in writing from the start. Perhaps she should have attended Sarah Lawrence College. For years, teachers had singled out her talent, and Kristin had spent countless hours alone writing television scripts, stories, and short novels. But her parents never showed an interest or offered encouragement. The idea of becoming a writer seemed like some silly dream far from reach.

It was only after marrying Hart and giving birth to Ollie and Lily that she revisited her true passion. At one point, Kristin believed that staying at home with small children might dry-rot her brain. She longed for adult conversation, and she found no solace in the company of other mothers with young children. All they wanted to talk about were matters concerning their fussy babies, misbehaving toddlers, selfish husbands, and invasive in-laws. So she began writing and sought refuge in the lives of her characters.

Kristin still made obligatory attempts to stay in touch

with her parents – primarily on birthdays and major holidays. Even today, William and Abigail prattled on about themselves exclusively. They never acknowledged the fact that their daughter had written two consecutive international bestsellers and created a hit series on HBO.

'Maybe we should try that again,' Hart was saying.

Kristin shook away the past and refocused. 'I'm sorry. I got distracted. Try what?'

'The London has a corporate suite.' He paused to give her an amorous grin. 'And it's vacant. What do you say?'

'I need to work. I'm behind on my book. Another time.' She began scanning the menu.

'Jesus, Kristin, give me a break.' Hart's lips tightened into a firm line. 'I'm trying here.'

'Trying what?' Kristin shot back. 'To get laid? Because your hotel's deserted and you've got a few business hours to kill?'

'It's not the worst idea,' Hart countered. 'A decent fuck might do you some good.'

Oh, you stupid, stupid man. If you only knew the real truth.

Shaking her head, Kristin gave him a condescending smile. 'The idea just isn't appealing, Hart. Ordering me a glass of wine and tossing off a sexy memory doesn't make me want to jump into bed with you. Because all I can think about is what an asshole you are.'

He pretended to turn his attention to the menu. But the slight twitch in his left eye gave him away. The man was pissed.

'Spend more time with Ollie and start kicking around the soccer ball with him again,' Kristin continued. 'Back me up when he steps out of line. Watch how you talk to me at home. Don't allow Lily to grow up believing that's what she should expect from a man in a relationship. Take Sinatra for a walk. Ask me about my career. And don't just leave it at that. Actually pay attention to my answer. Kiss me. Really kiss me. Because you want to. Not because it might lead to sex five minutes later.' She nodded, liking the sound of all of it. 'Yeah, start doing things like that. Who knows? You might get lucky next time.'

Hart slid out of the booth and stood there, his temples pulsing with rage. 'Who the hell do you think you are? Don't sit there and lecture me on how to be a better parent. Improve your own game first. Jesus, Kristin, you're no mother of the year. Ollie's a mess. Lily does whatever she can to stay at other people's houses. And where are you? Locked up in your office writing another book. You need to take a break.'

Kristin's cheeks were hot with fury. She rose up to face him. 'Why should I be the one to take a break?'

'Look around.' He gestured to the half-empty restaurant. 'The staff here agreed to a four-day workweek just to save all their jobs. The London is trying to stay alive. This tourism economy is giving me an ulcer. Meanwhile, you're at a point where you make money in your fucking sleep. You could take a break and give the kids the time they need and deserve. But you won't. Because you're cold and selfish – just like your goddamn parents.'

Kristin felt impaled by the comparison.

Hart pressed on. 'How are you any different? It's all about your books and your television show. Ollie and Lily are in the way. I'm in the way. You give the least amount that you can to all of us. And you expect me to romance you like Clark Gable to earn a little action? Fuck this marriage.'

Kristin stood there – completely shell-shocked – as Hart walked out. Her BlackBerry chimed, signaling an incoming text.

LILY FOX Going to Ramey's house after school.

KRISTIN FOX Ok.

She sent the reply with a profound sense of shame. Maybe Hart was not far off the mark in his brutal assessment. She channeled so much energy into her work, her erotic adventures with Cam Lawford, and her therapy sessions with Jennifer Payne. Oh, God. Was she really that selfish?

A pretty waitress approached. 'Mrs. Fox, may I get you anything?'

'No, thank you.' Kristin sighed. 'Obviously, we won't be having lunch today.' She opened her purse, took out a fifty-dollar bill, and pressed it into the girl's hand.

'No, that isn't necessary.'

Kristin's smile was insistent. The economic woes had forced thousands of food and restaurant workers on the Strip into unemployment. 'Every table counts in a four-day workweek.'

The expression on the girl's face was pure gratitude.

Kristin made a beeline for the parking garage. Driving home to Red Rock, she paid attention to her surroundings, and she saw a different Las Vegas, perhaps for the very first time.

There was the Echelon project, an eighty-seven-acre development that had abruptly halted. And across from Circus Circus, there was the heavily hyped, blue-mirrored Fontainebleau Tower, nearly complete but at a standstill and tied up in lawsuits. The Ritz-Carlton had shut down. Mammoth billboards promised free food and bargain-rate lobster and filet mignon specials. The decades of boom were officially over. The city was overbuilt. Down – or flat, if you were lucky – was the new up.

Hart was fighting against these tough conditions – for his career, for the livelihood of his employees, and, ultimately, for their family. The pressure had to be intense. Was she being unfair? Were her expectations of him unrealistic? All of a sudden, she felt a surge of affection and tapped out a quick text.

KRISTIN FOX I'm sorry. I do love you.

She waited anxiously for his reply. His BlackBerry was attached to him as if by nerve fibers. If he intended to respond, it would be immediately. The sound of the chime lifted her heart.

HART FOX I won't be home tonight.

CHAPTER SEVENTEEN

One of the finest female jazz vocalists Jennifer had ever heard was cooing a red-hot remake of Paul Simon's '50 Ways to Leave Your Lover.' She tossed back her head, lost in the moody music, the glorious sunshine, and the whipping wind.

Kurt Taylor grinned in the driver's seat of his ultra-sporty Berlina black Honda S2000, throwing the convertible into fifth gear, then sixth, showing off its impressive horsepower.

The man was dead sexy. Jennifer continued to marvel at his uncanny physical clone status to actor Christopher Meloni.

'Who *is* this?' Jennifer demanded to know as the music continued to sweep her away.

'Sophie Milman!' Kurt shouted above the wind. 'Isn't she amazing?'

Jennifer closed her eyes, nodding in blissful agreement.

This lunch excursion had been scheduled and rescheduled several times. But today everything synched, and Kurt insisted on escaping from the office complex and making a break for the Strip. His favorite sushi restaurant, Okada, was located in one of the big hotels.

'How long can you play hooky?' Kurt asked, cutting a sharp turn onto Las Vegas Boulevard.

In the distance, Jennifer could see their destination – the gleaming bronze fifty-story Wynn. The luxury hotel towered dramatically at the northern end of the Strip. 'I have a two o'clock,' she murmured, suddenly lamenting her afternoon responsibilities.

Kurt made a face, like a teenage boy who had just heard about his prom date's strict curfew.

Jennifer laughed at him. 'I take it your office is closed for the rest of the day.'

'Not closed, but definitely slow.' He glanced at her, his expression suddenly more serious. 'I had to lay off one of my hygienists last week. That sucked.'

'I'm sorry, Kurt,' Jennifer said. And she truly meant it. She felt for him, running a small business in these tough economic times, being responsible for the livelihood of a group of employees who become almost like family, and then having to make excruciating decisions based on grim financial realities.

Kurt shook his head. 'I've got over a hundred grand out there in uncollected billings. A lot of people just aren't paying. And the rest are putting off dental visits until an emergency sets in.' He sighed deeply. 'I don't know what's going to happen.'

They rode in silence for a few minutes, taking in all of the casino hotels and the massive billboards advertising big-name entertainment – Cher, Barry Manilow, David Copperfield, Joan Rivers, Donny and Marie, and Billie Shelton, who, incidentally, happened to be Jennifer's two o'clock appointment.

Kurt sped up the hill to the Wynn and handed the car over to a waiting valet. 'No joy riding.'

'Never, sir.' The handsome young man smiled, slipped into the front seat, and took off like a rocket.

Okada offered Asian-inspired opulence on a grand scale. Away from the hullabaloo of the Wynn's casino floor, it was like being teleported out of Las Vegas entirely.

Kurt had arranged for seating at one of the choice tables, centered just in front of the massive doors that slid open to expose a three-tiered waterfall, lush Japanese gardens, and a koi-filled lagoon.

The moment they sat down, a server was right there to deliver menus and hot wet hand towels. Just seconds later, another server presented them with fresh watermelon juice.

Jennifer marveled at the beautiful and peaceful atmosphere. She and Patrick rarely – if ever – ventured out for special meals. In fact, she could not even remember the last time they had enjoyed an extravagant date night. Workdays left him fatigued, depression rendered him ambivalent, and Saturdays were typically dedicated to Mia Sara. On Sundays, they stayed close to home to prepare for the week ahead.

Kurt beamed an excited smile. 'The best sushi in Vegas is right here. Nobu at the Hard Rock is great, too. But I give this place a slight edge on freshness and taste. Any special favorites?'

'I'm a novice,' Jennifer admitted. 'You lead the way.'

He flashed a bad-boy grin. 'Sake. I think we should indulge. What do you say?'

She shook her head.

'Don't make me drink alone. It's no fun.'

'I have a two o'clock,' Jennifer reminded him. 'And considering how much I struggled to remain focused in the couples session this morning, alcohol is not a good idea.'

'Okay, I won't corrupt you ... *today*.'

She smiled and sipped on the delicious watermelon juice, feeling relaxed and secretly delighted to be in Kurt's company. 'So how are Diana and the boys?'

'The kids are great – crazy, active, and happy. Sometimes I don't know whether I'm a father or a zookeeper.'

Jennifer laughed.

'Diana is working a lot. Apparently, the fucked-up Vegas economy means good business for divorce lawyers.'

Jennifer noticed that Kurt's tone changed when he turned the subject to his wife. There was a hostile edge to his voice. She proceeded cautiously and decided to offer a general take. 'Financial pressures are very difficult for marriages to endure. I've seen many couples survive infidelity but then throw in the towel over money squabbles.'

'It's more than that.'

She gave him a quizzical look.

'If I'm going to get into this, then I definitely need some sake.' Suddenly, he stopped, an expression of guilt crossing his face. 'This is wrong. You listen to other people's shit all day long. You don't need to listen to mine. Let's talk about something else.'

'It's not a burden, Kurt,' Jennifer assured him. 'If there's something bothering you, I'm happy to listen.' It was easy to say this earnestly, because she was eager for anything that kept her mind off her own personal, moral, and ethical troubles.

'Diana has shifted the direction of her family law practice,' Kurt began. 'Now she only represents men. Mostly fathers. She's developed a reputation – and it's well deserved – for being a barracuda on behalf of her clients. One of my patients – a very nice woman and a terrific mother – was on the losing end of one of her cases recently. Diana really put her through the grinder. Completely destroyed her. This woman lost custody of her daughters. And she's part of that hundred grand in overdue billings, because she can't pay. Diana wore her down to a crap settlement, and now she's doing temp work to survive. The sick part is that her ex-husband is loaded. He's just a cruel prick who wanted to come out on top in every sense. And Diana did the legal dirty work to make that happen. She's good at it, too. Being a mother of five helps. She really plays that up. Automatically, the judges seem to think that if a female lawyer like Diana is asking for full custody rights to go to the father, then there must be a good reason for it.' Kurt shook his head. 'I don't know. I love her. I just ... I just don't respect her anymore. I'm not sure if I even like her.'

Jennifer took a deep breath. 'I've changed my mind about the sake.'

Kurt laughed, clearly grateful for the moment of humor. 'Now we're talking.' He quickly flagged down the waitress and ordered miso soup, a variety of sushi, and two cups of Tamanohikari.

'You have to talk to her, Kurt. Really talk. The longer you wait, the wider the distance will grow.' Of course, Jennifer realized that this was wise advice she failed to follow in her own marriage. But that was the case with almost every working therapist.

The sake arrived.

Kurt raised his tiny porcelain cup. 'To cutting class like a couple of delinquents.'

Jennifer smiled, clinking her cup against his before taking a slow sip. It went down warm, smooth, and strong. Though no sake connoisseur, she could ascertain that this was the high-grade variety.

'I don't think she would hear me if I tried to talk,' Kurt said. 'Diana works like a crazy woman, and with five boys at the ages they are, there's no such thing as a sex life for us. Unless I'm in the shower – alone.' He grinned, shook his head, and bit down on his lower lip. 'I must sound pathetic.'

'No,' Jennifer assured him. 'You sound honest and normal. I'm afraid this is modern marriage. It's the reason why I don't have the capacity to add any clients to my practice. My schedule is full.'

'I want a friend,' Kurt said. 'A friend with benefits, you know? Someone to share romantic meals with now and then. Someone who enjoys sex. Someone in a position similar to mine. I don't have any intentions of leaving Diana. But I need some happiness and satisfaction of my own.'

Jennifer could not determine whether this was an announcement or an invitation. 'I don't think that would be a solution to your marriage, Kurt. I think that would be the end of it.'

He nodded and drank more sake.

'If you ever need a referral, I can recommend a very good marriage counselor.' She was sincere. But the offer still hit the air like the dim platitude that it was.

'I shouldn't be unloading all of this on you. I'm sorry. But you're easy to talk to. I guess that's why you do what you do. And ... I feel like we have a lot in common.'

This intrigued her. 'How so?'

'Are you happy with Patrick?'

'No,' Jennifer said matter-of-factly. 'I haven't been happy for many months.'

Kurt's eyes widened. 'That was honest.'

'It's that kind of lunch, I guess.' Now she drank more sake.

'I want to kiss you right now.'

Thankfully, the miso soup and sushi landed, providing a necessary distraction. Jennifer had never been quite so relieved to see a waitress. Her attraction to Kurt was powerful. If he had leaned across the table to put his mouth onto hers, she would not have stopped him.

He looked at her apologetically. 'Now I can shut the hell up and start stuffing raw fish into my mouth. That's probably a good thing.'

Jennifer smiled, took a quick taste of miso, and made a show out of getting her chopsticks ready. 'Okay, Mr. Sushi, what do you have for us?'

The mood lightened considerably as Kurt talked at length about his love of sushi – passed down to him by an uncle who lived and worked in Japan.

Jennifer got pushed out of her stagnant California roll comfort zone and into the more adventurous territory of sea urchin (firm with a slight nutty taste), mackerel (oily with a strong flavor), and squid (similar to chicken). But her absolute favorite was the artfully prepared restaurant signature Okada roll, a combination of lobster, avocado, and asparagus topped off with the most delicious sweet sauce.

When they were finished, Jennifer surveyed the damage. There was not so much as a single grain of rice left on the table. 'We are pigs.'

Kurt laughed. 'And we still have to order dessert.'

Jennifer held up a hand in protest. 'I can't.'

But Kurt would hear none of it. 'You have to at least taste this.' He gestured for the waitress and asked for the coconut panna cotta with passion fruit sorbet.

Jennifer placed her hands over what she felt was a swollen belly. 'I'm going to have to swim a mile to make up for this.'

Kurt grinned. 'It'll be worth it. Trust me.' He chuckled. 'I have a confession.'

'Another one? We don't need dessert. We need a priest.'

'I've been wanting to ask you to lunch for a long time.'

Jennifer was surprised and flattered. 'How long?'

'Let's see . . . I moved the practice to that location about two and a half years ago.' One beat. 'So about two and a half years.'

She smiled at him.

The dessert arrived, and at Kurt's insistent prompting, Jennifer enjoyed far more than a single taste of the silky custard and tart fruit sorbet.

'I hope we can do this again,' Kurt said. 'And it doesn't have to be a big production like this. Maybe we could just duck out for some coffee between appointments.'

'Kurt . . . I want to . . . I really do . . . but I don't think that's a good idea.'

His face registered genuine surprise. 'Why not? We're business neighbors. We're friends.'

'And we also crossed the line today. We shared things with each other that we should only be sharing with our spouses.'

Kurt's eyes blazed into hers intensely. 'We don't have to be miserable, Jennifer. I'm tired of being lonely. I think you're tired of it, too.'

'None of that matters. You have a wife and five children. I have a husband and a daughter. This has disaster written all over it. We think we're miserable now . . .'

Kurt reached for Jennifer's hand.

She pulled it away. 'I know what you're feeling. I feel it, too. And I'll feel it again when I go home tonight. But we can't be unmindful of the people in our lives. We could inflict so much pain on them. It's selfish, stupid, and dangerous to even consider . . . what you're considering. My advice – find an expensive call girl.'

Kurt's half laugh was bitter.

'I'm serious,' Jennifer said. 'Think of it as a form of therapy. The physical contact and release will do you good. And she can listen to you complain about Diana without feeling like a terrible person.'

'Really? Your advice for me is to go find a hooker? What kind of therapist are you?'

'I'm sorry, Kurt. I can't do this. I'm taking a cab back to the office.' Fighting back tears, Jennifer rose up and rushed out of Okada.

There seemed to be a dozen or more desperate taxi operators jostling for her business. A valet stepped in to get it sorted. She fished out five dollars for his trouble and slid into the backseat.

The driver talked nonstop. He lamented the Mafia losing its stranglehold on Las Vegas. According to the heavyset Angelo, the big corporations had come in and ruined the city. On any other day, Jennifer would have enjoyed this man's colorful take on the town, but she was barely listening.

Mia Sara was away at an overnight wilderness camp with her Montessori schoolmates, and the idea of going home to a night alone with Patrick filled Jennifer with dread.

He would settle for the least effort when it came to dinner – either fast food or a frozen entrée. And then he would spend what remained of his waking hours listening to Bill O'Reilly and Sean Hannity scream from the Fox News Channel. The thought of that was unbearable, today of all days, especially.

But Jennifer decided to call him anyway. For once, she was going to follow her own advice. They had to start talking, connecting, and relating. Otherwise, the next time a Kurt Taylor gave her the friends-with-benefits pitch, she might not be able to walk away from the table.

She tried his direct line at the newsroom first.

'Linda Danvers.'

Jennifer hesitated. 'I'm sorry. I thought I was calling Patrick Payne's desk.'

There was a pregnant pause. 'May I ask who's calling and what this is regarding?'

'I'm his wife,' Jennifer stated, unable to hide her irritation.

'Oh . . . please hold.'

After a brief silence, Patrick's editor, Hank Lucas, got on the line.

She was relieved to hear a familiar voice. 'Hank, it's Jennifer. I'm just trying to reach Patrick. Is everything okay?'

Another pregnant pause. 'Patrick doesn't work here anymore.'

She immediately went flush with alarm. 'Since when?'

'It happened several days ago.'

Jennifer was speechless for a moment as she tried to digest the news. 'I don't understand. He's been going to work every day.'

Hank said nothing.

'What happened?'

'I think you should talk to Patrick.'

Jennifer was humiliated. 'Obviously, I can't, Hank. He's gone off the rails to the point of putting on a convincing little play about still working there. Why did you fire him?'

'He didn't file a story. It was a big one – a front-page piece on the food bank. Then he came rushing in long after deadline reeking of pot.'

She closed her eyes as the taxi rumbled along.

'I'm sorry, Jennifer. I liked Patrick. He was one of my best writers. But the crackdown here is severe, and he was already on thin ice for regular disappearing acts.'

She rubbed her temples, sensing a monster headache coming on. 'Do you have any idea where he might be, Hank?'

'I've heard some of the staffers mention a screenwriting group that he started. I think they meet at the Coffee Bean on Flamingo. If he's not there, your guess is as good as mine.'

'Well, I didn't even know that much.'

'I'm sorry, Jennifer. Good luck. To both of you.'

'Thank you.' She hung up and called Billie Shelton. It rolled into voice mail. 'Billie, it's Jennifer Payne. I apologize for doing this at such late notice, but I have a family emergency and have to cancel our two o'clock. I'll be in touch soon to reschedule at your convenience.'

She sighed deeply and concentrated on her breathing. Be calm, she told herself, feeling the eyes of Angelo peer curiously into the rearview mirror.

'You okay back there?' he asked.

Jennifer inquired about the Coffee Bean on Flamingo and learned that there were two locations – one at the Venetian, the other further west. She directed him to the latter and stared morosely out the window as he made the turnaround.

It almost disappointed her to see Patrick's dingy maroon-colored Saturn in the parking lot. She asked Angelo to wait and rushed inside to confront her husband.

The place was packed. A line spilled out to the door. Every table and overstuffed chair was occupied. It took her a moment to fully scan the coffee shop. And then Jennifer saw him in the back.

He did not look like the depressed man she knew from home. He did not look like the unemployed man she had just heard about from Hank. Patrick Payne looked like a man whose world was in perfect harmony as he laughed, sipped his coffee, and casually touched the knee of the beautiful stripper/bikini model/whatever sitting across from him.

For a long time Jennifer just stood there watching, completely immobilized by the discovery. If there was an explanation for this, she had no interest in hearing it. Patrick could not bring himself to so much as show a sign of life with her, but he could be goddamn Cary Grant for this silicone bimbo.

She stormed out and got back inside the cab. As hot, angry tears misted her eyes, she thought about Cam Lawford. Jennifer had sworn over and over again that she would only see him that one time. But his number was programmed into her cellular as C.L. All she had to do was press the button . . .

He answered on the second ring. 'This is Cam.'

'Hi . . . it's Jennifer.'

'I was hoping to hear from you.'

She could feel him smiling over the phone – a warm, inviting, sensual smile just for her. Patrick had found a little piece of happiness. Jennifer deserved some, too. The words that came next were easy. 'I want to see you again.'

CHAPTER EIGHTEEN

'Are you having a good time?' Billie belted out in a singsong voice as she beamed a showgirl smile into the audience.

It was the same question posed at the same point in the same show every night. Five songs into the set, after her energetic, highly choreographed crowd-pleasing take on Katrina and the Waves's 'Walking on Sunshine,' and before her faithful rendering of TLC's 'Waterfalls.'

The first response – as always – was tepid.

'I can't hear you!' Billie admonished. 'Are you having a good time?'

And then came the enthusiastic ovation.

She always had to work a little to jar them out of their post-buffet fatigue syndrome. The juxtaposition never ceased to amaze her. Just two years ago, she'd been on a stage staring back at a youthquake of acid-tripping mosh-pit crazies. And now in her line of sight – the Maalox and Prozac crowd.

The predictability of performing in Las Vegas was slowly crushing Billie's soul. This song. That dance routine. This scripted joke. That staged audience interaction. Everything was so rigidly structured. At this point, she could do the entire show on autopilot.

The only moment that made her feel truly spontaneous

and alive was 'What's Love Got to Do with It.' That number tore out her heart each time. It conjured up enough on-the-sleeve emotion to mask the fact that she was a robot for every other part of the show.

Making a torch version of the song the centerpiece of *Rebirth* had been Billie's idea. Randall wanted it cut. But she fought like a tigress and prevailed, and from opening night on, it became *the* showstopper that earned the longest ovation.

The audience was responding as much to her anguish as to her killer pipes. On top of that fucking piano, Billie sang her guts out. She was singing to March Donaldson, the one that got away. And every night her heart broke all over again. The tears were always real, the voice quiver at the end always genuine.

March's profile as a Republican political analyst had grown more high profile than ever with an exclusive guest commentator deal with MSNBC. Just seeing his face or hearing his voice could shatter her to pieces, so in a move of total self-preservation, she blocked the cable channel from every remote that fell into her hands. The last thing she needed was a reminder of those dark days as the upstanding young GOP mover's dirty little secret.

As a matter of fact, it was March who suggested – the last time they'd been in bed together – that she record a new version of the Tina Turner classic. Billie had never forgotten his pillow talk idea. She wondered if he would ever see the show ... and if he would remember, too. It was their song, after all. 'What's Love Got to Do with It'? Whoever wrote that hit had posed a damn good question.

Like a vaudeville trouper, Billie gamely entertained for

seventy minutes. The people always got their money's worth. Her show easily lived up to the hype. The men, the women, the old, the young, the straights, the gays – there was something onstage to please everyone.

Her first encore, a ferocious cover of Michael Jackson's 'Workin' Day and Night,' drove home the impressive fact that few performers could rival Billie's remarkable stamina. Her ability to deliver solid vocals in the midst of aerobi- cized choreography was unparalleled.

The dance finale concluded with a daring overhead lift- spin-flip that never failed to elicit audible gasps. The high- risk move was a testament to disciplined rehearsals and the trust she placed in the talent and strength of John Phillip Harmon, who, at six-foot-three, was the tallest dancer in the show and a former cheerleader from the University of Iowa.

Billie bowed graciously to thunderous applause, then dashed backstage to facilitate her fifth costume change and prepare for her second encore, a stirring, appropri- ately bombastic version of Snow Patrol's 'Run' that would bring these tacky tourists to their bunion-burdened feet one last time.

When it was over, she professed her love to the seven hundred strangers, high-fived the band, group-hugged the dancers, and retreated to her dressing room to catch a few minutes of peace. Soon it would be back to the penthouse to suffer through dinner with Randall – the nightly activity that never failed to turn her mood as black as the desert night.

If Billie was grateful for anything, it was the rigorous performance routine. The grind protected her health. There was no faking the physical demands of *Rebirth*. She had to get enough sleep, maintain a peak level of fitness, and follow a strict nutritional protocol. The days of tanking up on booze, pills, and cocaine to medicate her through a gig were long gone.

Letting out a groan, Billie kicked off her spike-heeled metallic slingbacks and flopped down in her plum-colored strapless organza ruffled gown by Marchesa. Her heart was pounding. Her palms, armpits, and cleavage were prickling with perspiration. And she desperately wanted to smoke.

Lindsay – the cantankerous wardrobe mistress – knocked twice and burst inside the room. 'Take off that dress before you stink it up or burn a hole in it.'

Billie scowled, stood up, and raised her arms overhead, a lazy signal for Lindsay to do the honors if she wanted her demand met. 'I don't smoke anymore.'

'Really? Well, if you're not sneaking cigarettes, then I've got a dinner date with George Clooney.' With one fast tug, she stripped Billie down to her skivvies. 'I think we both know I'm about thirty years too old for that to happen.' And then Lindsay was gone.

Billie snatched her mobile from the dressing table to call David.

Someone answered on the third ring. There was raucous laughter in the background. 'Hey, girl, it's John Phillip. David just left with that delicious hunk of a boyfriend and forgot his phone. Imagine that.' More laughter.

For a moment, Billie envied their tight camaraderie, the way the dancers had formed such an instant, nurturing surrogate family. 'I'm dying for a fucking cigarette,' she said finally. 'I'm in my dressing room.'

'Hold on, darling.' John Phillip Harmon was a flaming, red-haired, take-charge super gay. 'Which one of you bitches is still smoking? The diva needs a nicotine fix.'

Billie grinned as she listened and waited.

'American Spirits will have to do in a pinch,' John Phillip said airily. 'Unless you want me to run out for your favorite brand. I don't mind. It'll just take longer.'

Billie sighed her relief. 'No, whatever you have is fine. Make it fast.'

Within seconds, John Phillip was at her door with three cigarettes, a matchbook from the dancers' favorite hangout, Lucky Cheng's, and a knowing smirk. 'I'm sure you realize this, but it's my duty to inform you that these things cause cancer.' He dropped his gaze to her exposed belly button. 'And birth defects. So I hope that lizard you married hasn't impregnated you.'

Billie lit up, took a drag, and blew an impressive curl of smoke. 'It would have to be an immaculate conception.'

John Phillip smiled – bitchy.

Billie smiled back – bitchier.

'We're all heading to the usual crime scene,' John Phillip said. 'Stop by later if you feel like it.'

Billie pulled a face as she thought about Lucky Cheng's. 'Drag queens and bad food? Thanks but no thanks.'

John Phillip shrugged. 'Your loss, honey.' He struck a vampish pose. 'I might bless the tragic souls with my Ann-Margret tribute, "Hold Me, Squeeze Me."'

Billie laughed.

Carly appeared in the doorway and gave them both a molten glare of impatience, then ignored the flamboyant dancer as she barked out, 'Randall is waiting for you in the penthouse.'

John Phillip pranced away, Carly stalked off, and Billie was left there, alone in her underwear, puffing away like a crazy girl, wishing she had a secret stash of cash somewhere that would allow her to disappear. Oh, God, why hadn't she listened to her former manager?

'Take a hundred grand and put it in a bank far, far away,' Amy Dando had told her when the CD sales and the tour revenues were clicking along. 'Shove it in a shoebox and bury it in the back of your closet if you have to. One day you're going to need it. Everybody should have a three A.M. get-me-the-fuck-out-of-here fund.'

Amy Dando was right. In fact, Amy had always been right – about every goddamn thing. But back then Billie was too arrogant and out of her mind to listen to anyone. So here she was, with nothing to show for her high-earning rock chick days and no access to the money she was pulling in as one of the top draws on the Strip. Randall controlled every dollar that she made.

Billie cleaned up quickly, donned a pair of face-eclipsing blackout Chanel sunglasses, and walked the gauntlet to the elevator that would take her to the London's most extravagant top-floor suite.

Randall was waiting for her at the small dining table on the balcony, wearing his typical brutal confidence. He gestured for the room-service attendant to remove the silver domes from the plates, then dismissed him with a curt wave.

For a moment, Billie just stood there, torn between sitting down and jumping over the railing. Finally, she slipped into her chair and cut into her asparagus with a glum expression.

Randall watched her intently. 'How was the show?'

'The same. Like always.'

He continued staring, his reptilian eyes penetrating, assessing, and calculating.

Billie turned her gaze downward, searching for a part of her steak that wasn't blood rare.

'There are a few other procedures I have in mind when we do the breast implants,' Randall announced.

Billie looked up in alarm. She hated surgery. She hated hospitals. Whenever she walked into one – or even drove past one – the memories of her long, painful stay at University Medical Center consumed her. It had been so unbearably lonely there after the attack, with only a few visitors to break up the endless hours.

Longtime friend Kellyanne McGraw had arrived at her side. But with a baby girl and stepson to care for in Sag Harbor, she returned home after three short days. She followed up with phone calls for several weeks, then eventually faded out. Todd Bana, the president of Billie's former record label, managed a single fifteen-minute drop-by while in Las Vegas for a New Year's Eve party.

The rest of her well-wishers had expressed their sentiments through flowers. Amy Dando sent an arrangement. And so did March Donaldson. A bouquet from him arrived every day for three weeks. The attention tricked Billie into thinking that he might appear in person. But she gave up that fantasy soon enough.

'I don't want any more procedures,' Billie said wearily.

'Implants might affect my dancing. Right now I know the routines and move really well.'

Randall's half smile was thin and cold. 'You can relearn them if you have to. Besides, it's not your decision.'

'It's *my* body,' Billie said with a defiance that surprised even her.

'That's debatable,' Randall remarked calmly as he shoved more red meat into his mouth and washed it down with wine. 'You were broken into pieces and almost dead when that maid found you. And I paid the hospital bills. You didn't have any medical insurance, remember?'

She glared at him.

'Anyway, those are minor points. Your *face* is mine. Everybody knows that.' A supercilious grin curled his lips.

Billie's fingers coiled tightly around her heavy steak knife. She fantasized about stabbing him with it.

'I'm thinking dimpleplasty,' Randall said matter-of-factly. 'It would improve your smile.'

Billie was aware of the latest plastic surgery craze. Vanity seekers wanted cute dimples like those modeled naturally by Mario Lopez and Cheryl Cole. But there were risks. Some surgeons compared the procedure to permanent scarring and warned that with age, a fake dimple could become a real disaster.

'I also want to shorten your toes,' Randall said.

Billie had just taken a sip of water and nearly choked on it.

'I couldn't sleep last night, and I found myself staring at your feet,' he explained. 'Your second toes are perhaps a quarter-inch too long.'

She searched his face for the joke that should follow. But it wasn't there. 'You're serious.'

'Indeed I am,' Randall clucked. 'After all of my efforts, do you really think I would allow my wife to walk around with a deformity?'

She stared down at her sandaled feet. Of course, they looked completely normal. This medieval notion – breaking a young girl's toes to ensure the appearance of tiny feet – was an ancient tradition in China. Elders called it foot binding.

'It's unnatural,' Randall went on. 'But surgery can correct it.'

'*You're* unnatural,' Billie countered savagely. 'Nobody is going to shorten my toes. My feet are fine.'

Randall waved off her protest as if it were a pesky gnat. 'Stop being so dramatic. You'll be under full sedation.'

Billie was aware of plastic surgery patients who developed body dysmorphic disorder. She had met some of them in Randall's office. They became obsessed with their outward appearance, and they could always pinpoint a flaw in themselves – no matter how slight. These discoveries triggered a desperate need to seek out corrective procedures. Right now Billie was convinced that Randall suffered from the same affliction – only his compulsion was focused on *her*. And it was beyond pathological.

He finished eating and pushed his dinner plate away. 'Enough about that.' He smacked his lips, wiping his hands and tossing off the napkin as if the subject had been settled. 'The more pressing matter is your contract renewal with the London. What did you learn from your evening with Kristin Fox?'

'Not very much,' Billie lied. 'I thought a girls' night out on the Strip would relax her, and it did – to distraction. I'll take her out for lunch.'

Randall gave her a venomous ray-gun stare. 'Like you took that dancing fag and his police detective boyfriend out for lunch?'

Billie just looked at him, stunned.

'You don't think I know about that?'

'What exactly is there to know?'

Randall regarded her for several long seconds, as if making up his mind about something. There was a strange gleam in his eyes.

Billie knew the look well. She had crossed some invisible line. And once again her punishment would come in the middle of the night. Randall would lie in wait until she slept. And then Billie would wake up to the taste of the gun's cold metal in her mouth, the sound of his dark threats to pull the trigger in her ear, and the sensation of her heart leaping around in her chest.

'You're spending too much time with him,' Randall said.

Billie drew back. 'With *David*?' She wanted to laugh, but the situation was too disturbing. 'How could you possibly find him threatening?'

'I don't,' Randall hissed. 'He's more of a ... *nuisance*. Carly has observed you using his phone, and the GPS report on the BMW shows that you went to his apartment.'

'He's practically a child. His friendship is—'

'*Unnecessary*,' Randall cut in harshly. 'I encourage the time with Kristin because it might prove useful to our negotiations. And for the time being, I allow the talk therapy sessions.' He reached for his spoon and cracked the burnt sugar shell of his crème brûlée. 'But this business with David is getting out of hand.'

Billie's mobile phone buzzed. She watched Randall watch her as she checked the screen. The incoming call was from David Dean.

'Answer it,' Randall said, his tone ominous.

She picked up, expecting to hear David make some comically bitchy demand about joining the group at Lucky Cheng's.

'Billie, we're at the hospital.' It was John Phillip on the line, sounding distraught.

'What happened?'

'Somebody attacked David. They just came out of nowhere and smashed his knee with a baseball bat.'

'Oh, my God.' Billie's stomach was in free fall. She could hardly breathe.

'It happened in the parking lot of Lucky Cheng's. He ran out to the car to look for my Ann-Margret wig.' John Phillip started to cry. 'It's bad, Billie. It's really bad. He might never be able to dance again. What kind of sick fuck would do something like this?'

'I don't know,' Billie managed to whisper, looking at Randall as she said it. But the truth was, she *did* know.

Confessions from the Man
Who's Satisfying Your Wife

By Cam Lawford

No Such Thing as an Easy Lay

I know female escorts who can just lie there. They call that a straight lay. If you expect them to so much as bend their knees, the rate goes up.

The women in this business – from the five-star-hotel hookers to the adult film performers who escort on the side – tend to be less classy, more crass, and generally rougher around the edges.

When a successful man takes a paid-for date to an important event, there's no hiding the arrangement. Other women can always sniff out a whore, even if she's wearing the most expensive dress in the room. A Badgley Mischka can only cover up so much.

But when I put on a tuxedo and go into the same situation, the reaction is different. Men regard me with wariness and envy, not disdain. They hold in their paunchy stomachs, wonder about their height, worry about their cock size, and finally remind themselves about their healthy financial portfolios.

A guy who hires an escort is a simple creature. He's usually looking for an easy screw or an outlet for some secret kink. The women who retain me are far more complicated. It requires work, real charm, emotional intelligence, and a sophisticated set of skills to satisfy them on a date.

Patience is definitely a virtue. The time I spend in bed with a woman is not always focused on sex. One recent client – Marianne – complained for an hour about her mother-in-law. She was pissed off that the woman had made a family photo album for her son, which included wedding shots from his first marriage, a brief and stormy union that ended in a quick divorce with no children involved. But her kids saw the pictures and started pelting her with questions about Daddy's first wife.

'Can you believe she disrespected me like that?'

Marianne must have asked me that question at least fifty times. So I listened. I made her feel like I really cared. I agreed that her mother-in-law was a manipulative bitch, that her husband was a pathetic mama's boy, and that she deserved more consideration from both of them. For Marianne, this was the ultimate foreplay. Pretty soon she was pulling at my clothes and begging me to make our second hour count.

Most of my clients are women of a certain position. They get stuck in different roles – career woman, mother, wife, daughter, sister, neighbor, girlfriend, community volunteer, you name it. But behind closed doors with me, they get to be anyone. When all is said and done, who they want to be is usually the woman they can't be at home – the biggest slut of the year. But they can play that role with me. I make it safe. I keep the fantasy level high. And I please them in a way that rarely makes them regret losing their inhibitions.

For the most part, it's a pleasure doing business with these women. And business is booming. I owe thanks to our sexually repressed culture, the loser husbands of America, and most of all, the women who dare to step out and find their own satisfaction.

CHAPTER NINETEEN

'Aaron, you may come back now,' Jennifer said.

The first-time client gave her a confident smile, stood up to his full towering height, and turned over the clipboard of preliminary paperwork as he strode into the room and made himself comfortable on the sofa.

She sat down and quickly scanned over the documents that summarized Aaron Rutter's medical and psychological history. 'We can do this two ways. You can begin by telling me your personal story from the beginning, or if there's a particular issue that brought you here today, we can start there.'

Aaron leaned back, spread his legs, and slid his hand down his inner thigh.

Jennifer struggled not to notice. This new client was undeniably attractive – breathtakingly handsome, hyper-masculine, and blessed with a broad chest and well-defined biceps that strained the fabric of his dress shirt.

'I can't seem to concentrate on work,' Aaron said.

'What's distracting you?'

'Women,' he replied simply. 'Women distract me.' He paused a beat and gave her a bold stare. 'Women like you.'

Jennifer experienced a frisson of discomfort. 'You'll have to elaborate.'

'I'm a contractor,' Aaron explained. 'Mainly high-end remodels. Kitchens are my expertise.'

She nodded for him to go on.

'I primarily deal with the wives. Most of them are smart, successful, attractive . . . just like you.'

Jennifer offered only the slightest smile.

'We have a lot in common, you and I.'

'How so?'

'We both listen to other people's problems.'

She waited for him to explain further.

'These women . . . these wives . . . they come to me with their problems. I'm their contractor, shrink, and best friend – until the husbands decide to get involved. They inspect my work, examine the bill, make noises about being ripped off. By this point, the wives are usually avoiding me. They're either embarrassed about revealing too much about their lives or trying to pretend like that quick fuck never happened.'

'You're playing a lot of roles here,' Jennifer observed. 'Carpenter, therapist, lover—'

'Penetrator,' Aaron interjected.

She looked at him intently.

'I prefer penetrator to lover. What these women want from me has very little to do with love.'

'Do you enjoy these roles?'

Aaron smirked. 'I could live without playing the therapist.'

'And what you're describing is the main source of your distraction?'

'That depends. Right now I find you distracting.'

Jennifer's gaze flitted across the hand casually draped inside his thigh.

Briefly, Aaron adjusted himself, making his obvious arousal more obvious. 'Do you want to know why you're distracting me?'

'This is your time. You can share anything that you choose to.'

'And they say men are noncommittal.' He laughed a little. 'You know, most of the talk out there is about women wanting romance and needing a real connection. But the women I meet – especially the married ones – crave a no-strings encounter as much as any man does. I bet the same goes for you.'

Jennifer said nothing.

'Am I right?' Aaron pressed.

'I don't think that's relevant.'

'Why?'

'For starters, you're not remodeling my kitchen.'

'Not yet. But you might go home tonight and decide that you want new countertops.'

'Let's try to keep the focus on you.'

'Tell me about your husband.'

'Aaron—'

'At least tell me what he does for a living.'

Jennifer sighed, growing exasperated, though not enough to end the session. She wanted to know where he was going. 'He works for the *Las Vegas Review-Journal*.' This was no longer true, of course. But Patrick was still getting up and pretending to go there every morning. 'He's a writer.'

Aaron nodded knowingly. 'Most of the wives I deal with have soft husbands – lawyers, bankers, executives. They've got carpal tunnel. I've got calluses. Women like a domi- nant, physical man. I can tear down a kitchen and rebuild it into something beautiful with my hands. Women instinctively respond to that.' His look was smoldering. 'You're responding to it. What would you do if I kissed you right now?'

'I would never allow that to happen,' Jennifer said. 'It's unethical.'

'Okay . . . you're fired. Now there are no more therapy rules to worry about. Problem solved.' And then in one breathless movement, Aaron was off the couch and all over her, one hand tugging a fistful of hair, his mouth hard over hers, his other hand already moving up her dress and beginning to probe between her legs.

Jennifer's body ignited instantly. His touch inflamed her in a way that rendered her astonished, ashamed, and excited all at once. The reckless endangerment made her shudder.

Aaron seemed emboldened by the desperate way her body was responding to him.

She gasped as his fingers finally found their way inside her.

His smile was ruthless. 'You're already wet.'

Jennifer felt paralyzed.

He held up his slick fingers as evidence. 'There's nothing wrong about this.' The belt came undone. The trousers went down. 'This is what you need. This is what you want. Isn't it?'

She managed a blank nod, squirming underneath his grip, halfheartedly fighting for an independence that her body clearly did not want.

Aaron was firm, insistent, purposeful, pushing the dress past her waist and twisting her panties to allow immediate entry. Skillfully, he shifted positions, planting himself in the chair and Jennifer astride him, practically impaling her. 'I'm going to wear you out.'

It was hard and fast and hot. And he fully carried out his erotic threat, screwing away every bit of the guilt and shame that clung to her for desiring him so much.

What amazed Jennifer the most was how authentic the scenario felt. Cam Lawford played his part so convincingly. For a few minutes, she actually believed that Aaron Rutter was a real client. If there were awards for sexual role play, then this man deserved a golden statue.

Now she found herself laughing at the situation. It was the complete submission. It was the glorious release. It was the disheveled mess she had become. It was all of that and more.

Cam got dressed in seconds. His shirt had never come off. He only had to pull up his pants. The action had been that urgent and furious. As he buckled his belt, he said, 'I love fucking you. It's the way you respond. The heat of your blood is so easy to feel. I really have to work to control myself when I'm inside you.'

Shyly, Jennifer retreated into her bathroom. She dampened a washcloth in cold water to freshen up. As she began putting herself back together, she was struck by how self-conscious that compliment made her feel.

Cam appeared in the doorway. He watched her for a moment, then gently took possession of the cloth and pressed it against her neck, cooling her instantly.

Jennifer's body shivered.

His smile was warm and intimate. 'You have so much passion locked up inside you. It's sexy to be with a woman whose body is like a volcano.' He kissed her forehead.

Jennifer closed her eyes, wondering if this kind of desire could be replicated with another man. Cam brought out a ravenous carnality that was unique to anything she had ever experienced before.

He grinned strangely. 'I think your dog is scratching at the door.'

Jennifer rushed to liberate Nancy from the outer office before she could do any damage.

The Bichon frise trotted inside and went straight for Cam, standing on her hind legs, begging him to pick her up.

He scooped her into his arms, laughing as she licked his face with sheer joy and abandon.

Jennifer could hardly believe it. Nancy was characteristically wary of men. Even Patrick had never earned such affectionate devotion. She clearly had a mad crush on Cam Lawford. The little bitch was a tramp. Just like her owner, apparently.

'What's her name?' Cam asked.

'Nancy.'

'After Nancy Drew?'

She looked at him with surprise.

'I noticed your collection,' he said, stepping closer to the bookshelf. His finger ran across the tightly stacked spines lined up side-by-side in order of publication date. He retrieved the very first one, *The Secret of the Old Clock*, and admired it.

'That's a first edition from over eighty years ago,' Jennifer said. 'My husband gave it to me on our wedding night.'

Carefully, Cam returned the book to its proper place. 'This is quite a collection. Were you a fan as a little girl?'

Jennifer nodded. 'Nancy was never preoccupied with boys or clothes or makeup. She was always the intelligent girl. She used her head.'

Cam grinned. 'Smart women must have an affinity for her. A senator flies me in to D.C. about once a month. She has a nice collection of these in her Georgetown condo. But nothing like this.'

Jennifer was immediately intrigued.

Cam seemed to pick up on her curiosity. 'I would tell you which state she represents, but that would give her away. I have to be discreet.'

'Of course,' Jennifer said, feeling just the tiniest bit scolded. She retrieved the small envelope containing his payment from her top desk drawer and presented it to him.

He made no move to count the money.

'I can't do this anymore.' Her voice was barely a whisper.

Cam looked at her with a sense of real understanding. 'This is the awkward part for most of my clients. You'll feel differently later.'

'It doesn't matter how I feel. This has to stop.'

He gestured to the sofa and her chair. 'You admire Nancy Drew because she solves mysteries, right? Isn't that what you do here? Solve the mysteries of people's emotions?'

Jennifer just stared at him, captivated by his analogy.

'Sex is a mystery, too – the things we like, the things we don't like, what turns us on. That's all we're doing here. We're exploring. We're solving your sexual mystery. You can't stop now, Jennifer. We haven't figured it all out yet.'

In that moment, she knew that he was right. A time would come, the right amount of loneliness and desire would strike, and Jennifer would pick up the phone to call him again.

When Cam opened the door to leave, Nancy stealthily darted out, running so fast that she was just a blur of white fluffy fur.

'Nancy!' Jennifer shouted, lunging after her in a state of panic, nearly colliding with Kurt Taylor.

Cam chuckled, letting rip a piercing whistle that sent the eager-to-please Nancy racing back in his direction.

Jennifer sighed her relief and snatched Nancy into her arms, unable to make eye contact with Kurt.

Cam nodded wordlessly and discreetly left the scene.

Kurt boomeranged a look from Cam's retreating form to Jennifer and back again, his face registering faint suspicion. 'I was just coming up to leave this Post-It on your door about grabbing a coffee later.' He gestured to the yellow square stuck to his index finger.

Shamefully, Jennifer wondered if she smelled of sex. Kurt probably thought that she was sleeping with a client . . . in her office . . . during a session. This had truly been a reckless move. 'Maybe tomorrow.' She could not tell him no outright. As bad an idea as it was, she wanted to be his friend. She needed one right now.

He nodded stiffly, glancing over the balcony to watch Cam slide into a shiny black Audi R8. Suddenly, Kurt's jaw slacked open. The malignant male envy was all over his face as he took in the sexy sports car's menacing grille and wide haunches, and when beautiful plumes of smoke puffed out of the twin chrome exhaust pipes as Cam roared out of the parking lot, Kurt openly swooned.

Jennifer's office phone jangled.

'I should get that,' she said, swamped with relief that she could put a quick and legitimate end to this moment. She disappeared inside, reaching it on the fourth ring. 'Jennifer Payne.'

'Hi, Jennifer, this is Amy from Visions Academy.' Her voice was sweet but carried a hint of concern. 'I'm here with Mia Sara. We understand that she had a doctor's appointment today, but Mr. Payne hasn't shown up to check her out, and we can't seem to reach him.'

Jennifer glanced at the clock, quietly fuming. Even if she left for the school right now, they would be at least forty-five minutes late for the annual checkup. 'Amy, I'm so sorry. It seems Patrick and I got our wires crossed. I'll call the doctor and reschedule. Please send Mia Sara back to class.'

'No problem at all,' the secretary said. 'These things happen.' There was a brief pause, and then Amy dropped her voice to speak quietly. 'Jennifer, we also need to update our contact records. I tried to reach Mr. Payne at the newspaper, but I was told he's no longer employed there. Does he have a new work number?'

Jennifer gripped the edge of the desk, hoping Mia Sara was out of earshot. 'Just use his mobile number for the time being,' she said evenly.

'I'll make a note of that,' Amy said.

'May I speak with my daughter?'

'Certainly.'

A moment later Mia Sara was on the line. 'Mommy, where's Daddy? He was supposed to pick me up.'

'Daddy's fine. We just got our schedules confused. That's all.'

'I hope Dr. Knox doesn't find us tiresome for missing the appointment.'

Jennifer smiled at the precocious statement. *Tiresome* was Mia Sara's favorite new word. And it perfectly suited the current situation. 'Don't worry, angel. I'm sure Dr. Knox has encountered this sort of thing before. Now enjoy the rest of your day. I love you.'

'Love you, too.'

Jennifer hung up and dialed Patrick's cell. As expected, it rang straight to voice mail. She slammed down the receiver, imagining him laughing it up at the Coffee Bean with that blond bimbo.

Her eyes burned into the rows of Nancy Drew novels lining the bookshelf. She could not ignore his behavior any longer. It was time to play girl detective and solve the mystery of Patrick Payne.

Where was her husband going when he left the house every morning? Did he have another job? Did he have a mistress?

CHAPTER TWENTY

Patrick had an obsession underneath the Strip . . . *literally*.

There were 350 miles of flood channels in Las Vegas, and more than seven hundred people called these dark and dirty underground tunnels home. Most of them took up residence directly below the famous boulevard. It was cool, comfortable, and quiet there, much better than homeless living on the streets above.

Cops never ventured down to run a hassle. The tunnels provided real freedom, and those who lived here were like a special family. Some had been doing it for years.

'Hey, man, I've got something new to show you,' Elijah said. The twenty-three-year-old was one of Patrick's favorite tunnel people. He had lost his job as a front desk worker at the Palms Hotel because of a random drug test that turned up positive for heroin. His addiction still had him in a tight grip. But he was a phenomenal artist, too.

Patrick followed him through the damp, cavernous space and into the official underground graffiti art gallery, where Elijah's massive murals of classic Vegas stars ruled. Next to his likenesses of Frank Sinatra and Wayne Newton was a stunning new portrait of Sammy Davis Jr.

'It's amazing,' Patrick marveled.

'The Candy Man can,' Elijah sang, revealing a newly chipped tooth.

'The detail, the accuracy – it's uncanny.' Patrick stopped there, having once made the near fatal error of suggesting that Elijah's talents were being wasted down here in the depths.

The tunnel artist's response to that insult had been a switchblade to Patrick's throat. 'This is our *home*, man! This is where we *live*! You think this is some *phase* we're going through? This is our fucking *life*!'

When the intense young man had withdrawn the weapon and walked away, Patrick had scribbled the rant into his notebook, grateful for the raw dialogue. His fascination with life in the tunnels, his belief that this bizarre world could be the set piece for an intriguing screenplay, inspired him to make regular visits no matter the safety threats.

In the beginning, he only managed to slip down sporadically. But now that he was no longer shackled to the newsroom, he had become a regular fixture, an artistic observer ignored by some, tolerated by most, and trusted by a few.

For the first time in years, Patrick felt happy and fulfilled. He began his morning routine by going straight to the tunnels, where he usually stayed until early afternoon. Then he met his writing group at the Coffee Bean to discuss their scripts, after which he followed Eva back to her house to vaporize. By the time he made it home, he was exhausted – and still stoned. Seeing him sacked out like a zombie in front of the television, Jennifer thought he was the same depressed lug, but he was different now and getting better every day.

'Check it,' Elijah said, 'I'm GQ all the way, man.' He did a proud peacock walk, showing off an expensively tailored blue dress shirt with a small stain on the pocket. 'Found this last night.'

Patrick was learning how easy survival in the tunnels could be. Living here did not necessarily mean going without. The simple acts of Dumpster diving and bin raiding at the mega hotels yielded incredible finds – plush bedding, good books, nice clothing, gently used toiletries, occasional medicines, office supplies, even musical instruments. Elijah's constant refrain was that he could always rely on one thing – rich tourists pitching out items of real value.

'How'd you do in the casinos last night?' Patrick asked.

Elijah dipped into the like-new designer man bag crisscrossing his chest and pulled out a thick wad of cash. 'Got to love those shit-faced gamblers!'

Money was still a necessity in the tunnels, mainly for food. Elijah had become a pro at credit hustling. He waited until late at night to prowl the casinos for money and credits left behind by drunken slot players. They never disappointed. Once Elijah had found over seven hundred dollars on one machine at the Bellagio. Of course, that was a rare jackpot. But if he worked hard and canvassed all the major casino floors, he could usually scrape together a thousand dollars on a good night.

Hanging out with Elijah and his tunnel buddies during the day was surprisingly entertaining. Talk radio was a favorite pastime. They blared Rush Limbaugh and Glenn Beck. Afterwards, they engaged in lively debate. All kinds had taken up residence here – Democrats, Independents,

conspiracy theorists, Marxist communists, radicals of inde-
terminate beliefs, and even a few Republicans.

'Where's Edie?' Patrick asked.

'She's reading,' Elijah said. 'I found a nice copy of *The
Girl with the Dragon Tattoo* in one of the bins, and she
can't put it down.'

Edie was Elijah's girlfriend. She ended up in the tunnels
after losing her job as a singer in a Vegas club and getting
kicked out of her apartment following a fight with her
roommates. Now she provided lead vocals in the tunnel
band that played in the makeshift nightclub every night.
Edie was a pretty brunette with a versatile, nearly pitch-
perfect voice.

There were several accomplished musicians living underground. Many had been fired from casino shows, usually
for drugs or alcohol. Shitty instruments or not, the boys
in the band could still rock out. They called themselves
the Neon Underground. And Patrick believed that what
they did was better than most of the ear pollution passing
for music on the radio.

The tunnels could be a strange and dangerous place.
Sometimes Patrick felt as if he were visiting in an alter-
nate reality. Everything they owned had to be stacked on
crates to avoid wetness, and the possibility of flooding
was always top of mind. Water sent down from a construction project on the Strip could do serious damage. The
tunnels filled up so quickly that a heavy rain could mean
death. Just a few months before Patrick started coming
down, a couple had actually drowned. And there were
also poisonous black widow spiders to contend with.

This immersion was essential to the screenplay, though.

He wanted his script to be authentic and authoritative to the experience of tunnel living. Before getting fired, Patrick had tried and failed several times to convince Hank Lucas to approve a news feature on Elijah and Edie and the plight of the tunnel people. Tired of getting turned down and eager to move forward, the idea to write the story as a feature film came to him as if by thunderbolt.

Sometimes Patrick experienced guilt about coming here to soak up the details. Van and Robbie made occasional nasty cracks about him 'whoring the tunnel freaks' for reasons of selfish creative gain. But the truth was, Patrick really cared about them. He had even reached out to a social worker friend about bringing special services into the tunnels. But the paper-pushing bureaucrat dismissed the idea, telling him that offering help in the tunnel environment would only encourage the illusion that it was a viable place to live.

So now the script had become as much a social cause as a personal passion project. Maybe *Neon Underground* would make a difference. Dramatizing a difficult subject could often shed more light on the issue. Patrick's frequent presence alone had promoted Elijah and Edie to some sort of power couple status within this subterranean counterculture. The buzz was that the Visitor was writing a movie about them, that they were going to be immortalized on the silver screen. Soon others were seeking out Patrick to tell him the story of how they got there, why they stayed, and what they wanted out of life. Listening to them pour out their souls gave him a newfound respect for Jennifer and the work that she did every day.

Elijah was strutting back and forth now, still orbiting

the moon over his clothing find. He gave Patrick his best Blue Steel *Zoolander* look. 'You can't tell me shit, man. I'm straight up ready for the runway.'

Patrick laughed. It felt good to laugh. And now he was feeling the laughs deep in his gut, a sign that the dark cloud of depression was finally breaking up. Even down here in the dank darkness, he could almost feel the sun shining on him. He was done with Lexapro, having gradually tapered off the medication from one tablet every other day, to a half tablet every three or four days, to none at all.

His libido was cranking up again, too. In fact, he almost felt like a normal man again because he thought about sex so much – sex with Jennifer, sex with Eva, even sex with Edie. A hot fantasy was constantly popping into his mind. He wanted to reach out to Jennifer, to connect with her in that way again, but it had been so long since they had shared that kind of intimacy. And he just did not know how to approach it.

The fact that he was lying to her hardly made their issues easier to deal with. He planned to tell her about being let go from the *Review-Journal* ... eventually. Jennifer would insist that he start job-hunting immediately. In a few months they would really be feeling the loss of his income. But right now he needed the time and space to incubate with his screenplay.

As Elijah entertained a small crowd of tunnel people who had gathered to watch his comical male model routine, Patrick considered his master plan. Hank Lucas calling him into his office and shit-canning him without so much as a day's severance had been a cosmic sign. He could see that now. It had ignited the fire in the belly he needed to get off his ass and finish his screenplay. The first polished draft was almost there. And it was great.

Eva had compiled a list of industry professionals who offered in-depth screenplay analysis, as well as agents and managers who actively read spec scripts to scout potential new clients. But before Patrick told Jennifer anything about this, he wanted already to be somewhere with it. Having tangible proof that his project was more than a loser's pipe dream was key. He needed his wife to believe in him again, to be proud of him.

Patrick had been living in Las Vegas for over twenty years and had never thought of himself as a gambler. But he was gambling now. The stakes had never been higher for him. Everything he cherished was on the fucking line.

CHAPTER TWENTY-ONE

John Phillip flounced into the room and dropped a small stack of magazines onto the king-size bed. 'These should take your mind off your misery.'

Billie glanced down to see *Inches*, *Steam Room*, and thankfully, at least one non-gay-porn offering – *Vogue*.

'That's nice,' David slurred, too loaded up on Vicodin to offer anything else.

The unknown assailant who smashed his knee with a baseball bat had done serious damage. The top third of David's patella had been broken in two places, the rest of it shattered to bone gravel. The impact of the blow severed tendons down his femur and in the quad muscle of his thigh. Doctors were anticipating one more surgery (there had been a knee replacement already) and a recovery that might take up to a full year. But considering David's youth, strength, and athletic body, all doctors were united in the opinion that he *would* dance again.

John Phillip fussed over him, adjusting his pillows, positioning remote controls within easy reach, and tending to his many floral arrangements.

Billie sat perched on the edge of the bed, monitoring him with aching guilt as he drifted in and out of the narcotic-induced sleep.

'Oh, honey, I'll have what she's having,' Trevor Dunne trilled upon walking in and taking a quick read on David's loopy state.

Billie smiled at the latest arrival, another gay dancer from *Rebirth* who also performed in *Peepshow* at Planet Hollywood.

Trevor glanced at the saucy reading material, then shot an annoyed look in John Phillip's direction. 'Way to keep Jimmy Osmond classy.'

'One had a frat boy theme, and the other had a college football feature,' John Phillip explained. 'He's hot for both. I couldn't decide.'

Trevor looked at Billie, rolling his eyes with bemused affection. 'And they say Sophie had a tough choice. Girlfriend had it easy.'

Billie covered her mouth to laugh.

'How's he doing?' Trevor asked.

'He's in good spirits,' Billie answered quietly. 'It's physical therapy day.'

Trevor smirked. 'Honey, I've seen the physical therapist. I'd be in good spirits, too. In fact, I might throw myself down the stairs just to get a little physical therapy for myself.'

John Phillip fluffed the comforter. 'We should let him rest. It looks like he'll be out for a few hours.'

Trevor waved an envelope bursting with cash. 'Ka-ching. The boys and girls of *Zumanity* took up a little collection.'

Billie knew the show. It was billed as 'the sensual side of Cirque du Soleil' and played at New York, New York.

Trevor tossed the money to John Phillip. 'I never thought

they'd be this generous, Jerry Lewis. You've restored my faith in humanity. People actually give a shit.'

'I'll deposit it,' John Phillip promised, proudly fingering the green. 'I set up a special bank account, a Facebook page, and a PayPal link.' He was beaming. 'We've raised several thousand dollars so far.'

Billie nodded encouragingly as she migrated to the outer sitting room. It touched her deeply that the community of Vegas dancers had stepped forward to support David. The hospital had been a revolving door of hot bodies coming in to see about the sweet young runaway Mormon. They were like a platoon of soldiers. One of their own was down, and everybody had rallied round.

John Phillip's reaction had been particularly impressive. The transplant from Iowa was to no one's surprise a dynamo in a crisis, showing immediate concern over the fact that David carried no health insurance and would be out of work for months. He tirelessly organized backstage donation campaigns at other shows on the Strip, at gay bars in the blink-and-miss-it Fruit Loop section of Las Vegas, and at Lucky Cheng's, the scene of the crime for the tragedy.

Billie had personally appealed to Hart Fox to provide a suite at the London for David's recovery. The idea of him bedridden and alone at his crappy apartment in the Dancers Ghetto was unbearable. He needed – and deserved – more luxurious surroundings. Plus, relocating to the London would mean more regular visitors to boost his spirits. His dancer friends could more easily drop by before or after their shows.

'You won't believe this,' John Phillip said. He was holding

a card and pointing an accusing finger toward a fruit basket on the coffee table. '*Get well soon. Love, Mom and Dad*. Are you fucking kidding me? Their son is brutally attacked, and they act like he's got a head cold.'

'It doesn't matter,' Billie said. 'He's got family *here*. He's got us.'

John Phillip flicked the offending card onto the cellophane-covered basket. 'Whatever. His parents suck. They're not fit to raise hamsters.'

Three knocks rapped on the door.

Trevor moved to open it, revealing Jagger and his partner, Gucci Marlowe, who looked more like a television detective than a flesh-and-blood one.

Billie had been introduced to the Vegas crime fighter at the hospital on the night of David's attack and was struck by Gucci's striking beauty and razor-sharp intellect. Her brain seemed to operate like a supercomputer. Billie got the impression that Gucci picked up on even the most nuanced physical and emotional details. Pity the guilty one who ever ended up on the receiving end of a Gucci Marlowe interrogation.

John Phillip raided Fiji waters from the minibar and passed around the bottles.

'How's David?' Jagger asked.

'Zoned out on pills,' Trevor put in. 'In other words, that bitch is doing better than we are.'

Gucci grinned, twisting the cap off her water as she eyed the fruit basket and stepped over to inspect the card from the injured dancer's no-show parents.

'Any luck on finding the monster who did this?' John Phillip inquired.

Jagger and Gucci shared a secret look.

Billie tensed.

'I don't hold out much hope,' Jagger said. 'There were no witnesses. And David got a better look at the bat than the person swinging it.'

There was an ominous moment of silence as the cringe-inducing image took hold.

'It's scary,' John Phillip said. 'There's a crazy, violent homophobe out there.'

'I don't think this was a gay bashing,' Gucci put in. 'They typically run in packs and taunt their victims before striking. Part of the appeal is feeding off the group aggression and the target's fear. David's case has none of those qualities. This was fast and deliberate. A stealth attack.'

'So what are you saying?' Trevor asked.

'I'm saying I don't believe this was a hate crime or that he was just in the wrong place at the wrong time. David was specifically targeted.' Gucci's tone was absolute.

Billie said nothing.

John Phillip and Trevor traded expressions of alarm.

'Do you recall him ever mentioning an ex who might have an ax to grind? Maybe an ugly breakup?' Jagger asked helplessly. 'He never mentioned anything to me.'

John Phillip looked to Trevor, then Billie, then back to Jagger. 'You were his first boyfriend that we know of.'

'Could there have been any recent or previous involvement with gambling or drugs?' Gucci pressed.

John Phillip shook his head. 'We live in the same apartment. We dance in the same show. I would know. He's clean. I know he denounced the Mormon religion. But he still lives like one.'

Billie could feel anxiety building to a pressure point. The private torment was unbearable. She knew Randall was responsible for this. And even worse, the sick motherfucker had done it because of her. She checked the time on her phone, realized that she was late for her lunch with Kristin, and quickly said her good-byes to the group.

In the elevator, she exhaled a deep breath. Her stomach was in knots. She felt like a criminal for concealing what she knew. But there was no other choice. She had no proof of anything, just a damning suspicion. And Randall posed too much of a danger to aggravate with accusations.

If Domestic Violence had taught her anything, it was this: Never underestimate what one human being is capable of doing to another. The thug had changed her as a person, and altering her physical appearance was just one way. Now she lived fearfully and accepted horrible indignities in a trade-off to simply stay alive and avoid bodily harm.

'I hate my life,' Billie hissed, stepping out of the elevator and into the parking garage, jolting as a Cadillac Escalade came careening around the bend at high speed. Probably some degenerate gambler who thought luck at the casino's blackjack table would go his way.

It occurred to Billie to leap in front of the SUV. The vehicle would crush her and slam her onto the garage floor. Certainly the body trauma and head injuries from hitting the cement would kill her instantly. But she couldn't rule out some miracle survival scenario. After all, she was one tough bitch.

An overdose of pills was an option. But with her luck, there'd be no peaceful end on that front either. Some asshole would find her in time and call 911, or she'd slip into a coma and wake up with significant organ damage.

There was one surefire way to put an end to her misery – the balcony. The penthouse suite at the London was on the thirty-seventh floor. All Billie had to do was climb over the railing ... and let go. The breath would get sucked out of her as she fell downward, time would slow as she approached the oncoming impact, and then it would all be over. That was a way out. And it would be a dramatic final exit, almost cinematic.

Why not end this charade? Everything in her life was a goddamn lie – her new career as a Las Vegas song-and-dance girl, her marriage to the surgeon-Svengali-psychopath, even her sessions with Jennifer Payne. There was so much Billie had to conceal for fear that her therapist would report matters to the police. The client confidentiality rule only went so far. If a therapist knew that a patient was in life-threatening danger, she had an ethical duty to alert the proper authorities.

Billie concentrated on pinpointing some aspect of her life that was purely authentic. But she couldn't think of a single example. Not even Cam Lawford could count as one. Sure, his kiss had stirred her soul, but she couldn't deny the fact that his hourly rate was ticking the whole time. Everything surrounding her was a huge fraud.

All of a sudden, an epiphany hit Billie like a phosphorous starburst. Maybe the answer wasn't ending a life of lies. Maybe it was beginning a life of truth. A wonderful feeling came over her as she slid into the front seat of the BMW.

If there was one thing she knew for certain, it was this:

Billie Fucking Shelton had survival in her DNA. She'd lived through shit that would've killed a bulletproof rocker like Keith Richards – even as a young man. And she'd live through this, too. But it was time to fight back. Yes! It was time to kick ass. And it was time to seek out the life that she wanted.

Billie knew exactly what she had to do.

CHAPTER TWENTY-TWO

'At the end of our last session you were telling me about getting involved with Hart and his decision to transfer you out of the Mirage training program,' Jennifer said.

'Yes,' Kristin sighed, not looking forward to excavating the old hurts and grievances. 'And like most twenty-two-year-old girls, I was too young and stupid to realize what an omen that was. Hart demanded most of my free time. My friendship with Jeffie suffered. And I was just going through the motions at Treasure Island. That hotel was like a big amusement park. I lost all my enthusiasm for the business when he pushed me over there.'

'At that point, did you imagine yourself marrying him?' Jennifer asked.

'Not really. Late one night he took me to the Las Vegas National Golf Course. I knew his intention was to propose. I could feel the butterflies, but they never took flight. I just had this pit of conflicted feelings in my stomach – hope and doom, love and ambivalence, excitement and dread. I'll never forget it.'

The memory swept Kristin away. She could still vividly picture the oldest golf course in the city, once a favorite hangout of the Rat Pack. It was only two miles from the

Strip yet far and away from the hotel and casino nerve center that dominated so much of their time. There were rolling fairways, glistening man-made lakes, and hundreds of palm, pine, and olive trees standing in fierce protection of the green. The scene was breathtaking in the moonlight.

'Hart drove a golf cart to the eighteenth hole,' Kristin continued. 'There was a white-gloved waiter in a tuxedo standing next to a candlelit table for two. He had Cristal in a silver champagne bucket, caviar, exotic fruit carvings, and these beautiful mini-desserts that looked like works of art. There was even a full symphony assembled on the green. They were playing that Frank Sinatra song, "Put Your Dreams Away."'

'It sounds incredibly romantic,' Jennifer said.

Kristin found herself reliving the moment when Hart guided her out of the golf cart and into his arms. He held her so close, led her into an impromptu dance, and sang along to the music in a perfectly melodious crooner's voice that she had no idea he possessed.

'What are you feeling as you remember all of this?' Jennifer asked.

'That I was a fool for allowing myself to be swept away by the fairy-tale staging.' Kristin paused a beat. 'Jeffie was right.'

Jennifer leaned forward. 'Right about what?'

'I called him the next day to relay every detail. And all he said was, 'I'm happy for you if this is what you really want.' I got so angry at him. It was such a stingy reaction. At first, I thought he was jealous or feeling left behind in some way. But then he told me that he didn't have a lot of faith in men who orchestrate big productions like that. He said it revealed more about Hart's ego than his feelings for me.'

'I take it all you wanted to hear was "Congratulations,"' Jennifer said.

Kristin smiled wanly. She was right back there, sitting on the bed in Hart's corporate apartment at the Mirage, holding the phone in her hand, debating whether or not to bang down the receiver in the middle of Jeffie's rant. 'His sense was that Hart just wanted a proposal story that would make other men feel outdone and make their wives and girlfriends swoon. He said that guys like Hart peak early in relationships, and he warned me that in five years I'd be wondering why the man who put all that imagination and effort into asking me to marry him couldn't bring himself to show me simple kindness.'

'You knew he was right, didn't you?' Jennifer probed. 'Deep down, in your heart of hearts.'

Kristin nodded. 'I got shipped off to Treasure Island the day after Hart showed up in Vegas. But Jeffie worked closely with him for months. He saw the way Hart treated people, the way he could be a charmer one minute and a vicious prick the next.'

'What was your response to Jeffie?'

Kristin felt a knot of emotion lodge in her throat as tears misted her eyes. 'I hung up on him. I didn't invite him to the wedding. Shortly after that, he left the Mirage for a position at a resort hotel in Acapulco. And we didn't speak again for eleven years.' She took advantage of the de rigueur box of tissues, dabbing at her eyes. 'Why are we going down this path?'

Jennifer's expression was warm. 'Because the past stalks the present in ways that we can't begin to imagine.'

Kristin shook her head shamefully. 'He tried to reach out to me over the years. I just couldn't let him back in, though. By then I knew how right he was. I missed him terribly. But I didn't want to face him. He would've taken one look at me and known.'

'You mentioned that you were estranged for eleven years. What prompted the reunion?'

'He showed up at my first book signing in Manhattan for *Come to Bed*.' Kristin smiled as the recollection took hold and played out moment by moment in her mind. The memory was powerful.

She could see Jeffie as if in 3-D, looking exactly the same, only more fit than ever in his cycling gear.

'I rode ten miles to get here!' he exclaimed.

Kristin rose up from the table to embrace him, instantly overcome with emotion. She had never stopped thinking about him. 'Oh, Jeffie!' she cried. 'I can't believe it! What are you doing in New York?'

'I live here now. I'm managing a hotel in SoHo.'

She took his hand. 'Please tell me you're free for dinner. I won't take no for an answer.' She glanced back to Leesa, her efficient publicist from New Woman Press.

Leesa nodded. 'We're having drinks with Toni Valentine at five. The rest of the evening is yours.'

Kristin squealed in delight and turned back around.

Jeffie was laughing. 'So I'm being squeezed in after the media mogul? I guess I'm okay with that.'

Kristin waved off Jeffie's teasing and reached for her

BlackBerry. 'Give me your number. I'll call you the second I'm done here, and we'll make a plan.' She glanced over to see a long line of readers queued up to meet her, to buy her novel. It was surreal. But all she wanted to do was talk to the best friend she had ever had.

Jeffie picked up on the impatient throat clearing of the woman behind him and quickly presented his copy of *Come to Bed*. 'Autograph, please.'

Kristin beamed, dashing back to take her seat at the table stacked high with her first bestseller. 'I'm sorry about that!' she called out to the crowd. 'I just ... ran into an old friend.' At that moment, their eyes met, and she knew that everything – the harsh truths spoken, the years of stubborn silence – was forgiven.

She inscribed his book,

> *For Jeffie. You were right, my insightful, darling*
> *friend. I would trade a million golf course*
> *symphonies for a kind conversation that made*
> *me feel cared for. Love Always, Kristin.*

When she called that evening to arrange dinner, the phone rang straight into voice mail. She left him several messages. But Jeffie never responded. For hours, Kristin waited in her lonely hotel room, haunted by their brief reunion, replaying every moment as she wondered why he had changed his mind.

The following morning, the answer was in the *New York Post*. Under the garish headline KILLER STREETS, Kristin read a brief news capsule reporting the death of a thirty-four-year-old cyclist who had been hit by a sanitation truck. His name was Jeffrey A. Nichols. It marked the fourteenth biking fatality in Manhattan that year.

By the end of the story, Kristin was overwhelmed with sadness, sobbing quietly.

Even Jennifer was tearful. 'There are certain people in a lifetime whom you meet and instantly love. Jeffie was one of those rare and beautiful connections that defies time apart, ugliness, and neglect.'

Kristin nodded, beginning to compose herself. 'I just regret turning away from him. I regret it so much. It's hard to reconcile. I ran from his honesty. And today that's the main quality I would treasure in a friend.'

'He wanted to see you live a life of truth,' Jennifer said. 'Are you doing that?'

The question tripped Kristin into an uncertain place. Sometimes the intangible promise of analyzing her life each week unnerved her. Was this helping? Was she changing? Or did it only serve to make her a more backed-up version of the same person?

Jennifer glanced at the clock. 'We're going to have to stop here for today.'

This was the aspect of therapy that Kristin hated the most. Just as she was settling in to reflect more fully upon her problems, the session would come to an end.

'By the way, Hart left me. He moved into the corporate suite at the London. I guess we can start there next time.' And then Kristin grabbed her purse, walked out, and got into her car.

'You've got to be kidding me,' Kristin muttered to herself as Frank Sinatra's 'Put Your Dreams Away' filled the cabin as soon as she started the engine. Immediately, she changed the Sirius radio channel to Outlaw Country. Anything but Ol' Blue Eyes.

Years had passed since she last heard the romantic classic. There should be a sentimental reaction. The music should mean something to her.

But she hated that fucking song.

CHAPTER TWENTY-THREE

'She doesn't try,' Dale Munso complained. 'She takes a hundred vitamins a day, she spends a small fortune on face creams, but then she never exercises.' His voice took on a mocking tone. '*I don't have time. I'm tired. It's too hot.*' He rolled his eyes. 'And then she cries and calls herself fat because a size ten won't fit.'

Julie Munso was seething. 'I don't like to exercise. I don't like to sweat. I never have.'

'You didn't have a problem sweating off some weight for your e-mail boyfriend,' Dale shot back.

Julie looked directly at Jennifer, her expression both hostile and desperate for female solidarity. 'I'm so glad we decided to do this. My husband has talked more since we got here than he usually does over an entire weekend.'

Now Dale zeroed in on Jennifer. 'That's only because she sleeps all weekend.'

Jennifer was struggling to hold it together. The Munsos deserved her full engagement. But refereeing this self-absorbed couple whose only open-air issues seemed to be that he wanted to have sex with an aerobics instructor and she wanted to take long naps seemed like the longest fifty minutes of her life.

That was frustration talking, of course. There were

serious matters to probe in the Munso relationship – the sexual impasse, the emotional distance, the lack of honesty, the infidelity. Could this marriage be saved? For now, Jennifer felt confident that the answer was yes.

Many couples facing similar issues toughed it out for the sake of their children. It amazed Jennifer how the buffer zones of hectic schedules and socializing with other families could Band-Aid seemingly irreconcilable differences. But that was precisely why she saw so many clients reeling from divorce after eighteen or more years of marriage. Eventually, the pretending, the ignoring, and the living without . . . just stops.

This brought to mind her situation with Patrick. Last night, Jennifer had come so close to snooping through his computer and cell phone for clues about his daily activities. To resort to that kind of privacy invasion would have been a new low for her. Another example of how desperately they needed counseling. But if she and Patrick ever found themselves sitting across from a therapist, she wondered if they would sound as tiresome as the bickering Munsos.

Jennifer jotted down a few notes in an attempt to stay in the game. Ten minutes longer. She could do it. As clients, they deserved her abiding curiosity, complete patience, and total focus. But hour after hour of people going on about unresponsive mates, misbehaving kids, passive-aggressive parents, difficult bosses, and selfish friends could take its toll. This was not necessarily a burn-out factor, just a human one.

'I sleep because I'm tired,' Julie was saying, her voice practically girded with steel. 'I get up at five in the morning.

I leave for work at seven. I get home after six. I take care of Preston by myself, because you're on another business trip. I'm tired.'

'Yeah, until it's time to have cybersex,' Dale remarked.

Julie turned on him, her eyes blazing. 'If you're going to keep bringing up Sean, then we're going to talk about *why* Sean came into the picture. Are you really ready to have that conversation? Because I am.'

Dale just sat there, rigid with silent arrogance.

Jennifer regarded him with sympathy. To her surprise, Dale had called back to announce that he wanted to work on his marriage and try couples counseling. And here he was making an attempt at that in his own limited way. It was far more than Patrick seemed willing to do with her.

Dale's wife was a woman who lived by bottom lines. Julie worked as a sales manager for a popular energy drink called Supergirl. Earlier in the session, she had described her marriage to Dale as a good business partnership, their successful products being a precocious seven-year-old son and a shared commitment to debt-free living.

Jennifer listened to her, occasionally struck by Julie's abrasiveness. She possessed a calcified quality that Jennifer recognized in many adult children of alcoholics, and with a few key background questions, it became clear that Julie's historically absent father was indeed a lifetime drunk.

Julie clung to superficial religious pabulum. But in Jennifer's estimation, her talk of 'God's plan' and sentences that began with 'Our pastor says' revealed more spiritual laziness than deep faith.

As Dale complained about Julie crying hysterically over episodes of *The Biggest Loser* and spending hours on

Facebook to keep up with acquaintances, Jennifer was suddenly struck by the vested interest couples have in the lies that keep their marriages intact.

Dale was obsessed with a looking-glass version of masculinity. It was important how everyone else saw him as a man. He went to great lengths to be affectionate toward Julie in public, but in the privacy of their home, he barely touched her. They coexisted like platonic room-mates but put on the false front of being a happy, frisky husband and wife.

This assessment was a painful reminder of Jennifer's life at home, of the way she and Patrick were vested in lies of their own. She had Cam Lawford and – to a lesser degree – Kurt Taylor. He had his fake job and his bottled blond stripper friend. And the sad truth was that pretending none of these things existed was the only thing keeping their family together.

She redirected her focus onto the Munsos. The goal was always to rearrange the landscape of a client's mind, to open up the possibilities of thinking and feeling differently. The main component of Jennifer's treatment modality was simple. She encouraged the high-strung workaholic to go unplugged and relax quietly for a few hours. She pressed the emotionally cold macho man to be more expressive with the people who loved him. She knew what to prescribe for Dale and Julie, too.

'We only have a few minutes left,' Jennifer announced softly. 'I want to give you some homework to do before the next session.'

Dale checked his Rolex and began tapping his foot.

Julie stared at the door.

'Try making love,' Jennifer said.

Dale and Julie first looked at each other, then back at her.

'There is no right time for passion,' Jennifer continued. 'Waiting for the magic moment that leads to the kind of graceful sex we see in the movies never works. Sometimes you just have to march into the bedroom and start the kissing, touching, and fooling around that leads to making love, even if you really don't feel like it. Eventually, arousal will kick in, and the enjoyment will be yours. Just give it a try.' She paused a beat. 'We need to stop here for today.'

A half hour later, Jennifer was eating a plum at her desk and reading an article in a psychology journal when the buzzer sounded.

Nancy was quickly whipped into a barking frenzy.

Jennifer hushed her on the way to answer the door.

Kurt was standing on the other side, holding out a tall Starbucks cup. 'Is this allowed?' he asked with mock sheepishness. 'One neighbor bringing another neighbor coffee?'

She smiled, actually happy to see him. 'Don't be glib.' And then she accepted his offering and invited him inside.

'It's just black. I didn't know how you liked it.'

'This is perfect. Thank you.' She sipped carefully. 'I'm glad you caught me. I was just about to leave to go for a swim, and I needed the caffeine.'

'Really? My root canal didn't show, and I've got two hours to kill. I was planning to squeeze in a workout myself. Where do you go?'

'Las Vegas Athletic Club – the location on South Maryland.'

Kurt nodded. 'Why don't you come with me to my gym. It's private. And there'll be a light lunch waiting for us after we swim.'

Jennifer hesitated.

'How can you say no to your caffeine superhero?'

This made her smile. In fact, he always managed to do that. She found herself caving in to the idea. 'Okay, but I have to be back by two o'clock.'

'Not a problem. Grab your bag, Esther Williams.'

They were speeding toward the 215 Beltway in his Honda S2000 when he inquired about Cam Lawford. 'So what's the story on the guy I ran into at your office last week? The one who drives the Audi R8 I'd trade one of my children for.'

Jennifer grinned nervously, grateful to be in a convertible where the sun and wind could mask the instant flush of heat on her cheeks. 'You know I can't say – client confidentiality.'

'*Really?*' Kurt replied with good humor. 'A guy looks like that and drives that car and still needs a shrink? It's erectile dysfunction, isn't it? You don't have to confirm it out loud. Just blink twice if I'm right.'

Jennifer laughed, revealing nothing.

Kurt blasted Michael Bublé's jazzy rendition of 'Heartache Tonight' as he roared toward the foothills of Red Rock Canyon, steering toward the Ridges of Summerlin. It was one of the most desirable addresses in the Las Vegas Valley.

When he zipped into the guard-gated Falcon Ridge subdivision, she assumed they would be stopping at a members-only clubhouse. But Kurt turned onto Meadow Hawk Lane and pulled into a private driveway.

For a moment, Jennifer marveled at the magnificent home, which looked more like a sophisticated, twenty-first-century postmodern sculpture than a residence. 'This isn't a gym.'

Kurt cut off the engine. 'It's my house. But there's a gym ... and a pool.' He grinned cheekily. 'I told you it was private.'

Jennifer felt tricked and practically squirmed in the passenger seat. 'Kurt, I'm not getting out of this car. Take me back to the office.'

'Relax. This is perfectly innocent. And we won't be alone. I'm never alone in the house.' He hopped out and motioned for her to join him.

Reluctantly, Jennifer followed Kurt through a side door that led directly into a dream kitchen that took her breath away – Miele stainless steel appliances, a Wolf range, and Vetrazzo glass countertops.

A pretty, plump, middle-aged Hispanic woman in a crisp white uniform was busy chopping fresh vegetables.

'Jennifer, this is Yolanda, our housekeeper slash nanny slash chef slash live-in lifesaver.' He rushed over to the woman's side, kissed her cheek, and snatched a baby carrot.

Yolanda beamed, revealing a brilliant white smile.

'You see those choppers? This lady's never seen a dentist in her life, and she's got prettier teeth than Jennifer Lopez.' Kurt popped a cherry tomato into his mouth. 'Yolanda, this is Jennifer Payne. We work in the same office park. Get her card before she leaves. She's a therapist. When this family officially drives you nuts, you'll need to make an appointment.'

Yolanda giggled.

Jennifer smiled warmly.

'Do we have any avocado?' Kurt asked.

Yolanda nodded. 'I picked up at farmer's market this morning.'

'Add a little of that to your creation. And make two. We'll eat out by the pool. She makes the best salad in Vegas,' Kurt bragged, leading Jennifer into an elegant living room that was all sea grass limestone floors and sleek white leather furniture. Adorning the walls, which stretched up to vaulted ceilings, were several large, colorful Tom Everhart originals depicting the *Peanuts* gang.

'Your home is amazing,' Jennifer gushed, her eyes falling on a recent beach portrait of Kurt, Diana, and their five boys. It was the first time she had ever seen his wife, a stunning brunette who closely resembled the actress Courtney Cox. 'What a beautiful family.'

Kurt smiled at the picture with a hint of wistfulness. 'That was a good trip. Five nights in Cabo.' He pressed a button, and the floor-to-ceiling windows parted like curtains, paving the way for them to venture out to an enormous zero-edge pool.

Kristin was momentarily speechless. The views were nothing short of majestic – prehistoric red rock formations on one side, the Strip and all its promise of glitz and glamour on the other.

'You can change in the cabana,' Kurt instructed. 'I'll meet you in the pool in a few minutes.' He disappeared inside.

The cabana was comfortable and beautifully appointed. In fact, it was more spacious than Jennifer's first apartment after graduate school. What a life the Taylors lived! His dental practice might be in a slump, but there was certainly no sign of a financial crisis on the home front.

She emerged wearing a black Speedo one-piece and a matching swim cap just as Kurt was entering the pool in a pair of tight blue trunks that brought to mind Daniel Craig's celebrated ocean scene in the Bond film *Casino Royale*. It was the kind of look that few men could pull off without embarrassment. A guy either had the body or he did not. And Kurt Taylor had it.

Jennifer joined him in the water. The temperature was soothing – just cold enough to encourage her to begin her stroke to trigger warmth. 'Oh, this feels wonderful.'

He grinned. 'How often do you swim?'

'At least five times a week. It keeps my head clear.' She adjusted her goggles. 'I'll probably swim for a half hour. Are you up for that?'

'*Without stopping?*' His tone was playfully incredulous.

Jennifer laughed. 'Yes.'

'I'll probably conk out after a few laps. But you do your thing, Esther Williams.'

Jennifer smiled and pushed away from the wall, gliding through the water in a smooth freestyle. The sensation was like a soft caress. Swimming had become her version of meditation. It gave her important reflective time as she moved back and forth, counting down her laps.

For the first several, Kurt was keeping up right beside her, but as she started her seventh length, she noticed that he had stopped. But Jennifer continued on, finding a steady rhythm and locking into it.

Lately, her time in the pool had allowed her the space

and solitude to rehearse lines for difficult conversations with Patrick that she never had. Today her mind drifted to some research she was reading which supported the theory that spouses who carry positive illusions about each other often enjoy stronger marriages.

She thought about the difficult married couple from earlier in the day – Dale and Julie. Where were their wonderful illusions? If she saw him as a sensitive man, he might occasionally act like one. And if he viewed her as a sex kitten, perhaps she might surprise him in the shower one morning.

As Jennifer examined the condition of her own marriage, she realized that she had no illusions about Patrick. Maybe the answer was to imagine him as honest, smarter, ambitious, and more attentive than he really was. But she could not do it. No matter how hard she tried.

Her loneliest moments occurred when she was alone with him. Sometimes the silence was unbearable. Jennifer was too young and vital to settle for a relationship like this. But she could not leave him. Mia Sara loved and needed her father too much.

Jennifer worried that her personal struggles might be rendering her ineffective with clients. Was she really doing them any favors? Should she consider a sabbatical of sorts until she felt better about her own choices and ability to do good work?

As she negotiated a flip-turn, a bitter thought came to mind. If she was the only one working, how could she possibly take time off? She picked up speed and cut through the water with a vengeance, feeling her heartbeat accelerate.

The exercise was important. And the opportunity to purge her innermost thoughts was liberating and replenishing. By not doing it, she ran the risk of becoming as depressed, angst-ridden, and self-delusional as so many of her clients.

It took discipline to not try too hard during a session. That was one of the worst things a therapist could do. Like trying too hard to sleep or trying too hard to make someone love you, it always failed. The stakes in her work were high. Not listening – or listening in the wrong way – could lead to an error in judgment that might send someone down the wrong path. Her influence did not end with the people sitting across from her. It extended to others in their lives as well – spouses, children, parents, siblings, friends. She tried never to lose sight of that heady responsibility.

Jennifer stopped swimming with a heaving breath. She had lost count of her laps but could feel the challenge of the workout in every limb. Slipping off her goggles, she saw Kurt kicked back against the pool's black marble wall.

He whistled. 'You went at it for thirty-seven minutes! I can run a half marathon in less than two hours, but I can't do that!'

She smiled and glided toward him, still taken aback by the phenomenal beauty of the surroundings. 'You could if you practiced.'

'Most of my time in this pool is spent doing cannonball contests with the boys.'

Yolanda waved cheerily as she prepped the outdoor dining table for their lunch.

Jennifer waved back. 'She's lovely, Kurt.'

'This household would perish without her.'

All of a sudden, Jennifer stopped to marvel at the impeccable, magazine-perfect conditions. 'I'd never think that five little boys lived here.'

'You should see the playroom downstairs. It's ground zero for testosterone overload. Diana has us trained to keep the main parts of the house like this.' His handsome face took on a serious expression. 'Jennifer, I want to apologize for the way I behaved at lunch. It made you gun-shy to simple outings like this, and I hate that. Thanks for giving me a second chance.'

Jennifer freed her hair from the swim cap. 'I hope things are better with Diana.'

'They're not better. They're not worse. They just . . . are. How about things on your end?'

'Patrick got fired from the newspaper.'

'Jesus. That's a tough break. I'm sorry.'

'It happened weeks ago, and he still hasn't told me yet. He pretends to go there five days a week. I don't know where he spends his time, other than at a Coffee Bean with a girl at least fifteen years younger who looks like a dancer from Club Paradise.'

'That could be innocent,' Kurt pointed out. 'Like this is.'

'It could be,' Jennifer murmured. She sighed heavily and gazed out toward the Strip. A fleeting image of Cam flashed in her mind. He was over there, ensconced in some luxurious hotel suite, making a woman forget her problems for a few hours.

She whirled around in the water. 'I saw them together once. He was animated and talkative and even laughing

... with *her*. He's never that way at home with me. It felt like such a betrayal. Sometimes I think it would've gone down easier to find them in bed together. Maybe I should be happy for him, though. He's been depressed for months. Finding someone he can open up to is a good thing, right?'

Kurt nodded. 'Kind of like us.'

Jennifer fell silent for several seconds. 'I've seen depression transform my clients in amazing ways. It can make people tougher and more optimistic than they were before. But sometimes I think depression is wasted on Patrick. He can't seem to see any possibilities.'

'Maybe he wants to find a new job before he confesses to losing the old one,' Kurt said. 'I could see myself reacting that way.'

Jennifer grinned wryly. 'Stubborn masculine pride?'

'Never underestimate it. Listen, I don't know Patrick from Adam. But he managed to hook you as a wife, so the man has my respect. Don't give up on him yet.'

Jennifer fought the urge to embrace Kurt. 'Thank you. You're a good listener. And wise counsel.'

'But a lousy swimmer.'

As she laughed, it occurred to Jennifer that over the course of her career, she had seen many marriages develop a depth of wisdom and emotion just from years of slugging it out. She prayed that would be the case with Patrick ... and with Kurt and Diana, too.

'So tell me, how is that brilliant little girl of yours?' Kurt asked.

'Oh, she's wonderful.' Jennifer could feel her own eyes shining. 'This morning I was driving her to school, and Taylor Swift's "You Belong With Me" came on the radio.

We sang along at the top of our lungs. She knew all the lyrics and sounded much better than her off-key mother. It was so much fun, though.'

Kurt smiled. 'I love those moments.'

'Patrick and I created this incredible little person,' Jennifer went on. 'As a couple, we've gotten a lot of things wrong. But we did that job right. I can't wait to see the woman Mia Sara will grow up to be. And I want us to do that together. I want to be partners again.'

'I want that, too,' Kurt said.

CHAPTER TWENTY-FOUR

'Husbands suck. Therapists suck, too. Here's to my Great Dane . . . and to our Julian,' Kristin toasted grandly, making her second Lava Flow disappear. The drink was an addictively delicious frozen blend of piña colada and strawberry daiquiri. She signaled a passing cocktail server – a gorgeous brunette who probably dreamed of being tapped on the shoulder by a producer promising to make her the next Megan Fox – and motioned for another.

Billie raised her Voss water in the spirit of things and crunched down on a lobster taco.

Here they were at the Mirage's Bare Pool Lounge – under an orange umbrella, on a luxurious daybed, in front of the infinity Jacuzzi. The place could only be described like this: Imagine the classiest strip club in the world hosting a barbecue/lawn party for the genetically blessed. *That* was Bare.

Prepared by Light Group's executive chef Brian Massie – who had made the hotel's Stack restaurant a passionate favorite for New American cuisine lovers – the poolside menu was heaven. Ditto the service. If a wannabe starlet was not sashaying by to present frozen fruit kabobs, then she was offering up an iced towel soaked in flavored water or shot glasses filled with mango smoothies.

Kristin munched on a king crab fry drizzled with truffle oil and dunked in artichoke dip. 'This was a brilliant idea,' she murmured, settling back to stare at the Nevada sky.

Billie was scoping out the scene behind ridiculously large Tom Ford sunglasses. 'Isn't that Leonardo DiCaprio over there?'

Kristin rose up to see. Leo was tan, shirtless, in good but not great shape, rocking a pair of board shirts and holding court with a short male buddy and a bevy of model types. 'I feel like I watched him grow up. Is it sick for me to want him?'

Billie chortled. 'Take it easy, Mary Kay Letourneau.'

Kristin shoved her playfully.

'You're not that bad, I guess. Somewhere out there is a *Twilight* mom with a shirtless photo of Taylor Lautner as her screensaver.'

Kristin grinned as the third Lava Flow arrived.

On the reserved daybed next to them was a foursome of attractive guys in their late twenties nursing what appeared to be brutal hangovers. From what she had over-heard, one of them had accidentally dialed his fiancée at home while rifling through his jeans for dollar bills to toss to the lap dancer at Spearmint Rhino. His future bride had listened to every 'oh, baby' and 'you're so hot,' before texting him with the news that their wedding was off.

'Dude, what are you going to do?' the friend in the Ole Miss hat asked.

'Fuck if I know,' the newly single man answered, looking only half worried as he shrugged and ordered a Raspberry Sin.

'Every schmuck thinks he can handle this town,' Billie

snickered under her breath. 'But it can really take a bite out of your ass.'

They people-watched in silence, temporarily entertained by a muscle-bound reality star's failed attempt at joining Leo's coveted clique. It was living proof that high school never ends.

'I'm doing a weekend in Malibu with . . . *Julian*,' Kristin announced. 'Hart will have the kids, and . . . I need to get away.'

'Be careful,' Billie trilled.

'Of what?'

'A two-hour booking is infatuation. An entire weekend? That might be love.'

Kristin sighed. 'I suppose I'll either get him out of my system or become a real goner.'

'I wonder if he's ever fallen for one of us,' Billie mused.

Kristin gave her a curious glance.

'I mean, you know, a *client*.' Billie let the idea roam around as her gaze remained fixated on Leo and company. 'Or vice versa. Sometimes I think he's just a dumb jock. And then he says something, and I'm like, "You sneaky son of a bitch, I've been waiting for a man to say that to me my whole fucking life."'

Kristin smiled. 'I know what you mean.' She snatched another king crab fry. 'Maybe you can book him for the weekend after.'

'Yeah, right. Your husband is a real slave driver. There's only one dark night a week for *Rebirth*. Besides, I could never pay the weekend fee.'

Kristin did a double take. 'If that's the case, it really *is* time to renegotiate your contract.'

'It's not that. It's Randall. He controls every dollar that I make.'

Kristin looked at her strangely.

'It's so bad that I've been snatching watches from his collection and blaming it on the maids.'

'You're kidding.'

Billie shook her head. 'I couldn't think of any other way to pay. Randall doesn't allow me access to much cash . . . if any.'

Kristin was lit with a quick anger. 'That's absurd!'

Billie took the third Lava Flow out of her hand and gently set it down. 'I need to tell you something. And I need you to be sober when you hear it.'

'I'm fine,' Kristin insisted, feeling an odd sensation in her belly. She had never seen Billie so serious.

'Before I was attacked by Domestic Violence, I'd hit rock bottom. My career was over, I was bankrupt, I was an addict, I'd burned every personal and professional bridge at least once and in some cases even gone back and torched them again.'

Kristin nodded with empathy. She remembered some of the more sensational stories. 'But you've changed—'

'The point is that's where I was at the time of the beating,' Billie cut in. 'There was no one in my corner – no family, no friends, no business allies. I'd never been so alone.'

Kristin was almost moved to tears and put her hand over Billie's. 'I'm so sorry.'

Billie took a deep breath. 'Randall showed up at the hospital. He was attentive. He promised to make me beautiful. In the beginning, I thought he was some kind of guardian angel. I was just so grateful to have someone who cared that I never suspected that there could be darker intentions.'

Kristin vividly remembered the first time she met Randall Glass. It was at the London's Waterside Inn for a quiet dinner celebrating the opening night of *Rebirth*. She had encountered the ugly man/beautiful woman syndrome before. Usually, she could assess the aspects of an unattractive man that made him appealing to a woman far out of his league physically. It could be charm, intelligence, a sense of humor, power (always alluring), and perhaps – for all its simplicity and crassness – wealth.

But Randall repulsed Kristin in every way. The fact that Billie had chosen to marry him completely perplexed her. And the fact that perfection seekers placed their vanity in his surgical hands left her puzzled as well. He was small and reptilian, cold and controlling, arrogant and prickly.

Kristin had researched the subject of domestic abuse while writing *Come to Bed*, even going so far as to conduct in-depth personal interviews with some victims. Their stories were as individually distinctive as fingerprints and yet very much the same. There was always a man who had come into their respective worlds, held them back, and squeezed the life out of them.

That night at the Waterside Inn Kristin had picked up a vague sense of this. She did not know enough to be certain. It was just a gut instinct, an intuitive feeling. She knew Billie Shelton to be a force of nature, a hurricane in Rock & Republic denim. But Kristin walked away from the evening believing that a life with Randall would downgrade her into nothing more than a faint gust of wind.

'He won't stop with the surgeries,' Billie said. 'Now he wants to do breast implants and dimpleplasty and shorten my toes.'

Kristin knew the horror was all over her face.

'That's not even the worst of it.' Billie appeared visibly relieved just to be confiding in someone, as if an enormous burden had been lifted. 'He watches practically every move I make. And if he's not doing it, his assistant is – Carly. They monitor my phone. They keep a record of my mileage. They track my schedule from morning to night.'

'This is awful,' Kristin said softly. 'Billie, you can't live like this.'

'I want out. But Randall's dangerous. He really is. Sometimes he wakes me up in the middle of the night and shoves a gun in my mouth. One day he'll pull the trigger. I know it.'

Kristin stopped breathing. She believed every word. The veracity was right there in Billie's terrified eyes. 'You have to call the police.'

'And say what? There isn't a mark on me. It'll be my word against his. I'm the ex-rock star, ex-drug addict, ex-you-name-it. He'll tell them that I'm delusional or that I'm suffering from some panic disorder stemming from the attack. I know how that bastard thinks. There's a dancer in my show – David.' Billie was tearful now. 'He's just a sweet kid from Utah. His parents threw him out when they found out he was gay. Randall didn't like me spending time with him. And when he found out that I was using David's phone, I think he hired a street thug to assault him. It happened in the parking lot of a club.

Someone slammed a baseball bat right into David's knee. He won't dance again for at least a year.'

Kristin just stared back in shocked silence.

'I know Randall was behind it. There was a sick smile on his face when I told him what happened.'

The chilling story sent a shiver down Kristin's spine. What else could Randall be capable of? Right away her thoughts arrowed to concerns for her own safety, not to mention Ollie's and Lily's, even Hart's.

Billie seemed to pick up on this fear. 'The only reason he allows me to spend time with you is because he wants me to find out anything that might help him negotiate bigger money from Hart.'

'You have to get away from him.'

Billie's eyes blazed with anger. 'I know. I need to get away from Las Vegas, too. This town isn't for me. I can't dress up like a princess and sing covers anymore. I'm not a baby Cher. I'm a rock-and-roll girl.' She shook her head regretfully. 'Years ago when I was really bringing in money, my manager told me over and over again to squirrel a big chunk away. If only I'd listened to her. I wouldn't be sitting here dumping all of this on you. I'd be gone.'

Kristin's mind zeroed in on the check that was recently deposited into her corporate account. A prolific producer with a first-look development deal at Sony had optioned the film rights to her second novel, *The Guy Next Door*.

It was an unexpected windfall. The book's themes of closeted suburban homosexuality and Southern mega-church religion made for difficult subject matter at the multiplex. But one bullish producer had charged for-ward and was already close to attaching Ryan Reynolds,

Matthew McConaughey, and Patrick Dempsey to the project.

The Hollywood money looked good on Kristin's balance sheet. She did not need it, though. And she would not miss it either. But it could help Billie. More than that, it just might save her life.

'Is two hundred fifty thousand enough?' Kristin asked.

Billie's mouth dropped open.

'Sex in suburbia has been good to me. I'm a rich woman.' Kristin reached out to reclaim the third Lava Flow and started drinking again. 'I'll set up a joint account. Randall won't be able to get anywhere near it. I'll arrange for a good amount of cash for emergencies, plus a check card to make day-to-day purchases and travel easier.' She paused a beat. 'You'll need a mobile phone that he can't trace. I'll open another account in my name. What's your preference – iPhone or BlackBerry?'

Billie was still speechless. 'The iPhone, I guess,' she whispered finally. 'I'll pay you back. I promise. I'll pay back every—'

'This isn't a loan, Billie. It's a solution. This money fell out of the sky for me. I'll never miss it. And if you need more, I'll have all my numbers programmed into your new phone. All you have to do is ask.'

Billie's eyes filled with tears. 'I don't know what to say.'

Kristin clutched Billie's hand tightly. 'Just tell me that running away will work. Tell me that Randall won't come after you.'

Billie shook her head ferociously. 'He won't find me. And after I get my bearings, I'll go public with my story. That sick bastard will never touch me again.' She stared at Kristin for several long, intense seconds. 'Are you sure that you want to do this? It's a lot of money.'

'I don't care about the money. I just want you far away from him. I can go to the bank today.'

Billie took in a deep breath. 'No, I need time to put my plan together. Enjoy your Malibu getaway. Next week I'll have everything in place.'

'Are you sure you'll be safe?'

'Yes. Randall is slow and methodical. That's how I need to be.'

Kristin prayed that Billie was right. The emotions of losing Jeffie were still so raw. She could not bear to see another friend's life snuffed out too soon.

Confessions from the Man
Who's Satisfying Your Wife

By Cam Lawford

Gigolos Get Sentimental, Too

Being great at sex and great in bed are not the same thing. One takes skill and practice, the other interest, sensitivity, and humor. Most men don't realize this. Hence, the reason I have a successful career.

Some of the women I see are just going through an adventurous, self-indulgent phase. More often than not, it's a temporary thing. And it usually ends after a few dates with a kiss and a nice parting gift – a designer shirt, a high-priced gadget, and in one rare instance, a new car. My Audi R8 was given to me by a lottery winner from Lake Geneva, Wisconsin. She wanted to reward the man responsible for her first multiple orgasm.

For some women, sex takes on less importance. What they really want is just to be heard. One of my regular clients is the regal wife of a powerful Fortune 500 CEO. We meet on the first Thursday of every month at the Mandarin Oriental, and she has a fine French meal by star chef Pierre Gagnaire sent up to the room from Twist, the hotel's five-star restaurant.

As we eat, I listen to her worries for her three children and complaints about her maid. Amanda is struggling with her weight. Clark is dating the wrong girl. Pierce is a hothead on the tennis court. Consuela is inept at polishing silver and mean to the social secretary. Our encounters always end with a long embrace and a chaste kiss on the lips. It breaks my heart that she needs me so much for something that requires so little. But I'm glad that she found me. There are opportunists who prey on that kind of vulnerability and loneliness.

An heiress to the BMW fortune was one such victim. She got played like a harp by a Swiss gigolo running a classic con. He researched her habits, arranged for an introduction at a spa retreat, and seduced her into a passionate affair. Soon he was making up a story about running over a mobster's baby and needing a big payoff to keep from getting killed. She loved him, she believed him, and she showed up at a Holiday Inn with millions in cash to save him.

I try to keep a business mind, but I'd be lying if I didn't admit that emotions come into play. I'm a romantic. At one point or another, I feel something real for all of my clients. It could be lust, affection, empathy, protectiveness, or sadness.

Sometimes it's love. And when I do feel love, and the woman is in my arms, and the only thing existing in the world at that moment is the two of us, a certain question secretly rolls around in my head as I look into her eyes: Could I run away with you?

I wonder about that with the bestselling novelist. I wonder about it with the buttoned-up therapist. I wonder about it with the song-and-dance star, too. But only one of them makes me wonder most of all.

And she's the one who makes me answer yes.

Part Three

OBSESSION

For a loser, Vegas is the meanest
town on earth.
HUNTER S. THOMPSON

CHAPTER TWENTY-FIVE

'Don't forget your lunch, sweetheart,' Kristin said.

'But Daddy's coming to the school to have lunch with me,' Lily said. 'He's bringing Johnny Rocket's.'

Kristin betrayed no reaction, even though this was the first she had heard of it. 'Well ... take it anyway. Just in case he gets stuck in an important meeting.'

Lily grabbed her *iCarly* lunchbox and hugged Kristin tightly. 'Will you stay with us at the hotel this weekend? *Please.*'

She stroked her daughter's cheek. 'I'm sorry, darling. I have a short business trip to Los Angeles. But I'm sure your father has all kinds of exciting plans. You're going to have a wonderful time.'

Lily's eyes glazed over with sadness. 'I wanted us to have high tea at Buckingham Palace. Ollie won't go with me. He says it's gay. How can tea be gay?'

'It can't be, darling. And I'll talk to Ollie about this. Now run along. The bus is here.'

Lily rushed out.

Kristin nearly lost it at the sight of Sinatra lapping up milk from Lily's abandoned Lucky Charms. Anything dairy always gave him terrible diarrhea. 'Sinatra!'

He froze in fear before trotting into the living room.
Beep! A horn blasted from the driveway.
Sinatra started to bark.
'Ollie!' Kristin called out. 'Carpool is here!'
A text alert chimed from her BlackBerry.

HART FOX Send lunch with Lily. Noon meeting just came up.

KRISTIN FOX I figured.

HART FOX Tomorrow looks iffy. I'll pick up kids Sat.

KRISTIN FOX I leave Fri for speech in L.A. Keep schedule as is.

Beep!
'Ollie!' Kristin screamed.
Finally, he emerged, moving slow and dressed slovenly in an oversized wrinkled polo, stained khakis, and battered Converse sneakers.
Kristin noticed new patches of blemishes on his forehead and chin. 'Did you take your medicine?'
'Yeah. It doesn't work. Can't you tell?'
'I'll call the dermatologist.' She gently squeezed his shoulder and handed over an insulated bag stuffed with bottled water and fresh fruit. 'Here. Try to cut back on the sodas and sugary snacks. That'll help.'
Ollie nodded morosely.
'One more thing – please have high tea with your sister this weekend. And stop telling her that it's gay.'

'What's gayer than sitting around drinking tea and eating little finger sandwiches?'

'We don't use that word as an insult.'

'I'm using it as an adjective.'

'You know what I mean. Just indulge Lily for an hour. It would mean so much to her. And I'll treat you for the effort when I get back.'

'Okay,' Ollie mumbled. He trudged toward the kitchen door, then stopped and turned around. 'Is Dad ever going to sleep here again?'

Kristin hesitated. 'I don't know, sweetheart.'

'Is it because he's such a dick sometimes?'

'Don't say that.' She looked at her son imploringly. 'He loves you, Ollie. The problems your father and I have ... they have nothing to do with you or Lily.' She started to cry. Everything was such a goddamn mess. What would become of them?

Ollie stepped forward and awkwardly embraced her. 'Don't cry, Mom. We're going to be fine.'

The sweetness of his gesture only made her cry harder. He was attempting to take care of her. The role reversal shamed Kristin into pulling herself together. She patted his back and reached for a tissue to dab her eyes.

Beep!

'Tyler's mom's implants must be hitting the steering wheel again,' Ollie joked.

Kristin smiled in spite of herself. The woman's DD enhancements *were* ridiculous.

Ollie grinned slyly as he walked out.

Kristin treasured this moment with her son. For the first

time in a long time, they were not at war. It was almost enough to get her through the rest of the day.

Fueled by guilt and a profound sense of failure – and working against her better instincts – she reached out to Hart.

KRISTIN FOX We need counseling.

HART FOX Why? It hasn't helped you.

Kristin's thumbs were poised on the tiny keypad, ready to tap out a profane response. She resisted, though. Hart could be so mean. But she was not going to play that game.

She searched for Sinatra to take him on a walk, apologizing in baby talk for yelling at him as she kissed his sweet, enormous face. Great Danes were such gentle giants, full of loyalty, good intentions, and a constant need for affection. Sinatra was a maddening responsibility at times. But she truly adored the clumsy beast.

'Hello!' Elaine Dayan called out from across the street, her groomed-to-perfection Coton de Tuléars sniffing curiously around a mailbox.

Kristin waved. It never failed. Every time she stepped outside the door with Sinatra, there stood Elaine with Sonny and Cher.

'I haven't seen Hart in several days. He must be out of town.'

Kristin was in no mood to tap dance around the truth. 'He moved out, Elaine. I'm not sure our marriage is going to survive.'

She was positively gobsmacked. 'Oh, you poor thing . . . I didn't know . . . I'm so sorry.'

Kristin continued walking with Sinatra. Saying the words out loud had been strangely liberating. The energy that went into parceling language and dodging the truth could sometimes be more exhausting than just spitting out the harsh reality.

Picking up the pace, she headed back to the house and directly upstairs to her office. Sinatra went down for a nap and would be out for hours. Everything was quiet . . . and suddenly lonely.

It occurred to Kristin how isolated she had become. In her family and personal network, she could count Hart, the kids, the limited contact she had with her parents, and some casual tennis friends at the Red Rock Country Club. The last true friend she had enjoyed – someone whom she truly loved and knew her inside and out – was Jeffie. And just as Kristin was growing so fond of Billie, she would soon be losing her.

There were other people in her life. Some of them she had become quite close to over the years – her publisher Toni Valentine, her literary agent, her television and film agent, her editor at New Woman Press, her publicist. But these were business relationships first. If she ever chose to change representation or publishing houses, the ties would be severed.

During the early days of her career, there had been other writers in her private circle, women she met with to swap rejection horror stories and critique new work, plus others she had bonded with at writing conferences. But the moment her success kicked in – and it happened quickly and in a big way – all those friendships suffered and eventually petered out, undone by professional jealousy.

Of course, there was Cam. What category did he fit in? He was her lover. He was her friend. But she paid by the minute for that. And yet, second to her children, he had become the most important person in her life. She felt breathless anticipation for tomorrow's Malibu getaway. The line between fantasy and reality had become disturbingly blurry.

'Get a life, Kristin,' she hissed to herself, pushing a gnawing hunger pang out of mind as she started to review the most recent pages of *Kiva Dunes Road*.

After a few minor edits, she started clacking away and went at it for hours, the pages practically writing themselves. She would have a completed first draft in a few weeks. Then she could start the invigorating process of revising, rearranging, and cutting. Reaching into her secret junk food drawer, she snatched a Reese's Peanut Butter Cup, determined to keep pushing forward.

An old snapshot of Jeffie was Scotch-taped to Kristin's monitor. He was the model of inspiration for the character Jaron, the only unmarried member in the core group of characters. The novel would be dedicated to him. Jaron – just like Jeffie – spoke X-ray truths that were not always welcome and sometimes better left unsaid. Creating him and getting inside his head was bringing Kristin great joy and melancholy. It was like breathing Jeffie back to life and grieving him at the same time.

When Lily dashed into her office to report on her school day, Kristin realized with a start that it was already late afternoon.

'Darling, go tell Ollie to take Sinatra for a walk. Will you do that for me?'

Lily nodded eagerly and disappeared, always delighted to deliver orders to her older brother.

Kristin reached for her BlackBerry and started making babysitter calls. Finding someone on such short notice seemed unlikely. But she lucked out with Ben Fillion, a skinny, freckle-faced eighteen-year-old college dropout who was just down the street and sitting on his parents' sofa after being laid off from a restaurant job – his third in as many months. Grateful for the work, he showed up an hour later, wearing distressed jeans and a T-shirt emblazoned with the phrase, YOUR FUTURE EX-BOYFRIEND.

Ollie and Lily adored Ben. They thought he was 'the coolest guy ever.' Kristen left them to a Wii tennis showdown while she ventured upstairs.

Sinatra followed her, napping in the master bathroom as she showered, applied makeup, and dressed. It was important that she look good for this mission. She selected a black belted Jil Sander dress with half sleeves and an A-line skirt. The final verdict was attractive yet serious with a hint of sex appeal. Perfect.

The London was buzzing with activity when she arrived. An impressive line for Billie Shelton *Rebirth* tickets snaked around the Palladium Showroom box office. Shoppers populated the Harrods boutique, and guests were queued up for the evening dinner package at the Buckingham Palace Experience.

In the wake of a decline in large group and convention bookings, major hotels and casinos were being forced to

'Believe it or not, I'm getting married again.'

Kristin laughed. 'Really?'

Mitch nodded proudly. 'She's a great girl. You'd like her. Sophisticated. Works at one of the art galleries in the Caesars mall. I'm hoping this fifth time will stick.'

'I hope so, too. No one can say you're not persistent.'

'One day I should sit down and tell you all about these crazy-ass women I've married. You could write a book about it.'

Kristin grinned. 'Let me guess – it would be a bestseller.'

'Most definitely.' He said this with no trace of modesty or self-awareness.

'If I had a nickel for every time somebody told me that, I could cover the attorney fees for all four of your divorces.'

'Well, if you ever run out of ideas, consider it a standing offer.'

Kristen smiled. 'I'll do that.' She paused a beat. 'Any chance Hart is still in his office?'

An odd look skated across Mitch's face. 'I was just back there, and I didn't see him.'

Kristin wondered if the entire London staff knew that Hart was living in the hotel. She left Mitch and made a beeline for the elevator that would take her to the twenty-third floor. He was staying in suite number 2314. Kristin knew this because Lily had taken to doodling those digits onto every available writing surface as a declaration of her weekend destination.

Kristin's intention was to catch Hart off guard. Calling ahead would afford him the time to steel himself against anything close to productive exchange.

A young woman answered the door wearing a London spa robe.

The possibility that she might have the wrong room never entered Kristin's mind. The girl was pretty, blond, not a day older than twenty-two, and positively glowing with the intoxicated energy of infatuation. Basically, she was Kristin from fourteen years ago. The only difference was the hotel.

'You must be in the management training program,' Kristin said.

The girl looked mortified.

Kristin brushed past her to seek out Hart. She found him naked on the freshly rumpled bed, punching a text into his BlackBerry.

He glanced up, made no attempt to explain the situation, and shamelessly went back to his message.

The girl's cheeks were pure scarlet as she skulked around retrieving her clothes and throwing them on as quickly as possible. 'I'm ... sorry ... I ... I love your books.'

'Thank you,' Kristin said acidly. 'Don't be surprised if you're in the next one.'

'Come back later, Heather,' Hart said with infuriating nonchalance as the girl scampered out the door like a spooked rodent.

Finally, Hart pressed Send. And only then did he meet and hold Kristin's gaze. 'You should've called first.'

Her emotions toward him were completely frozen. 'Let's go downstairs for a drink. We need to talk about the kids and determine how we're going to do this.'

'I already know how I'm going to do it. You want a drink? Go have one.'

'You can't hurt me, Hart. I don't care about what happened here. I realize that we're finished. But we have to come together for Ollie and Lily. This could have serious consequences for them if we're not careful.'

His chuckle was patronizing. 'The kids are fine.'

'Ollie called you a dick today. Does that sound *fine* to you?'

Hart shrugged. 'Show me a twelve-year-old boy who doesn't think his father's a dick.'

Kristin shook her head. 'You're pathetic. I can't believe I wasted fourteen years of my life with you. And that's exactly what it feels like – a goddamn waste.'

He rose up from the bed and started to get dressed, shooting a look at the discarded comforter and twisted sheets. 'Should I bother to make it up?' His tone was rhetorical. 'Nah. Why bother? I'll be fucking her again in a few hours.'

There were so many things she could say to trump his management trainee slut. But Kristin refused to sink to his level.

Hart buttoned his striped dress shirt and let out a satisfied sigh. 'Heather is so *tight*. I'd forgotten how good that feels.'

Kristin could not resist. 'Your erections have gotten softer with age. I hope she doesn't mind.'

Hart's face tightened. 'Funny. That only happens to me with you.'

Kristin instantly regretted the sniping. She did not want to play dirty. She just wanted to talk about their family. The marriage would dissolve. That seemed inevitable. But how could they proceed in order to manage the least amount of damage to Ollie and Lily?

'Hart, please. It's obvious that you don't care about me. But I refuse to believe that you don't care about the kids.'

'If you care so fucking much, why aren't you home with them right now?'

'I thought it was important for us to talk.'

'For you maybe.' He reached for his tie and quickly looped the knot. 'I don't have anything to say.'

'What is this?' Kristin asked.

He gave her a bored look. 'What is what?'

Kristin shook her head wearily. 'This is pointless. I thought you could behave like an adult.' She started for the door. Her hand was on the latch.

'I hired an attorney,' Hart announced to her back.

Kristin froze for a moment, then slowly turned around. 'Someone had to go first.' A feeling of heartsickness washed over her.

Hart slipped on his square-toe black leather Ferragamo loafers. They had been a present from her for his forty-ninth birthday and still looked brand new.

'I'll get one, too,' Kristin said.

Hart's expression was like granite. 'I don't care what you do. But here's what's going to happen – I'll be petitioning for full custody of the kids and half the proceeds from your writing.'

Kristin just stood there, shocked silent.

'I supported you for years while you pursued that bull-shit career. You got lucky and struck gold. I deserve my share for propping you up to make it happen.'

Her insides became an instant cauldron of rage. '*Propping*

me up? You did everything to tear me down! You were never supportive! You ridiculed me! You told me that I was wasting my time!'

Hart's smile was thin. 'And look where it got you. Tough love, baby. Works every time.'

Kristin gave him an excoriating look. 'Why don't you just man up and call this what it is – insecurity and jealousy.'

He scoffed at her.

'You can't handle my success, Hart. You need me to be smaller than you. You always have. But I'm not. I'm bigger. My success is mine. I did it alone. I did it in spite of you. And that just eats away at your inflated ego, doesn't it?'

There was hatred in his eyes.

Kristin pressed on, going for the jugular. 'My career is still growing. But you've peaked. That's what the real problem is. Vegas is in shambles. And it won't be coming back anytime soon. Not the way that it was. You're going to spend the next several years fighting to keep the London's financial bleeding to a minimum. And then it'll be time to retire.' She paused a beat. 'That is if you make it that long. They might want to bring in someone younger.'

Hart's left eye was twitching. His hands were shaking. He was practically imploding with fury.

Kristin had never seen him so angry. The possibility that he might strike her hung in the air. But instead of being frightened by what Hart might do, she felt emboldened by the fact that speaking her truth had rattled his cage to such a degree.

Wordlessly, Hart pocketed his wallet, keys, and BlackBerry. He moved toward the door.

Kristin was far from finished. She stood in his path. 'If you want to go after the money I earned like some gold-digging bitch, try it. But don't you dare make noises about custody. The idea that you'd use Ollie and Lily to get back at me is disgusting.'

'I've hired Diana Taylor,' Hart said. 'Getting fathers full custody is what she does best. She's a real piranha.'

'This isn't a game, Hart.' Her voice was suddenly pleading with reason. 'The kids are suffering. And how much do you even know about their day-to-day lives? What kind of medicine does Ollie take for his acne? What days does Lily have gymnastics? When is her next competition?' Kristin threw the questions at him like darts. 'You don't know anything. You're not involved. And if you chose to be, it wouldn't last. What are you going to do? Send them down to play in the casino while you have another romp with Heather? I won't let you do this.'

His laugh was cold and mocking. 'You *won't let me?*'

Tears sprang to her eyes. 'Just leave the kids out of this. It's not fair. We don't even have to fight it out with lawyers. There's mediation.'

'Maybe I'm doing this for the kids. Did you ever think about that?' His gaze was intense. 'Maybe you're an unfit mother.'

Kristin fought for restraint. A violent impulse was vibrating in her solar plexus.

'People talk.' His tone was suddenly ominous. 'What were you doing at the Flamingo in the middle of the day?'

She feigned confusion as a cold and immediate fear clenched her stomach muscles. 'What are you talking about?'

'You've been spotted there. You've also been spotted at the Paris. Someone mentioned seeing your car leave the Palazzo, too. That Bentley you had to have is pretty conspicuous. It's not the car to sneak around in.'

She tried to put him off with a pugnacious attitude. 'Who says I'm sneaking around? Am I on some kind of lockdown? I can't have lunch with a friend at a hotel restaurant?'

'I'd buy that if you were a lady who lunches. But you're not.'

Kristin struggled to remain stoic. Was he just repeating idle gossip? Had he retained a private investigator? How much did he really know?

'I've got online access to all of our accounts,' Hart went on. 'I know about the cash withdrawals. You've got a secret.'

Kristin glared at him. 'The only secret worth knowing is why I didn't leave you a long time ago.'

'You still haven't,' Hart pointed out. 'I left you.' He searched her face carefully. 'And I'll find out what your secret is ... if you give me a reason to.'

She showed no sign of fear. 'We both have secrets. I just walked in on one of yours.'

'I have a girlfriend. So what? That's something I'd be willing to share with the kids. I'd be willing to share it with a family court judge, too. Can you say the same?' His eyes blazed into hers. 'My guess is no.'

'You're grasping, Hart.'

'Am I? Those withdrawals add up into the thousands. What did you spend all that money on?'

She remained cold-water cool. 'I run an expensive household. I don't have the luxury of just calling up room service like you and your college girlfriend.'

Hart's eyes gleamed with smug triumph. 'I don't know what you're hiding. But I have a feeling it's a lot more interesting than those hack novels you put out every year.'

Kristin looked at him as if seeing him for the first time. 'How did we get here?' Her voice was etched with sadness. 'When did we start being so cruel to each other?'

Hart was unmoved. 'That sounds like a question for your shrink. I'm done, Kristin. But first I'm taking the kids and half your money. You can have the house and that fucking dog that shits like a horse.' He attempted to step around her.

Kristin refused to let him pass. 'I will *not* let you do this!' It came out as a shriek, instantly straining her vocal cords, and in a fit of emotional frustration, she proceeded to beat Hart's chest with both fists.

He shoved her away with such force that she sailed across the room, bounced off the bed, and hit the floor hard. The impact stunned. Her wrist hurt. Her knees smarted from carpet burn. Tears of rage filled her eyes as she looked up in total defeat.

But Hart was already gone.

Kristin just lay there on the floor, massaging her sore wrist, wracked by convulsive sobs. If ever there was a rock-bottom moment in her life, then this was it.

Her purse started to ring. She crawled across the floor to dig for her BlackBerry, not even bothering to check the ID screen. 'Hello?'

'Are we still on for Malibu?' It was Cam.

She felt her spirits lift. In fact, they soared. 'Yes.' Her voice broke a little on that one word.

'Are you okay?'

'I will be,' Kristin said softly. 'I wish we could leave tonight.'

'Why can't we?' Cam asked. 'There's a United flight to LAX at eight thirty. We could be making love on the beach by midnight.'

'Are you crazy?' She was half smiling as she asked this.

'Maybe. A little bit. Get crazy with me.'

And that is exactly what Kristin did. She rushed home to arrange for Ben to spend the night and see Ollie and Lily off in the morning. Hart would pick them up from school for the weekend. Ben would feed and walk Sinatra. With everything set, she packed a small Prada suitcase and drove to the airport, convertible top down, Katy Perry's 'Teenage Dream' blasting on the stereo.

CHAPTER TWENTY-SIX

'Are you decent?'

Billie glanced at her dressing-room door. The male voice behind it rang familiar. 'Come in.'

Hart Fox slipped inside, flashing a smile. 'Another fantastic show. You send them out in a good mood. It makes them want to drink and gamble more. Thank God for that.' He laughed, leaning in to kiss her on both cheeks.

Billie found Hart incredibly sexy. He exuded self-absorbed swagger and confidence. And he always smelled so damn good, his cologne an earthy, vibrant mixture of basil, mint, and cypress. She wondered why Kristin couldn't make it work with him. Granted, he was an asshole. But hot men who operated on a high level always were.

'Randall asked us to cancel the grip-and-grins,' Hart said.

With Carly gone for the night and no one to play the role of ferocious gatekeeper, Billie had braced herself for a tedious gauntlet of fake smiles and awkward snap-shots.

'I do have one special fan waiting outside,' Hart whispered conspiratorially. 'He says he's an old friend of yours from New York. March Donaldson. I've slipped him in under the radar.'

Billie struggled to contain her reaction, even as she felt an instant flush of heat hit her cheeks. She managed an easy smile. 'As long as he promises not to talk politics.'

'I'll have him sign a waiver.' Hart grinned. 'It's a pleasure to see you, Billie. The show is great. Every hotel on the Strip would kill to have you, and I couldn't be more proud to see your name on the London's marquee.' He started for the door. 'I'll send March in. And I'll have some champagne and strawberries brought in as well. Would you care for anything else?'

'I'm dying for something fizzy,' Billie said. 'But I don't drink anymore. Maybe some club soda or ginger ale?'

'Of course.' And then Hart Fox was gone.

When March Donaldson walked through the door, he was more handsome than she remembered . . . and remarkably thinner, a fact that stood out in the skinny cut of his shiny black Dolce & Gabbana suit.

Billie started to rise.

'Don't move an inch.' He closed the door behind him. 'You more than earned the break.' Bending down to take her hands and kiss her cheek, March settled onto the leather ottoman directly in front of her. 'Jesus, Billie, you're fucking unbelievable. I've never seen you look so beautiful. Your voice is unreal. And those moves. Holy shit! I had no idea you could dance like that.'

She smiled demurely. But it was false shyness. The truth – she couldn't have engineered a more satisfying reunion with this bastard. Their last time together had been at the Hudson in New York. She was in love with him, they were both coked out of their minds, and in answer to her simple, desperate plea that they share a meal together in public at the hotel restaurant, he'd walked out on her and never spoken to her again.

But now he was coming to her on different terms. Las Vegas was Billie's town. Advertisements for *Rebirth* were plastered on countless billboards, across buildings, and all over the airport. To get this close, he had to make special calls, trade on his good Republican name, and plead his case as the proverbial old friend. It was more effort than March Donaldson had ever made on her behalf before.

Billie lit a cigarette, took a drag, and gave him a cool once-over. 'You've lost weight. Are you sick?'

March shook his head, grinning. 'I'm into triathlons now. I just qualified for the Ironman World Championship in Hawaii. The training changed my body.'

She nodded knowingly. 'All that long-distance swimming, biking, and running. You must be avoiding something.'

He took possession of her cigarette and stole a quick drag. 'My coach would kill me for this.'

'Your life coach?'

'My training coach.'

There was a knock on the door. A room-service attendant rolled in a cart carrying a silver champagne bucket, a tray of glistening strawberries, and an iced-down bowl of miniature club sodas and ginger ales. 'Courtesy of Mr. Fox,' the young man said dutifully. And then he went about the business of uncorking the chilled bottle of Salon 1995 and filling two delicate flutes before quietly disappearing.

March tilted an eyebrow. 'We should toast.' He passed the cigarette back to Billie and reached for the two glasses.

'I'll skip the champagne. Just open one of those for me.'

March looked at her, a question in his eyes.

'I stopped drinking,' Billie explained after another drag. 'No more drugs either. Not even pills. I just sneak one of these every now and then.' She flicked what remained of the cigarette into her declined bubbly.

March raised his glass and offered her a club soda. 'To nine lives.'

Billie clinked her bottle against his flute. 'And nine times to die.'

They took perfectly synchronized sips.

March's expression turned serious. 'You're lucky to be here.'

Billie just looked at him. She didn't feel lucky.

'I should've visited.'

'You're not that kind of guy.'

He winced. 'I did send flowers.'

'Several times, as I remember.'

March drank more champagne. 'I never imagined you as a doctor's wife.'

She grinned coolly. 'Nor your wife.'

'Are you happy?'

Billie was torn between continuing to play out this look-at-me-now fantasy and stripping down to the horrible reality.

'You look happy on that stage,' March answered for her. He laughed a little. 'Are you really the same Billie Shelton who used to spit Jagermeister onto the first few rows?'

This made her smile. 'It's funny. They don't like that as much here in Vegas.'

March regarded her with something close to awe. 'I'm on my way out to L.A. to do Bill Maher's HBO show. But I had to stop here first. I had to see *Rebirth*.'

'What was your favorite number?' Billie asked.

March thought about it.

She was patiently waiting for him to say, 'What's Love Got to Do with It.'

'I guess it would have to be the last encore, "Run." You nailed it.'

Billie was shocked.

'Of course, the eighties geek in me might have to say your cover of T'Pau's "Heart and Soul." I've always loved that song.'

'What about the Tina Turner number?' Her voice was just above a whisper.

March's shrug was indifferent. 'That's never been a big favorite of mine. The audience loved it, though. And you sang the hell out of it.' He finished his champagne and refilled the glass.

Billie couldn't speak. For more than two years she'd clung to March's pillow talk suggestion that she record a cover of 'What's Love Got to Do with It.' She exhausted herself fighting Randall to include the song in the show. Every goddamn night her soul bled for this son of a bitch as she sang the number and thought about him from first note to last. And the pathetic truth was that March didn't even fucking remember. Hearing her perform it live had meant nothing to him.

All of a sudden, Billie struggled to breathe. The pangs of anguish and humiliation hit so quickly and with such intensity that she felt physically ill. Exhaling deeply, she sipped slowly on the club soda, hoping the sensation would pass, even as the terrible loss began to sink in.

She'd been holding on to a silly fantasy that March Donaldson might one day come to Las Vegas, hear her gut-wrenching interpretation of what she believed was their song, and storm backstage to take her back to New York.

'I should go,' March said, drinking down his second glass of Salon. 'I'm meeting some people at Surrender.' He stood up. 'I might be getting my own show on MSNBC. It's still early stages, but the buzz is positive.'

Billie nodded encouragingly. 'I hope it happens for you.'

'Will you watch?'

She gave him a faint smile. 'I'll set my TiVo. That way I can fast-forward through your rants against gun control, same-sex marriage, and Wall Street regulations.'

'That'll be the whole show,' March remarked dryly.

Billie rose up stoically. 'Thank you for coming tonight. It was good to see you.'

March cupped her face in his hands and studied her for several long seconds. 'You really are beautiful, Billie.'

She embraced him just as the tears began to mist her eyes. It felt so wonderful in his arms – warm, safe, familiar. March didn't love her, though. He only loved himself, his career, his political ambitions. The man was a true toxic narcissist.

As Billie continued to hold him, though, the desperation in her heart came close to overwhelming her. She shut her eyes and willed him to pick up on the thoughts she was too terrified and too ashamed to express out loud.

Take me with you.

He's a monster.

Finally, March drew back. 'I really have to go. My fiancée is waiting.'

'So there's a number two,' Billie said, her tone carrying a tinge of bitchiness as she thought of his first wife-to-be, Amaryllis Hartman, the ice princess fashionista with the old money Connecticut pedigree.

'Her name's Kimberly. She's Senator Ashe's daughter. We're getting married on Martha's Vineyard next year.'

'Of course you are,' Billie said. 'I'd expect nothing less.'

March brushed her cheek with his lips. 'Take care.'

Billie watched him walk out. And then she gave in to the full gamut of emotions that his surprise visit had stirred up. Crying like a baby, she smoked a second cigarette, then a third, feeling foolish for even once entertaining the daydream that March Donaldson would rescue her from this nightmare.

Kristin was the only person who could save her now.

CHAPTER TWENTY-SEVEN

'I used to drive a hundred miles per hour. I'd close my eyes, I'd take my hands off the wheel, and I'd think, "Maybe this will kill me."'

Jennifer was still waiting for the Billie Shelton breakthrough. This was not it. 'You're speaking metaphorically, of course.'

'I guess. Anyway, that was the thought in my mind. It was, like, a little voice. I used to hear it all the time – before every drug bender, on the night Domestic Violence beat me.' She tripped off into a faraway place. 'It's weird ...'

'What is?' Jennifer prompted.

'Deep down, I knew that it wouldn't ... kill me, I mean. I always had this invincible feeling. You know, an instinct that nothing would ever kill me. Maybe I'd hit rock bottom. But I'd never die. It made me fearless in my self-destruction. I don't feel that way anymore, though.'

Jennifer eased forward. 'Feel what way?'

'Invincible,' Billie clarified. 'Now I know that I could die.'

There was a message in the words that Jennifer did not understand. In a perfect world, therapy was a place for serene reflection, for truths to be slowly sought after, calmly suffered through, and then safely arrived at. This was not the path to get to that place. Somewhere in Billie was a horrible secret lying in wait. Jennifer could sense it. Her emotional instinct bell was clanging.

'I feel like we're talking in circles, Billie.'

'Oh, I'm sorry.' But clearly she was not. 'Let's get down to specifics. Which scab do you want to pick at today – my mother's cancer? My father's suicide? That time the bratty neighbor boy stole my fucking bicycle?'

Jennifer ignored the sarcastic rage. 'What are you most afraid of?'

Billie did not answer this.

For a millisecond, Jennifer saw a flash of the truth she had been seeking. It was buried there, deep beneath the veneer of the washed-up rock star toughness, in the place where Billie's heart should be. And just as quickly, it was gone again.

'We're not reaching each other,' Jennifer lamented quietly.

'*I just want to feel loved*,' Billie sneered, being at once intransigently avoidant and cruelly mocking. 'Does that help your diagnosis?'

Jennifer sat there in the psychological muck, a good therapist feeling like a bad one. The transference was obvious. Billie was projecting fears and frustrations onto her. The countertransference was also obvious. Jennifer was projecting her own failure to solve the mystery back onto Billie.

'Let's regroup,' Jennifer said. She sounded more upbeat than she felt. There was a certain style of thinking, an operational language, a way of reframing a person's life story to Jennifer's work method. But Billie was not responding to it. 'Pretend that we're two friends meeting for coffee and conversation. What would you want to talk about? It can be any news about your day. There's no requirement for the discussion to be about anything dramatic or important. We're just two girls talking.'

Billie looked pale and short of sleep. Whatever anxiety she was hiding wrapped her like an aura. But the offer of easy banter seemed to trigger a frisson of comfort. A long silence stretched.

Jennifer waited patiently. She had to switch tracks. Probing was about as welcome to Billie Shelton as a roach in a key lime pie. Her private world of disassociation, her terrible, horrible pain, could not be broken into.

Finally, Billie began to talk. 'I've been thinking about a friend of mine who died . . . Liza Pike.'

Jennifer winced as the name entered the atmosphere and seemed to hover there with sobering significance. A few feet away, the late feminist firebrand's work commanded space, respect, and reverence on the bookshelf. *Whore* was the treatise on sexuality that always got the adolescent girls to open up in Jennifer's teen group sessions. *Stupid Girls* was the polemic that made thirty-, forty-, and fifty-somethings cry about the choices they had made and the women they could still become.

'We weren't on speaking terms at the end of that summer . . . when she died.' Billie's voice had a haunting quality. 'God, I was such a mess. I was hooked on drugs. I'd just had my heart ripped out by some asshole guy. I'd just started things up with Domestic Violence, too. We'd rented a house in the Hamptons for the season. It was me, Liza, and Kellyanne. But I left in August. I ditched them to shack up with my new rapper boyfriend. I abandoned her. Sometimes I wonder how things would've turned out if I hadn't been such an awful friend. He killed her in the middle of the afternoon. Did you know that?'

Jennifer nodded wordlessly. She was well read on the circumstances of the murder.

'Just me being there on that day could've made all the difference. It might've changed the trajectory of everything.'

'You can't think that way.' She reached out to touch her hand, to tell Billie she was with her, to let her know that she cared.

'Why not?' It was a child's question in a child's voice. Through sympathetic eyes Jennifer watched Billie's grief. 'Because Liza was being stalked and targeted by a very sick young man. He was mentally ill, Billie. He was *obsessed*. Nothing you did or didn't do could've changed anything. Leonard Tidwell was determined to harm Liza.'

Billie's eyes flashed fire. 'God, I hate him. Assuming there is a God. His will makes no sense to me. Liza was successful and disciplined. She was championing causes and forcing intelligent debate. She was even in love and thinking about children. How could God bring an end to her life and let me go on to live this one?'

Jennifer just stared helplessly. There was no adequate answer to that big question. A major spiritual crisis was far more than she expected from her two-girls-at-Starbucks experiment. And though it was a step in the right direction, the survivor's guilt was still a smoke screen. Billie's real demons had not come to the surface yet.

It was ten minutes before the hour. 'We're going to have to stop here for today.'

When Jennifer was alone, she sat there for a long time, feeling drained. She thought about Billie ... about Cam ... about Patrick. On some level, they each presented their own mystery.

Rows and rows of Nancy Drew novel spines stacked up tauntingly from the bookshelf, as if the teen sleuth role model from Jennifer's youth were daring her to go out there, to solve the puzzles, to get the answers.

What was Billie hiding?

Why did she desire Cam so much?

Where was Patrick spending his time?

On impulse, Jennifer grabbed her purse and rushed out of the office. After all, Nancy Drew never cracked a code sitting on her ass. She was racing down the steps as Kurt jogged into the courtyard on the finishing end of his daily run.

'Where's the fire?' He looked hotter than a radiator. Plus, he was funny, adorable, and actually cared about her distress. A state-of-the-art man factory could not build a husband this good, even with George Clooney available for spare parts.

'It's in my head.' Jennifer smiled but did not stop moving. Sliding behind the wheel of her Camry hybrid, she decided that Diana Taylor should be committed for at least three days of psychiatric observation. Allowing a man like Kurt to wonder and wander was not the sign of a lucid woman.

As Jennifer pulled into the parking lot of the Coffee Bean on Flamingo, she began to question her own sanity, too. The Saturn that had seen better days, driven by a man who had seen better years, was right there in a prime slot near the door, leaking oil, exposing lies, and stirring hurt.

Her grip on the steering wheel was tight. Her knuckles were white because of it. The conservation-friendly vehicle that would get her two thumbs up from Al Gore idled silently as Jennifer considered whether to storm inside or to drive away.

But before she could make a decision, Patrick stepped out and into the sunlight. He did not see her. And how could he? His eyes were too focused on the young blond who sparkled like a rhinestone in a garbage can.

Granted, she wore clothes – tight ones with obvious designer labels. The clothes, however, were not the point. Her body was – the drum-tight butt, the pert, pushy, post-operation breasts, the plumped-up porn fantasy lips. If people ever had to go by the MPAA rating system, this woman would get the NC-17.

Patrick laughed at something she said. And then he tumbled into the passenger seat of her Lexus RX in a way that told Jennifer it was familiar territory for him. The conversation they were having distracted the girl from starting the engine.

Jennifer's eyes welled with tears. How many times had she tried to talk to Patrick? For months and months he had pushed her away, refused to engage on any level, starved her to the point where she was actually paying a man to fill the desperate and lonely void.

When the SUV pulled out onto the street, Jennifer followed it on pure impulse. Everything blurred around her – the signage, the traffic, the landmarks. The only thing that existed was the matador red Lexus with the EVALICK vanity license plate. She stayed in hot pursuit until it stopped in the driveway of one of the few inhabited homes in the Silverado Ranch neighborhood.

Patrick hopped out of the car as if he knew this place well. And then he noticed Jennifer's Camry. He did a double take. The shock, shame, and fear on his face played out like a slideshow. He motioned for the Pamela Anderson in training to go inside.

Jennifer made eye contact with her rival, expecting to see some callow expression of triumph or dismissal. But it was kindness and tender regret that beamed back before the girl turned and disappeared into the house.

Patrick was standing in the street on the driver's side. Jennifer zipped down her window.

'This isn't what it looks like.' His voice was pained.

She could not even glance at him. She just held the steering wheel at ten and two o'clock as she stared straight ahead.

'Her name's Eva. We're just friends. I swear, Jennifer. There's nothing going on between us.'

'Tell her I know exactly how that feels.' She shifted the Camry into gear and tore down the road. Up above, the throbbing staccato of a police helicopter roared. But it was not loud enough to drown out the Taylor Swift song on the radio, the one that Mia Sara loved, and the one that Jennifer was sobbing to right now, 'You Belong With Me'.

CHAPTER TWENTY-EIGHT

'What does that say?' Cam whispered. He angled his wrist so Kristin could read the face of his Cartier at precisely the moment he plunged into her.

'Eleven ... fifty ... eight,' she rasped.

'I told you we could be making love on the beach by midnight.' His mouth feasted on her neck and shoulders as he moved in the slow, corkscrew motion that made the most vital part of her sing in rapture.

Kristin was always amazed by how completely he filled her up. She opened wider, even when there was nothing left to give him, and he still found a way to reach farther, go deeper, take more, create additional space for himself. This body – her body – was Cam's rightful home. And she clamped down on him and prayed he would never leave it.

'Relax for me,' Cam whispered, his stomach slapping against her stomach, their bodies greased with sweat, gritty with sand, and desperate for passionate release.

She obliged him, even as she feared the climax. The joy of his fulfillment would bring the panic of her emptiness. That is why the musical rhythm of sex with Cam possessed such a terrible reassurance. Eventually, ultimately, the point reached its purpose, the goal got to its gain, and the lust found its ending.

Slower ... softer ... faster ... harder.

Kristin was dimly aware of his strokes, of his hot-to-the-touch body, of his incredible eyes grilling into hers, communicating the magic moment. It was pitch black in front of the Malibu Beach Inn. Down there on the shore, the waves were crashing. Up here on the beach, she was, too. And in the midnight darkness, a brilliant orgasmic light illuminated her mind. They called this strip of seashore Billionaires' Beach. And Cam Lawford was definitely making her feel like one.

He moaned out his exquisite pleasure, a primal, animal-istic cry to the Pacific and everything living in it and around it that wanted to listen.

'Oh, God! I love Malibu!' Kristin howled at the glorious peak.

His body collapsed onto hers. He was shaking, slightly at first, then more violently as the small laugh became a bigger laugh. 'I love Malibu? *Really?*'

She looked up at him from the brink of the wonderful abyss. 'Well, don't you?'

All of a sudden, Cam hushed her with a finger, and for a long, embarrassing second, they lay there in the guilty silence of two not so clever lovers.

A rich-looking fiftyish couple embarking on a late-night beach walk strolled rigidly past them, awkwardly pre-tending not to see the carnal criminals.

'Are they gone?' Kristin whispered, her face buried in the deep ridge of Cam's pectoral muscles.

'I think so.' The laugh that came next was carefree, like a high school boy caught making out under the bleachers with a hot girl. As busted moments go, it was one to be proud of by guy standards.

'Do you think they'll complain?' Kristin hissed.

'Only because they got here too late,' Cam hissed back. 'We put on quite a show.' He popped her bare bottom and recovered her sand-blasted jeans and top, handing them over with a quick kiss. 'Let's take a shower and open up a bottle of wine.'

In a flash, he was dressed, climbing the rocks underneath their private balcony, hoisting himself up and over the railing with the ease of a lifetime athlete. He reached out his hand, beckoning her to follow him. 'Come on, baby. I'll lift you up.'

Kristin hesitated for a nanosecond. And then she carefully negotiated the treacherous terrain. But at the crucial point, her fingertips could barely touch his.

Heroically, Cam stretched out to what could have been his own peril. When he claimed her wrists, he brought her up as if her ninety-eight pounds were ninety-eight ounces, twirling her around in satisfied triumph. 'You pick the wine. I'll start the fire and put on some music.'

Their one-bedroom suite was beautifully appointed. The floor-to-ceiling views were panoramic and faced the water. The décor was a charming blend of California chic and Zen tranquility. It felt like an oceanfront refuge just for them.

Kristin shivered and stepped closer to the slate-bordered fireplace that crackled with flaming orange heat.

Cam was concentrating on his DJ role as if it were hard science. His handsome brow furrowed adorably as he studied the catalog of four hundred preloaded CDs, searching for the perfect soundtrack for what was turning out to be the perfect weekend. He pressed some buttons. And suddenly the lush saxophone intro of Sade's 'Smooth Operator' filled the suite.

Kristin smiled in delight, swaying to the jazzy beat as she opened a small production pinot from Dragonette Cellars, a premiere vintner in the Santa Ynez Valley. The logo on the gold label was an old alchemist symbol for 'the elixir of life.' Offering Cam a glass, she wondered, ever so briefly, if he might be her elixir.

He clinked his glass against hers. 'Do I know how to start a weekend or what?' One sip later, he pulled her into the shower and under the steaming jets.

With luxurious laziness, they lathered each other with Molton Brown Re-charge Black Pepper Body Wash before rinsing off and slipping into matching robes to finish their wine.

The moment Kristin climbed into the king-size bed and felt the clean crisp crush of the Frette linens, her energy began to fade.

Norah Jones was singing 'Don't Know Why.'

It seemed like the appropriate song. Because Kristin did not know. Just a few hours ago, she had been fighting with Hart. Now here she was with Cam in Malibu. This felt worlds apart from the ugliness she left behind in Las Vegas. Nothing made sense. And yet everything did. She nuzzled against him and slowly drifted off to sleep.

When Kristin woke up, she was alone. The bright sunshine floodlit the suite with a kaleidoscopic brilliance. Groggily, she rose up and went out onto the balcony, instantly energized by the visual feast that was the pale blue sky. The ocean breeze ruffled her hair and cooled her skin. In the distance, she saw two surfers, and she watched them ride the waves as the salty air practically licked her good morning.

Down on the beach, a runner was approaching. The sun had him in its lustrous glow, casting his long shadow like a good omen across the golden sand. Kristin grinned as the profile clarified – the proud aquiline nose, the sensuous mouth, the strong jaw. It was Cam.

He waved and jogged to the space just below their balcony. 'What's up, sleepyhead?' His smile was warm, bright, and happy.

Kristin could see the sweat glistening on his honey-brown flesh. The scent of Cam's liquid charisma seemed to carry in the wind as the molecules of last night rearranged themselves in her mind. 'I guess I fell asleep.'

He stood there Viking proud, watching a gull swoop down, hands going to his hips as his breathing relaxed. 'I guess you did.'

She looked at him, thoroughly guilty of lust in the first degree. God, he was extraordinary. Feeling a zing of naughty courage, she opened her robe and flashed him.

Cam did not merely climb the rocks to get to her. He attacked them like a warrior. In a blink, he moved up and over the balcony. His body was slick with perspiration as he pulled her into his arms, smelling of sun and sand and masculine musk.

Kristin could feel his arousal straining against his running shorts.

'There's only one thing better than sex in the morning.'

She peered up at him for the answer.

'Sex in the morning at the beach.' And then he tore off her robe, dragged her back into bed, and made her a true believer.

They surrendered to civilian sanity around noon and wandered into the hotel's Carbon Beach Club restaurant, electing to sit outside, blessed by the ocean view and serenaded by the tumbling surf.

Kristin marveled at the tranquil, sun-kissed surroundings as they drank cold beer and shared a dozen oysters on the half shell.

'You're having a Malibu moment,' Cam said. His voice was singsong, youthful, irresistible.

She smiled at him. 'How do you know?'

'Because I recognize the shift. I've seen it before. This is where I grew up.'

'Here? In Malibu?'

'Actually, we call it *the Bu*. You should know that. I'd hate for you to walk around sounding like a tourist.'

She laughed a little. 'I bet you were a holy terror.'

They ordered lunch – a Greek salad with salmon for her, a lobster club sandwich for him. Cam regaled her with tales from his days as a member of the MLO, Malibu Locals Only, a local gang made up primarily of surfers and skater punks.

'So Cam Lawford was a gangbanger,' Kristin teased.

'We were scrappy, a little territorial, nothing too dangerous. The worst I got into was spray-painting "MLO" all over town. And I deflated a few tires on the cars of the guys who drove in from the Valley.'

The waiter brought another round of beers.

Cam cocked his head to one side and stared at her with

his blue forever eyes, sizing her up, sorting her out. 'I hope you brought pages to read to me later. You know I'm hooked on *Kiva Dunes Road*.'

With a crushing sense of disappointment, it dawned on Kristin that she had not.

Cam pantomimed devastation by taking the butter knife and aiming for his heart.

'I'm sorry,' Kristin wailed softly. And she was. Reading to him was one of her favorite things in the world. 'I packed in a whirlwind. I'm lucky to have underwear.'

His eyes flashed purified sex. 'That's the last thing you needed to bring.'

Kristin blushed and stabbed her fork into a black olive. 'I brought a few pages with me. Maybe I'll read to you this time.'

She looked up in astonishment. 'Something you've written?'

Cam nodded with a sly grin. A hint of pride crept at the corners of his edible mouth. 'It's sort of a book, sort of a journal. I haven't really decided yet.'

'What do you call this work in progress?'

'*Stud Diaries*.' He threw the title down like the gauntlet that it was, his eyes gleaming like blue diamonds bathed in starlight.

'I'm intrigued,' Kristin said. And indeed she was.

The rest of the day passed in a blur. He took the wheel of the rental car and showed off his twenty-one-mile-long strip of a hometown. The busy Pacific Coast Highway (PCH to natives) ran straight through it. Most of Malibu hugged the Pacific coastline, but the city also extended a few miles up into the Santa Monica Mountains.

Cam drove her to the Point Dume State Preserve and led her to the top of the coastal bluff where they could look out and see Catalina Island. After that, he zipped over to the shopping paradise Malibu Lumber Yard. While Kristin browsed the Tory Burch boutique, he held her purse like a doddering old husband.

As dusk approached, Cam insisted that she experience her first Malibu sunset. 'Most of the city faces south, not west, so we can't go to just any seaside joint.'

They hit Sunset Restaurant and settled into a white leather banquette just in time for nature's spectacular light show. Cam ordered a carafe of wine and a plate of cheeses as Kristin embraced the elegant yet beach casual atmosphere.

She gazed through the giant picture window. The sky was cloudless. The sun was a glowing ball of phosphorescent postcard-perfect colors. And the dark blue carpet of the ocean was dotted with foamy white peaks of cresting waves.

'It's so beautiful,' Kristin murmured. But the sentiment failed to do the remarkable scene justice, and she felt foolish for uttering it. The woman who made big money with words was using the language of pedestrians.

This focused her mind on Cam's words. The promise of hearing *Stud Diaries* had hovered in her consciousness ever since lunch. In fact, she could not stop thinking about it.

Kristin drank some wine, and settled back against the cushion. 'Okay, I'm ready.'

The half-stricken look on Cam's face told her that he knew what she was ready for. He pulled the folded pages from the back pocket of his jeans and smoothed them out on the surface of the table. For the first time since Kristin had known him, he actually appeared nervous.

She understood his reluctance – a novice writer reading his work to an established writer, and a step up from that, a bestselling writer. As author games go, this was high-stakes poker.

Cam gulped the wine for the liquid courage he needed it to be, cast down his eyes, and began to read . . .

Confessions from the Man Who's Satisfying Your Wife

By Cam Lawford

Sex Education

Most tourists don't realize that prostitution is a crime in Las Vegas. The legal brothels – like Sheri's Ranch resort and spa, which is forty-five minutes away in Pahrump, Nevada – are located outside the city limits.

For high-end escorts like me, this confusion makes booking dates easier. It creates a bolder and more reliable clientele. Once that plane from wherever-the-hell sets down at McCarran International Airport, they take the idea of Sin City to heart.

Sunday is the best working day to meet new clients. Usually, it's their last night on the Strip, and they don't want to leave without doing something really crazy. Everybody wants a 'What happens in Vegas, stays in Vegas' story to tell . . . or not tell.

My typical customers are married women, thirty to fifty. But there are exceptions – like the nineteen-year-old Disney Channel star toplining one of the network's most popular sitcoms. Her mother is the overbearing stage manager type. Think Dina Lohan. Now exponentialize the crazy. She's determined to keep her meal ticket daughter's squeaky-clean image intact. And this nutcase figures that hiring me zeroes out the chance of some loser snapping naughty cell phone pics of Little Miss Disney Princess and selling them to TMZ.

It was a bizarre setup. Dina Wannabe made all the arrangements. This woman scheduled the booking, reserved the suite, procured the drugs and alcohol, and tried to set the tone for the date.

'Lauren is stressed and needs to let loose,' she told me. 'Snort coke with her, get her drunk, and give her some wild sex.'

My theory is that Dina Wannabe was projecting the freaky things she wanted onto her daughter, because nothing I did with Lauren (not her real name, by the way) represented anything close to that. The girl was just happy to hang out and get away from her mother.

We ordered cheeseburgers, fries, and sundaes from room service. Lauren wanted to see an adult movie for the first time, so I ordered *Batman XXX: A Porn Parody* on pay-per-view. It kept us laughing for a half hour or so. She called the sex scenes 'retarded.'

Finally, we turned it off and snuggled up to watch *Valentine's Day*. After that ended, we snacked on gummi bears while she told me all about the professional hockey player who was tweeting her. His name was Cory, he was twenty-three, he played for the New York Rangers, and she already knew that she wanted to marry him. Our time was up. So I kissed this sweet girl on the forehead and sent her back to the mother/manager who will eventually ruin her life.

Do I sound like the kind of menace to society that should be targeted, arrested, and locked up? Because the next day I was just another case taxing the overwhelmed Clark County justice system.

THE STRIP

It started with a call generated from my Internet ad on Eros. Most of my business is referral. But I keep some online marketing in play for the leaner months. December is always slow, for example. The potential client on the phone was a man looking to book a date with his wife.

I wasn't a big fan of that scene. For starters, the crazy-husband-with-a-gun incident in Summerlin still haunted me. I begged off. Then the guy offered to pay double my rate. He said his wife had seen my photograph and only wanted me. They were coming in from Dallas for a health insurance convention and staying at Caesars Palace. I did a fast Google search while he talked, and the information verified. I said yes to a one-hour appointment.

I met them in their suite and sensed something amiss right away. Mike was forty, looked forty-five, and wore most of the extra twenty pounds he carried around his middle. Patti was under thirty, possessed the lean body of a runner, and probably still got carded whenever she ordered a drink. They didn't give off a married couple vibe. And there was a staged quality to the sex toys on display.

The room phone rang.

Mike slipped into the bathroom to answer it.

I tried to make small talk about Dallas, and Patti's vague answers left me wondering if they really lived there.

Mike rushed back in to announce, 'She wants to see you naked.'

This seemed normal. If I were a woman married to Mike, I'd want to see me naked, too.

'It's a thousand for full services, right?' Mike asked.

'Full services alludes to prostitution, and that's illegal,' I said. And then I took off my shirt. 'I'm just here to entertain.'

'Show me everything,' Patti said.

I locked eyes with her as I slipped off my jeans. Usually, I can feed off a woman's desire for me. I wasn't feeling it with Patti, though. Her mind was somewhere else. My fingers were on the band of my underwear when it dawned on me what this might be. But I realized too late.

A plainclothes police officer burst inside the room. 'You're under arrest for soliciting. We're Las Vegas Metro. Get dressed, stud.' He flashed a badge.

I closed my eyes and cursed myself for not following my initial instinct, which had been to turn down this date in the first place. I zapped an accusing look at Mike and Patti. 'This is entrapment.'

The third cop waited for me to get my jeans and shirt back on before clinking on the handcuffs. 'You say entrapment. We say prostitution. Hope you've been nailing a good lawyer.'

I never imagined that this could happen. With so many murders and drug deals, not to mention all the underage girls being pimped out against their will in this sleazy, sex-crazy town, I just assumed that the upscale escort trade would be the last item on a police team's punch list.

'Let's go.' The officer who made the arrest took firm hold of my arm.

'You must feel like Eliot Ness right now,' I cracked. 'Way to serve the community.'

'Shut the fuck up, smartass.' He pushed me into the adjoining suite and shoved me inside a bathroom full of handcuffed women. I could barely squeeze in. There were eleven of us stuffed in the small space.

'Can you believe this bullshit?' a gorgeous blonde in full

nightclub party gear griped. 'My stolen car gets no attention, but this is the sting of the century!'

'Hey, Cam.'

I shifted to my left and saw Kara Kent standing two girls back. 'They got you, too?' I turned to face the door. 'Well, law enforcement has done its job, ladies. The Strip is safe tonight.'

There was a delicate chorus of laughter.

I'd met Kara at Tao when I stepped in one night to save her from an aggressive college punk who was haggling over her rate. The recession had younger guys seeking out the high-end girls. These dudes traveled to Vegas and didn't want to blow money on expensive drinks for some chick who might turn them down. But with youth came stupidity, arrogance, and general ass-clown behavior.

Kara and I became fast buddies. Sometimes we met for breakfast or coffee to swap client stories. No matter how good mine were, she could always top them. The list of men's sexual hang-ups went on and on. Once a week we did a Costco run together to buy condoms in bulk. It was always funny to see the looks we got as we pushed our carts side by side.

Kara had followed a boyfriend to Vegas. He lost his job at one of the big casinos and moved back home to Florida to live with his parents. She stayed, found work as a stripper at one of the better clubs, and then started escorting on the advice of her yoga instructor.

She was very pretty in a girl-next-door kind of way and reminded me of a young Sandra Bullock. Kara wore minimal makeup and dressed in regular clothes. No one would ever pin her for being a call girl. She looked like a down-to-earth coed who worked part time at the Gap. And men went ape shit for her. Kara was busier than most of the girls who dolled themselves up like walking porn fantasies.

I ended up in jail with three rowdy drunken tourists, a shoplifting black drag queen, and maybe half a dozen random guys in for assault or petty robbery. I stayed there for twelve hours.

I had put in my one phone call to a regular client, a high-powered single attorney who booked me for a standing date at the Aria twice a month.

She answered her cell on the second ring. 'What the fuck, Cam? The way this works is *I* get in touch with *you*.'

'You said to call if I ever got in a legal situation,' I reminded her.

'You got busted.'

My silence was confirmation.

She sighed. 'I'll send an associate.' And then the line went dead.

The lawyer who showed up in court was Will Blaylock – baby-faced, cocky, and smoothly competent. I asked him to handle Kara's case as well and to bill me for both. He worked identical deals with the prosecutor.

We had each been charged with two counts of solicitation on account of the two officers. Trial could be avoided and all charges dismissed if we performed twenty hours of community service and completed an online sex education course. We separately agreed and were both released on our own recognizance.

Kara and I hopped in a cab together feeling dirty, exhausted, pissed off at the system, and hungry as hell. I told the driver to stop at the closest restaurant. A few minutes later, we were crawling into a booth at Blueberry Hill. An ancient waitress took our order for coffee, pancakes, and bacon.

I looked at Kara.

She looked at me.

'Well, it's official,' I said. 'I'm a whore.'

CHAPTER TWENTY-NINE

Kristin was speechless.

Cam's writing was not just good. It was *great*. And for a moment, she was so pulled into his world, so captivated by the mood he created, that she wondered if he might be better at the storytelling thing than she was.

He stared at her, his eyes conveying a gravity usually reserved for 3:00 A.M. meetings in the White House Situation Room. It was a million miles from let's-have-sex-again. And the message was unmistakable. Cam Lawford wanted to be a writer – a serious writer, just like her.

Kristin's tongue snaked over a top lip that needed a fresh coat of Dior's Pink Lust. But this was no time to helicopter to the ladies' room. 'It's good, Cam. It's better than good. It's sad and funny and shocking and titillating and everything else that keeps the pages turning. You have a voice – tough in some spots, sensitive in others. But it's real . . . and highly commercial. I wanted more. You knocked me out.'

Cam took a deep breath, banged back the wine, and made half the cheese plate disappear. The smile that came next would have killed her marriage were it not already sitting on the conveyor belt at the relationship cremat-orium. 'Shit.'

Kristin grinned. The newbie already had writer's block. 'You'll have to do a little better than that for your segment on *The View*.' She imagined Cam would be author catnip for the television bookers. The man was heavy-duty visual dynamite. In fact, it hardly seemed fair that he should look like this *and* write like this. Somewhere in the world an ugly man with no talent was cursing God for being so stingy and cruel.

Without asking permission, she reached across the table and took possession of the pages.

Cam shifted in his seat, as if the closer inspection might somehow put the rave review in turnaround.

Kristin scanned the sample, deciding that *Stud Diaries* read even better than it recited. Plus, the formatting was solid, the spelling and mechanics spot-on. She knew of superstar names at the top of the publishing tree that turned in half-literate disasters and expected their over-worked editors to do the rest. So nobody could say that Cam Lawford was not ready for his literary close-up.

'I'd like to show these pages to my publisher, Toni Valentine.' The idea landed in her head and on the table microseconds apart.

The Lawford baby blues gleamed. Granted, the business of books was not Cam's game. But the replacement math of his life experience played out all over his drop-dead-handsome face. He was replacing media mogul Toni Valentine with Miami Dolphins owner Stephen Ross. And it still added up to one big fucking deal.

Kristin reached for her BlackBerry. 'Toni has a house in the Colony. If she's here this weekend, we'll fax her the pages and try to meet for brunch tomorrow.' Pressing

Toni's mobile contact, she watched Cam empty the wine carafe.

'Where's my book?' Toni asked immediately. The woman did not deal in hellos.

'You'll have it soon,' Kristin promised.

'That's what you said a month ago.'

'We must have different operating definitions of soon.'

'Just get it in. If you don't deliver in time, I don't have anything for the summer slot that can come close to generating your numbers. Jobs are at stake. Not yours or mine. But there are others at New Woman Press who like this crazy thing called employment.'

'I'm really close, Toni. Don't worry. I won't let you down.' She paused a beat. 'Are you in Malibu this weekend?'

'For a spell. I'm leaving for London on Sunday. Why?'

Kristin glanced at Cam. The wine was gone. Ditto the nuclear-level confidence. He looked like an actor waiting in the holding area of a casting call with fifty Johnny Depps. But Cam even made insecurity sexy.

'I'm here with a friend. We're at the Malibu Beach Inn. There's something I want you to read, Toni. It's only eight pages. And if you like it, there's someone I want you to meet. Are you free for brunch tomorrow?'

'Possibly,' Toni said. It was cool water, not cold water.

'Great. I'll fax the pages to your house.'

'I'm on my way to meet a group at Nobu. I'll take a look later tonight or in the morning. Let's say Geoffrey's at eleven. I have a standing reservation.'

Kristin was more encouraged. 'We'll see you there.'

'Only if the fax interests me. If I don't show up, you

can't go wrong with the shiitake omelette. It's heaven on a plate.' *Click*.

Kristin explained Toni's cliffhanger protocol.

Cam looked a little dazed, a lot confused. 'You don't fuck around.'

'Neither does Toni Valentine. If she gets on board, it'll be a life changer.' As Kristin gave voice to this, she wrapped her mind around it, too.

That phone call could have been step one in the making of Cam Lawford, Celebrity. He would become public property. Everybody would step right up to claim a piece of the sex god. Kristin could very well lose him. And suddenly, it occurred to her that – subconsciously at least – perhaps she wanted to. Maybe this was her way of letting go of the fantasy.

'I don't want the entire weekend to be about my book,' Cam said. 'We came to Malibu for you.'

Kristin was stunned. It seemed impossible that a twenty-four-year-old who looked like this could not only say those words but also mean them – in this time, in this culture, at a point when narcissism seemed more generational epidemic than individual disorder.

'You're sweet.' Here she was again with the language of the hopelessly ordinary. First the sunset was *beautiful*. Now Cam was *sweet*. Still, it was economical and fit the moment. Why compose a sonnet if she was footing the bill for the bed, the food, the drink, and the boy?

'Labradors are sweet.'

Kristin laughed. Apparently, he did expect a sonnet.

'Seriously, though, I want to thank you. Reaching out to your publisher on my behalf was very generous.'

'You have talent, Cam. It was an easy thing to do.' She sighed knowingly. 'The hard part is going to be the hours between now and eleven o'clock tomorrow. I'm sorry about the whole will-she-or-won't-she bit. But that's classic Toni.'

Cam shrugged in a way that told her he was trying hard to get back into cool demeanor mode. 'Terra makes an amazing martini with organic vodka and bleu cheese olives. We could have dinner, get drunk, and go back to the hotel and make love all night.'

Kristin gave him a wicked smile. Cam the author was good. But Cam the stud was better.

He started looking sick at 11:10 A.M.

'It's still early,' Kristin assured him. 'This is Saturday. And this is Malibu. *Casual* is the law. Isn't that what you told me?' She convinced herself that the lobbying for calm was exclusively for Cam's benefit.

At the table next to them, Goldie Hawn screamed with laughter. Whatever the joke was, her brunch companion – Kurt Russell – thought it was funny, too.

Cam cut a humorless glance to the almost ageless star couple as he massaged his temples. 'How many martinis did I have last night?'

'Four,' Kristin answered.

'And how many times did we fuck?'

'Five.'

His mood brightened – a little. 'Really?'

'Yes, but the fifth time wasn't your best work. In fact, if it had to stand on its own, I'd want a refund.'

Jennifer Aniston strode through the patio entrance.

Cam appeared to be the only patron at Geoffrey's Malibu

who was disappointed – if not outright offended – by the sun-kissed beauty's arrival.

The classic eatery was built high above Pacific Coast Highway and nestled within gorgeous flora, every table carefully arranged to provide a spectacular view of the ocean.

Kristin sat there, sipped her mimosa, listened to the sound of the waves crashing on the shore, and prayed to God in heaven that Toni Valentine would show up.

'It's eleven fifteen,' Cam said. He looked worried. He sounded worried. He stopped the waiter to ask for a gin and tonic.

Kristin was not quite ready to round up pallbearers. But she was officially concerned, though it seemed criminal to be fretting about anything at all in such breathtaking surroundings. She gazed out at the endless blue sea and rolled around the idea of one day moving to Malibu.

It was interesting to observe the scene makers and scene seekers populating Geoffrey's waterfront patio. Though Cam was too busy pouting behind his John Varvatos aviators to notice, he was generating significant attention. The nobody who looked like he invented masculine sex appeal had Rita Wilson ignoring her lobster Cobb salad – and Tom Hanks. Her husband might have two Oscars, but he did not have Cam Lawford's face and body.

'She's here,' Kristin said.

Cam the damned metamorphosed into Cam the blessed. He stood up like a skyscraper growing in time-lapse photography. Every woman, every gay man, and even most of the straight ones seemed to take a deep breath. The Diesel jeans hugged the ass that the first Mrs. Pitt could not stop staring at. The distressed cotton fabric of the fitted Green Lantern tee gripped his upper arms like it wanted to *be* his upper arms, and if it had a change of heart, Goldie looked ready to push Kurt off a cliff and take the job.

Toni Valentine witnessed the floor show as she approached the table like twenty minutes late was military-mission punctual. 'Kristin, you sneaky little bitch. I pay people obscene amounts of money to find me the next *It* thing, and you show up out of nowhere with this delicious piece of . . . *material.*'

All three of them laughed.

Kristin embraced Toni and introduced Cam.

'I've already visualized your book cover,' Toni told him. 'How do you feel about being naked with a football under your arm?'

'Like I should skip brunch and hit the gym.'

Toni smiled, took notice of Kristin's champagne morning glory, and signaled for the waiter to bring a second mimosa.

Cam gestured to make it a third. The need for the sad drinker's gin and tonic was ancient history.

Toni Valentine rocked bohemian glamour with her blinding white kurta, faded denim, and avalanche of silver and turquoise jewelry. The Wellesley girl from the Upper East Side of Manhattan had little-boy-short black hair, eyebrows a millimeter too thick, a crooked front tooth, and nostrils that flared just the tiniest bit too much. But the imperfections – and her refusal to correct them – only intensified her striking beauty.

At forty, she had divorced a rich adulterous husband, taken no settlement, and started New Woman Press with one hundred and twenty dollars, a free logo from a graphic designer friend, and a dream. Books segued into movies, the big screen into television, the boob tube into music and Web ventures. Soon Toni was high dealing in magazines, newspapers, and radio as well.

The Valentine apocrypha was legendary. A woman playing a man's game and not only doing it well but kicking his ass always set tongues wagging. The big boys could be such little girls at times. But the proven truth was this: Toni Valentine possessed a brilliant mind and style to burn. She was tough, creative, analytical, inquisitive, vengeful, unpredictable. And right now at Geoffrey's, she was commanding more attention than the Pacific Ocean.

Toni reached into the vintage Hermés Kelly bag that was older than she was, snatched out the crumpled fax that had lured her, and crashed it onto the table like a hand grenade. Coal-dark eyes flashing, she smiled like a mad media bomber. Explosions of sex and scandal made her heart beat faster. And the impression lingered that she wanted to pull the pin and make *Stud Diaries* go *boom*!

'There better be more, and it better be just as good. I need a book, not a pamphlet.'

Cam's confident grin shimmered in the sunlight. His belief in himself put the table immediately at ease. It was scrumptious to watch. The NFL dreams had died with the knee injury, but new ones were dancing in the azure emeralds behind the designer shades. Surrounding him on the power patio were major players who could easily buy and sell him over Geoffrey's famous shiitake omelette. But talent – and knowing you had it – was a great leveler. Cam did not need to have stood next to the movie star's son as an angel in the nativity play to get here. His entrance ticket was all on the page.

'I thought of a subtitle on the way over,' Toni announced dramatically. '*Confessions from the Man Who's Satisfying Your Wife.*' She threw it down on the table and watched it pop like a firecracker.

Kristin experienced a chill. It was provocative. She could even hear the cable babblers expressing faux outrage as they greedily recounted the salacious details over multiple news cycles. The book was already a bestseller. The only thing left to do was print it and ship it.

'Not all my clients are married,' Cam pointed out.

Toni dismissed this minor detail with an airy wave of her hand. 'It doesn't matter. Most of them are.' Her eyes zeroed in on him. 'I can see *Stud Diaries*. I can also see another book just like it – more stories from the escort trade that didn't make the first. So save some hot ones. Then I see novels. Jonathan Franzen rules the dude lit world, but women don't hire a sitter to camp out at his book signings. They will for yours. I see a parallel career as a talking head, too. You could be *the* authority on women and sex and what husbands should do to keep their wives from raiding the emergency fund for one afternoon of pleasure.'

Toni's words sprayed into the air like machine gun fire. But nobody was ducking. They were listening. *Hard*.

'Of course, I see a movie,' she went on. 'Richard Gere made them drool in *American Gigolo* over thirty years ago. That's before Christ in Hollywood time. And this is just me talking out loud. I haven't given this much thought. But I have a rough-cut vision in my head for how I want to position you.'

Kristin watched Cam absorb the Toni Valentine verbal assault. She could practically hear the *ram bam* of his strong young heart against his rib cage. He looked to her as if seeking some clue about what to say.

'I guess I need to find an agent.' His delivery was half declaration, half question.

Toni laughed, exchanging glances with Kristin. 'That'll be the easy part. The main thing is to finish my book.'

Underneath the table, Kristin's hand found Cam's knee and squeezed meaningfully. He did not know this, but Toni Valentine only used the personal pronoun for discussing a writer's work if she was in all the way and ready to move heaven and kick earth to make it a success.

Cam slid a silver-colored jump drive across the table. 'Here's the rest.'

Toni gestured extravagantly to Cam, as if introducing a prizefighter that she managed.

Kristin turned slowly toward him, stunned by this evidence of assiduous attention to his writing.

The waiter loitered to explain the menu and take their orders. It was the shiitake omelette for Kristin, the challah French toast for Cam, and the crab cake Benedict for Toni.

While they waited for the food, Toni spun tales of Geoffrey's previous incarnation as Holiday House, a small resort/hotel/bar that pulled in classic stars of a bygone era – Frank Sinatra, Lana Turner, Ava Gardner. The gossip was that JFK had started his affair with Marilyn Monroe in this very spot.

'Are you a sex addict?' Toni asked Cam. The question hit like sniper fire. Nobody saw it coming – not the budding literary wunderkind, not Kristin, and certainly not Goldie, who halted the famous giggle to eavesdrop on the answer.

Cam drank deep on the mimosa. 'Every man is at some point. The urge to be with as many females as possible is evolutionary. I don't like the term *addict* as it relates to this, though.'

Toni's gaze was locked and loaded. 'Why not?'

'Because sexual cravings are innate.'

'So are hunger cravings,' Toni argued. 'Are you saying the binge eater can't be called a food addict?'

'Sex is more specific,' Cam countered. 'It represents a curve of normal behavior. There's a beginning, a peak, a plateau, a decline.'

Kristin was fascinated. She followed the points back and forth, like she would a ball in a good tennis match. Toni was Federer, hitting strong, whiz-bang shots, and Cam was Nadal, thwacking back with equal power.

Toni's smile was a flashbulb. 'You give good debate. I like it.' Her discovery that he could swim in midlevel intellectual waters without drowning brought out a dreamy sigh. 'You may be right. I hate the sex addict label, too. It's pseudoredemptive bullshit. I mean, let's face it. Tiger Woods never got caught with a hare-lipped carnival worker.'

Cam's laugh was contagious.

Toni's grin was suddenly shrewd and assessing. 'Okay, I have to ask. How do the two of you know each other?'

CHAPTER THIRTY

'Honey, everybody knows that diamond is the hardest mineral in the universe,' John Phillip gushed. 'Well, let me just say that I know from firsthand experience that Black Diamond is the hardest *man* in the universe.' One beat. 'But only because the clumsy bitch fell on me during rehearsals.'

'No!' David Dean screamed, his sweet face a masterpiece of shock, delight, and eagerness to hear more as he looked to Billie for confirmation of the news.

'Yes, I put him in *Rebirth*,' she admitted with a sigh, smiling at her young friend. 'Only for you. And one of the conditions might've been that he come see you after his first show tonight. You know, just to say hi.' Her voice fell to a hush. 'Don't tell Jagger.'

David clapped in delight. 'Oh, we've already agreed that Black Diamond is my one free-pass fling. Jagger's is Kobe Bryant.'

'Mine is Justin Timberlake,' John Phillip put in.

Billie gave him a look. 'You're single.'

'I know, darling,' John Phillip trilled. 'But when I do meet Mr. Right, I want this bit of business about being free to sleep with JT already worked out.'

'He's a very efficient queer!' Trevor Dunne piped in.

Billie let out a throaty cackle. She stood there on the edge of the bed, at the edge of the group, sadness swirling inside her. Oh, God, would she ever miss these crazy, delightful, loyal boys.

Three knocks rapped the front door of the London suite. Billie slipped quietly away to open it.

Kristin stood on the other side, tiny in stature but in no other way. She walked forward quickly and held out a white padded envelope bleeding a pink and orange KRISTIN FOX, INC. logo. 'Plenty of cash, a check card, all the banking info, and a new iPhone.'

Billie held the package in her hands. It felt like the escape from hell that it was. 'I need one more favor.'

Kristin looked deadly serious. 'Name it.'

A surge of adrenaline raced through Billie's bloodstream as she floored the borrowed Bentley down Las Vegas Boulevard. The glorious sense of freedom was all-consuming. She felt like a wilted flower opening up to the healing properties of the morning sun. She dismissed the notion of keeping her appointment with Jennifer Payne and merged onto I-515 South, taking the Eastern Avenue exit and pulling into Pioneer Loan and Jewelry, the city's oldest pawn shop.

The money to be made here hardly mattered. After all, Kristin had just set her up in cash-flow heaven. This transaction would be about the symbolism. And when it came down to the business of ending relationships – especially bad ones, more especially abusive ones – symbolism mattered.

Billie strutted inside the place where desperate sales were

made. She slipped off her wedding ring, crashed the impressive sparkler onto the counter, and announced her firm intention to get rid of it.

A cheap and bored-looking girl called out, 'Malcolm!'

The slick specialist who sauntered over reeked of cigarettes and drugstore cologne. He smoothed out a neatly groomed goatee as he put on a little play about sizing up the diamond's cut, clarity, carat-weight, and color. First came his smile, which revealed small sharp teeth and the smarm of a lifetime bit player. Then came the ripoff – his insulting offer that was a fraction of the ring's real value.

'You must think I'm on drugs,' Billie said. 'Or maybe you hope that I am.'

Malcolm narrowed his cold, seen-it-all-and-don't-give-a-shit eyes. 'Times are tough. You think you can do better someplace else? There's the door.' He handed back the ring.

'Ooh, tough negotiator,' Billie mocked. She knew this type. He was the stripe of worm that drank his way through college, the short man on campus who kissed the girls and made them cry – of boredom, the C student who faked out a general business degree and dreamed of the corner office but settled for the dingy closet with a time clock. This would almost be too easy.

'They trained you well at the used car lot,' Billie said. 'Or did you get your start going door-to-door with vacuum cleaners?'

Malcolm the hardliner became Malcolm the annoyed. 'That's my price. Take it or leave it.'

'Only a junkie needing a fix would take it.'

'Like I said, there's the door.'

The ring meant nothing to her. A decent salesman with a nice personality could've schmoozed it away from her for a song. But Billie suddenly harbored a strong dislike for this pawn shop manager with the receding hairline, the bitten-down fingernails, and the face so etched with arrogance that it looked like a natural rock formation. She didn't want the money-grubbing prick to win. At least not by too wide of a margin. 'I bet you already have a short list.'

'A short list of what?'

'People to call when you get a high-end piece of jewelry. Never mind. You won't have to bother.' The ring went back onto her finger. 'I came here to sell, not to get fucked.' She spun around and started for the door.

'Hold up,' Malcolm said. 'Maybe I should take another look.'

She tossed the ring into the stale air.

He caught it and went through the motions of a careful reinspection. Suddenly, the new price was five hundred dollars more.

'That's better. But now I just feel like I'm getting fucked after a cheap dinner.' She signaled for him to throw it back.

He bumped up the offer another five hundred.

Billie smirked. 'Now I just feel like you threw in some supermarket flowers to go along with the bad restaurant and terrible sex.'

Malcolm glowered. 'How much do you want?'

Billie named a figure three thousand dollars more than his original offer. It was low enough to make him close the deal and high enough to make him sick about doing so. She completed the necessary paperwork and walked out with a thick wad of cash.

Just outside the door, Billie noticed a cute guy in his early twenties angrily clutching a few pawn tickets as he lit up a cigarette and slumped against the brick wall.

He'd been in the store unloading an iPod, laptop, and Canon Sure Shot digital camera, making noises about losing his job and needing to pay rent. His eyes met hers. 'So how bad did you get screwed?'

'I didn't come for a fair deal. I came for instant gratification.' She stepped closer and gestured for a smoke.

He obliged and fired up another Kool Light.

Billie took a drag and surveyed him from head to toe – sharp haircut, clear skin and eyes, retro Atari tee, skinny Gap jeans, and Adidas trainers.

He put out a hand. 'I'm Jensen.'

'Billie.' She shook firmly.

He held up his pawn tickets. 'A couple hundred bucks. Can you believe it? At this rate, I'll get evicted *and* lose all my favorite shit.' He laughed bitterly. 'Vegas ain't my town.'

'Maybe your luck will change.'

'Oh, yeah, when? I followed my girlfriend here. She's a waitress at Prime at the Bellagio. The bitch dumped me for a bass player three months after we moved. I lost my job at the Palazzo, got brought in at the Luxor, and just lost that, too.' He dragged deep on the Kool Light. 'Last hired ... first fired. Story of my life.'

'What do you do?' she asked.

'Waiter, banquet service, bartending, anything really. I'm trying to save money to make my first short film.'

Billie instantly liked this guy and wanted to help him. He reminded her of Shayne Cutter, a screenwriter she met at Sunset Beach on Shelter Island a few years ago in the Hamptons. She seemed to have a knack for random encounters with budding young filmmakers.

Jensen's eyes widened with sudden recognition. 'Wait a minute. I thought you looked familiar. I've seen your billboard on the Strip.'

She managed a wry smile, amused by the fact that he had zero awareness of her previous incarnation as an indie rocker girl and tabloid train wreck.

Jensen ping-ponged a look to the Bentley, to the entrance of Pioneer, then back to Billie. 'Since when do headliners need to come here?'

She took a final drag of her cigarette, tossed it onto the ground, and killed it with her heel. 'Vegas ain't my town, either.' Palming a fat stack of hundred-dollar bills into Jensen's hand, Billie started for the car. 'Good luck, Spielberg.'

Jensen stared wide-eyed at the fistful of cash.

Billie peeled out of the parking lot and drove back toward the Strip. The opportunity to pay something forward felt good. Kristin had helped her. She'd helped Jensen. That's the way the world was supposed to turn.

At a traffic light, Billie slowly fingered the money left over. A perfect stranger was happy. Now it was time to treat herself to some happiness, too. Blissfully, she placed a call on the new iPhone that Randall and Carly knew nothing about.

He answered on the third ring. 'This is Cam.'

'It's me.'

'Courtney Love . . . I thought you'd never call.'

'I hate that bitch.'

His laugh, like every other part of him, was sexy as hell.

Billie made the Bentley go faster. 'I'm on my way there.'

'Good. Come straight up to the room. Thirty-six forty-one.'

'Believe it or not, I've got cash for you today.'

'That's too bad. I was hoping for keys to a boat this time.'

'So how was Malibu?' Billie asked.

'Interesting. I got a book deal.'

'A *what*?'

'You heard me.'

'You're writing a book.' Her tone suggested that he stood a better chance of performing brain surgery in the middle of a hurricane.

Cam laughed. 'Yes. Is that so unfeasible? Tori Spelling has written a couple of them. I figure I can do it once. It's called *Stud Diaries: Confessions from the Man Who's Satisfying Your Wife.*'

She marinated on the news for what seemed like an age.

'Are you still there?'

'I'm here.' And Billie was there – on the phone, at the hotel, in the lobby. She experienced the vague sense that someone was watching her. Suddenly, in her peripheral vision, she saw a sweep of processed blond hair.

Carly.

Billie spun quickly. Her heartbeat racing, she frantically scanned the area. And then she felt foolish. It was nothing more than a trick of her paranoid mind.

After leaving David's suite, Billie had hopped on and off the London's faux Tube station several times, not to mention taken every measure in the parking garage to make certain nobody was following her. She had driven a borrowed car and used a mobile phone activated in someone else's name. These maneuvers could elude a trained CIA operative.

'Don't worry,' Cam was saying. 'I'm changing the names to protect the guilty.'

'It's not that.'

'What is it then?'

As the question sailed over the cellular connection, Billie could visualize Cam's strong jaw, with its beautiful, masculine cleft, jutting out defensively. 'I'm just surprised.'

'That I can actually compose a sentence? I do have a degree from Penn State. There's more to me than my cock.'

'Oh, forgive me. Is *Stud Diaries* an existential study on the meaning of life?'

Cam sighed the sigh of the exasperated. 'Are you on the elevator yet? I haven't decided whether I'm going to kiss you or spank you when you walk in the room.'

'I'll be up soon,' Billie murmured, searching the lobby for Kristin. 'I didn't know you were a writer.'

'Apparently, I am. Kristin introduced me to her publisher, Toni Valentine. She loves my work.'

'I bet she does.' There was more topspin on the delivery than Billie intended.

'Okay, it's definitely going to be a spanking.'

She laughed at Cam and hung up, lingering in the people graffiti as she waited for her friend.

Finally, Billie saw Kristin approach in all of her simply red Bottega Veneta glory, moving fast, as she always did, a case study in pint-sized blond superiority, only with the brilliant career, the megabucks, the razor-sharp mind, and the selfless generosity that made such attitudes tolerable.

They met at the lip of the Wynn casino chaos.

Kristin smiled guiltily, holding up a Chanel bag. 'I should be writing. But instead I'm shopping.'

'I hear you're helping turn Julian into the next Xaviera Hollander.' The edge in Billie's tone said that this didn't exactly top her list of most desirable developments on earth.

'That's Toni Valentine's plan,' Kristin pointed out. 'I just made the introduction. But I've read some of his stuff. It's very good.'

'I don't want to be a pathetic chapter in Cam's version of *The Happy Hooker Goes to Vegas*. Do you?'

The gigolo's literary liaison gave her a quizzical look. 'He has a story to tell. As a writer, I respect that. And he wouldn't use a book to hurt us. The portraits are veiled anyway.'

With a stab of regret, Billie shook her head. 'Maybe on some level I want him to stay a secret. If he writes a book like this, the whole world will know about him.' She handed over the valet ticket to the Bentley. 'God, you must think I'm an ungrateful pig. You give me a quarter of a million dollars, and I'm shoveling shit about you playing career guru to Julian.'

Kristin's eyebrows arched, and her perfectly painted lips quivered slightly. 'If you need *anything*, Billie, anything at all . . .'

She squeezed Kristin's hand. 'You've already done so much for me. I'll pay back every—'

'No—'

'Yes,' Billie insisted. 'When I get my act together, I'm paying back every dollar.' She laughed a little. 'What if some other broken-down bitch needs to get the hell out of Dodge?'

'Then start a foundation,' Kristin said. 'Pay it back that way. I've released the money in every sense – no restrictions, no expectations. Use it however you need to. Go get the life you deserve.' Her eyes were misty as she spoke the last words.

Billie didn't do emotional good-byes, but tears were rolling down her perfectly sculpted cheeks.

Kristin embraced her tightly. 'I'm going to miss you.'

A wave of sorrow shook Billie to her core. The Vegas revelers orbiting all around ceased to exist. Right now, for her, it was all inside, where the feelings lived. She loved Kristin. How could a woman share so much? Nothing was off-limits, not her discovery of a good man, not her mountain of money. And all she wanted in return was the kind of happy ending for Billie that she wrote about in her steamy summer novels.

'*Thank you.*' Gratitude wasn't Billie's thing. But she uttered these words with every atom of sincerity within. And then she gulped in a lungful of air and raced across the casino floor to the resort elevators.

When Cam opened the door to room 3641, she fell into his arms. Her body, so strong and so powerful from the workouts and dancing, seemed to go weak in his presence. The breaths against his chest were coming in shuddering gasps.

Cam held her close and gently stroked her hair.

At first, the sound of his heartbeat soothed her. But then the tears rained down, and she couldn't even speak through the sobs. The horrible men of her past – March Donaldson, Domestic Violence, Randall Glass – had poured on the hurt in all the potent places, in her heart, in her soul, in her very essence. And the sadness was crashing at this particular moment, with this particular man.

Somehow Cam was a link to the deepest part of her. She couldn't explain it. But he seemed to know the pain she was feeling. The guy who got paid to fake emotion was the closest thing to a real man Billie had ever known. Through the tears, her eyes found his, and they held fast, making her wonder . . . again.

Finally, she spoke to him. 'Have you ever fallen for one of your clients?'

'Maybe.'

'That's not really an answer.'

'It's the only one you're going to get until I know you better.' His voice was soft, creamy, like a low ballad.

Billie could feel his fingers tracing the contours of her neck . . . her shoulders . . . her arms. And when his sweet warm breath bathed her face, she instantly knew the difference between this man and all the rest. Sex might be a business for him. But it was also a tender art. There would be no crass declarations of erotic war, no brutal negotiations, no greedy threats, no dirty promises, no cruel bedroom battles.

Cam Lawford was pure harmony.

His finger slipped under her chin and lifted it up to meet the gentle intimacy shining from his blue eyes. 'Billie ... Billie ... Billie,' he murmured, as if loving the sound of her name. 'You make this job so damn easy ...'

CHAPTER THIRTY-ONE

Jennifer's office telephone jangled.

It was past 7:00 P.M. Calls after regular business hours often signaled client trouble – a breakdown, a suicide attempt, a domestic disturbance, a sudden death.

But when she picked up, it was Patrick on the line. 'You're working late.'

'I'm just finishing up.'

'I tried your cell a few times.'

'Did you?' She reached for her mobile. 'I must have it on silent.' There were four missed calls – two from Patrick, one from Kurt, and one from Cam Lawford. The last name on the screen triggered desire and panic in equal measure.

'Mia Sara just left for her sleepover at Kylie's. It's just the two of us tonight,' Patrick said.

'Actually, you have the night to yourself. I meant to call earlier. I have a client situation.' They had barely spoken since the confrontation in front of Eva's house. And she felt no inclination to start talking now.

'You just said you were finishing up.'

'Here at the office, yes. But now I have to go offsite. It's . . . complicated.' It was the truth. It was a lie. And the words tripped off her lips with an ease that troubled her. Who was she becoming?

'Is there any risk of danger?' Patrick asked. There was genuine concern in his voice.

'No, nothing like that,' she assured him. 'I'll be fine.'

Over the course of her career, Jennifer had experienced some frightening incidents. Once, while in graduate school, she had foolishly attempted to stop a sullen teenage boy from leaving a session. For her effort, she got a black eye, a few cracked ribs, and a broken arm. Another time she had been cornered in the parking lot by a sexually abusive stepfather.

'We could go out for a late dinner,' Patrick suggested. 'I have a craving for Red Lobster.'

Jennifer sighed softly. 'Maybe another night. I don't know how late this will go.' She cringed as the storm of guilt rained down. Patrick's affinity for chain restaurants annoyed her. Red Lobster was the last place she wanted to be tonight. She knew the drill. He would order the Admiral's Feast, contribute little to the conversation, complain about being too full for dessert but ask for the warm apple crumble anyway, and fall asleep as soon as they got home.

Just imagining the evening killed her soul a little bit, especially when compared with the night she had planned with Cam. But this only intensified the guilt. At least Patrick had called. He was making an effort. And she was betraying him. Again. None of this swayed her, though. Jennifer wanted – she needed – to be with Cam tonight.

'I sent something to your Kindle,' Patrick said.

He occasionally surprised her with a download to her electronic reader, his way of attempting connection. Once she had turned the device on just after takeoff during a flight to Chicago to find the Kindle edition of her all-time favorite novel waiting – F. Scott Fitzgerald's *The Great Gatsby*. This was something. But she wanted more from Patrick.

'What is it?' she asked.

'Just take a look,' he said vaguely. 'And let me know what you think about it.' He sounded different – less morose, more confident, a touch mysterious. 'Will you do that?'

'Yes . . . later.'

All of a sudden, CAM LAWFORD CALLING lit up the screen as the mobile phone vibrated in her hand.

'I have to go. A client call is coming through on my other line.' Just then a stunning realization hit. Between the two men, Patrick actually intrigued her more at this moment. He had not elicited her interest in months. But he had it now. She hesitated. 'I'll read it. I promise.'

Jennifer hung up and switched phones. 'Hello?'

'Change of plans,' Cam said without preamble.

Her heart dipped in disappointment.

'I need to push back our time by an hour. Is that a problem?'

Her relief was instant. 'No, that's fine.'

'I'm a popular guy today.'

She could feel the stirrings of jealousy. Who had he been with? What had they done together? Part of Jennifer was desperate to know. The idea of being with a man who had just slept with another woman – or two or three – should disgust her. But instead she was emboldened by the challenge. She wanted to be more desirable than the others. She wanted to be so good that Cam would wonder whether or not he should accept payment.

'I'm in a suite at the Wynn.' His voice was thick. It sounded like he was stretching in bed. 'Room thirty-six forty-one. There's a key for you at the front desk.'

'Under *my* name?' Her voice went up an octave.

'Relax. I left it under Phyllis McGraw.' He laughed a little. 'Dr. Phil's the only shrink I know of. It was either that or Dr. Laura.'

Jennifer smiled.

'I want you to come in, enjoy a glass of wine, and strip for me. How does that sound?'

'Like a wonderful way to end the day,' she purred. Her anticipation intensified, and the hour-long delay seemed like an eternity.

'Good girl. That's what I want to hear. See you soon.' He hung up.

Jennifer attempted to busy herself with some overdue paperwork – client billings, insurance forms, office expenses. But her excitement to see Cam made it impossible to concentrate on the tedious work.

She gave up and was walking Nancy around the courtyard when her mobile rang again. Glancing down, she saw that it was Kurt. After a brief internal debate on whether or not to answer, she picked up. 'Hello?'

'Hi.' In the background was the noisy outdoor soundtrack of active children and stressed-out parents. 'Can you hear me?'

'Barely.'

'I'm at a baseball game. Imagine that. I just wanted to say hi.' There was a commotion. 'Shit. Dalton just spilled his Sprite inside a mother's purse. And she looks pretty pissed about it. I better go. Maybe I can smooth things over with free teeth whitening.'

'Good luck.' She signed off, laughing. Kurt never failed to make her do that. It was a blessed quality in a man. Once upon a time, Patrick had been able to make her laugh. But he had lost that ability. In fact, he could barely make her smile anymore. Still, as she thought of him, the Kindle mystery intrigued her.

On her drive toward the Strip, it occurred to Jennifer that this would be her second visit to the Wynn this month. The first occasion had been an emotional affair. This occasion would be a physical one. Oh, what an honorable wife she was.

She was approaching a billboard for Billie Shelton's *Rebirth*. It glittered with neon magic and reminded Jennifer that Billie had missed her 2:00 P.M. appointment. A gnawing instinct lingered that Billie was not merely holding back in therapy but hiding what was really happening in her life.

Jennifer pushed the disturbing thought out of mind as she pulled into the hotel's valet line. Waiting for service, she impulsively grabbed the Kindle from her handbag and fired up the device, anxious to see what Patrick had sent.

The new addition to her library was a PDF document. She activated the file, and the cover page instantly materialized.

NEON UNDERGROUND
By
Patrick Payne

Fascinated, Jennifer explored it further, determining that it was a 120-page screenplay. She was surprised and instantly proud of him. To talk about writing a film was one thing. To dabble at doing so was another. But to sit down and complete a script demonstrated an ambition, passion, and discipline that Jennifer had not given Patrick credit for. She began to read.

CREDITS OVER

EXT. LAS VEGAS STRIP — NIGHT

The neon-drenched boulevard and all its promise of flash, cash, and excess. Celine Dion's 'My Heart Will Go On' is playing. In front of the Bellagio, the famous fountain's dancing waters leap in time to the song's dramatic crescendo.

INT. BELLAGIO CASINO — NIGHT

With one spin left, a drunk, well-heeled gambler is pulled away from a Fireball Frenzy slot machine by a pair of expensive call girls promising a better party upstairs. The next hand on the game is smudged with dirt and grime. It belongs to a slender, early twenties handsome white male, dressed in an ill-fitting suit and shoes. He plays the remaining spin. The machine comes alive with jackpot

lights and sounds. An easy thousand-
dollar win.

INT. UNDERGROUND TUNNEL — NIGHT

A pretty but tired-looking white female
in her early twenties is bathing her
infant in a makeshift shower constructed
from an old office watercooler. She is
tender and loving to the baby but indifferent to his crying. The area around
them is dark and wet.

'Ma'am?'

Jennifer jolted and glanced up with a start.

A cute, college-aged parking valet was smiling down on
her with robotic politeness. 'Welcome to the Wynn Las
Vegas.'

She had been so utterly absorbed with Patrick's screenplay that she forgot where she was. It even escaped her
notice that the valet had already opened the door in anticipation of her stepping out of the car.

Jennifer considered driving away. Part of her wanted to
find a coffee shop, finish reading *Neon Underground*, and
then talk about it with Patrick over dinner at Red Lobster.
But another part of her wanted to go upstairs to Cam
Lawford for what she swore would be the last time. And
that part of her won.

She surrendered her vehicle to the valet and hurried inside.

A boorish Texan making a stink about his suite's
obstructed view monopolized the front desk.

Finally, she secured the envelope waiting for 'Phyllis McGraw' and rushed past the casino to the bank of resort elevators.

The ride up seemed to last forever. There were half a dozen stops to let guests on and off. Every delay loomed like a sign from God. It pushed her closer and closer to abandoning her unfaithful mission. But Jennifer managed to convince herself that she needed Cam Lawford, if only one more time. She thought of the glass of wine that was waiting. She thought of the total erotic abandonment that was waiting, too.

The elevator arrived at the thirty-sixth floor, and when the heavy door opened, nobody inside made a move to exit.

'Anybody for thirty-six?' The friendly prompt came from the older Jewish man standing next to the control panel.

'Oh, that's me.' Jennifer slipped out and walked toward room 3641 in a dizzying state of moral conflict.

For the first encounter with Cam, she had been nervous yet determined. For the second, she had been tentative yet passionate. And during their last meeting – at the CityCenter's techno glam Aria Hotel – she had gone after him with the ferocity of a she-wolf. But this time, as she approached the scene for marital crime number four, Jennifer felt something completely different . . . a deep and abiding loyalty to her husband. In fact, she could not get Patrick out of her mind.

It was not too late to turn back. She stood in front of the door, wracked with guilt and fraught with indecision. But the thought of Cam on the other side of it, and the memory of how he could make her body feel, propelled her forward.

She silently cursed herself for being so weak as she slid the key card into the slot, waited for the open-sesame of the flashing green lights, and stepped inside.

It was eerily quiet.

Jennifer advanced farther into the room. And then her shameful desires metamorphosed into unspeakable horror.

She started to scream. But the noise died in her throat as she zeroed in on the shocking sight. He was sprawled naked on the bed with a blank expression in his eyes, a serrated bullet hole in his forehead, and a pool of dark red blood staining the white sheets. The air in the room was dead.

And so was Cam Lawford.

CHAPTER THIRTY-TWO

Eva Lick hit the Coffee Bean on Flamingo Road wearing her trademark Juicy Couture tracksuit and a spotless pair of Puma sneakers. With Jee Vice Cat Eye sunglasses blacking out her heavily made-up baby blues, she was an arresting vision of voluptuous youth.

Patrick watched from a two-top table in the corner as two baristas slyly signaled each other, checking her out as she stood in the middle of what was now a sudden rush line.

The dude with a nose ring and a slim arm covered in tribal tattoos – the same slacker who had prepared a lackluster double espresso for Patrick – got the privilege of fulfilling Eva's request for a hazelnut latte. But this time he approached the task as if the key to his future depended on it.

Eva flashed a brilliant smile and contributed generously to the tip jar before turning around and searching the area for Patrick. When she finally spotted him, she stopped cold, did a double take, and silently exclaimed, 'Oh, my God!'

Patrick just grinned, sipping slow on his steaming espresso as he closed up his razor-thin MacBook Air.

Eva slid into the seat opposite him and ran a hand down his smooth cheek. 'What happened to Kris Kristofferson?'

Patrick dusted his freshly buzzed head. 'He's sitting in a dustpan at my barbershop.'

Eva gave the image turnaround a critical once-over, taking in the closely cropped haircut, clean-shaven face, Land's End gingham-print oxford, smooth Paper Denim jeans, and Cole Haan loafers. 'Are you announcing a run for Congress?'

Patrick laughed. 'Not exactly. I am running for the office of better husband and father, though. That's the reason for the change. This is how I used to look . . . before I lost my way.'

Eva did a second-round assessment as she sipped her latte. 'You definitely look younger.' She grinned sweetly. 'I'd vote for you.'

Patrick shifted uncomfortably. 'Eva, I don't quite know how to say this . . .'

'You're kicking me out of the critique group.'

Patrick shook his head vigorously. 'Are you crazy? Before you came along, we were just a couple of losers with Hollywood fantasies. Now I've got a complete screenplay, Robbie has a pitch meeting for *Mancation*, and Van is finally coming around to moving on from his class reunion idea. You're Viagra for this group.'

'*Really?* I'm an erection pill? That's gross.'

Patrick gave her an embarrassed smile. 'Sorry, bad metaphor.'

Eva studied him. 'This must have something to do with your wife.'

'Kind of,' Patrick admitted.

'Does she think that we're sleeping together?'

'It's crossed her mind. Mainly because I haven't been

sleeping with her. I've been absent in a lot of ways lately.'
He sighed. 'I don't want Jennifer to leave me. We have
some serious work to do to get things right between us,
and I have to show up for that.'

Eva looked at him strangely. 'Why are you telling me
all of this?'

'Because ... I need to pull back on our friendship. I
can't meet you for coffee like this anymore. And I can't
spend afternoons at your house getting stoned.'

'But I can stay in the critique group?'

'Yes, of course.'

'Good.' Eva breathed a sigh of relief. 'That's cool. I get
it. Save your marriage. Whatever.' She paused to drink her
latte. 'You know, I've been tinkering with a new adult
screenplay. Porn parody is going gangbusters right now.
What do you think of this?' She scribbled *DyNASTY* onto
a napkin. 'I could play Sammy Jo, Krystle Carrington's
trampy niece. I've been watching the first few seasons on
DVD. It's a classic. My script could be hilarious *and* sexy.
The costumes would be a riot, too. All those shoulder pads!'

Patrick was taken aback – and more than a bit wounded
– by how Eva had accepted his announcement with such
nonchalance. 'Do you understand what I just said?'

'Yes, Patrick.' Her tone dripped with patronization. 'Did
you expect me to burst into tears and flail around on the
floor of the Coffee Bean?'

Jesus, he felt like a fucking idiot right now. The humiliation was all over his face.

Eva reached out to touch his hand with her smaller,
softer, perfectly manicured one. 'I'm sorry. That was mean.
I'm going to miss you. Seriously, I am. But I knew that

this was a temporary phase for you. It was only a matter of time before you wised up and started paying attention to your wife again. Why should I be upset? I support that. I'm just glad you didn't do something dumb like make a pass at me, because I probably would've jumped into bed with you. You're smart. And you're a nice guy. I never sleep with men like you. I usually end up with the stupid jerks.'

Patrick felt a surge of protectiveness toward her. 'Why?'

Eva considered the simple question. 'I don't know. Because Ryan Reynolds is dating someone else?' She laughed at her own joke. 'I'm sure living in Vegas has something to do with it.'

'I wish you would rethink this porn ambition. You're so savvy about the movie industry. You're a good writer, too. Why not set your sights on something mainstream?'

Eva shrugged. 'I don't have a college degree. I look like this. Who's going to take me seriously? I'm sure I could make the rounds and get some meetings. But they'd be, like, "Hey, baby, I could make you the next Diablo Cody." I'd end up having sex for an empty promise and feeling like a prostitute with a bad business plan. I'd rather have sex for money and feel like a career woman.'

'You're too young to be so cynical.'

'I've been on my own since I was seventeen, Patrick. There's nothing I haven't been exposed to, but I've managed to keep my head on straight. And I know how ugly the adult industry is. But I'm shrewd. Most girls get talked into believing that the more they do the more popular they'll be. I'll never fall for that. I won't do anything on screen that I wouldn't want to do with a boyfriend I loved.'

She smiled at him. 'You just watch. I'm going to be the classiest porn star you've ever seen. And I'm going to have a screenplay credit, too.'

Patrick raised his espresso. 'To the next ... shit, I can't even name a famous porn star.'

Eva drank up in honor of the incomplete sentiment anyway. 'Most of them are train wrecks. I'm creating a brand new mold.'

'So when are you moving to Los Angeles?'

'I'll probably wait until they foreclose on my house. Until then, I'll just save up as much money as I can.'

He looked at her with real admiration and gratitude. 'Thank you, Eva.'

'For what?'

'For helping me break out of my funk. I owe a lot to you.'

Her eyes sparkled. 'You know, I just realized that you've never seen me perform. You should come watch me dance. Robbie's been to the show.'

Patrick held up his hands and shook his head. 'I'm sure you're fantastic. But I don't do strip clubs. I'm the guy who wants to cover the girls with a blanket and sign them up for computer classes.'

Eva laughed. 'We don't get many of those at the Crazy Horse.'

Patrick shrugged helplessly.

'Anyway, I'm talking about *Bite*, the show at the Stratosphere. It's more than just topless girls dancing around. There's a storyline, aerialists, great music. I could get tickets for you and Jennifer.' Eva grinned saucily. 'It'd be a sexy date night.'

Patrick smiled. 'I'll talk to her about it.'

She finished her latte and tossed a glance at the service counter as if considering a second one. 'Did I tell you that I lost my job at the Seven boutique?'

'No, what happened?'

'Business is off, and they wanted me to switch over to nights, but I make more money at the Crazy Horse, so ... that was that. My real estate license came through, though, so now I can work on that during the day.'

Patrick was stunned. 'You're going to sell houses?'

Eva nodded.

'You do realize that Las Vegas is the deepest crater in a very bad housing market.'

'Of course I do. You've seen the neighborhood I live in. But I still want a piece of the action. Or whatever's left of it.' There was a gleam of ambition in her eyes.

Patrick could not believe it. This girl was either completely delusional or one balls-to-the-wall entrepreneur. At such a brutal time in the market, there was not much in between when it came to those diving in. 'You're insane.'

Eva smiled. 'I've got a digital camera with a wide-angle lens, and my business cards should be ready in a few days. I'm all set.'

Patrick leaned forward and splayed both hands on the table. 'Vegas isn't just part of the overall housing recession, Eva. It's the *crash*. If you're making money in real estate in this town, then you're probably less of a Realtor and more of a con artist. Do you know what you're getting into?'

Suddenly, Eva stood up. 'Take a ride with me. I'll show you my first project area.'

Patrick still wondered if she was living in some kind of fantasy world. 'Fine.' He gathered up his things and followed Eva out to her Lexus. Sliding inside the luxurious SUV, he fingered the rich leather and polished wood-paneled interior.

Eva turned the engine over and peeled out of the parking lot, coasting in the direction of western Las Vegas, one of the hardest hit areas of the city's housing crisis.

Patrick relaxed and went along for the ride.

The twenty-four-hour party atmosphere along Las Vegas Boulevard could be misleading. People were still gambling, shopping, drinking, eating, dancing, and spending with shameless extravagance. But the real story was beyond the Strip's neon bubble.

Patrick had been in the trenches for the local political beat, getting the bleak stories firsthand. Home values were abysmal. Retail outlets were empty. Jobs were scarce. Food banks were struggling to meet demand. Even the city's oldest art museum had gone bust.

But at its core, Las Vegas was a gambler's town, and people were always willing to make big bets on the future of it. So why not Eva Lick? Perhaps this cockeyed optimist in Juicy Couture was on to something.

They were driving through a subdivision of suburban dream homes. It looked like a gated community designed exclusively for young, upwardly mobile families – immaculate landscaping, a homogenous sheen of strict design covenants, a clubhouse with a pool and sports activities. But the postcard-perfect environment was eerily uninhabited.

'I want to show you something,' Eva said, cruising down a deserted residential lane. 'Pick a house.'

Patrick gave her a curious glance.

'Any house. Just pick one. It doesn't matter.'

He shrugged, deciding to play along. 'Okay ... ahead on the right. The one with the terra-cotta shutters.'

Eva pulled into the brick-paved driveway and cut off the engine.

'Is this one of your listings?'

'No, it's a foreclosure.' Eva swung out and started toward the back of the house.

Patrick followed her.

'I looked at one of these last week,' Eva remarked, checking side doors and windows for entry possibilities. 'The owners left their dog behind. Poor little guy was scared to death and starving.'

Patrick's nod was all-knowing. 'The city's overrun with abandoned pets. It's a terrible problem.'

Eva tried the sunroom door. It was open. 'Voila.' She grinned in triumph.

He hesitated. 'Isn't this breaking and entering?'

'Actually, it's just entering.' She grinned and stepped inside.

Patrick stayed close behind her, shocked at the deplorable condition of the property. He had laid eyes on some elaborately trashed foreclosed homes, but this one took frustration-fueled destruction to a new level. Doorknobs, hinges, copper wiring, carpet, appliances – everything had been crudely gutted. Black mold was spreading along the walls and ceiling. Red paint was splattered throughout. There were green handprints everywhere, some belonging to adults, some belonging to children. And profane messages had been angrily smeared onto doors, walls, and counter surfaces.

FORECLOSE THIS!

THE SYSTEM SUCKS!

TRY TO SELL IT NOW, BITCH!

FUCK THE AMERICAN DREAM!

'The original owners did this,' Patrick said. 'People have a right to do whatever they want before the bank seizes a property.' He stood in the middle of the destruction, of what had once been a family home, taking it all in.

'What are you thinking about?' Eva asked quietly.

Patrick looked at her somberly, making the connection that the people who did this and the people who lived in the tunnels were not so far apart after all. 'I'm thinking that nobody imagined regular working people would ever fall through society's cracks this way.'

Something in the corner of the open-plan kitchen captured his attention. It was a pile of debris – remnants of Chinese takeout, Mountain Dew cans, stained bath towels, battered running shoes, and old mail.

Eva pointed at the mess. 'Looks like a squatter was here.'

Patrick grimaced. There was a sense of suburban apocalypse to what was happening all around, and standing in the middle of this hell pit, his dream of seeing *Neon Underground* get made into an important film became more powerful than ever. He looked at Eva. 'So what's your plan?'

She opened her mouth to speak, then suddenly went catatonic.

'You're in my house.'

Patrick spun around.

A man stood there with a shotgun. He had scraggly black hair, several days of beard growth, and wild, crazy eyes. He was dressed in dark jeans and a tattered Ed Hardy T-shirt. On his left ring finger was a simple gold wedding band. 'You shouldn't be here.'

Patrick noticed the family portrait in a large pewter frame propped up against the living room wall. A clean-cut handsome husband, his pretty wife, their three adorable children. The man in the photograph was the same man with the shotgun. He pointed the barrel squarely at Patrick's face.

Eva cried out in horror.

The man jolted briefly, then steadied his aim.

Patrick swallowed hard. On sheer human instinct, he threaded Eva's damp palm into his own and squeezed tight. 'Take it easy, man.'

'Are you from the *bank*?' The last word was pure rage.

'No, we're not from any bank,' Patrick said, amazed at the calmness of his own voice.

'So what? Are you looking for a *deal*? I lose everything, and you come sniffing around to buy my house for next to nothing?'

Patrick could not move, think, or breathe. Time seemed to stop. He just stood there clutching Eva's trembling hand, fearing the absolute worst. This could not be happening. This could not be real. But it was. Only two words came to his terrified mind, and they barely croaked out of his throat. 'Please don't.'

But the man's finger still groped for the trigger. 'Fuck you.'

Patrick closed his eyes. There was just enough time to pray that Jennifer knew how much he loved her, to hope that she would remarry a good man who could be a father to Mia Sara, to mourn every milestone he would never see his daughter reach – her first date, her senior prom, her college graduation, her brilliant career, her wedding, her baby.

A single blast exploded.

Slowly, it dawned on Patrick that he had felt nothing, that he was still alive. He opened his eyes. Eva was still alive, too.

'That was just a warning shot.' The man raised the rifle and started to laugh, softly at first, then louder, more convulsively.

Suddenly, Patrick realized that the man was sobbing. He began to inch toward him in a nonthreatening way. 'Everything's going to be okay, sir ... nobody got hurt here ... why don't you let me have the gun ...'

Taking possession of it was easy. The man had collapsed in total despair. Patrick gestured for Eva to call for help. And then he put his hand on the man's shoulder, as he had done so many times in the tunnels, one human being comforting another, listening to the cries of a once happy life in ruins.

CHAPTER THIRTY-THREE

This was the last time Billie would ever sing 'What's Love Got to Do with It.' She belted out every note like a diva possessed, scaling impossible-to-believe heights, riffing and running vocal acrobatics that brought spontaneous eruptions from the sold-out crowd.

By the end of the song, tears were streaming down Billie's face, and for the first time, the tears were *not* for March Donaldson. She was crying for the life that she would be leaving tonight – the show, the dancers, the musicians . . . the surge of mass love from an appreciative audience.

It was never a career she imagined for herself, but she was proud of her success in Vegas. Many talents had tried and failed here. But she'd done it. From the first show to this last one, Billie Fucking Shelton owned the Strip – lock, stock, and neon.

The thunderous ovation seemed to go on and on, intensified by her emotional waterworks. They loved her. And in this sad, surreal, full-of-regrets moment, Billie – for perhaps the first time in her career as a performer – loved them back.

She spotted Randall and Carly at one of the front tables

to the far left of the stage, and the instant she saw them, her rainbow moment turned ugly and dark.

Everyone in the Palladium Showroom was up on their feet, applauding enthusiastically, begging for more.

But Randall and Carly remained conspicuously seated.

Billie turned away, disturbed and confused by their presence. Having sat through the show innumerable times during workshops and rehearsals, Randall had stopped coming after opening night. And Carly typically flitted in before and after curtain to deliver green tea elixirs and schedule instructions. Whatever the reason for them being there was, after a few more songs, it would no longer matter.

Billie gave the crowd one more bow, wiped away her tears, and blew a kiss as the band began to play the opening strains of 'Chasing Pavements.'

The dancers were at once fluid and as precise as a military troupe, showcasing perfectly synchronized choreography.

Billie fell into step between John Phillip Harmon and Trevor Dunne, determined to give her final *Rebirth* audience everything and more. This show was for David Dean.

She got through the Adele number and segued directly into a fiery version of the Stevie Nicks synthesizer-driven floor stomper, 'Stand Back.'

Billie locked eyes with Randall, emphasizing the aggressive STOP hand gesture for his benefit, boldly displaying her naked wedding ring finger.

Did you know that I sold that meaningless rock to a pawn shop, you hideous bastard?

And did you also know that I used the money to

*hire a real man to make love to me, you thimble-dick
freak?*

Randall iced her down with an eerily cold stare. He
pantomimed his fingers into the shape of a gun, and silently
mouthed out a single word. 'Bang.'

The distraction rattled Billie's muscle memory, causing
her to jumble a half movement in the middle of an intri-
cate step.

This sent John Phillip into an awkward position, then
Black Diamond, though both recovered quickly and got
back into groove.

When the lead guitarist ripped into an extended solo
with his Gibson Firebird, Billie darted backstage for another
costume change. 'Nice save,' she said breathlessly to John
Phillip.

'Honey, as long as we don't fall flat on our ass, they
never notice.'

Billie took his hand and squeezed hard. 'I need to see
you after the show. Come to my dressing room.'

The bossy wardrobe assistant pulled Billie toward a
discreet changing area. 'Tick tock,' Lindsay Lee scolded.
'This is your gig. Nobody out there wants to see me wearing
this.'

Billie stepped out of the slinky Marc Bouwer gown and
squeezed into a custom-made sequined catsuit that left
nothing to the imagination.

Lindsay zipped it up.

Billie spun around.

Lindsay carefully pressed the garment's billowy decol-
letage to Billie's tit tape. 'There. Now the girls won't come
out to play.'

Billie grinned. 'Thanks, you haggard old bitch.'

Lindsay grinned back. 'My pleasure, you no-talent slut.'

Billie might actually miss the woman.

As the opening chords of the Eurythmics classic 'Here Comes the Rain Again' commenced, Lindsay popped Billie on her Spandex bottom. 'Don't keep them waiting. They already wish they'd gotten tickets to *Jersey Boys*.'

Billie laughed. And then she vaulted back onto the stage to make these people forget there ever was such a thing as Annie Lennox. She went through the remainder of her set list with passion and verve, turning out high-energy renditions of 'Love Is a Battlefield,' 'Da Ya Think I'm Sexy?' and 'Band of Gold.'

After wowing the crowd with Michael Jackson's relentless dance floor powerhouse, 'Workin' Day and Night,' Billie was practically running on pure adrenaline, exhausted from the emotional upheaval, the slow-burn lovemaking with Cam Lawford, and the intense song-and-dance effort.

There was one more costume change. She had a final turn at Snow Patrol's 'Run.' This would be her last song on the Strip. And she intended to make it memorable.

Picking up on Billie's inward distraction, Lindsay remained quiet as she assisted in peeling her out of the catsuit and slipping her into the exquisite Marchesa dress with the rich plum hue and all-over silk organza detail.

'You're on fire tonight,' Lindsay gushed, tending to some minor adjustments with the gown's glamorous ruffles. 'You're out there doing this like it's your last show on earth.'

Billie clasped Lindsay's leathery, square-cut-nailed hands. She spoke in a soft, earnest tone. 'Who knows? It might be.'

Lindsay smiled. 'Well, don't let the drunken crowd's applause fill your head with delusions. I still can't tell whether this is a high-end Vegas show or karaoke night at Barbie's Dream House.'

Billie started for the stage. 'Love you, bitch.'

'Right back at you.'

She sashayed out to an uproarious reception and stood in front of the million-dollar microphone covered in pavé diamonds, an over-the-top touch of glitz created especially for *Rebirth*.

The piano man began the haunting melody of 'Run.'

Billie felt uncommonly intimate and fully exposed as she began the ballad.

It became her most melting, vulnerable version of the song ever. She sustained the pitch, focused her vibrato, and soared effortlessly.

By the end, the audience was on their feet again.

'Good night, Las Vegas!' Billie shouted. She lingered for a moment. 'And good-bye!'

Backstage she exchanged quick embraces with the band, the dancers, and the crew, making a point to establish eye contact with John Phillip before slipping away to her dressing room.

Carly was already waiting there with a thermos of green tea.

Billie accepted it with an openly hostile attitude. She gave Carly an intense stare. 'Why do you do this for him?'

Carly's eyes narrowed. 'Do what?'

Billie drank deep on the tea. 'Run after me like a

demented handmaiden. Keep tabs on me like some stalker. Are you really that unskilled?'

'Where's your gratitude?'

Billie laughed at her. 'For you? Babycakes, I don't have any.'

'I'm talking about your gratitude for Randall,' Carly hissed. 'He *created* you.' She displayed the ring finger of her left hand. The wedding heirloom that Billie had pawned earlier in the day fit perfectly. A strange expression clouded Carly's face. 'If he'd given me this ring, I never would've taken it off. You don't deserve him.'

The shock of seeing the ring she'd pawned barely registered as Billie regarded Carly with sudden pity. 'You're right. I don't. And as much as I hate you, I don't think you deserve him either.'

Carly shook her head. 'I was nothing before I met Randall. Do you know what they used to call me in high school? Paper or Plastic. They said a bag would have to be put over my head in order for anybody to want me.'

Billie was silent. It seemed impossible that the pretty girl in front of her had endured such cruel bullying about her looks. She only knew of two procedures that Randall had performed on Carly – a breast enhancement and lip-plumping injections. Obviously, there'd been more.

'Do you know what that's like?' Carly asked. 'To be taunted and laughed at about how ugly you are?'

Billie began to feel very tired. Glumly, she drank more tea, wondering how long this impromptu live reading of *Memoirs of a Fucked-Up Childhood* would last.

'Paper or Plastic,' Carly went on. 'That's what they called me. They wrote it on my locker. They yelled it out in the hall, in the cafeteria, even in class. They brought paper and plastic bags to prom and passed them out to my date. He was the fattest boy in school. But he earned a big laugh because he handed me the paper one and said it would be easier to breathe through.' Carly's voice had taken on a lost, faraway quality.

Billie's groan was equal parts fatigue and frustration. 'Kids are mean. Your prom date was a jerk. High school was humiliating. It's supposed to be that way. But it was a long time ago.'

Carly stared back with an intensity that bordered on madness. 'You don't get it.'

Billie's eyelids began to feel heavy. She experienced a moment of dizziness. 'What's to get?' she murmured. 'Besides bored out of my mind.' She moved to sit down and dropped onto the ottoman, losing her grip on the thermos, which tumbled to the floor. For several long seconds, she stared at it. The energy to pick up the stainless steel cylinder just wasn't there. Where was John Phillip? She had to see him before . . .

Carly lunged forward and grabbed Billie's arms in a vise-like grip, shaking her angrily.

Billie was too weak to put up a fight. She just sat there motionless as Carly began a hysterical tirade mere inches from her face.

'You don't know how lucky you are. You showed up in the news, and Randall lost all interest in me. He said there were raw elements to you that I didn't have. So he turns you from a rock has-been left for dead into a beautiful star with her name in lights on the Strip. And how do you repay him? You pawn your wedding ring and whore around at the Wynn with some gigolo. You're a dirty, selfish, ungrateful bitch!' Carly drew back her hand and unleashed a powerful slap across Billie's face.

The blow was jarring. Her head reeled to one side. But everything seemed to be happening in a strange and detached slow motion. If pain had accompanied the strike, Billie couldn't feel it.

Now Carly was waving a padded white envelope in Billie's face.

She could barely keep her eyes open. The corporate logo looked vaguely familiar. Slowly, the realization dawned on her. It was the packet from Kristin – the cash, the check card, the iPhone, all the things she needed to break free. *How did Carly find it?*

Carly was smiling. 'Did you really think Randall would let you run away?'

Billie tried to speak. But no words could make it past her lips. They just died there, as if she were paralyzed. What was wrong? The room began to sway. She tried to focus her vision. Dual images began to take shape. There was one Carly, then a second Carly. No, it was Randall.

'Hard to believe she's still sitting up. That dosage would've put down a horse. Help me get her to the penthouse.'

Billie could hear Randall's reedy voice through the internal fog. No, please, no . . . she had been so close. Where was John Phillip? He could get a message to Kristin.

'What's wrong with her?'

Billie heard another voice. She tried to make out the third figure in the dressing room. It was John Phillip. Oh, thank God!

'She's been fasting,' Randall explained. 'And not in a smart way. She's dehydrated and exhausted.'

'Poor thing,' John Phillip said. 'She nearly performed herself to death tonight.'

Billie began to fade in and out of consciousness. Everybody sounded as if they were talking underwater. She put up a ferocious battle to stay alert, to speak out loud. Whatever they'd given her, she could fight it off. Back in her wild days, she'd defied all physical laws and tested medical limits with her high tolerance for drugs and alcohol. No fucking way was some spiked tea going to take her down.

Randall and Carly flanked her on each side, carefully assisting her toward the elevator.

Even in Billie's rapidly intensifying delirium, she could still sense John Phillip behind them.

'Take good care of our diva,' he said.

Billie started to scream inside her head.

John Phillip, please stop them! They drugged me! She's crazy! He's going to kill me! Call Kristin Fox! She'll know what to do! Oh, God! Why can't you hear me?

The elevator doors closed.

Billie exhausted herself trying to speak. But no matter how hard she tried, nothing came out. She could feel her stomach react to the fast rise upward.

And then everything turned to black.

Confessions from the Man
Who's Satisfying Your Wife

By Cam Lawford

A Good Life

This morning I had sex with the wife of my childhood comedy idol. I'll call her Mrs. S. It was a strange way to start the day.

Growing up, I was a huge fan of her husband's TV show. The series ended when I was thirteen, but it still plays on cable 24/7. In fact, I watched an episode the other night when I couldn't get to sleep.

He's in Vegas for a two-night engagement at the Caesars Palace Colosseum. I only recognized his wife because she's been all over the media promoting her new cookbook.

Mrs. S was kinky. She had a fantasy about doing it in her husband's new Aston Martin DBS Volante. And by new, I mean Mr. Funny Man drove it to Las Vegas straight from the dealership. He made his wife fly alone. That way he could establish a *connection* with his new baby in private.

When he performed stand-up concerts, his routine was to sleep until late afternoon, so she asked me to meet her in the parking garage of Caesars at 9:00 A.M. She brought a bucket of vanilla buttercream frosting and flung it across the backseat in huge globs before we got down to business.

It was messy and delicious and crazy and hot. In addition

to being a sex freak, Mrs. S was a yoga freak. This woman got into positions that I didn't know were physically possible. After we finished, we sat there and laughed at the condition of the superstar comedian's car. It was a total wreck. Frosting was smeared on the front windshield, the back windshield, and every place in between.

She hated his obsession with cars and played this stunt every time he bought a new vehicle. One of the parking attendants got a big tip to have it washed, detailed, and returned by 4:00 P.M. Then Mrs. S thanked me for helping her break in his latest toy, paid me, and left.

I zoomed to my apartment, showered, chugged down some Muscle Milk, and headed back to the Strip to check into my suite at the Wynn. I was seeing a client who needed total discretion, so I booked the room under my name. I like the Wynn because the mood is quiet, elegant, and sophisticated.

My second client of the day happened to be headlining at one of the big hotels. Massive billboards of her beautiful face and smoking hot body have been assaulting the Strip for months. It'd taken several dates to coax her from erotic massage (which I do well) to sex (which I do best).

She seemed timid, unsure of herself, almost sad. At first, I figured it was the Beyonce/Sasha Fierce alter ego dynamic – shy and reserved in private life, a firecracker on the stage. But her vulnerability went far beyond that.

When she broke down crying in my arms, I held her for a long time. I told her everything was going to be okay. And then I made love to her until she felt like the most important, protected, treasured, and desirable woman in the world. It was beautiful. For both of us, I think.

My last client of the day wasn't scheduled until the evening, so I decided to hang out by the pool. I set up outside the Terrace Pointe Café and ordered a blue cheese burger with crispy fries. I needed to eat. The only nourishment I'd consumed all day was half a bucket of frosting and a bottle of Muscle Milk.

I was just finishing my late lunch when a young woman approached me. She was a processed blonde, mid-twenties, fake tits, plumped lips, and pretty in an uptight executive-by-day/slut-by-night kind of way. I wondered if I had a sign on my back that said THIS COCK FOR HIRE, because she just marched right up and boldly asked me how much.

There was something kooky about her. She kept twisting her wedding ring like she wanted me to take notice of it. No psycho bells were going off in my head, but this chick definitely had a crazy girl quality. It was sort of a turn-on, though. Sex with neurotic women is usually damn good. I figured this one was just another unhappy wife. I could give her some satisfaction and then walk to the bank with a nice payday.

We settled on 6:00 P.M.

CHAPTER THIRTY-FOUR

'I don't have a drinking problem,' Julie Munso said archly, her body language talking defiance. 'I drink socially. That's all.'

'Problems with alcohol aren't limited to solitary drinking,' Jennifer pointed out. 'Were you alone when you called me last night?'

'No, I was at a wine bar with some girls from work.'

'Do you remember our conversation?'

Julie paused. 'Not every part. But I remember the broad strokes. I told you that I appreciated what we were doing in therapy . . . that your insight has been helpful. Something to that effect.'

Jennifer gave Julie a direct gaze. 'Actually, you told me that you loved me.'

Julie scoffed as if the sentiment were meaningless. 'I was a little tipsy. I love everyone when I drink. I probably told our waitress the same thing.'

'You also told me that I was more of a sister than a therapist. And you were tearful.'

Julie shrugged. 'I don't think I should be held accountable for every word that comes out of my mouth at happy hour.'

Jennifer nodded reasonably. 'Perhaps not.'

Julie's face tightened. 'Did Dale say something to you about my drinking?'

'We're not here to talk about what Dale discusses in his individual sessions. You know that.'

Julie slumped back against the sofa. 'I don't think this is working for me.'

Jennifer glanced at the clock. 'You felt quite differently about twelve hours ago. What changed?'

Julie did not answer.

In a previous session, Dale had relayed a revealing story about his wife. The incident happened after a dinner party with friends. Too much wine was consumed. As it so often does, the conversation turned to sex. Saucy banter went back and forth between the other couples, the impression clear that the marriages enjoyed a healthy and frisky sexual component.

Dale had expressed shame to Jennifer, not only for the envy he felt sitting there, but for the fraudulent way he played along, throwing out zingers that indicated his bedroom was a red zone of sensual heat instead of the sleep factory that it really was.

Julie was drunk and unusually affectionate on the ride home, lamenting the lackluster state of their sex life, professing her love, and promising to bring more erotic fun into their marriage. She attempted to perform fellatio while Dale drove. But in the middle of her effort, she vomited. They rode the rest of the way in tense silence. While Dale cleaned up the car, Julie stumbled inside and passed out with her clothes on. The next morning, she pretended as if nothing out of the ordinary had happened.

Jennifer surmised that this was a pattern with Julie – drinking too much followed by declarations of love. But with sobriety came a return to her hardened shell. The calcified girl who refused to apologize or accept complicity in a problem always showed back up to undo the work of the overly sentimental lush.

'This doesn't help me,' Julie was saying, apparently bashing therapy as a general concept. 'It's stupid. Talking everything to death doesn't do any good. It just makes things worse. And you charge what – one fifty an hour?' She checked her watch and seemed to be silently calculating how much money had evaporated so far.

'The examined life isn't for everyone,' Jennifer allowed. 'Some people never get comfortable with self-disclosure. Freud described talk therapy as an effort to convert hysterical misery into uncommon happiness.'

Julie let out a frustrated huff and stared at the floor.

Jennifer struggled to maintain focus. Her mind was teetering on tumult. It required determined concentration to sit here. Otherwise, every thought in her head would be consumed by the horrifying discovery of Cam Lawford's body and the fear of what might happen next.

She fought to stay in analysis mode. As a therapist, it was important for her to recognize the clients she could help and the clients she could not. Jennifer began to wonder if Julie and Dale Munso were in the latter category. But the answer to that question was the answer to most big questions in life – not a clear yes, not a clear no, just a solid maybe.

At least Julie and Dale showed up. They talked. They sort of listened. In their own damaged little ways, they were trying to improve matters. But they were both rigid thinkers who saw solutions to problems in extremes – seek solace in an e-mail affair, say yes to the willing girl at the hotel, never express your true feelings. This is how they lived their lives.

'It's time for us to stop,' Jennifer announced in her kindest voice. 'I want you to think about a few questions for our next session.'

'I'm not sure there's going to be one,' Julie said, standing up. 'I haven't decided yet.'

Jennifer smiled easily. 'We can leave it at maybe. I'll keep the time open for now. Just let me know within the next few days.'

Julie nodded stiffly and headed for the door. 'What am I supposed to think about?'

'What makes you happy? Do you think you're a good wife?' Jennifer's voice was soft and free of judgment. 'If you decide to continue, I'd like to start there.'

Julie left the office.

Jennifer began to pace the small confines of the counseling area as Nancy observed her curiously. Within the treatment scenario, she had effectively compartmentalized her anxiety. But the moment it ended, she could no longer contain her agitation.

'Jennifer?' A male voice was coming from inside the reception suite. It belonged to Kurt Taylor.

She took a moment to breathe, hoping her raw nerves would calm, then opened the door, surprised that she had never heard the bell.

Kurt stood there dressed in an expertly tailored designer suit. He was holding two Starbucks drinks. 'I saw your client leave just as I was pulling up, so I assumed it was safe to pop in. I got you a vanilla chai.'

'Thank you.' Caffeine was the last thing Jennifer needed in her system. But she was grateful for the distraction. She gave him an up-and-down glance. 'You must have a very important root canal.'

Kurt grinned. 'I got a frantic call from a producer of one of the local morning shows. Their expert on teeth grinding had to cancel at the last minute.'

Before Jennifer could respond, a beautiful brunette and a handsome black man stepped inside the waiting room.

Nancy dashed excitedly to greet them.

The woman spoke first. 'Jennifer Payne?'

'Yes.'

'Detective Marlowe, Las Vegas Metro.' She brandished a badge and identification. 'This is my partner, Detective Smith. We'd like to ask you a few questions.'

Jennifer's insides liquefied with fear as she felt the color drain from her face. 'Of course.' She busied herself with the task of securing Nancy into her crate, purposefully avoiding eye contact – with the detectives, with Kurt – in order to mask her overwhelming panic. Could they hear the powerful drumming of her heart? It was beating that loud inside her chest.

Kurt lingered.

Jennifer glanced at him, urging him with her eyes to leave. 'I'll catch up with you later on.'

He nodded to the detectives and walked out.

Detective Marlowe seemed to take mental note of the exchange between them.

Jennifer experienced a numbing sense of dread, concluding quickly that this woman missed no small detail or nuance. She gestured for them to join her inside the counseling suite and closed the door. 'Please. Have a seat.'

Detective Smith took the offer and made a joke about not wanting to get into the details of his unhappy childhood.

Detective Marlowe remained standing.

Jennifer cleared her throat. 'What's this about?'

Detective Marlowe spoke up first. 'The murder of a twenty-four-year-old white male – Cam Lawford. Did you know him?'

Jennifer eased down onto the leather chair where she held court for sessions five days a week. It was a comfortable place for her, and it made her feel more in control of the situation. She made the instant decision to be truthful. But what came along with that was a release of all the pent-up fear, sadness, and shame that had been spiraling inside her like a tsunami since discovering Cam's body the night before. As she opened her mouth to speak, she suddenly burst into tears.

Detectives Marlowe and Smith traded knowing looks.

Jennifer could not stop crying. The therapist who was the voice of reason, the psychological professional who was the rock of emotional support, had become a basket case in her own treatment office.

Detective Marlowe handed Jennifer a tissue and attempted to comfort her. 'Would you like some water before we continue?'

Jennifer just wiped her eyes as the overwhelming emotions began to subside.

Detective Marlowe stepped over to the water carafe. She filled one of the glass tumblers to the halfway mark and presented it to Jennifer. 'Take your time.'

Jennifer nodded gratefully. Slowly, she drank it down.

Detective Marlowe eased onto the sofa next to her partner. 'You knew him.'

'Yes.'

'In what context?' Detective Marlowe probed.

Jennifer cleared her throat. 'Professionally, I guess. I was ... I was one of his clients.'

Detective Smith spoke next. 'When was the last time you saw him?'

Jennifer closed her eyes for a moment and took in a calming breath. 'Last night. I had an appointment to meet him at the Wynn. When I walked into the room and saw his body ... I ... I should've called the police right away. But I just ... panicked. I'm ashamed to admit that I went into self-preservation mode. I didn't want to explain my reasons for being there. It was too potentially embarrassing and damaging to my professional reputation ... to my marriage. So I left. I drove back here to collect my dog. I took a call from a client. And then I went home.'

Detective Smith was jotting furiously onto a small spiral notepad. 'What time did all of this happen?'

'Around nine o'clock. We were originally scheduled to meet at eight. He called to push it back by an hour.'

'And what time was that?' Detective Marlowe asked.

Jennifer thought about it carefully, wanting to be as accurate as possible. 'Sometime after seven.' She covered her face with her hands and realized that they were shaking. 'I can't believe I just left him there.'

'The hotel room was registered in his name,' Detective Marlowe said. 'How did you get inside?'

'He left a key for me at the front desk.' Jennifer got up and reached into her bottom desk drawer for her purse, retrieving the envelope embossed with the Wynn logo and scrawled with *Phyllis McGraw* in Cam's handwriting. The key card was still inside. She handed it over to Detective Marlowe.

'How long were you in the room?' Detective Smith inquired.

Jennifer exhaled a deep breath. 'Not long. I let myself in. I saw his body on the bed. I realized that he was ... dead. Of course, I was terrified. I didn't know if someone was still in the room or if they might come back. It all happened very fast. I don't know. Maybe a minute or two. I'm not exactly sure.'

'Did you notice anyone suspicious in the corridor or on the elevator?' Detective Smith asked.

Jennifer reflected back. 'No.'

Detective Marlowe stood up and swept an assessing gaze up and down Jennifer's bookcase. 'How often did you retain Cam Lawford's services?'

'Three times over the past several weeks,' Jennifer replied quietly. 'Last night would've been our fourth meeting.'

Detective Marlowe turned around. 'How did you meet? Most women encounter the Cams of the world in cougar lounges or expensive hotel bars. You don't seem to fit either scenario.'

This was precisely the area that Jennifer was hoping to

avoid. But there was no way of dodging it. 'One of my clients saw him regularly. She talked about him during our sessions, and he captured my interest. I contacted him.'

Detective Marlowe perused the bookcase again. She pulled *Come to Bed* off the shelf and held up the best-selling novel. 'Would that client happen to be Kristin Fox?'

Jennifer hesitated. 'Client information is confidential.'

'Unless you want to use it to ramp up your sex life,' Detective Marlowe countered.

Jennifer remained silent. The thought that she might need a criminal lawyer occurred to her.

Detective Smith picked up his vibrating mobile and stepped off to the side to answer it.

'I'm investigating a *murder*,' Detective Marlowe continued, her tone more forceful now. 'So far, there's an intimate connection among the victim, you, and at least one of your patients. If you choose not to cooperate—'

'Gucci,' Detective Smith cut in as he shut down his phone. 'The shooting in the Paradise Cove subdivision that was radioed in on our way over here?'

She nodded in acknowledgment.

'No homicide. No injuries. But three people are being questioned at the scene, and one is a Patrick Payne.' He turned to Jennifer. 'Is that your husband?'

She nodded wordlessly as he scribbled an address onto a blank sheet, ripped it out of his pad, and handed it over. Jennifer tried to wrap her head around the shocking realities. Cam Lawford was dead. Patrick had been involved in a shooting.

Detective Marlowe moved on, treating the moment like

the business-as-usual that it was to someone in her field. 'Just a few more questions. Did Cam ever mention any kind of conflict – with a client, a client's husband or boyfriend, anyone?'

Jennifer's eyes clouded with tears. 'I've told you everything that I know.'

Detective Marlowe studied her carefully. 'Were you aware that he was writing a book about his life as a male escort?'

'No, I wasn't,' Jennifer said, shuddering inwardly at the implications of what that could mean.

Detective Marlowe handed over her business card. 'Don't leave town over the next few days. I'm sure we'll have more questions. And call me day or night if you happen to recall any details, no matter how trivial. Even the smallest thing could be important.'

Jennifer nodded earnestly. She watched them leave. The moment the door closed she rushed to her desk to call Patrick. It became a staring contest with the dial pad. The art of phone number memory was gone. She scrambled to find her mobile and used the automatic contact feature, praying that he would pick up.

It rang and rang until his voice mail activated.

Jennifer heard the interior bell jingle, then a soft knock on the door. Instinctively, she knew who it was and dashed to open it. 'Kurt, there's been a shooting. It's Patrick. He's not hurt, but I don't know what's going on.' She gave him the crumpled address.

'I know where this is. Come on, I'll drive you.'

She grabbed her purse and tried Patrick's mobile again on the way out. Kurt's hand was in the small of her back, guiding her toward his roadster and into the passenger seat.

He jumped in and revved the engine. 'Buckle up.' And then he roared out of the parking lot, weaving through traffic like a speed demon.

Jennifer tried Patrick's cell again and again. 'He's not picking up.'

'It's not much farther,' Kurt assured her, turning into what appeared to be an abandoned cul-de-sac.

She tried to make sense of the desolate surroundings. The neighborhood looked overrun with foreclosures. Why was Patrick in this area?

Kurt pointed to signs of life ahead.

Two squad cars ... a Lexus SUV ... three officers standing in the front yard talking to the young blond Eva ... a fourth officer leading a handcuffed man toward the curb ... Patrick – the clean-shaven, almost preppy Patrick she had fallen for – sitting on the front steps of the house looking shell-shocked.

Kurt stopped in the middle of the street.

Jennifer got out and raced across the neglected lawn, ignoring the policeman who tried to stop her, desperate to reach her husband.

When Patrick saw her, he stood up and moved to meet her part of the way. There was instant relief on his face. There was pure love in his eyes. And he embraced her with the kind of strength, warmth, and emotional intensity that said he was not only grateful to be alive but grateful for her as well.

Jennifer clung to him for several long, silent seconds.

He was safe. Nothing else mattered. The details were meaningless.

Patrick drew back and kissed her deeply.

When she came up for air, she held his smooth face in her hands.

'Jesus, Jen, I thought I was a dead man.'

'But you're okay, darling . . . you're okay.' She embraced him again, even more tightly this time as the image of last night's gruesome discovery flashed in her mind. Cam was dead, Patrick was alive, and Jennifer was at once terribly sad and deliriously happy.

He kissed her again. 'Let's get out of here.' His hand claimed hers in a way that seemed to convey that everything between them would be good again.

Jennifer glanced up. The officers were huddled together in a group. Eva was standing alone on the periphery. Kurt was, too. The two of them looked like interlopers. And in a sense, they were. But introductions went around regardless – Eva Lick, the screenwriter in Patrick's critique group; Kurt Taylor, the dentist in Jennifer's office park.

They gathered and talked of life flashing before your eyes and God's intervening hand before the subject turned to the former owner of the property, the same man who had been taken away by squad car, sirens screaming.

His name was Rick Carroll. He had been unemployed for eight months. The mortgage company refused to adjust his balloon interest rate. When the foreclosure commenced, his wife left him and took the kids to live with her parents in Scottsdale. He had been squatting in his own home.

When the youngest police officer stepped in with an

offer to drive Eva home and she accepted, the quartet broke apart.

Kurt insisted on driving Patrick to his car, which was still parked at the Coffee Bean on Flamingo. The three of them squeezed into his sporty two-seater and made the journey together in preoccupied silence.

'He seems like a good guy,' Patrick said as Kurt drove away.

'He is,' Jennifer said simply.

'Eva's a good girl, too.' He glanced at his car, then seemed to think better of it and gestured to the Coffee Bean entrance. 'Let's go inside for a bit.'

Jennifer made the necessary calls to cancel her appointments for the day. She finished reading *Neon Underground* as he sat there pretending to thumb through the *Las Vegas Review-Journal* but mainly watching and waiting for her reaction.

Finally, she closed the Kindle case and looked at him. 'It's wonderful, Patrick. It's sensitive and gritty. It's uplifting and heartbreaking. It's honest and impossible to believe. It's everything a film like this should be.'

He beamed with pride and reached out to touch her fingers.

They sat there for hours, drinking ice-blended coffees, crunching on biscotti, and reconnecting to each other. And Jennifer felt closer to him than ever before.

'Let's go home,' Patrick said. There was a glint of bad-boy mischief in his eyes. 'If we leave right now, I'll have about an hour to show you how happy I am to be alive before it's time to pick up Mia Sara.'

Jennifer grinned as a counterproposal came to mind.

'The Strip is closer. We could get a cheap hotel room. That would give you an extra twenty minutes to show me.'

'Jesus, Jen,' he marveled with a dirty laugh, clearly delighted with the idea. 'Since when are you so naughty?'

It was a question Jennifer would never answer. She just stood up, took Patrick's hand, and led him out the door.

CHAPTER THIRTY-FIVE

Slowly, Billie came up from the deep.

When she lifted her eyelids, everything bombarded her all at once – the terrible dryness in her mouth, the familiarity of the penthouse ceiling, the sunlight streaming in through the open blinds ... the fact that her fingers were wrapped loosely around Randall's black matte Beretta Storm pistol.

Realizing that she was still wearing the ruffled Marchesa gown from her show, she released her hand from the gun and pushed it away in disgust, struggling to piece together the last hours. And then she saw him.

Randall was sitting in the loveseat close to the fireplace, watching her with intense and hostile eyes.

Billie started to remember blurred fragments of time. The *Rebirth* show ... her dressing room ... Carly ... Carly and Randall ... John Phillip ... and then the blackout. Finally, she spoke. 'What did you do to me?' Her voice was mangled.

'It's not what I did to you,' Randall said. The detached calm in his tone was chilling. 'It's not what anyone else did to you. It's what you did to yourself.'

Billie noticed the padded white envelope emblazoned with Kristin's corporate logo on the Eames coffee table in front of him. Suddenly, the memory of her failed great escape came flooding back.

'You're garbage, Billie,' Randall said. 'You always have been. I thought I could change that.' His cold stare rendered her practically immobile. 'You were a broken-down piece of trash when I found you. I saw something then. But I don't see it anymore.'

Billie's heart filled up with the tiny hope that Randall was finally letting go. For months he'd positioned himself as her only frame of reference, isolating her, distorting her mind-set. But entrapment wasn't love. And tyranny wasn't attention. A part of her would always be grateful to him for the miraculous way that he'd saved – and dramatically enhanced – her look. Gratitude only went so far, though. This hideous, thin-lipped freak could have everything – her money, her career. She simply wanted out.

'It'll be better in the daylight.' His voice was eerily casual. 'More commotion. More witnesses. A bloodier scene all the way around. I'm sure Hart will keep the house dark tonight. That'll be a nice tribute to you. But by tomorrow, he'll find a way to book the venue. A few days after that, you'll be forgotten.'

Billie looked at him strangely.

'I'll have to remind housekeeping to burn those sheets. No matter how many times you wash, the stench of a whore never comes out. Have you ever noticed that?'

Billie moved to get out of bed. She wanted this dress off her body. She wanted a hot shower.

'You let that bottom-feeder defile your body. *My* masterpiece. The temple *I* created.'

Billie was struck by the expression on Randall's face.

His fixated gaze was nothing short of deranged. His eyes glowed like a wild animal's.

'I've never touched you. And I *made* you. How could you let him contaminate my creation? And you paid him to do it. I'll say it again. You're garbage.'

'You're insane,' Billie whispered.

'No, I'm not. You are. Crazy people throw themselves off the twenty-ninth-floor balcony.' He leaned forward to run his fingers across the white envelope from Kristin. 'I know you had other plans. But plans change.'

Billie shook her head, a knot of frustrated emotion lodged in her throat. She was more fatigued than frightened. This vile bastard's torment had worn her down. She'd leave with nothing. She'd leave naked if she had to. 'I want out.'

Randall pointed to the balcony. 'The only way out is down. That way.'

Billie didn't so much as flinch. 'Go to hell.'

'What are you going to do?' Randall taunted. 'Leave me? Try it. I'll find you. And when I do, I'll put you under and take it all away. That's not your face. It's *my* face. I just made the mistake of creating something beautiful from garbage. You can't take that with you. I won't let you. It's mine.'

Her eyes zeroed in on the gun like a laser, calculating whether or not to make a move for it. But Billie determined that Randall was closer to it now. And so she started to inch toward the bathroom. A phone was in there. She could lock the door and call for help.

But before she could make the attempt, Randall lunged fast and began dragging her onto the balcony. The sinewy strength of his small, wiry body caught her off guard, and she stumbled in her nosebleed Louboutin heels as he pushed her toward the railing.

'You're going to jump.'

'No!' Billie screamed. But only the sky and wind could hear her terrified protest.

Randall stared at her with a bizarre, peaceful expression. 'It's better this way. You can die while you're still beautiful. I don't want to go through the business of taking back my face.' He held up his hands. 'Making you ugly isn't what these instruments were made for. But if you force me to do it, I will. One morning you'll wake up, and everything I gave you will be gone. You'll be the same disfigured whore that the maid found in that stairwell. Is that what you want?'

Billie shook her head, tears streaming down her face, fully realizing that he was demented enough to make good on his threats. There was no place for her to go. She felt like a cornered, wounded animal.

'Jump.'

'Randall, please, let me—'

'Nobody cares about you, Billie. That's why I chose you in the first place. There wasn't anyone around to ask questions. No family, no friends, no lovers. You were an empty, lonely canvas in that hospital room. I took something broken and disgusting and turned it into something magnificent. But you dishonored that. And now you're worthless to me. So jump.'

Randall's words practically gutted her. Billie couldn't refute any part of his savage assessment. She was completely alone. She always had been. Maybe jumping was the answer after all.

'I know about the visit from your pretty boy politician.' His smile was cruel. 'I saw and heard all of it.'

Billie just looked at him. Of course he had. Her dressing room was under audio and video surveillance. How could she have expected anything less?

'You've been singing that song for him, haven't you? "What's Love Got to Do with It"? I never wanted it in the show. But you kicked and screamed to keep it in, because you thought it meant something. March Donaldson didn't give a rat's ass. He bummed a smoke, drank some free champagne, and took off to meet a woman he's not ashamed to be seen with.'

Billie turned away from him. She peered over the railing, the wind whipping her organza ruffles into a frenzy as the words blistered and burned. At this moment, jumping appealed to her more than ever.

'Come on . . . do it.'

The snake hiss of Randall's voice seemed to be coming from inside her head. If the only way to escape him was to die, then it was a small price to pay. She was so close to vaulting over the rail. But something held her back. It was a vision, a shimmering reflection of the past, a fleeting memory of her former self.

Billie Shelton was a fighter. Right or wrong, good or bad, rich or poor, she'd always entered the room throwing punches, kicking ass, taking names. And Liza Pike, her late feminist friend, would expect nothing less from her now. In fact, to give in to the abuse and sadism of this man would be the ultimate betrayal of their friendship and Liza's legacy as a crusader for women.

If Billie caved in to him, she wouldn't meet her friend

in the afterlife. Liza would shun her in heaven. So even in death, Billie would be alone again. This notion fueled her soul. She had something to live for. And that something was Liza's memory.

Angrily, Billie spun around, adrenalized by a new will to survive. 'I've got a better idea, you sick fuck. *You* jump.'

'I've got no reason to.'

'You're a short, ugly man with a tiny dick. That's reason enough.' Billie smirked. After all these months of playing victim to his oppressive games, it felt so good to lash out at him.

Randall stood his ground, grinning like a gambler who knew he was holding all the cards. 'It makes sense for you to jump. You murdered someone. You don't want to go to prison.'

Billie studied him carefully, seized by an ominous fear. 'What are you talking about?'

'Why do you think you woke up with my gun in your hand?' Randall asked. 'Last night you went back to that ex-jock hustler and killed him.'

At first, Billie didn't believe it. But the fact that she could recall nothing between passing out in her dressing room and waking up with the Beretta in her hand filled her with a steadily mounting terror.

She shook her head in rigid defiance, refusing to accept the possibility that Cam Lawford could be dead. Her mind ran images of him in that suite at the Wynn, so alive and so vibrant, so young and so gorgeous, so . . . sweet.

'You're lying,' Billie said finally, her voice a fraction of its full compass.

Randall's expression was flat. 'Your rent-a-dick is dead, you can't account for your whereabouts last night, and you woke up with the murder weapon in your hand. Think about the ramifications of that. And think about this – on top of everything, I *will* take my face back. You won't go anywhere with it. Not even prison. So do yourself a favor. Jump.'

All of a sudden, Billie noticed the watch on Randall's wrist – the Tiffany Mark T-57, the same one she'd stolen from his collection to give to Cam as payment.

Randall smiled in triumph, picking up on her observation, raising his arm to show off the reclaimed timepiece.

Just then Billie noticed Carly creeping into view behind him. She didn't understand this girl's morbid infatuation. She could only surmise that Carly had formed the same kind of trauma bond often found with children of incest, prisoners of war, victims of torture, and members of cults, people who would do anything out of loyalty to their abusers.

Something clicked in Billie's mind as the situation became clear. 'Oh, my God,' she whispered. 'You made Carly do it.'

There was a gleam of pride in Randall's eyes.

'What have you done to her?' Billie asked.

'I saved her from a lifetime of ugliness, and now she's my slave girl.'

Still unnoticed by Randall, Carly stood there, statue still, listening.

'Paper or Plastic,' Billie said.

'She'll always be that girl,' Randall said coldly. 'There's

only so much these surgical hands can do for a beast like her. I've done enough to make her presentable. And she thinks I'm a God for it. She worships me.' He paused a beat, gazing at Billie longingly. 'The way you should worship me. Your face is my finest work of art.'

Billie made the quick decision to press him further, sensing she might be able to create a distraction. 'Carly's face is a work of art, too.'

Randall scoffed angrily, as if offended by the idea. 'She was a dog before, and she's still a dog, just a mildly prettier version of one. That's not art.' He held up his hands again. 'These instruments can perform magic. But they have their limits. Still, she's an obedient mutt. I'll give her that. I told her to kneecap that dancing faggot, so she did it. I told her to put a bullet in your gigolo's pea brain, and she did that, too. The bitch knows how to play fetch.'

Quietly, Carly slipped out of view.

Billie's heart crashed with disappointment.

Randall stepped forward. 'I want one last look at you.' His eyes burned into her with a vicious intensity. 'Now. It's time. Jump.'

'Dr. Glass?'

Billie took a sharp intake of breath.

Carly was standing behind Randall again, this time with the Beretta Storm in her hand.

He turned around, observed her for a moment, and showed no sign of concern. 'Put that away. She's going to jump.'

Carly just stared at him.

Randall looked annoyed. 'I said put that away.'

There was a sudden and complete madness in Carly's eyes. 'Show me your hands.'

Randall regarded her more carefully now. 'What are you—'

'Show me!' Carly shouted.

With a seething reluctance, Randall raised his hands in the air.

Carly stepped forward and fired a single shot. The bullet blew through the center of his right palm.

Billie cowered in horror as the scene unfolded.

Randall screamed out in agony, sinking down to his knees, staring in disbelief at the exit wound in the back of his hand.

Carly moved even closer and fired again. The next shot ripped off his index and middle fingers.

One of the fleshy, bloody digits landed across the toe of Billie's Louboutin shoe. The other finger flew off the balcony to the Strip below. Randall's anguished cries were deafening.

Carly remained emotionless. She closed in on him, grabbing his left wrist and raising his arm. 'Open your hand.'

Randall could only wail and stare at the bloody stump that was once the primary instrument of his livelihood and art.

'Open it!'

His left hand remained a tightly closed fist.

Carly pressed the gun's muzzle into the base of his knuckles, fired a third shot, and showing no mercy, pumped out a fourth bullet that amputated his thumb.

Billie covered her ears to mute Randall's tortured squeals.

And then Carly turned the Beretta in her direction.

Billie stopped breathing. She shut her eyes to the inevitable and wondered if Liza Pike had felt this calm when she knew Leonard Tidwell was going to kill her.

CHAPTER THIRTY-SIX

'We live in a violent world,' Jennifer said.

Kristin took a deep breath and dabbed her wet eyes with a tissue. 'I still dream about him.'

'It's going to take time.' Jennifer's voice was soft, her cadence soothing. 'But you're doing all the right things – coming here to sort through your feelings, establishing a rewarding set of routines, spending time with your children. The shock and hurt will subside. The important thing is to not run away from the pain.'

Kristin nodded gratefully to the beat of Jennifer's encouragement. It had been weeks since the death of Cam Lawford rocked her life to its very core. She was still sorting through the emotions.

'How are you feeling about the divorce?'

'Better. Hart has abandoned the idea of a custody battle and going after my money.'

'That's certainly a more civil approach. What brought about the change?'

'The hotel conglomerate he works for promoted him to CEO. It'll mean living overseas part time to manage the final construction and opening of a new property in Macau.'

Jennifer raised a curious eyebrow.

'The Strip is overbuilt,' Kristin explained. 'Investors are

forecasting that no major building will break ground in Vegas for at least a decade. Asia is the new promised land for casino growth.'

'This is a major change for the family. How do you feel about it?'

'About my future ex-husband spending half the year in Asia?' Kristin grinned. 'Like I won the divorce lottery.'

Jennifer smiled.

'Seriously, though, the opportunity has been transformative. The company wants him in the center of the most profitable action. Professionally, Hart's at a pinnacle point in his career, and that's made him less adversarial. Besides, he doesn't have time to act like an asshole, because he's too busy taking crash courses in Cantonese and Portuguese. I asked for the house and Sinatra, and he agreed with no argument. We're just waiting on a court date.'

'And how are the children?' Jennifer asked.

The change in subject brought an instant smile to Kristin's face. 'The three of us have a new nighttime ritual.'

'Tell me about it.'

'We climb into my bed, share a pint of Ben and Jerry's, and everybody gives a high-low report about the best and worst parts of their day.'

Jennifer beamed. 'That's wonderful, Kristin. You're building protective walls around your family. Research has shown that simple childhood rituals are what trigger the most precious memories in adults. When Ollie and Lily grow up, those bed talks will continue to be so meaningful.'

Kristin nodded. 'It's been amazing. The other night Ollie said that the high point of his day was being in Barnes and Noble and seeing an end cap display for *Come to Bed* and *The Guy Next Door*. He bragged to his friends. He told them, "My mom wrote those books." It almost made me cry.'

'He's proud of you,' Jennifer remarked warmly.

Kristin felt a pang of bittersweet joy. 'I was worried that the divorce might tear our family apart. But I feel like we're stronger than ever.'

'I think everyone in the family has found a certain peace,' Jennifer said. 'Divorce isn't always destructive. If a situation is toxic enough, it can be healing, too.'

'They're not even sad about their father being so far away for six months,' Kristin went on. 'They're more excited about being able to visit him. Lily has spent hours doing Internet research on Macau. Apparently, it's one of the richest cities in the world. Did you know that?'

Jennifer grinned. 'No, I didn't.'

'Neither did I.' Kristin sighed and gave the sleeping Nancy a few gentle strokes.

'How is your work progressing?'

'Better, I guess.'

Jennifer waited for more.

'It's been difficult getting back to it. But I'm in my office ... I'm trying.'

Jennifer's expression was sympathetic and supportive. 'I once read a quote by the author Rosellen Brown. She was giving advice to other writers and she said that the best thing you could do was show up, pay attention, and tell the truth.'

Kristen sat there for several long seconds. 'I have to write my way through this, don't I?'

Jennifer's smile was comforting. 'It won't be easy. Part of what you do requires living events twice, first as an experience and a second time through your writing. But ultimately, I think that process can work miracles, especially for someone like you.'

Kristin considered this. The final pages of *Kiva Dunes Road* remained unwritten, a block that continued to irritate her. 'So why can't I finish my book?'

'Maybe ending the novel is also a subconscious ending to your friendship with Jeffie. His presence has been such a vital part of this project. In many ways he came back alive for you. Perhaps you're not ready to say good-bye.'

'There's some truth to that,' Kristin allowed. 'But not finishing this novel is also a great way to avoid starting my next one. I'm calling it *Love for Sale*. I'm dedicating it to Cam. He was so much more than the one-dimensional stud the media has made him out to be. But the world will know that soon enough. Toni Valentine is still publishing his book. I read it in Malibu, and even in draft form, it was incredibly good.'

'Its release doesn't concern you?'

Kristin shook her head. 'He doesn't name names. Granted, there are clues here and there ... about certain people, certain circumstances. But only true intimates could put those pieces together.'

She knew about Jennifer and Cam. And now Jennifer knew that she knew. But this was as far as the matter would ever need to go. 'He was wonderful ... wasn't he?'

Jennifer's gaze was direct. 'Yes, he was.'

Her eyes gleamed with philosophical insight. 'I believe Mary Pipher said it best about my profession and yours,'

Jennifer said. 'Writers and therapists ... we expose the unexposed.'

'I like that,' Kristin said, tripping off into a distracted place for a moment, thinking of Billie. She missed her, wondered where she was, and hoped that she would hear from her again.

Jennifer glanced at the clock. 'We're going to have to stop here for today.'

Kristin drove home with a burning desire to write.

Sinatra was sacked out and entertaining no ideas of a neighborhood walk. It literally required pulling him out the front door to coax him into getting some light exercise.

To no surprise, Elaine Dayan was across the street with Sonny and Cher. She waved anxiously. 'Hello, there! I'm still saying my little prayers and hoping to see Hart's car in the driveway one of these days!'

'Start praying for world peace instead!' Kristin shouted back with upbeat cheer. 'He's moving to Asia for part of the year!'

Elaine looked completely astonished. It was as if someone had just told her that little people lived inside her salt-and-pepper shakers. 'Asia?'

Kristin nodded enthusiastically and vaulted down the sidewalk. She gave in to Sinatra's sluggishness and cut their jaunt short, rushing back to sequester herself for some major productivity.

The inspiration was total. Her fingers danced across the keyboard, producing the kind of text volume and clickety-clack that brought to mind a typing pool girl from a 1950s office.

The last pages of *Kiva Dunes Road* practically wrote themselves. Kristin keenly understood the journey of heartbreak her characters went through. She knew the bottomless feelings of disbelief and devastation triggered by someone you love filing emotional bankruptcy and erasing you from their life without explanation or negotiation. In her novel, one character was doing it to another. Years ago, Kristin had done it to Jeffie. As far back as childhood, Kristin's parents had done it to her. And at different stages during their fourteen-year marriage, Kristin and Hart had done it to each other.

She was proofing the last page when Lily padded in from school, dropped her backpack with a loud thump, and rested her chin on Kristin's shoulder.

'Hi, Mommy.'

'Hello, sweetheart.' She kept her eyes on the screen for a moment, spotting and correcting two minor typos. 'You smell like grape soda.'

'I had a Fanta on the bus.'

'You're not supposed to drink on the bus.'

'The driver never sees anything. He's usually texting the whole time.'

'That's a comforting thought.' Kristin rearranged the closing sentence, clicked Save, and breathed out a dramatic sigh, still staring at the monitor.

'Are you done?' Lily asked.

Kristin nodded. At a moment like this, there were no two words more beautiful in the English language than ... THE END. Her heart was soaring.

Barbra Streisand was singing on Pandora Radio.

'I think this song is pretty,' Lily murmured.

Kristin tilted her head against her daughter's. 'Me, too, sweetheart. Me, too.'

'I'm starving. Who wants pizza?'

'You do, apparently,' Kristin murmured. 'Go call in the order. I'll be down in a few minutes. I want to hear all about your day.'

Lily dashed out of the room.

Kristin opened a new Word document. It was her custom to start a novel as soon as she finished one. She set up the title page, gave it a careful look, and sighed deeply.

LOVE FOR SALE
A Novel
By Kristin Fox

And then she started to write . . . THE FIRST TIME SHE SAW HIM HE WAS RUNNING ON THE BEACH IN MALIBU. HER VALUES CHANGED IN AN INSTANT. SHE WANTED TO QUIT HER EXISTING LIFE AND FOLLOW HIM. SHE WANTED TO SELL EVERYTHING SHE OWNED AND BUY HIM. HIS NAME WAS BROCK LAWSON, AND AS IT TURNED OUT, HE WAS FOR SALE . . .

CHAPTER THIRTY-SEVEN

VEGAS WOMAN FACES MURDER
CHARGE IN DUI ACCIDENT

The lurid headline screamed out at Jennifer. Absorbing the pain of clients was the most difficult aspect of her work. She wondered if her stamina for tragedy was sustainable.

Close on the heels of Cam Lawford's murder and the disappearance of Billie Shelton came even more horrific news – a car accident involving Julie and Dale Munso. The gory details were still being played out in the media.

According to news accounts, they were leaving a friend's fortieth birthday party. It was after midnight. Julie was driving. The crash occurred just past the dangerous intersection of Jones Boulevard and Tropicana Avenue in the southwestern Las Vegas Valley. Their 2010 Mercedes sedan was traveling northbound on Jones when it veered left and smashed into a Porsche in the center of the southbound lanes.

The black box recovered from the wreckage clocked Julie's speed at the time of impact at 88 mph. Witnesses from the party reported that she had been drinking and arguing with Dale throughout the night. At .13, her blood-alcohol level registered beyond the legal limit.

To the amazement of first responders on the scene, Julie and Dale escaped serious injury. They were taken to Spring Valley Hospital for treatment of minor wounds. But the two passengers in the Porsche – Zoe and Calvin Vargas – had been killed instantly. She was an actress on a new cable drama about professional tennis called *Love/Thirty*. He was a junior agent at United Talent Agency. They were both twenty-five and had just been married at the famous Graceland Chapel on the Strip.

Metro police arrested Julie in the emergency room. It was her second DUI in four years. She had just been indicted on two counts of depraved-heart murder and was currently awaiting trial.

With a heavy heart, Jennifer pushed aside the *Las Vegas Review-Journal*. 'Is there *any* good news?'

'Not in there,' Kurt said. 'That's why I read this.' He held up the slick, oversized glossy *Vegas*, a magazine that featured the face of Billie Shelton under this month's masthead. Of course, by the time the issue hit subscriber mailboxes and newsstands, its glittery cover girl had become an unsolved mystery.

On Tuesdays and Thursdays, Jennifer and Kurt made a regular retreat to his palatial home in the Ridges for a half hour of swimming and a full hour of lunching.

'Diana and I finally went to see Sebastian Craig,' Kurt announced.

Jennifer was visibly surprised. She had given him the couples counseling referral weeks ago and then never heard another word about it. 'How did it go?'

'It was intense,' Kurt said, stabbing the last bite of avocado from Yolanda's delicious chef salad. 'But we didn't walk out feeling angry or defeated. We agreed to go once a week.' He smirked. 'You didn't tell me he was so old. I hope we don't kill him.'

Jennifer laughed. 'Don't worry. Sebastian is wise and wonderful and will probably outlive all of us. I'm thrilled that you're doing this, Kurt. You and Diana will thrive from it.'

'I just want us to be happy.'

'All happiness is limited,' Jennifer said. 'The key is learning to live with the sadness and the joy.'

'He said something similar to that.' Kurt gave her a cheeky look. 'Do all therapists read from the same script?'

'On second thought, maybe there is the risk of you killing him.'

Kurt laughed. 'So how are things with Mr. Hollywood?'

A smile broke out on Jennifer's face like a brand-new morning. 'Patrick's in Los Angeles this week to meet with Harrison Beck. He's agreed to direct *Neon Underground*.'

Kurt's brow furrowed as he put his brain computer to work placing the name. 'Isn't that—'

'The director of *Watch Her Bleed*,' Jennifer finished.

'Yeah, a film student was obsessed with that movie and killed Beck's girlfriend, right?'

Jennifer nodded somberly. 'Liza Pike, the writer. He hasn't made a film since then. But he loves Patrick's screenplay, and he's ready to work again. It's *the* buzz project in Hollywood, at least this week. Everybody wants to read the script that brought Harrison Beck out of hiding. Now Patrick's manager's phone is blowing up with calls. It looks like Sony might offer him an overall development deal.'

'Jesus,' Kurt muttered. 'The best thing the guy ever did

was blow off work and get stoned that day. Look what it led to.'

'Yes, that's exactly what he plans to share with Mia Sara's class at the school's next Career Day.'

Kurt laughed. 'I'm just saying.'

Jennifer rolled her eyes with exasperated humor. She adored her friend. She enjoyed her work. She loved her husband. She cherished her life.

Billie's thousand-yard stare on the *Vegas* cover was haunting her, and she reached out to flip the magazine over, revealing a Roberto Coin jewelry ad on the back. Much better.

'What's the matter?' Kurt asked, pushing away his salad.

'I'm still bothered by my failure with Billie Shelton. I don't like to admit defeat. I keep asking myself, "What did I miss?" I should've seen the warning signs.'

'Not if she didn't want you to see them.'

Jennifer looked unsure. 'I don't know. Billie was exhausting in her volubility. She talked about everything and talked about nothing at the same time. In retrospect, I can see the manic defenses more clearly. She was outrunning her life by never slowing down to think about it. And now she's just running. It makes my stomach hurt. I hate to fail. I'd like a do over. Next time, I know that I could help.'

Kurt studied her for a moment. 'You're being too hard on yourself. You can't make people reveal themselves any more than I can make them floss every night. Do you think I blame myself for a patient's tooth decay?'

Jennifer laughed. 'Well, when you put it that way ...'

'Listen to me. I'm a doctor.' One beat. 'By the way, Yolanda made cupcakes.'

'Oh, I can't.'

Kurt waved off the decline. 'You'll hurt her feelings. She does everything from scratch. We'll split one.'

'You're impossible.'

'Actually, I'm quite practical.'

Jennifer groaned in frustrated amusement and stared out at the phenomenal view of the Strip, still thinking of Cam, still thinking of Billie, still pondering the question that floated in and out of her analytical mind with disturbing regularity.

Whatever happened to Billie Shelton?

EPILOGUE

Billie Shelton was dead of a drug overdose. A skateboarder found her body near Venice Beach.

Billie Shelton went down in a yacht that capsized in St. Tropez. A Saudi prince owned the vessel.

Billie Shelton was in a private plane that nosedived somewhere in the Colorado mountains. The search-and-recovery team never found her remains.

The stories, though always murky and far-fetched, contained just enough specific detail to sound remotely plausible. Somebody would post a rumor on Twitter. The item would be retweeted. Facebook users would spread the word like VD. And then TMZ or RadarOnline would report the alleged news. The Internet had become the official echo chamber for Billie Shelton death folklore.

But she was very much alive on the *Crimson Tide Beauty*, a brand-new forty-two-foot Bruno and Stillman fishing boat anchored ten miles from Montauk Point off Long Island, New York.

'Bluefish make a good live bait,' Parks McGraw informed her.

Billie smiled at the adorable seven-year-old. 'Is that so?'

His nod was gravely serious. 'I'm the first mate, so it's important for me to know that kind of stuff.'

Tucker McGraw embraced the boy from behind, tousling his long, surfer dude sun-bleached hair. 'So what's biting today, son?'

Parks peered out into the beautiful emerald green waters that shimmered as clear as quartz crystal. 'Definitely tuna and striped bass,' he said authoritatively. 'And you know what, captain?'

Tucker smiled broadly, winking at Billie. 'Lay it on me.'

'I smell a thresher shark. A big one.'

Billie spun around to point an accusing finger at Kellyanne. 'You didn't say anything about sharks!'

'They're not, like, Jaws,' Parks assured her. 'Threshers have a super-long tail that swats at smaller fish. It's how they hunt. I heard about a fisherman who got decapitated by a thresher tail, though. So be ready to duck.'

'Parks, you're scaring Aunt Billie,' Kellyanne admonished lamely as she fussed with three-year-old Holly Elizabeth's life jacket.

Tucker nudged Billie teasingly. 'That only happened once.' One beat. 'That we know of.'

Billie playfully slapped Tucker's thickly muscled arm. 'If I die on this boat after everything that I've been through, I'm going to kill you.'

Parks gave her a quizzical look. 'How will you kill him if you're already dead?'

'Don't worry about that, little boy,' Billie snapped good naturedly. 'Just watch out for the sharks.'

Today marked Billie's six-week anniversary as a guest at Tucker and Kellyanne's Sag Harbor home. It had been a blessing to reconnect with her friend. Their connection went back to college days, a relationship sealed in the crucible of spring break partying with Liza Pike. And now it was grown-up bonding – with Kellyanne's children Parks and Holly Elizabeth, even working the occasional counter shift at the family business, McGraw's Fish Market. But the time had come to launch her next move.

Holly Elizabeth squirmed away from Kellyanne. A few determined steps later she was tugging on her father's cargo shorts. 'Up, Daddy!'

Tucker scooped his gorgeous daughter into his arms and smothered her neck with silly kisses.

'He spoils her rotten,' Kellyanne drawled as she and Billie slowly drifted toward the boat's bow and sat down. 'I couldn't help but notice a new suitcase on the bed before we left.' There was real disappointment in her voice.

'It's been six weeks. If I don't leave soon, Tucker's going to use *me* as live bait,' Billie joked.

'Oh, that's not true, and you know it.' Kellyanne stole a glance at her husband. 'In fact, I think Tucker might have the tiniest little crush on you.'

Billie cackled. 'Can you imagine? Me and Tucker McGraw? We wouldn't last five minutes. And four of those would be him running away as fast as he could.' She tracked him for a moment. He was handsome, strong, even-tempered, kind, hard working, dedicated to his children, and devoted to Kellyanne. This boat had even been named after her, a nod to her days as *the* campus stunner at the University of Alabama.

It was a wonderful life for Kellyanne in the Hamptons. Holly Elizabeth, lovingly named after Tucker's late first wife and Liza Pike, was Kellyanne's physical clone. And even though Parks was technically her stepson, their connection defied the qualifier. She was his mother, and he was her child. Kellyanne worked outside the home one day a week, and that was only during the summer, as cohost of a Plum TV morning talk show called *Coffee on the Beach*. Yes, it was a wonderful life here ... but not the kind of life for Billie.

'I just want you to know that you can stay,' Kellyanne said earnestly. 'As long as you want to, as long as you need to.'

'I'm not going far.'

'Back to New York?'

Billie nodded. 'I can be anonymous there. New Yorkers don't gawk. I don't think I could ever go back to Las Vegas. And Los Angeles would be too much of a fishbowl for me.'

'The kids will miss you. They love their Aunt Billie.'

'I used to hate children. I thought they were a pain in the ass. Actually, I still do. I just like yours, I guess.'

Kellyanne laughed. She gazed ponderously into the water, then back at Billie. 'Liza would be so proud of you.'

'You know, I think she might be orchestrating my next career move from heaven.'

'What do you mean?'

'This morning I had a Skype video conference with Toni Valentine.'

Kellyanne's eyes widened. 'Wow. That's a big deal.'

'I know. The Liza connection immediately put me on a different level with Toni. Her ideas are really exciting, and for the first time in my life, I feel like my best work might be ahead of me.'

'That must be a wonderful feeling.'

'It is,' Billie murmured, basking in a contentment and optimism for the future that she'd never experienced before.

Toni Valentine was a media mogul who didn't deal in mere media releases. She dealt in media assaults. And even though her pitch to take Billie from death hoax to rock priestess was coming through via Skype with a grainy image and a half-second delay, it still carried the maximum punch.

'The album is over,' Toni had declared. 'Releasing a brilliant collection of songs is no longer enough. Don't get me wrong – you still need great music. But that's only part of the package. You have a story to tell – your *Dick Magnet* indie days, your addictions, your relationship with March Donaldson, Domestic Violence, the plastic surgery, your stifled life in Vegas, your love affair with Cam Lawford, your feelings about his murder, the circumstances of your husband's shooting. I want to team you up with a good ghostwriter, someone who can pull the raw truth out of you for a kick-ass, tell-all memoir. I'll make it a bestseller, Billie. How would you like to have the number one CD, the number one nonfiction book, and the number one cable reality show in America? All at the same time. That's what I can make happen for you. Now you'll have to work harder than you've ever worked before to put it all together. But I can position you to be a big star. Bigger than you ever imagined.'

As seductions go, Toni Valentine had Billie's clothes off at hello. She wanted everything that Toni promised. And this time Billie would be ready for it. There was already a new batch of song lyrics scribbled into a notebook, and her mind constantly hummed with melodies and chord progressions.

'I Never Saw It Coming' was about Domestic Violence. 'Under His Scalpel' was about Randall Glass. 'Republican Boy' was about March Donaldson. 'Plastiholic' was about Carly McPhee. 'I Got More Than I Paid For' was about Cam Lawford. And 'Bitch Has My Back' was her ode to Kristin and female solidarity. The style was classic Billie Fucking Shelton – in your face, darkly humorous, shockingly honest ... and, last but not least, outrageously authentic. The sequined cover girl from the Strip was no more.

Save yourself.

Those were the two words Carly had uttered out loud after firing four shots into Randall's hand.

For a long moment, Billie had watched him writhe in agony on the balcony before a final bullet to the head ended his life. And then she desperately collected the envelope from Kristin, ran out of the penthouse, and never looked back. She got on the first available flight to New York, took the Jitney to the Hamptons, knocked on the door of Tucker and Kellyanne's small cottage in Sag Harbor, and disappeared from the world by losing herself in their domestic routine.

But there was still no escaping the aftermath of Carly's bloody rampage in Las Vegas. The story became a tabloid sensation. Carly confessed to the murders of Cam Lawford and Randall Glass and the assault on David Dean. Media vultures dug out her homely high school senior portrait and gave face time to her tormentors of yesteryear. They lunged for their minute in the spotlight, expressing shock and dismay that the paper-or-plastic girl had gone on to commit such violent acts.

Cam's memoir continued to be the topic of feverish speculation. Months before its release, *Stud Diaries: Confessions from the Man Who's Satisfying Your Wife* was breaking all preorder sales records for Toni Valentine's Fahrenheit Books imprint. The actual book was under fierce embargo, being guarded by armed security in the warehouse until its release.

And whenever the gossip feed trickled to a slow drip, the inevitable question always presented itself: Where is Billie Shelton? One day she'd answer it – on her own time, in her own words, on her own terms. But until then, let the death hoax rumormongers have their fun.

'Aunt Billie! Come look! It's a thresher!' Parks shouted.

She watched as an enormous creature jumped fully out of the foamy sea and negotiated a dazzling, dolphin-like turn.

'This might be too much excitement for Holly Elizabeth,' Kellyanne said, rising up to join the others at the stern. 'Are you coming?'

'In a minute,' Billie said. For a long time she just watched them on the other end of the boat, wondering if she'd ever experience that much love, togetherness, and comfort of her very own.

And then Billie reached into her denim pocket and pulled out the gift from Cam Lawford. It was a note scrawled in his masculine handwriting on petite pale cream Wynn stationery. It was a note she discovered folded up and tucked inside her handbag. But most important of all, it was a note that revealed the answer he promised to provide.

Only once ... and only you. Love, Cam.

AUTHOR'S NOTE

Special note on *The Strip*: The characters Billie Shelton, Liza Pike, Kellyanne Downey, Tucker McGraw, Parks McGraw, March Donaldson, Jab Hunter, Todd Bana, Amy Dando, Toni Valentine, Robbie Breslow, and Domestic Violence were introduced in the novel *Tan Lines*.

Visit the author online at wwww.jjsalem.com.

extracts   reading groups
competitions   books   new
books   discounts   extracts   extracts
competitions   new   events   reading groups
books   new   books   extracts   discounts   events
events   books   reading groups
extracts   books   new   titles   reading groups
interviews   events   new
events   extracts   extracts   books
discounts   interviews
new   books   events   events   new   books
events   new   interviews   extracts
discounts   extracts   discounts   books

www.panmacmillan.com

extracts   events   reading groups
competitions   books   extracts   new